For Colin J. Northwood,
who has been a constant source
of wisdom and encouragement.

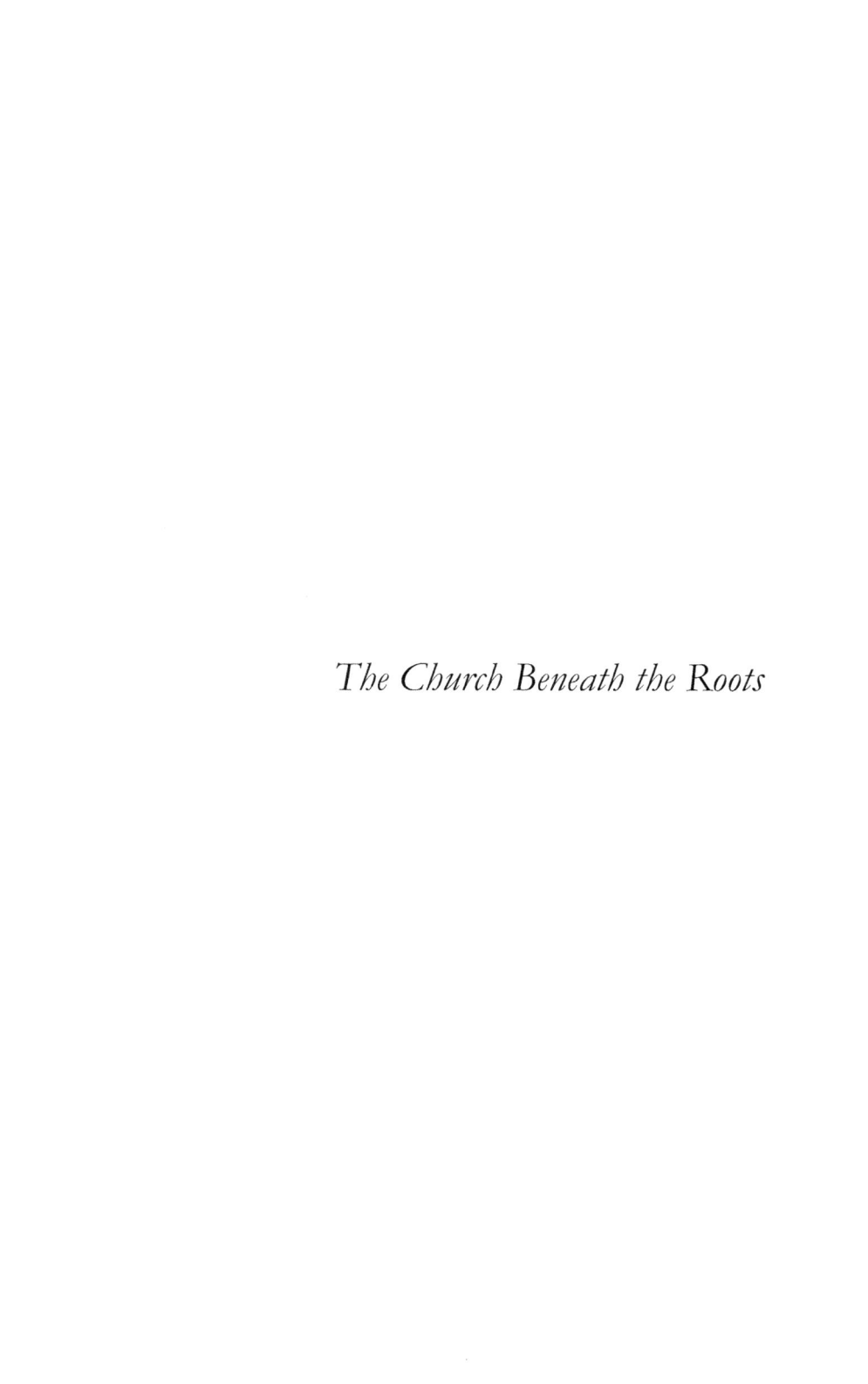

The Church Beneath the Roots

PROLOGUE

1968

Captain Hank Friese eyed his copilot with growing concern. First Officer Ted Lombardi hadn't checked his flight instruments in a while, nor heeded the intermittent radio chatter. Instead, he tapped a nauseating belch from his chest, then resumed his unconscious fumbling of the rock his son had given him. He'd been turning the object over in his hand for the past fifteen minutes, as if praying on a rosary.

"Stomach still bothering you?" Hank asked.

"Just isn't sittin' right," Ted replied, shifting uncomfortably in his chair. "Not since camping. Mighta been those sandwiches we brought along... Ham seemed on its way out."

The stone's peculiar surface glimmered in the morning light, casting a rainbow across the flight deck. The longer Hank looked at it, the dizzier he became. And yet, he found himself staring into it for longer and longer intervals.

"You find that up in the mountains?" Hank asked, mesmerized by the richness of the stone's color. He'd never seen black so pure. His eyes unfocused in the little void it appeared to rip in Ted's hand. Hank imagined himself falling in.

1

"Yeah," said Ted, swallowing hard. "Jason found it on the hike. I figured he'd want to keep it, but he gave it to me before I left this morning. Said it would keep me safe."

"He still worried about you flying?" Hank asked, quickly glancing at the altimeter and then returning his gaze to the stone.

Ted snorted in amusement, but the motion seemed to cause a bolt of pain to arc through his abdomen. He dropped a hand onto his belly and looked over at Hank, noticing the captain's fixation with the stone.

"Last night, he dreamed about a crash," said Ted. "He's prone to nightmares. It's always something."

"That's a shame," Hank replied. "You should bring him up here one of these days. Show him how boring the job really is."

Ted tried to speak, but a groan of discomfort came out instead. Beads of sweat collected on his brow, and he tugged at the collar of his uniform.

"Listen, why don't you hit the lavatory?" Hank said, finally looking up at his copilot's face. "I'll call Lila up here with some water and crackers if need be. Better out than in, man."

Ted's eyes darted around the flight deck as if he'd only now realized he was on an airplane. His breath hastened, and his neck visibly quivered with the pounding of his heart. He continued turning the stone in his hand.

"You think we turn out like our fathers, Captain?" he asked, ignoring Hank's suggestion. "You know...the good and the bad."

"Not sure I...get your meaning," Hank replied, losing his train of thought. His eyes grew heavy studying Ted, and their weight pulled his attention back down to the stone.

It was a lovely, jagged thing, not some common pebble fished out of a creek. Its black seemed to emanate from an impossible distance. In a few moments, he became lost in it again.

"Do we become them's what I mean," Ted went on, wincing in pain as he spoke. "Is it inside you all along?"

"Inside...you..." Hank echoed, watching every movement of Ted's fingers as they glided over the stone. He imagined snatching the thing away, and how good it must feel to hold.

"Little kids," Ted blurted out, his voice a flood of sorrow. "Just...just bad thoughts. More and more."

Hank barely registered the strange admission. All he could do was fixate upon the weird rock.

"I swear I never touched 'em, though," Ted went on. "I couldn't live with myself."

"Oh yeah," Hank mumbled absently, "kids are great..."

His mind wandered to a place it had never been before, and teetered there at the edge of awareness. Then suddenly, every thought and memory and desire within Hank collapsed all at once into the darkness of the stone. He could no longer resist. Hank reached out and took it for himself, surprised that Ted seemed to give it up willingly. The moment it rolled into his palm, a strange feeling washed over him, some revolting decoction of fear and lust.

"I try to ignore it," Ted continued, squirming in his chair while he spoke. "But I feel it growing bigger. Makes me sick. Sick all the time now." He palpated his belly with a hand, as if searching his guts for a thing that did not belong. "I don't wanna be like him, Hank. I *hate* my father."

Ted's voice receded with the rest of the world as Hank lost himself in the stone. After peering into its depths long enough, he began to perceive distant lights within it, lonely stars trembling in the furthest reaches of space. They whorled into strange constellations and blinked in and out of existence.

"I'm afraid of the hunger," said Ted, his voice breaking with emotion. "Afraid of the ache. Even now, I feel it rotting me from the inside."

Hank gasped when his thumb came down on the bladed edge of the stone. It sliced deep, almost to the bone, but no pain came screaming across his hand. Instead, every bad feeling in Hank's body escaped with the blood running down his wrist, and the spreading warmth made him realize how cold he'd been all these years. His heart raced and his breath quickened at the immense pleasure overtaking him. He examined the wound, and a thought occurred to him that felt like the answer to all of life's great questions. It felt divinely inspired: *a revelation.*

Hank turned to his copilot with wild eyes.

"You want me to see if I can get it out?"

A long silence hung in the air. A sense of spiritual harmony pervaded the flight deck, and grins spread across both men's faces. Ted looked at the stream pouring down Hank's arm, and at the stone that had caused the wound.

"Oh God, yes," he finally said, wiping away the sweat that now dribbled down his brow. "Can you really?"

Hank nodded with joyful confidence. He sliced his own finger again, this time in demonstration, and then gently pushed Ted back in his chair.

"Just hold still."

Hank unbuttoned Ted's shirt, exposing a roiling belly. He ran his fingers across Ted's abdomen as he'd done to the stone, beholding it with the same sense of wonderment. He traced a bloody symbol onto the skin.

"Wait!" Ted cried out as Hank prepared to make an incision. He pointed a shaking hand at Hank's face. "How can you see like that?"

Another long silence filled the air. Both men burst into laughter and then quickly shushed each other as if trying to keep a hilarious secret.

"You're right," Hank said, realizing his mistake. He looked down at the stone for a moment, then plunged it into his eye with a twisting motion. Kaleidoscopic patterns of light and color exploded across his vision. Hank could now see more clearly into the void.

"Mother of God," he said, looking around the flight deck in awe. The sight returned him across long years to the innocence of boyhood, and there he felt a comfort he'd since learned to live without. *"I'm home."*

Ted's snickering grew to uncontrollable laughter. With his remaining eye, Hank could see drops of sweat flying off Ted's face with each bellow.

"Oh shit," said Ted, now clutching his stomach to prevent it from bursting. "I think... I think I *hear* it." Mad babble erupted from his lips, and his tongue wagged around his mouth as if trying to escape on a forgotten curse.

Hank sliced into his other eye, methodically prying back the rest of the veil that had obscured his vision all these years. He rued the lifetime he'd wasted as a blind man, but at least now, he could see: the shape of Ted's soul, the sickness upon it, and the endless vistas of darkness cradling the two of them and everyone else on the plane.

"Now I see," Hank crooned. "I *see* it, Ted."

He loomed over the feverish man, soothing him with a hand to the cheek. Hank listened to the prayer Ted had begun to recite: a thing morose and indecipherable, uttered through him from across the dark.

"I hear it!" Ted cried out between the strings of guttural nonsense. "It's a song!"

"I hear it too, my friend," Hank replied, stroking the copilot's hair and beholding the illness that festered within him. He thrust the stone into Ted, slicing through his abdomen in the shape of the bloody symbol he'd drawn. "They're singing for us, buddy."

The sensation of cutting into Ted's body was transcendent for Hank. He felt the calamities of his soul called to order with each thrust. All his life had led up to this single act; it was his ultimate purpose, and he would be judged on it alone. He needed to remove all the pain and sadness from Ted to make room for the joy of salvation. As he reached inside to retrieve the malady that had affixed itself to the first officer, the prayer grew louder—both on Ted's voice and the ones chanting from the void. Brilliant, warm colors erupted from his spirit, showering Hank and the lightless cosmos around him while he ripped and tore at the infection. Everything was wet.

Ted screamed with ineffable passion now, unleashing verse upon verse of the song coming through him. It resonated inside of Hank, empowering him to do the work he was destined to do. The noises attracted the attention of the passengers in the cabin, their worried voices harmonizing beautifully with Ted's melodic prayers. The plane began to buck and snort over waves of turbulence, and Hank reveled in its soothing rhythm.

Stewardess Lila Jackson poked her head into the flight deck.

"What in the Sam Hell are you boys on about in here?" she asked—and then fell silent while she took in the scene.

Hank looked up at her, watching the terror gather on her face in radiant swirls. He could see through her as well—every emotion, every secret, every burden.

He would help her with all of those.

But first, he had to finish helping Ted.

The first officer now lay quiet in his chair, head bouncing lifelessly with each shudder of the plane. Hank craned over him, slowly removing and inspecting various things he'd excised from Ted's abdomen. Organic wonders dangled from every console, hung carefully to align with the stars that guided Hank. Rivulets of glowing liquid dripped from them and covered Hank's face and arms. Its warmth felt orgasmic.

Unable to speak, Lila instead croaked in horror, drawing Hank's attention. He looked up at her again, now cradling a snarl of Ted's illness in his hands. When he extended it to her as an offering, she found her voice and screamed.

"Yes, that's it!" Hank said. "They want us to sing too."

Lila fell backward out of the flight deck, crashing into the bulkhead behind her. She turned and fled, but Hank could see her no matter where she went. He could see everything now.

Hank turned to the control panel and set the plane to a moderate descent. Then he stood up and hung the infected viscera around his shoulders, imagining himself adorned in the vestments of a priest. By the light of the stars, he would consecrate this plane and everyone on it. He would free these poor souls from the disease of mortality.

Hank barged into the cabin and was met with the ghastly noises of his passengers. They too were becoming aware of the truths he'd discovered through the black stone, and now a few of them were praying and shrieking. Their eyes rolled back in their heads, no doubt from the immensity of their dark revelations, and they clawed at their own faces or pulled at each other's hair. Those unaffected around them looked on in fear, and when they beheld Hank's new eyes, they too began to scream.

Hank gripped the stone like a lancet in one hand and urged for calm with the other. He shushed the man closest to him and said in a gentle voice, "Don't be afraid, my dear. You won't feel a thing."

He then slashed the man's throat in one rapid flourish, baptizing the nearby passengers in the lustrous fluid that erupted from the wound. Although they screamed, the dying man himself looked up at Hank with an expression of relief and smiled wide-eyed as he crumpled in his seat.

"Be purified!" Hank cried out. "Throw off this wretched flesh!"

He drifted down the aisle, gazing into the souls of the passengers and longing to free them from the prisons of their bodies. Hank laughed as passengers attacked one another, as they prayed in nameless tongues, and as they cowered in fear at the sight of him. And they too began to laugh, until the entire plane filled with the music of the void. Two men grabbed hold of Lila, who had been crouched in a terrified ball at the back of the plane, and dragged her toward Hank. He peered deeply into Lila's eyes. Hidden galaxies swirled behind them, begging to be discovered.

"You'll see too," he said in a nurturing tone. "Here—let me help you."

The men held Lila's head still while she screamed in protest, but before Hank could relieve her of her blindness, a voice called out from behind him.

"Choose us," a young woman said, rising from her seat. She wore a tranquil expression and gazed fearlessly into Hank's new eyes. Her hands moved slowly over her pregnant belly, and inside it, Hank could see a most luminous soul—shared between a set of twin girls.

"Remarkable," he said breathlessly, forgetting the stewardess and turning to face the pregnant woman. "Truly a gift from God."

The woman moved past her convulsing husband and came face-to-face with Hank. The plane shuddered furiously as it descended through a cloud bank. In the cockpit, alarms blared.

"Teach us," the woman said, unblinking. "Teach us to sing."

Part I:
DREAMS

Chapter 1

1968

It was once believed that some caves in the Rocky Mountains are passageways to other realms, open only to the dead. Were a living person to enter one of these, they risked falling into *Knûth-Sōkáān*—the void between worlds, where even the spirit is forgotten. But the ones who told of this left the Rockies long ago, having fled the region after an age of brutal winters. Other peoples have since come and gone, weaving their own legends about the mysterious tunnels.

Down through the centuries, the caves of Pale Peak and its mountain neighbors have earned a particularly sinister reputation. They are said to cause fright and wonder in anyone who dares peer inside, and even hunger like winter wolves for the souls of the living. Their mouths whisper to passersby with promises of irresistible delight, and the mysteries of their depths call out to faraway children in their beds.

As a boy, Onwé Lopez had dreamed of the cave near his family's reservation on Pale Peak. He'd seen it in person while hiking with his father up to Mirror Lake, but he'd never stopped to inspect it. Onwé remembered the legends his father had told him about the cave—of wild animals and bandits and vengeful spirits—and heeded his warning never to explore it.

But in the dead of night, that maw of rock and all its pregnant darkness loomed in Onwé's mind. He dreamed of following his old man inside, and of shadowy things dragging him down into a bottomless chasm. He dreamed of undiscovered riches beneath the earth, and of lost, precious heirlooms of his people waiting to be reclaimed. As the decades passed, that cave became a thing of grim curiosity, feeling at once repulsive and alluring. Onwé grew up. But he never ceased to wonder.

Now, as he walked in the shadow of Pale Peak, Onwé realized the dreams had returned. Fragments of a nightmare came to him over the duration of his hike, and as he passed through forest and field, he tried to assemble the pieces. He remembered a boy and a copse of trees, and something moving in the distance. A storm, however, washed the color out of the world, and all of it blurred together in the fraying of memory.

Just like in his dream, today was dark and wet. The mountain's icy breath seeped through the pines all around Onwé, nipping at his ears and jangling the various charms affixed to his old hiking staff. It was late autumn now, and though the first snows were still weeks away, a month of rain had pummeled the land to a soggy pulp. The season had been unusually wet, and each squall seemed to portend the bitter winter to come.

Up ahead trotted Numi, a precocious Husky mix who loved the outdoors even more than her owner did. She sniffed every rock and flower, and ran circles around the trees in fruitless attempts at catching the chickarees that scrabbled over their branches. Throughout the eight years of her life, she and Onwé had explored almost all of the mountain and its foothills—except the western face, whose terrain was treacherous and shrouded in dark woods.

Today's journey would take them to Ash Hill, which rose above that eerie forest and offered a view of the distant mountains beyond it. It was a place for days that demanded a particular solitude. There, Onwé could escape his troubles—at least for a little while. Normally, the hike to get there was about an hour, but today it had taken more than two.

Onwé hardly paid attention to the trail as he wandered. Instead, he focused on the dream until its pieces came together and a little story played out...

The boy tugged Onwé's arm with one hand and gestured at a nearby tree with the other. Something dangled in it, twisting in a hateful wind. The boy had dread in his expression, but it wasn't clear if it was the swaying object upsetting him or the structure in the distance behind it.

"Lōnán!" the boy called out.

Father.

Onwé rubbed his eyes, trying to remember what had stood just beyond the tree. He thought at first it might have been a house, but it could have been a statue, or a cave. The faster he cycled through the images in his memory, the quicker they faded, and eventually, Onwé's mind returned to his surroundings. The dream vanished like mist on the morning slopes.

Onwé had had this nightmare many times before, or at least variants of it. He knew the boy was Akántha, his best friend from childhood, and he sensed that Akántha wanted to show him something. But Onwé always woke up before he could discern the thing through the heaving woods. After all these years, it remained obscured in the place just beyond the edge of his memory.

And what had Akántha meant by "father"?

More than two decades had passed since the boy's

13

disappearance, but the dreams rarely abated. At the worst times, they were terrifying, haunting Onwé in the dark of his home and weighing ceaselessly on his thoughts. He'd tried his best at interpreting the ones he could make sense of, and he'd scoured the wilderness for any place that looked like the tree line from his dreams. Alas, the forests and rock formations of Pale Peak all pretty much looked the same, and no amount of exploring had unraveled the mystery that had brought Onwé's life to ruin. The question echoed in his mind today as it had since 1944:

What happened to Akántha River Stone?

Numi's cheerful yipping pulled Onwé back to the present. She approached her master and gazed up into his eyes, perhaps noticing something was bothering him. He gave her a strong pat, which sent her zipping off down the trail in excitement, then bounding back to him again. As they rounded the bend, the pines thinned, and a grassy hill came into view against a gray sky.

"Looks like you found it," Onwé said to the dog. He quickened after her, his spirit renewed by the sight of an important landmark.

By the time he reached the top of the hill, Numi was already rolling around in the grass, dirtying the white of her coat. Onwé gave her some water from his canteen, then leaned against his hiking staff and took in the view. Emerald grass fluttered in the wind all around him, and a dozen yards ahead, the hill dropped off sharply toward a tree line far below. That was the edge of a woodland he'd never explored, and he prayed it was not where Akántha had gone all those years ago.

"Bears out there," Onwé's father used to say, trying to scare him as a boy. "Biggest ones around. *Man-eaters.*"

Long ago, Onwé had spent many mornings here with his father, sitting on a fallen log and trading stories or practicing the old language. It was one of the few places he could still feel

14

his dad's presence, and so Onwé had named the hill after him. With those memories embedded in the landscape, he could call upon his father's wisdom with each visit and be united with him through their mutual love of the outdoors.

Truly, Ash Hill was a beautiful place, not least for its spiritual aspect. The wild woods below sprawled out to a horizon of distant, jagged peaks tearing at the open sky. All around, rock formations jutted from the earth, which had served as fortresses for Onwé and his childhood friends. High above, the forbidding peak towered over the land, casting much of it in shadow. A rush of wind set the world shivering around Onwé and, for just a moment, chased away the dreary thoughts of all the people he'd lost.

But then, a mechanical sound arose: the roar of distant engines. Numi's ears perked up, and she jumped to her feet in search of the noise. It changed in pitch as it approached, and through the clouds overhead appeared a small jet. It sputtered against the choppy air and pitched back and forth on its axis, surely thrashing the poor souls on board. Onwé had seen plenty of aircraft pass over the mountain through the years, but none before had ever come this low, nor flown so erratically.

The plane's awkward glide turned to a spiraling dive, heralded by a shriek of its engines. It plummeted hundreds of feet in a matter of seconds, filling the valley with a hideous noise as it cut against the wind.

"Holy shit," Onwé said, already feeling in his body what his brain didn't want to admit. This plane was going down.

A moment later, it slammed into the earth in a burst of flame. The explosion echoed across the mountain, terrifying Numi and sending hundreds of birds soaring into the air throughout the valley. The dog fled to Onwé, who stood fright-frozen at the edge of the dropoff, and cowered there beside his feet. A terrible silence then followed, and plumes of smoke wafted from the distant trees.

"...*Holy shit,*" Onwé repeated, trying to regain control over his body. "Oh my God. Those people..."

He crouched down to console Numi. She licked at him nervously, reading his expression and growing more alarmed with each passing moment. The two remained pressed together in shock, until another loud pop erupted from the crash site.

At the sound, Onwé sprinted back down the trail. It would take a long time to get back to town, but he had to notify the tribal police. If anyone had survived this crash, they were now depending on him to send help.

"*Té'nak'yani!*" Onwé yelled, the dog already blazing past him. "Home, Numi! Home!"

Chapter 2

By the time he got back to the reservation, Onwé thought he might drop dead right there on the steps of the police station. It was a small wooden building at the edge of town, host to six police officers for the two thousand citizens of Autumn Ridge. He slammed a fist against the old door and called out to anyone inside, gasping for air between cries. Numi trotted nearby, breathlessly milling about in search of rain puddles to lap up.

The door finally opened, and a man in his sixties emerged. It was Steve Winépo, police chief and old friend of Onwé's father. Before the two exchanged words, Steve saw the urgency in Onwé's expression and whistled to his men inside. Two more officers approached.

"Plane crash," Onwé wheezed. "I saw it... I saw it go down."

"Just breathe, son," Steve replied, visibly shaken by the fear in Onwé's eyes. "Tell me what happened."

The notion of planes being swallowed by the Rockies wasn't exactly a surprise to the tribal police. Nearly every year, there was some report or other about a small craft disappearing over the mountains, and most of them were the military's business. On the rare occasion someone from the reservation actually saw it happen, Steve simply placed a call to the state government and then never heard anything more.

This time was different, however. The crash had occurred on Cold Valley's doorstep, and therefore, the Bureau of Indian Affairs might want to know about it—especially if any survivors found their way to the reservation.

"Why don't you go home?" Steve bade Onwé after listening to his story. "Try to rest up. I assume the BIA agents are gonna want to speak to you directly." He placed a hand on Onwé's back, gently urging him on his way.

"What about a search and rescue or something?" Onwé protested. "What if those people are alive? Shouldn't you call the ranger station?"

"Believe me," Steve replied, "we're on it."

The officers retreated into the department and closed the door, leaving Onwé by himself on the rickety porch. He collected Numi and ambled through the public square, exhausted and unnerved, wondering how long a rescue effort would take to assemble.

High above, the clouds began to part. Great sunbeams came stabbing through, illuminating the town against a backdrop of ominous dark. The rain would soon return, but for now, Autumn Ridge looked like a holy beacon on the grim mountain. Wet windows glittered all around, and the water dripping from rooftops sparkled with golden light.

The town's jarring mixture of poverty and beauty crossed Onwé's wires. He loved and hated Autumn Ridge, and at times, this war of emotions drove him up the mountain—to places like Ash Hill—in search of momentary peace. As much as he hated to admit it, this place was a part of him. Onwé had been born and raised here. He'd buried his parents in one of the cemeteries. He'd married and had a son. But even though Autumn Ridge was his home, neither he nor his people belonged to it, and it certainly did not belong to them.

The Cold Valley Indian Reservation was not a place built by the families who lived on it. Instead, it was one of many fragments of someone else's homeland, stolen by invaders from far away, shattered with guns and pens and broken promises. This land's previous inhabitants had been wiped out or relocated, and its new dwellers—all from different places—had been forced here with no regard for their historical relations to one another, corralled into a square that existed only on paper.

Those borders had not been forged through victory and alliance by Onwé's people. Rather, they were sketched on legal documents by bureaucrats half a world away. The schools and neighborhoods enclosed within them had been drawn up in distant offices, and the whole design of the reservation supported one simple goal: to ensure the Indians of the Rockies were "civilized" within a generation or two.

Onwé dropped onto one of the carven log benches lining the town square and soaked up the warmth of the sun before it vanished again. His hiking staff rested against one leg and Numi against the other, and he watched his neighbors as they passed by, unaware of the horror he'd just witnessed. The unpaved roads on which they walked led to houses on the north side of town, and to the south, a little grocery store and an even smaller library. None of the buildings were in good condition. Some of them should have been condemned long ago, but the people made do with what they had.

In fact, the only structure that looked well maintained was the church. It loomed on a hill above the town, glowing even on stormy days in its fresh white paint. The great cross on its steeple always seemed to cast a shadow over the ramshackle houses.

Laughter and cheering erupted nearby. In the river that spilled down the mountain and flowed through the town, a group of Onwé's neighbors celebrated their baptisms. Just as he turned to look, the junior pastor lifted a woman from the water and cried out, "Faith Sommers, you are born again in the Holy Spirit! Go forth in grace and righteousness!"

Onwé snorted with contempt as the woman threw her arms around her husband. The church had been warned the water was contaminated by runoff from the old mines farther up the mountain, but they didn't seem to care. Nor did they care that this river was probably sacred to the tribe who'd once lived on Pale Peak. He imagined those Natives might even spin in their graves beneath the church now standing here, had they been given the dignity of proper burials.

The sight of his neighbors abandoning the Old Way with such enthusiasm dug at the core of Onwé's frustration. He belonged to a lost people who could no longer remember their true home, and who had allowed themselves to be shepherded by false prophets. Everything about Autumn Ridge felt wrong.

As the newly minted Christians plodded by, Faith and her husband waved at Onwé there on the bench. He cast his eyes down, pretending not to have seen them and wishing he could disappear. Onwé wasn't alone in his rejection of the church; on some days, a few guys in town would hold traditional ceremonies in the field across the river, singing loudly enough to disrupt these baptisms and enraging the mirthless lead pastor whenever he was present.

Still, beneath the indignation Onwé felt toward the church, there flickered a longing for that hope and community he saw in the faces there on the riverbank. The converts had forgiven the church for all the evils it had wrought upon their elders, and now they even seemed happy. He watched them disappear into the town and then brushed the feeling off. His thoughts returned to the crash and what could have gone so wrong inside the plane.

The north road led uphill, where Onwé and the dog drifted

past tottering, rustic houses. They arrived at an old building on the edge of the woods, a house better kept than most of the others due to Onwé's skill as a handyman. Inside, he rested the hiking staff against the wall and patted Numi, who plopped onto her favorite blanket—a tattered blue quilt made by Onwé's grandmother.

"Rest up, girl," he said, gazing into her tired eyes. "We might need that nose of yours pretty soon."

Chapter 3

That evening, a knock stirred Onwé from a fitful nap. He'd drifted off in his old armchair, where he'd spent many nights reading in the drone of Numi's snores and the fire's crackle. The dog excitedly pawed at the front door. It could only be one person.

The sound occurred again, this time in a rhythmic pattern he recognized as the *secret knock*, which he and his boyhood friends had used to summon each other from their homes.

Onwé opened the door to his oldest friend, Luke, whose mere presence sent Numi ballistic. She leaped into his big arms and assailed his face with a barrage of licks.

"There's my pretty lady," he said. "Good Lord, what's Daddy been feeding you? Elk?"

Luke's playful banter drove Numi to run a circle through the living room and back at him for more. Onwé watched this cycle repeat a few times. He could never understand what it was about the man that affected his dog so much.

"It's true love, you know," Luke joked.

"Chipmunks have the same effect," Onwé replied in a sarcastic tone, gesturing for Numi to settle down. "Clouds too, sometimes."

Luke wiped his boots and headed straight for the fire. He removed his jacket and tossed it over the back of the armchair, then rubbed his hands near the flames.

"Looks expensive," Onwé said, eyeing the coat. He often picked on Luke for his choice of clothes, most of which came from the church donation box reserved for members of the congregation. The clothes were often nicer than the ones given out at the community-wide charity events.

"It's warm," Luke replied flatly. "All I care about."

"M'hm." Onwé sat down in the chair and studied his friend. Luke was tall and naturally muscular, one of the better-looking men on the rez. Women in town liked him almost as much as Numi did, owing especially to a tight haircut and a jaw hacked from stone. But in all the years they'd been friends, Luke had hardly given so much as a wink to any lady who'd crossed his path.

"So what's up?" said Onwé.

Luke traced a finger over the various trinkets dangling from Onwé's hiking staff. It was an old heirloom, like everything else in the house, left behind by Onwé's father. Elaborate carvings adorned its surface, whittled over the years in an effort to preserve an art form handed down through his family for generations. At the top dangled a leather string with a pouch containing things Onwé had found on his hikes: an animal tooth, an old coin, a bullet casing. Just below the pouch was a homemade bracelet crafted by Akántha, which fastened a small metal cross in place.

"You should try wearing this." Luke tapped the cross and turned to Onwé. Before his friend could retort, Luke offered, "...but this is a good start."

"Voth send you up here for something?" Onwé asked, suspicious that Luke was on some sort of mission for the church. The lead pastor, Burke Voth, had used Luke to pressure Onwé into conversion once before. It didn't go well, and a quiet bitterness had existed between Onwé and the pastor ever since.

"No, man," Luke said, softening his tone. "I ran into Steve. He told me to come check on you. Wouldn't tell me why. I stopped by earlier, but you didn't answer."

Onwé exhaled, relieved to avoid another confrontation with Luke over their religious differences. It'd become such a point of contention over the years, it sometimes resulted in long periods of silence between them. At times, Onwé could admit he tended to be the one to pick the fights. He knew their relationship would be less fractious if he eased up.

"I must have really been out of it," he said, glancing over at Numi, who'd returned to her blanket to watch the two men chat. "After what happened today, I thought I'd never sleep again."

"That bad, huh?" Luke replied. "You good? Wanna talk about it over some grub in town?"

Just then, there came another knock at the door, followed by an unfamiliar voice calling out, "Mr. Lopez? Are you home?"

Out on the porch were three men Onwé had never seen before, dressed in uniforms similar to those worn by the forest service rangers on the southwest side of Pale Peak. With them was Steve Winépo, looking positively out of his depth, and John Tall Rock, head of the reservation's tribal council. Luke and Numi spilled out into the cold evening air behind Onwé, and everyone began exchanging greetings.

"Onwé," Steve said, pointing at two of the men, "this is Paul and Vince, special agents of the Bureau of Indian Affairs."

Vince, the older of the two men, shook Onwé's hand. Paul simply nodded.

Steve gestured at the third stranger, a chubby man with freckles and curly orange hair. "And this over here is Warren.

24

He's from the...uh...Safety..."

"National Transportation Safety Board," Warren said. "Here to chat with you about what you saw, if it's not too much trouble, sir."

"What the hell did you see?" Luke asked, slapping Onwé on the back. "This guy get kidnapped by aliens or something?"

The joke died in the frigid air.

"No, Luke," said John. "He saw a plane go down. The government sent these folks to investigate."

Luke stared at Onwé with shock.

"How... Where?"

"That's what we need to determine," John said, approaching Onwé and dropping a meaty arm around his shoulder. "I'm sure you've had a long day, but we could really use your help figuring out where it landed."

Because of his position, John Tall Rock commanded great respect among the townsfolk—even the converts. But for Luke and Onwé, he was even more than a tribal elder. John had always been something of a father figure to them, and for that reason, they tended to heed his requests.

"Somewhere in the valley out west," Onwé said to the group. "I was on that hill my dad and I used to hike to, and I saw the plane crash a few miles out. You guys setting up for some kind of rescue op?"

There was a brief pause. Warren cleared his throat.

"Mr. Lopez, when you saw the craft go down, was it a gradual descent? Did you see it roll or slide at all?"

"No," Onwé said reluctantly. The horrible moment replayed itself in his head.

"Steep, then. Was it a hard impact? Loud boom?"

"...Yeah."

"Hm," Warren grunted. "Any fire?"

"One big fireball," Onwé said with a sigh.

"And did you happen to notice if the plane slowed down

at all before the crash?"

"No, sir," Onwé replied, arriving at the conclusion before Warren could say it. "I don't think anybody had their foot on the brakes."

Warren shot a grim look at the BIA agents.

"I'm sorry, Mr. Lopez," said Paul, the younger of the two agents, "but we're not expecting survivors. We find that people don't tend to survive the sort of crash you've described."

The finality in his voice cut like a hot knife, but it only confirmed what Onwé already knew inside.

"But there's still important work to be done," Vince added, trying to salvage the request they'd come to make. "Mr. Lopez, we want you to help us find the crash site. We're looking for a cause, and if we can identify it, maybe we can prevent it from happening again. Plus, if anyone survived, you'd be a hero for finding them, that's for sure."

"You'd have to get started at dawn," Luke interjected. "If it's as far out as Onwé says, that's a half-day's hike, at least. And you're bushwhackin' it. No trails at all. Can't risk the light."

"Actually," Vince said, removing his trapper hat to scratch at a mane of gray hair, "we were hoping to get started tonight. We've got supplies for both of you, assuming you'll come. Tents and bags and all. Documenting and photographing the crash will take several hours, so we need a full day out there tomorrow."

"Well," Onwé said hesitantly, "I can show you where I was standing when it happened. But Luke and I have never been out to where it crashed."

As he spoke, a rush of wind came shrieking through the town, silencing the men until it passed.

"Mr. Lopez," Vince protested, "maybe you don't know the way, but you've got all kinds of survival experience, don't you? John here told us your daddy used to take you guys huntin' and campin' all over the mountain. I'll bet you guys could keep us helpless city folk alive for a day or two while we do our jobs. Teach us about the land, protect us from the wildlife, that sort of thing. What do you say?"

Onwé couldn't tell if he was being complemented or insulted, but Vince's tone struck him as condescending.

"You need an Indian guide?" he said. "Is that what this is?"

"No, no," Warren replied. "It's just...we're not exactly mountaineers, Mr. Lopez. We figured a couple of fellas who are comfortable with the terrain—"

"Why not just take a helicopter out there?" Onwé interrupted. "You'll find the crash a hell of a lot faster."

"No can do," Warren said. "After this incident, the FAA's called a no-fly on the whole area for the next forty-eight hours on account of the forecast. We're hoofin' it out there, rain be damned. And we could really use your expertise here."

"Expertise?" Onwé said, venting his frustration through a hollow laugh. "I'm a handyman, Warren. Hit the gift shop. Ask for a shaman. Maybe a vision quest will reveal the coordinates of the wreckage." He turned to head back into his house.

"Nán'tāvúy," John scolded, embarrassed by Onwé's rudeness.

Like his father and many other folks on the rez, Onwé tended to be unwelcoming to outsiders, especially those who came on behalf of the federal government.

"Mr. Lopez," Warren called out, "what if—"

"I'll take you," Luke interrupted, trying to defuse the situation. "I've been out there before."

Onwé stopped at the threshold of the door and spun around.

"You?" he asked, incredulous. "When?"

"Long time ago," Luke said, averting his guilty eyes.

"You went alone? That's not like you at all."

"Not alone," Luke said. His gaze went vacant as he excavated a long-buried memory. "Akántha showed me the way."

Chapter 4

By nightfall, the group of men had pressed far across Pale Peak. A stiff wind propelled them along the trail out of Autumn Ridge and delivered them to the foot of Ash Hill, which glowed an eerie silver beneath a river of stars. The weather had kept, but the earth was still damp underfoot, so Luke hauled a bundle of dry firewood on his back. The other guys lugged packs of their own, and Numi trotted at the head of the line. Forgoing her typical whimsy, tonight she moved with a quiet vigilance, squinting in every direction at shadows in the gathering dark.

The men chattered amongst each other, making small talk. Onwé dipped in and out of it. His mind kept returning to Luke's strange admission, but he'd decided to postpone the interrogation until after they'd returned safely.

"Why does the Bureau care enough to send you fellas out here anyway?" Luke asked the men over his shoulder. "Nobody from the rez was on that plane; I guarantee it. Seems like cleanup is a job for the state."

"Safety of the folks on reservations is our number one interest," Paul said from the rear. "Anything that threatens life or livelihood out here is our business."

Onwé laughed. "Is this guy new, Vince?"

The senior agent's hesitation confirmed Onwé's suspicion.

"How long you been on the squad now?" he asked Paul. "A month?"

"...Seven weeks," Paul admitted.

Onwé briefly moved the circle of his flashlight over Paul's young face, revealing a look of embarrassment.

"People go missing every year in Cold Valley," Onwé said, with a bit of agitation in his voice. "Do you know how many of our women we've lost in the past decade? The BIA always tells us they just ran off to the city or some nonsense. Come to think of it, the government never sent in the cavalry for our friend Akántha either."

"It's true," Luke said, adjusting the shoulder straps of his pack. "He was an eleven-year-old boy, Paul. Broke his mother's heart. Tore up the whole town."

An awkward lull fell over the conversation, and the mountain filled it with a gloomy symphony. Owls and crickets sang in the distance, hidden waters lapped against stone, and pines shuddered in the night wind.

Onwé shined the light at Vince, isolating him in the harsh beam.

"No, I reckon your plane had someone important on it."

A low growl issued from nearby. Every flashlight beam fell on Numi. She stood rigid at the edge of the trail, peering out into the trees where the moonlight died. The fog-choked woods gave Onwé the creeps, and he loathed the idea of crossing into them at night. Whatever Numi sensed out there, he hoped it was only passing through.

"So, uh, what's it mean anyway?" Paul asked, seizing the opportunity to change the subject. "The dog's name."

"You know when it's so cold you can see your breath in the air?" Luke said. "That's *numi*."

"Dogbreath," said Paul. "Good name. Growing up, I had a cat named Barf. Not shittin' you."

"It's a good thing." Luke approached Numi and petted her into a state of relaxation. "The breath indicates the presence of the soul. Some of our people believe wicked things live here in the forest. No matter how cold it gets, you never see their *numi*."

"So y'all believe in the soul too?" Paul asked, kicking a large pine cone off the trail as he walked.

"Not exactly the same way as the Christians," Onwé said, heading off Luke. "But yeah. Sort of."

The group made its way to the top of Ash Hill and halted at the steep ridge on the other side.

"The plane went down out there," Onwé said, pointing to the wooded valley below.

While the agents prepared their descent, Luke and Onwé paused for a moment, each noticing the other's hesitation.

"Looks a bit creepy out there, doesn't it?" Paul said with a grin on his face. He was a handsome fellow, probably brash, and looked more like a greaser than a federal agent.

Luke smiled back, but Onwé didn't.

"That's a nameless place down there," said Onwé, tightening his grip on his father's hiking staff. "One big pit of nothing."

"It's just federal backcountry," Warren replied, studying a map with his flashlight. "We crossed the reservation's border a mile back."

Luke climbed down to Warren's position and moved his light over the treetops.

"We name places on the land to mark important memories for our people," he said. "That's how we keep our history. No one comes down here, so there are no memories. No memories, no names. Nameless place. Make sense?" Luke gazed back up at Onwé and offered a hand to him.

"You coming?"

Onwé sighed, his breath billowing into an icy cloud.

"Fuck it."

He pulled his long hair back into a ponytail and hiked his pack up on his shoulders. Then he clambered down the hill and followed Luke into the murky woods.

Chapter 5

Onwé had always revered the feral majesty of Pale Peak: the bristling pines, the golden valleys, the wind-scoured cliffs. Even in the overgrown cemetery above Autumn Ridge, he could find a sort of primal comfort. But here, in the nameless place, he felt only his own trespass reflecting back at him from the walls of towering trees. A chill unlike any he'd known before gnawed at his bones, of a sort no fire could banish. Onwé was unwelcome here, and the forest seemed to whisper it through an eerie breeze.

The journey quickly became too cumbersome in the dark. A deer trail snaked between blackened pines, taking the men single file on a meandering tour of the woods. Luke kept his light trained on the spaces between the trees, occasionally pausing to find his bearings. He searched for something but refused to say what, even when prodded by the others. Finally, he halted the march at a little grove.

"This is where we make camp," said Luke.

No one challenged him; they'd had their fill of scrambling over logs and stumbling through a night that seemed to bid them turn back.

Within the hour, the party had set up tents and built a fire. Onwé shuddered under its warmth, realizing how much he longed for hearth and home. Numi huddled near Luke, ears swiveling wildly at each distant noise, eyes chasing the shadows that danced with the firelight. All around them, the pines loomed overhead, eavesdropping on the conversations wafting up with the smoke.

"So y'all been outdoorsmen your whole lives?" Warren asked between mouthfuls of trail mix. He shook the bag at Luke.

"Pretty much," Luke replied, accepting a handful of the snack. "Onwé's dad used to take us all over the mountain as kids. Hiking and camping are pretty much the only things to do around here. Only *good* things, anyway."

"Ah yes, the great Ashthenôví." Vince nodded at Onwé and raised a canteen.

"How do you know my father?" Onwé asked, genuinely surprised to hear an outsider speak his name, much less pronounce it correctly.

"Oh, the BIA's got a file," said Vince, chuckling at the thought. "Man like that tends to draw attention."

"A man like what, exactly?" Onwé eyed Vince from across the campfire.

"Strong-willed. Stubborn. Meanin' no offense, of course. I read he once helped one of our agents out of the community center—through the window glass."

Luke cracked up and elbowed Onwé, who tried to conceal a smirk of his own.

"Isn't he the reason Autumn Ridge got a grant to build that library?" Vince continued.

"He fought for a lot of things," Luke said. "Ash was a great leader. Even Big John can't fill his shoes. Only thing he

34

couldn't get us was a grant to relocate everybody down to Lake Namarjo with the rest of our people."

"I heard about that," Vince replied. "Guess the BIA felt it had already written enough checks back then."

"Is that the truth?" Onwé asked. He'd always wondered if his father had simply pissed off the wrong people and worn out his luck.

Vince looked down at his canteen, apparently uncomfortable with the question.

"Cat got your tongue?" Onwé pressed.

A mournful howl arose from somewhere far off in the night, silencing men and crickets alike. Numi sprang to her feet and went stiff as a statue. After a moment, she sniffed at the cold air and peered intently into the darkness. The group exchanged discomforted looks.

"Transportation Board got you out hikin' in the dark pretty often, Warren?" Luke asked, noticing the apprehension on the man's face.

Warren hesitated, then offered an admission. "Just...one other time."

"Oh?" Luke said. "Do tell."

"I shouldn't," Warren replied, "I could lose my job."

"Who are we gonna tell?" Onwé asked. "In case you hadn't noticed, folks here don't go out of their way to talk to the feds."

Warren rubbed his tired eyes and shifted his weight. He stared into the fire as he spoke.

"Canadian Rockies, three years ago. Similar circumstances. Plane went down—one of ours. No mayday."

"No shit?" Paul said, intrigued. "You guys find it?"

Warren shook his head.

"Just a few pieces. Nothing like you'd expect in a wreck of that size. No passengers at the site. But..."

"But what?" Onwé said. The fire popped, startling the dog.

"But, uh, there was this cave about a mile away. We found some bodies in there."

"Bodies, but no plane?" Onwé repeated.

"That's right."

"Weird," Luke and Paul uttered simultaneously.

"Creepy," replied Warren, adjusting his coat around his bulk. The memories appeared to play out before his eyes, causing him to shudder.

"We've got creepy stories too," Onwé said, resting another log on top of the flames. "If you city boys aren't too yellow, that is."

Paul offered a lay-it-on-me gesture.

"Federal government's trying to sell this land off for development," Onwé said. "Upscale cabins or some shit. It's for the rich folks down in Orchid Valley who need a summer getaway, you see. My dad fought it for years. He wrote dozens of letters on behalf of the tribal council. This land was sacred to the Pozi. He wanted it returned to them."

"That's y'all, right?" Warren interrupted, pointing at Onwé with a stick of jerky he'd fished out of his backpack.

"We're Nauktí," Luke replied.

"Then who's the Pozi?"

"The people who lived in this region before the Gold Rush hit," Luke said.

"Oh, they're still here," Onwé continued, "under your feet. But they get up and walk around at night. That's why we don't come out here, Warren. We fear the *Kááth'matsiká*—the *skin-eaters*. They sniff out hikers and flay them living. Bury 'em upside-down. Revenge for what the miners did to them."

Warren's gaze darted back and forth from Onwé to the woods behind him. Onwé flashed a quick grin at Luke, who had already picked up on the ruse.

"In fact"—Luke dropped his voice to a fearful whisper— "our people say this place is forbidden. When the rain comes, the soil loosens and the *Kááth'matsiká* rise from the earth. On some nights, you can hear their cries on the wind. That means they've found their prey and are calling the others to the feast."

Another animal call echoed over the valley, and Luke snickered at its perfect timing. Numi flinched and headed over to Onwé, who wrapped her up in a big hug. The agents remained quiet, now focused entirely on the strange and mysterious sounds filling the woods around them.

"Sleep tight, fellas!" Luke said cheerfully. He patted Warren on the back and headed to his tent. "If you hear the souls on the mountain calling to you, don't listen."

Chapter 6

Onwé stayed up to chat with the agents a while longer. They kept the fire roaring into the night, talking about Vietnam and the recent death of Martin Luther King, Jr. Onwé apologized for his earlier hostility and explained some of the grievances his people had against the government.

At some point, the conversation came to a natural lull. The silence felt awkward at first, then odd, then eerie. A sluggishness came over Onwé's mind, and he realized how tired he was. He looked to the others and saw Vince carefully examining his own arms by the light of the fire. Warren tinkered nervously with the camera he'd brought to document the crash site. Paul ate handfuls of chips with nauseating fervor.

Onwé felt drunk. He rubbed his eyes for a long moment. When he opened them, the fire had died down to smoldering embers. Numi waited beside it, but the agents were gone.

"Guuuys?" he said. "Where'd you go?"

He listened through the wail of wind and bending wood. Footsteps crackled in the brush nearby. Numi whimpered.

"Vince?" Onwé called.

A blast of cold air assailed him and washed away his torpor. Onwé realized he was all wet; it must have rained again. The ceaseless dripping of the trees made it difficult to identify other sounds, but Numi's body language confirmed something was lurking out there in the dark. His mind conjured the silhouette of a large man at the tree line, circling the camp for hours and babbling strange words. It felt more like a distant memory than a figment of his imagination.

Numi cried again, fixated on something Onwé could not see.

"What is it, girl?" he whispered.

The dog didn't respond. She held still and kept her eyes trained on a point in the dark.

A branch snapped. A shape moved through the gloom. Numi bolted after it, more curious than aggressive. She slinked into the dark, giving chase to whatever loomed there. Onwé raced after the dog, calling out to the other men in the party as he ran. No one responded to his cries.

He flew over logs and between rows of pines, squinting through the mist in the starlit woods. His fear grew to panic. Onwé shouted the dog's name a dozen times, but she never responded.

Numi was gone.

The sounds of retching and mechanical whirring echoed from nearby. Bursts of light arced through the trees, temporarily blinding Onwé. Goosebumps rippled across his arms as the forest filled with laughter. He came upon Paul, who was hunched over with his hands on his knees, violently emptying his stomach onto the ground.

Warren stood a few feet away, snapping photo after photo and cackling malevolently. He weaved around the sick man, trying to find the perfect angle, howling with glee each time Paul loosed another volley.

"What the fuck's going on here?" Onwé demanded.

"I…I'm fine," Paul said, gasping for air.

"What did you eat?" Onwé asked. A camera flash went off right beside his head, causing an explosion of stars to float across his vision.

"And what the hell are you on about!" Onwé shouted, swatting at the huge camera.

Warren ducked the attack, snapping more photos and giggling feverishly. The flashlight's cone revealed that his pupils were grossly dilated. His greasy orange hair clung to his face, and drool hung from his open mouth.

"It was…tumors," Paul said, trying to stop himself from retching again. "Warts and tumors everywhere… Giant pustules all over the trees. I was…I was *eating* them. Oh Christ, the *smell* of it." He fell to his knees and vomited once more.

Warren laughed so hard at Paul's suffering he could hardly breathe and, for a moment, ceased taking photos.

"I think I lost track of time," Onwé said, comforting Paul and helping him back to his feet. "I don't understand it."

"Warren was sleepwalking," said Paul, glaring up at the chubby man snapping photos of him. "He was standing right here, lookin' off into the woods. Something out there was making him laugh."

A tortured groan echoed in the distance.

"Oh my God," a man cried, his voice freighted with agony. "Oh my God, someone help me. Jesus, help me."

Onwé spun around.

"Is that Vince?" he asked.

The men followed the voice to a little stream that cut through the woods. Vince was kneeling beside it, splashing water on himself and murmuring prayers.

"Vince! You okay?" Onwé asked, kneeling beside him.

Warren approached a moment after, trying to stifle his own laughter as he beheld the man's condition.

"It's b-blessed," Vince said. "It's holy w-water. It'll k-kill them." He shivered violently, dousing himself with more handfuls of water. Blood gushed from a large wound on his forearm, staining his pants and dribbling into the stream.

Onwé knew right away the amount he was losing could kill him.

"Get me a towel or something!" Onwé shouted at Warren. "Anything I can tie!"

Warren just stood there, clutching his mouth in an effort to hold back the laughter. The camera dangled from a strap around his neck and bounced on his heaving gut.

"Here," Paul said, removing his jacket. He handed it to Onwé, who then grabbed Vince's hand and tried to pull him away from the stream.

"No!" Vince threw himself back into the water. "They're in my veins. Little eggs right now, but when they hatch, they look like this!" He scooped a hunting knife out of the water and waved it around, causing Onwé and Paul to jump back. "When they're b-big enough, they attach to the back of your neck and get ins-side your head. I'll get m-mine out, and then I'll do yours. It'll be okay!"

Vince sat on his knees and lowered his head. He angled the knife downward over his neck, intending to dig into his own spine. Onwé leaped atop him, kicking Vince's hand so hard the weapon clattered across the stones. Paul dogpiled on and held Vince in place while Onwé tied a crude tourniquet with the jacket.

Upon seeing the melee, Warren lost control of himself and burst into another fit of laughter. He resumed his unhinged photography, crouching and coming in for closeups of Vince's horrified face. But the flash bursts appeared to stun Vince. The senior agent blinked away the madness that had gripped him and looked up at his friends as if seeing them for the first time.

"Please tell me Luke is in his goddamn tent," Onwé said to Paul.

"I haven't seen him," Paul replied, spitting the foul taste from his mouth.

"Look around," Onwé said. He pulled Vince to his feet and gave him a hard shake. "We gotta get you home, pal. Keep it together for me."

The red light of dawn had now conquered the sky, and the woods began to reveal themselves. The men returned to camp and found it a wreck: someone had torn apart the fire pit, tents had collapsed, and supplies lay strewn across the ground. Luke was nowhere to be found.

"He's not here," Onwé said, voice tightening with anxiety. "We have to find him. Fast."

The terrible feeling from the day he'd lost Akántha rushed to the surface. The world spun around him. He feared Luke could be injured, or worse. Onwé could not survive another loss of that magnitude.

"Likōté!" Onwé screamed, calling out to Luke by his birth name. "Numi! Where are you?"

Vince and Paul joined in and began calling for their missing companion. Warren staggered around like a child following his parents, giggling as he walked.

They made their way through the forest, and a dog's barks rose in the distance.

"Numi!" Onwé shouted. "Guys, follow me!"

Golden light had begun spilling into the valley from the east, revealing a cave set into the base of a tall ridge.

"There." Onwé pointed.

He raced down the hill toward the cave. Beside it was a tall tree, and sitting against its trunk was Luke. Numi stood next to him, sniffing and licking his face.

"Líkōté!" Onwé called.

He rushed over to his friend, who looked pale and drained of spirit. It took considerable effort, but the man climbed to his feet.

"What happened, brother?" Onwé searched both Luke and the dog for injuries. "Why the hell are you all the way out here?"

Warren approached the trio, laughing obnoxiously. He snapped pictures of Luke and the dog, but then began sobbing as he moved.

"Will you take that fuckin' thing away from him!" Onwé shouted at Paul.

Despite the situation, Luke had a preternatural calmness about him, and his expression seemed more withdrawn than frightened.

"Just sleepwalked is all," he said.

Without another word, Luke started walking back toward camp. He ignored Vince and Paul when he passed, and didn't seem to notice Warren's camera at all.

Onwé looked back at the cave and tried to see inside, but its darkness was impenetrable.

"Did you go in there?" he called out.

Luke ignored the question.

Warren's attention fell on the cave, and he slowly lowered his camera. Snot and tears and sweat covered his face, dripping from his mouth as he whimpered. He walked up to Onwé and stood beside him, peering into the lightless void—and gasped.

The insanity possessing him seemed to dissipate, as if drawn from him like poison into the blackness itself. Warren blinked several times, wiped his face, then turned and left in silence.

Chapter 7

"So, what happened?" Onwé finally asked.

It had been an hour of wordless hiking, and the question had practically fallen out of his mouth after rolling around in his head for so long. He and Warren had decided they were in the best condition to press on to the crash site. The others had packed up and returned to Autumn Ridge. For all the drama of last night, Luke acted strangely unfazed and seemed sober of mind enough to help Paul and Numi get Vince back to civilization.

Unlike Luke, who'd refused to share any details about his experience of the grim incident, Warren spoke candidly about his. He'd suffered visions of some hideous animal imitating a man, dancing in circles around the camp. It helped the others into coffins in the ground while Warren looked on, paralyzed with laughter.

"We sang together when the coffins were buried," he said, "me and the weird man. Well…it…*tried* to look like a man."

"What do you mean?" Onwé asked. "What was it?"

Warren stopped in his tracks and checked the compass, then shot a disquieted look back at Onwé.

"I have no idea. But it *wasn't* a person."

"What did you sing?" Onwé asked, disturbed by the mental image. The two continued on, ducking between trees and romping through tangles of ferns.

"I can't understand it," Warren replied, "but somehow I knew the words. '*Soul me ah do, soul me ah do, I'm a...naked soul...*' Something like that. The song was so sad it made me feel crazy. Like I was experiencing every emotion all at once."

Onwé wondered if he and his companions had disturbed something long forgotten by passing through these woods. He remembered his grandmother's stories about the creatures of the night. Although Onwé and Ash weren't as practiced in Nauktí tradition as Old N'wenthāil, they had heeded her warnings to respect the mountain and the spirit-beings that dwelled on it.

"After we sang," Warren continued, "it asked me to follow it."

"To where?"

"A house?" Warren said with uncertainty. "A house in the woods...maybe near a cliff."

"Did you see this house?" Onwé yanked his foot free from a tangle of wet brush.

"High up in the distance," Warren replied. "I didn't want to go, but I followed anyway. Like I was being pulled along. The thing kept singing to me as we walked, even when I told it to stop. Then I realized I was holding my camera, so I started taking pictures of it to show you guys. I woke up right there in front of the cave, standing next to you."

"Strange," Onwé mumbled to himself.

"Do your people, uh...have any legends about this sort of thing?" Warren asked hesitantly.

"A few, actually," Onwé conceded. "If my grandmother was still around, she'd say this was a curse on the night wind, or a wandering spirit. Or maybe one of the elders of the earth, who were here long before people came into the world.

"But this is a mountain, Warren. Toxic gasses, high altitude, contaminated water... All kinds of things here can make people sick. Hell, some of the folks on the rez say there's magnets and magic stones under the Rockies."

Onwé tried his best to reassure Warren and himself, but deep down, he was afraid. He wished now more than ever that he could speak to N'wenthāil, who'd passed just after Akántha's disappearance. She, like most Nauktí, believed dreams were puzzles to be solved.

As the two men carried on, the conversation returned to the sort that occurs when the sun is high and the woods are bright. They traded many questions; Warren inquired about life in Indian country, and Onwé asked about the wider world. Long ago, Onwé had inherited a vast collection of old books from his father, who'd believed reading was a means of unshackling Indians from their mandatory Christian education. These books had sparked in Onwé a hunger for more knowledge of life outside the reservation, but he, like most people in his community, had never been more than a few miles away from it.

The conversation was silenced when Warren halted once again, staring up at the trees ahead, or perhaps at the soaring mountaintops that peeked over the canopy.

"You find the plane?" Onwé asked, hoisting himself up a muddy embankment.

Warren simply pointed, unable to take his eyes off whatever it was he saw. As Onwé joined him, he, too, stopped dead in his tracks.

The sight gathered in Onwé's mind only as irreducible components: light, shadow, color, and shape. A composition formed, though it was one his brain could not interpret for several moments: a person, a tree, a web of red vines. But then his awareness gathered.

A corpse stared back at him, bent over a branch high off the ground. The spine had snapped and jutted skyward, the skin draping off the body in melted gobs. Intestine and other viscera dangled onto the branches below, mysteriously red and raw, as if unexposed to the heat that had baked the flesh.

More bodies flanked the ruined corpse, hanging from other branches in odd positions. Most of them were charred, and some were little more than glistening skeletons. The tree groaned under their weight.

"You think they fell out of the plane or something?" Onwé whispered.

Both men approached with caution, moving as if they'd trespassed on hallowed ground. The blood had blackened on the wood, but the organs still looked fresh.

"They're only in this one tree," Warren replied in a hushed tone, "and I don't see any damage to it."

Onwé's foot caught on something stiff, and he nearly toppled over.

It was a pair of legs sticking straight up out of the ground.

"Shit," Onwé grunted, recoiling in disgust. The feet were bare, and the calves had been gnawed away by animals.

"Someone put these here." Warren surveyed the nearby woods for anyone lurking about. "The bodies are arranged." He began documenting the scene with his camera, but this time, he didn't laugh at all.

"We should leave," Onwé said, entirely rattled by the gruesome scene. "We have to get out of here."

"I've got to do my job," Warren replied, steadying himself with slow, deep breaths. He stood over a bush, fighting against a barrage of dry heaves.

The two men crept onward, searching for any signs of the plane. They came upon a rocky mound with a gaping hole at its base. It was a natural stone tunnel shaped like a well, wide enough to swallow John Tall Rock's truck. At its mouth lay the corpse of a young woman, mangled but unburnt. One of her arms hung over the rim of the tunnel as if encouraging the men to enter. Much of the face was still intact, and a sharp black stone the size of a walnut protruded from her temple.

A dreadful sensation crept over Onwé's body, worse than the feelings already haunting him in the presence of so much death. The specter of doom was upon him, and Onwé fought the urge to run as fast as he could back to the reservation.

"That's nine," Warren said. His hands trembled as he raised the camera to his eye. "Plane had twenty-two on it."

"Who were these people, Warren?" Onwé demanded. "Luke and I did our part. The least you can do is tell me what's going on here."

"I don't know that much," Warren replied, seating himself next to the corpse and dangling his feet into the abyss as he studied her. "It was some businessman's jet. Important people heading to California. That's all I know."

"Important people," Onwé repeated. "Does the FAA think this was an accident?"

Warren took a few more photos of the woman and shook his head.

"Our boys already spoke to the widows of the pilots. I guess one of 'em was acting weird after a camping trip here in the mountains. Him and his kid."

Onwé swatted a pebble with his hiking staff and watched it skitter into the hole. It bounced against the walls of the tunnel and disappeared into its depths. Warren leaned in, listening as carefully as he could.

"Rest of 'em could be down there," he said, taking a photo of the gloom to momentarily illuminate the tunnel. The flash revealed a throat of bleached-white stone that seemed to pipe all the way down to Hell itself. "I have to catalog them for my report."

Onwé scoffed at the notion.

"Are you out of your fucking mind?" he said. "Have you ever even been inside a cave or a mine?"

"No," Warren admitted, pulling a flashlight out of his pack, "but I'm really hoping you have."

Onwé shook his head.

"Remember what I said about toxic gas? Radon, carbon monoxide, sulfur. A lot of these caves connect to the old mines all over Pale Peak. The government that's paying you to scope them out is the same government that dug up all that uranium here in the forties for their bomb. The excavation ruined our land, and this cave right here could be contaminated."

"I guess I didn't realize." Warren peered into the hole with even more hesitation than before.

"That crap seeps into the rivers here too," said Onwé. "We have to hike all the way up to Mirror Lake to get edible fish. I didn't much like seeing Vince sticking his face in that water."

"Does the Bureau of Indian Affairs know about this?" Warren asked, incredulous. "I bet Vince could file some kind of complaint, couldn't he?"

"Lots of Indian reservations are built on contaminated land," Onwé concluded. "You'd think they *want* us dead."

Onwé turned his attention back to the stone in the woman's skull, but as he looked at it, he began to feel nauseous. He caught himself shuffling toward the hole and narrowly avoided plunging in headfirst.

"I'll say a prayer for these people"—he backed away from the lip of the tunnel—"but I'd sooner take a baptism than follow your giddy ass down there. Let's split. *Now.*"

Warren relented and saddled up.

"I'll call it in," he said. "Hopefully they'll send teams with proper gear."

As they marched back into the forest, Onwé thought he heard a faint voice from the tunnel.

"Nope," he mumbled.

——————●◎●——————

After another hour of searching, the wreckage was still nowhere to be found. Onwé and Warren decided to make for Autumn Ridge rather than sleep another night in the nameless place. They spoke less on the journey home, but the mountain filled in the quiet with a rolling storm. They trudged through rain and mud and lashing wind, stopping only to check the map and compass under cover of a waterproof jacket.

"There's more you're not telling me," Onwé called over his shoulder to Warren when they reached Ash Hill. "The missing plane, the cave, the bodies... It's just like what you said about that crash in Canada."

A look of distress flashed across Warren's face. Whatever he remembered from the experience, he didn't like talking about it.

"There's a lot of stuff they don't let us say about incidents like these," he offered, wiping a mop of orange hair out of his face. "But yes, there are similarities. No connection between the people on the planes. More just the circumstances are shared: small jets, sick pilots or passengers, flying over mountains."

"Sick?"

"The Canadian pilot acted strange too. There were some kids onboard, and he wanted to, uh, to make them...*sing*."

"Make them *sing?*" Onwé repeated, trying to understand the strange tone of Warren's voice.

"We got the flight recorder," Warren said, visibly shuddering. "Everyone onboard was screaming. Especially the kids. Pilot kept dipping the plane. The more the kids cried, the more he did it. I heard him laughing and begging for more. The sound of it, Mr. Lopez... I still can't get the sound of it out of my head."

Chapter 8

Warren and Onwé arrived back in Autumn Ridge that evening soaked to the bone, just in time to witness a Nauktí ceremony in the field beside the town. Eight men were standing in a circle, dancing and clapping rhythmically while a man in the center beat a drum. The drummer sang long, melodic refrains, and the dancing men chanted, *"Wáj'chu! Wáj'chu! Wōulm'ai! Wōulm'ai!"* in aggressive bursts.

"Some kinda war cry?" Warren asked in a cavalier tone.

"It's how our people honor a man who's become an elder," Onwé explained. "There's another one for women. It's...calmer."

As they passed through, Onwé caught sight of Pastor Burke Voth glaring at the ceremony from across the little river. He was a tall, thin man who always seemed to cast too long a shadow, and his deep voice carried well beyond the pulpit from which he condemned Indian traditions. For now, he stood in silence, beholding the ceremony with fatherly disappointment, but Onwé knew the occasion would be denounced in next week's sermon. It always was.

"Is it true what you said about the Pozi?" Warren asked, breaking the unfriendly stare between Onwé and Voth.

"Nah," Onwé replied. "I mean, they really did lose a battle against the pioneers. They lost everything, in fact. Some of their descendants are right here on the rez with my people." He pointed at two women approaching Voth to chat.

"And the skin-eaters?" Warren asked.

"Every culture's got creepy stories," Onwé said.

The two men bade each other farewell. Warren headed off to link up with the BIA agents, and Onwé set off to find Luke and the dog.

The church glowed warmly in the twilight. It was not usually occupied this late in the evening, but tonight the ministers held a barbecue on the back lawn, and many people from the town had gathered. Free food and community were some of the church's most effective means of attracting new adherents into the congregation, and for this reason, Onwé tended to avoid the monthly event. Tonight his gut told him Luke would be there, searching for spiritual comfort after what had happened to him in the nameless place.

Onwé passed the welcome sign, which read in huge letters: **Jesus Is Lord in Cold Valley.** He followed the path around back, where he waded through a crowd of his neighbors while they ate and made merry beneath several large tents. Some of them expressed shock to see him in attendance, given his family's reputation for hostility toward Voth, but others smiled and welcomed him to the affair. Even Brother Duncan Campbell—or "Duncan the Dunker," as Akántha's mother called the junior pastor—looked delighted to see Onwé. But their warmth burned him, and he tried to politely distance himself from the festivities by refusing the plates offered to him. Instead he asked for Luke, but no one seemed to know where he was.

At last, Onwé spotted Luke through a window. The man sat alone inside the church, unnoticed by the congregation carrying on in the field.

"Thank God Ash isn't here to see this," Luke said as Onwé wiped his shoes and stepped inside the building.

The warmth instantly thawed his bones, and Onwé tried to ignore the cozy feeling that flooded him. He leaned his trusty hiking staff near the door, wondering whether Voth would be confused at its little Christian cross displayed alongside a tangle of heathen idols.

"Now you can't say I wouldn't do anything for you," Onwé replied with a wink. He sat down in the pew next to Luke and took in the austere surroundings. "Well, you guys got nothing on the Catholics, that's for sure."

Luke didn't laugh. Instead, he gazed ahead, eyes unfocused. He seemed lethargic, except for the tense way he picked at his fingernails in his lap.

"You okay, brother?" Onwé asked.

"I'm alright," he said. It was an obvious lie.

In recent years, Luke had turned to the church when things got tough—first as a member of the laity, and more recently as an outreach organizer. He did whatever he could to stay involved, and as such, a lonely man had found a family. That's how it worked for most of the people of Cold Valley: Christianity had softened on reservations over the last two decades, and in turn, Indians had begun to warm up to it.

"You guys find your way alright?" Onwé asked, trying to get anything out of his friend. "How's Vince?"

"It was a nice walk home," Luke said with agitation in his voice. "All things considered. Vince will be okay."

"About that," Onwé said, turning to face Luke directly. "Everybody else shared their story. You feel like telling me what went down?"

Luke's gaze remained fixed on the empty lectern.

"I barely remember."

"What were you doing all the way out there?" Onwé said. "Did you go inside that cave?"

Luke stopped picking his nails. A memory appeared to strike in his mind. His expression became grave, and he stiffened like a corpse, unable to relax his muscles for a long moment. He finally looked up at his friend, and in that moment, Onwé saw how Luke's eyes gaped in horror at what he'd seen. How they *screamed*.

Onwé's mouth went dry. In his thirty-six years, he'd never seen Luke so frightened. The terror was contagious.

"What the hell happened to you?" he demanded. "Tell me, Líkōté!"

"My name is *Luke*. And nothing happened. I thought I heard someone calling my name. But I was just sleepwalking. That's all. That's it."

"There's something wrong with that place," Onwé said, remembering the bodies up in the trees. He didn't mention what he and Warren had found, knowing it might stress Luke out even more.

"I wouldn't know."

"I was so scared when I couldn't find you," Onwé admitted. "I kept thinking of the day Akántha went missing."

Luke abruptly stood up and headed toward the door, trying to conceal his frightened reaction to the name.

"Is that who you heard?" Onwé asked, realizing he'd struck a nerve.

"Numi's in your house," Luke said flatly. He didn't look back.

"What did you see in that cave?" Onwé called out. "Why won't you tell me?"

Luke paused at the door. He took a breath and pushed it open.

"I just saw black," he said. "All the way down. Like the

space between dreams."

With that, Luke stepped outside, ignoring his fellow parishioners and disappearing into the night.

Chapter 9

The next morning, Onwé set off to Moya River Stone's house on the other side of town. After N'wenthāil's death, Akántha's mother and Onwé had grown even closer, and she became the elder he consulted on dreams and matters of Nauktí spirituality. But the loss of her son had left Moya with a mercurial temper, and as the community slowly Christianized during Voth's tenure, she'd become increasingly isolated.

Now, Moya lived alone in the weather-worn house left by her parents, who had died of typhus long ago. Onwé kept the place up whenever he could, but his skill and supplies were limited, and as he knocked on her front door, he made a mental note to replace its weather stripping. A frail woman with stormy gray hair emerged and looked relieved to see him.

"I thought it was that little pecker Samuel," Moya said, waving Onwé inside. "He's been stopping by more often since he found out about my sight."

"How's that going, by the way?" Onwé asked, noticing Luke seated at the table in front of a bowl of oatmeal. Luke kept his gaze down.

"Gettin' dimmer all the time," she replied, looking out the

window to the eastern valley. "Can't watch the hawks much anymore. I can still make out faces just fine, though."

Onwé made conversation with the two about goings-on around town. Eventually the talk turned to the past, as it always did, and the ice in Moya's expression melted under the warmth of fond memories. She teased Luke for his long legs as a boy and the clumsiness they'd caused him, and she told stories about Ashthenôví reprimanding the kids for playing pranks around the town.

"I dreamed of him last night," Moya said, more an admission to herself than an announcement to the room. "My son came home to me."

Onwé shot a glance at Luke to see how he'd react, and as expected, his friend continued staring into the empty bowl, trying to pretend he hadn't heard mention of Akántha.

"Was it a good dream?" Onwé asked.

Moya sat on her old couch, sinking so deeply into it she nearly vanished. Over the lonely years, both she and it had worn down to ruin. The onslaught of solitary winters had eroded her body, and the crush of sorrow had left its riverbeds on her face. Her spirit seemed to flee her body each time she talked about Akántha, so Onwé never mentioned him unless she brought him up first.

"No," she said, dragging a blanket over her bony lap. Moya wasn't even sixty yet, but she was weak, and moved the way Old N'wenthāil had in her final years.

"No?" Onwé repeated.

"I heard a noise." She pointed at the little bed in the corner of the room. Beside it was a window with a view to the nearby woods. "When I looked outside, I could have sworn it was him."

Onwé, Luke, and Akántha had begun many of their adventures right there at that tree line while Moya watched lovingly from inside. She stood up with the blanket and walked over to the window, looking for her son as she had every night for two decades.

"He used to pop out right there at sunset," she continued. "But in the dream, it was late at night, and the moon was full. I saw Akántha standing there with no clothes on, looking away. He didn't turn around no matter how loud I called his name. He just kept staring up at the moon. He looked frozen to death."

Luke finally lifted his gaze. He shot a look of pained helplessness to Onwé, who returned one in kind. Neither of them knew what to say to Moya during these times, so out of respect, they didn't speak at all.

"Then I was up in the air with the hawks," she said, "and the town was destroyed. Buried under a mudslide. I floated down into a hole in the ground. And then I woke up."

"*Néthédi* Moya," Onwé said, addressing her by her elder title, "he's returned to my dreams as well, and—"

"I have to be going," Luke interrupted, pushing himself away from the table and bolting for the door.

Just before his hand grasped the knob, a gentle knock resounded from the other side, and for a moment, Moya held her breath, as she must have done any time an unknown visitor arrived on her doorstep.

Luke pulled open the door to reveal a sprightly eighteen-year-old white boy with sandy hair and big blue eyes.

"Morning, Luke!" he said with his trademark church-cheer.

"Good morning, Samuel," Luke replied.

The two knew each other well; Samuel Cotter was on the reservation working his hours for entry into theological school. Around town, he was a glorified errand boy for Voth and his clergy, but Moya saw him as a well-meaning pest.

"Hello, Mr. Lopez," Samuel said. "It was great to see you at the barbecue!"

"Just don't tell anybody," Onwé replied, half-joking. He'd never been overly kind to Samuel, but knowing the business Moya was bound to give him, he forced a smile.

"I'm sorry to intrude," said Samuel, "but I just wanted to come by and see if Ms. River Stone needs anything from the store."

Moya responded with a frigid stare from across the room. Samuel looked to Luke and Onwé for support, but found that as long as they stood in Moya's house, the men deferred to her level of hospitality.

"Sorry, just...just making my rounds," he went on, trying to ward off the uncomfortable moment. "I'd be happy to walk with you down to the church this evening too, Ms. River Stone. There's going to be a truck full of all kinds of new things. Coats and shoes and non-perishables, stuff like that. A gift from the Valley Commission."

"Tell you what, Samuel," Moya said, approaching the door and stepping in front of Luke, "if that church ever goes up in flames, I'll let you walk me down there to warm my bones."

The doe-eyed cheer evaporated from Samuel's face. He looked to Luke and Onwé once more but found no defenders.

"Sorry again, ma'am," he said, clearing his throat. "May I have your permission to include you and your son in tomorrow's sermon? It's about triumph over grief. One of our young members just lost her father—"

"Begone," Moya snapped, impaling the boy with a fiery glare. She tugged at her leather-string necklace, retrieving a little sage pouch from beneath her shirt. It dangled in the open now—a symbol of spiritual resistance to the new religion.

"Sorry," he replied, his face reddening with embarrassment. He turned and left.

Onwé felt bad for the little twit. He knew Samuel meant well, and the same was probably true for most of the missionaries on the reservation. But history ran too deep. Moya had survived the most brutal era of Christian boarding schools, and had witnessed the abhorrent treatment of her parents by men of the cloth. She could never forgive the church for what it had done to her people, even if it had become more docile in her adult years.

Luke closed the door and turned to Moya, trying to contain his fury.

"How can you treat him like that?" he demanded, raising his voice beyond what was acceptable for a person addressing an elder. "What's that boy ever done to you, besides leave medicine at the door when you're sick?"

"He's one of the bricks in our prison," she replied. "None of them looks responsible up close. And the Valley Commission isn't here just to give out soup and sweaters."

Luke breathed a frustrated sigh.

"They probably gave you that blanket, *Néthédi*. And the breakfast you made for me. Have you forgotten our people's teachings about strength through community? About honoring those who honor us?"

"I'm not the one who's forgotten the Naukti way, *Likōté*," she spat.

"My name is *Luke,*" he replied, with as much sass as he dared.

"Enough," Moya said. "I can't stop you from carrying the cross. But neither you nor Samuel, or even Voth himself, is gonna drag that thing in here."

"Samuel doesn't need you to defend him, brother," Onwé added. "He knows what he signed up for. Working with Moya is...*character-building* for him."

"I'm ashamed of you," Luke said to Onwé. He ripped the door open and zipped up his jacket. "Samuel knows what you did to your son, and he still treats you with great respect. It's taken him half as long as you to figure out how to be a decent man."

Onwé's breath caught in his throat. What had happened with Tíwé was off-limits for discussion—Luke knew this well.

When he finally found his voice, Onwé called out, "What the fuck is your problem, man?"

Luke just kept walking.

Chapter 10

Onwé stepped out onto Moya's porch, and a nearby argument drew his attention. He looked over to see Pastor Burke Voth and two members of the church holding an animated discussion with Moya's neighbor Karl. The man was seated in a rickety chair, defensively clutching some kind of object that rested on his lap, while the pastor and his short-haired acolytes loomed over him.

"Why can't you all just leave me alone?" Karl pleaded. He shooed the men away, but they remained in place, trying to reason with him about the thing he held.

Onwé approached slowly, trying to ascertain the nature of the conflict before anyone noticed him. As he drew closer, he saw the argument was over a warding stave, and knew that Karl could probably use a hand.

The stave, not unlike Onwé's hiking staff, was a large wooden stick adorned with symbols of ritual. Rabbit fur and dyed yarn striped the handle in a color pattern announcing the clan of Karl's Ineho ancestors, and a crest of deer antlers rose proudly at the top. Eagle feathers, no doubt collected from high up on the mountain, dangled from a band Karl had affixed to a few of the antlers' points. A few pouches, probably full of herbs, hung from the leather strips that fastened the whole thing together. In the distant past, Inehos constructed warding staves to protect their families from vengeful winter spirits. Then, in the first bloom of spring, they burned these totems, destroying the curses they'd ensnared.

"God save these stubborn souls," Voth lamented under his breath. He sensed Onwé's approach and examined him with a side-eye. The two men had not spoken in months, nor had a full conversation in years, and tended to avoid each other whenever possible.

"These pricks wanna take it away from me," Karl complained when Onwé moved to his side. "It's just for my daughter's birthday."

"We don't want to take it away from you," one of the converts retorted. "We're just asking you not to build these anymore."

"Technically, it violates the Code," said the other, producing an old pamphlet from his jacket. "Members of the reservation should avoid wicked conduct, including the construction or worship of savage idols."

"Savage idols," Karl angrily repeated.

The Code of Indian Offenses was a blanket ban on most Native rituals. It had paralyzed the spiritual backbone of many Indigenous cultures on its passage in 1883, and had empowered the federal government's project of "civilizing" Indians with armies of missionaries. Onwé knew sections of the Code by heart, having been forced to learn it in boarding school as a young teen.

"You guys really have *nothing* better to do?" Onwé said to the church members. Recent converts tended to be overzealous, and they agitated Onwé the most.

"We're keeping the peace, Mr. Lopez," Voth said. "It was Mr. Ortega here who broke it."

"What are you gonna do?" Onwé pressed. "You gonna

call the Bureau agents up here to drag this man off his porch? It's a *stick*, Voth."

In decades past, Karl's affront would have been punishable with jail time, but now, the Code was more selectively enforced. And while some churches still called down fire and brimstone on other reservations in the U.S., the Cold Valley Baptist Church tended to operate with a gentler hand. Onwé knew Voth wouldn't retaliate but through an agonizing sermon or three.

"Maintaining the spiritual health of this community is my *personal* charge," Voth replied, taking a step toward Onwé. Although he was a lanky man, Voth liked to use his height to remind disobedient Indians of his primacy in Autumn Ridge. "If I can do that without involving the Bureau, I will. But I'll not have anyone practicing magic or any other Indian mischief on this reservation."

Onwé felt an ugly mixture of intimidation and pity. Other ministers had passed through Cold Valley over the years, but none as grim and soul-weary as Burke Voth. The man was a singularly brooding creature, having lost the exuberance of his younger faith to generations of frigid Indians, and now fought tooth and nail to grow his congregation and wrest the traditionalist holdouts from Hell's maw. Onwé had always imagined Voth would've been happier lording over some Dark Age fief. Alas, he'd been born in the twentieth century and thus had only Indian country to domineer.

"Karl's an atheist, for fuck's sake," Onwé said, glaring up into the pastor's icy blue eyes. "Everyone in town knows that. Even his own daughter gives him crap for it. He sure as shit isn't summoning demons with this thing."

"It keeps them away, actually," Karl said, jabbing the antlers at one of the converts. He used a spooky voice to add, *"The ones who can only walk on snow."*

"You think you could build one that keeps church mice

away?" Onwé replied, sneering at Voth as the man bristled with ill-concealed revulsion.

Voth was troubled to his core by Indian totems; there was something about them he could not help but abhor. Most of all, he hated feathers, and often denounced them in sermons as symbols of Indian rebellion.

"I'm not that powerful," Karl said, leaning back in the old rocking chair and glancing up at Onwé. "But your granny, Old N'wenthāil, was. She'd have cast these clowns out. Sent your ass back to Alabama, Mr. Voth."

"That's enough from you," Voth snapped. He motioned for his congregants to leave, and they faithfully obliged. Then he ripped the stave from Karl's grasp and hurled it onto the deck, shattering the antler rack.

"Pagan iniquities will not go unpunished," he growled, "in this life or the next."

He turned and bounded off the porch, leaving Karl and Onwé stunned into silence. Both men had known Voth for decades, but neither had ever seen him outright bully a member of the reservation. Onwé briefly considered rushing him, but he knew too well the impunity of missionaries, whose acts of violence were so easily lost in the paperwork of the federal bureaucracy. There simply was no recourse.

"Oh, about your daughter's birthday," Voth called over his shoulder, "might I suggest a nice quilt instead?"

Onwé turned to Karl, who sat motionless in the chair, trembling with rage.

"Fuck that guy," Onwé said. "I'll help you rebuild it. I see antlers on my hikes all the time."

Karl didn't blink for a long moment. His eyes darted around, as if scanning through a million thoughts at once, until they landed on one in particular. Finally, he stood up and looked right through Onwé, scarcely aware of his presence.

"I'll show him a *savage idol,*" he grumbled, scooping the

whittling knife off the ground and retreating into his house. "I'll show him."

Chapter 11

Autumn Ridge was a mere outpost on the edge of a vast wilderness. No towns lay westward of it for a hundred miles, and its supplies came up a single winding road from Lake Namarjo to the east, the largest city on the reservation. Just southwest of Pale Peak lay Orchid Valley, a burgeoning resort town full of tourists Moya called "Winter Whites."

Most of the clergy of the Cold Valley churches lived there, but not Burke Voth. He'd lived on the reservation in one place or another for half his life, starting in Lake Namarjo. Eventually, he was reassigned to Autumn Ridge to replace his ailing father as lead pastor.

It was here in Onwé's town where Voth had truly consolidated his power. The man had no official relationship with the Bureau of Indian Affairs, but over the course of his tenure, he'd asserted himself over their agents on the rez. In time, he'd become the eyes and ears of the federal government in Indian country. As his influence grew, so too did his prestige among the other churches in the Cold Valley Baptist Association, until finally he'd become a member of its central leadership—a clutch of priggish old men who called themselves the "Valley Commission."

The Commission oversaw the distribution of badly needed supplies to Indians throughout the rez. They managed the allocation of funds raised from donors countrywide, and even tried to act as an intermediary between the BIA and the tribal council. Voth preferred it this way. He knew Indians were more likely to convert if their stomachs depended on it. And so, his proclamations became unwritten laws in Autumn Ridge, and when he warned a man not to practice certain heathen rituals, that man obeyed.

Usually.

Likewise, when Voth made his occasional appearance at the meetings of the tribal council, John Tall Rock and Moya River Stone, alongside four other respected elders, grudgingly yielded the floor. Today, the council had convened in its dingy hall before noon. Onwé waited outside in the cold to walk Moya home.

Eventually, she emerged, but not to leave. Instead, she motioned Onwé inside—a gesture no elder had extended to him before—and the two stood before the council. Voth stood opposite them, having refused a seat, and was flanked by Paul, Vince, and Warren. Vince's arm was wrapped in a thick bandage, no doubt having been stitched up by Dr. Farmer at the town's medical center.

"Onwé," John said, standing to address him, "we've brought you here to discuss what you and these gentlemen found in the woods."

"We've heard about it from Warren," Voth added, "but we thought it was important to include you."

Onwé wanted to lash out at Voth for his behavior toward Karl, but he knew enough to show only respect before the council. He hoped someday he'd occupy a seat as his father had before him, and knew demonstrating patience and wisdom would play a role to that end.

"I'm grateful to the council for inviting me," Onwé

replied. "But did Warren tell you what we *didn't* find? There's a whole plane out there that's up and disappeared."

"Have you told anyone outside this room about the crash?" Moya asked, grabbing Onwé's hand. She looked concerned, even frightened.

"No, *Néthédi,*" he replied. "Just Luke. And Steve, when I first reported it."

"I've spoken with my superiors back at the Bureau," Vince said. He looked fully recovered from his ordeal at the campsite and even spoke with an overly professional tone. "They don't want any discussion of this matter beyond those involved in the investigation until further notice."

"Why the secrecy?" Onwé asked, already imagining the nefarious reasons the BIA would seek to cover up the crash.

"We just don't want a public panic," John interjected. "Arranged corpses and other mysteries... People would be terrified. We don't have the big picture yet, so the government's going to send a few more men out here to comb the area."

"And we feel it would be disrespectful to the victims to spread rumors of an odious death," Voth added, searching the elders for their nods of support.

"Agreed," said Tavshii, another elder. "The spirits wander without a proper funeral. If hundreds of people speak of them, it could draw them out of the forest and into Autumn Ridge."

It was clear the elders believed in the risk of attracting the restless dead, but Onwé suspected Voth had other reasons for the gag order. Was he trying to prevent news of the crash from spreading to Namarjo, and potentially beyond the rez? Onwé imagined the government wanted to keep the public eye away from Cold Valley at all costs, for fear its many problems might become newsworthy. The country was already ablaze with civil rights movements, and the American Indian Movement had just kicked off months earlier. Was Voth trying to insulate the rez from the changing world around it?

"I understand," Onwé conceded, deciding that now was not the time to debate. "I'll do as you ask, *Ik'sháathí* John. And I'll talk to Luke too."

"We already have," John replied, offering a warm smile. "He's also agreed to respect our wishes."

With that, the meeting ended. Onwé walked Moya arm in arm back to her home. The clouds had finally passed and the sun shone down on the mountain, but a deep chill remained in the air.

"You think they hate us?" Onwé asked. "The Bureau, I mean."

"Not when we do as we're told," Moya grumbled, her *numi* vanishing in the breeze.

After seeing Moya home, Onwé headed out to visit Tíwé. A few years ago, the boy and his mother had moved to her father's house down in Lake Namarjo, leaving Onwé alone on Pale Peak. Tíwé tended to avoid his father, but on occasion, Onwé was able to get the kid to agree to meet him at a thicketed pond where the two used to catch wood frogs.

The pond—Mudhole, as they'd named it—sat halfway between the lake and Autumn Ridge. It took a little over an hour to walk to, but the downhill stroll made it feel like only minutes. Onwé always liked the journey; from the road he could see the great valley and its rivers to the east, as well as the web of trails snaking up the foot of Pale Peak.

Onwé buttoned up his old jacket as he walked. The wind had begun to pick up, and it whipped across fields of grass and ageless stone. On it sailed a fleet of clouds that threatened to douse the world in frigid rain. He worried about the storms that rapidly descended on the Rockies, but was more than willing to take the risk. Today, he needed to see his son.

Numi led excitedly, knowing she'd soon get to play with her old friend Zeus, a German shepherd who'd gone with Tíwé in the separation. Onwé followed distantly behind her, once again lost in the reveries that come to lonely wanderers. He pondered the fact that Akántha had returned to three people's dreams in the same week, and that each person had been shaken by the experience. Onwé wanted to dismiss it as an eerie coincidence, but Nauktí spirituality weighed on his mind: his people believed the dead were far away, and hopefully, they stayed there. When a long-deceased person came out of the twilight of memory to haunt someone's dreams, the Nauktí saw it as a foul omen.

But why would Akántha leave the grave to frighten his mother and friends? What could have compelled him to return like this in the cloak of night?

Onwé knew what Moya would say. Because her son's body had never been recovered, a proper burial was impossible, and thus his spirit had not completed its pilgrimage to the world beyond. All these years, she'd hoped and prayed for the discovery of Akántha's remains, that she might put his soul—and her own—to the rest they both deserved. But fate had been cruel to Moya in denying her that simple wish, and crueler still to dangle a hideous visage of her son before her sleeping eyes.

Onwé sensed a deeper mystery at play. His nightmares were disturbing too, but in them, Akántha did not seem intent on scaring anybody.

It seemed like he was trying to deliver a message.

Onwé wondered if the boy was finally ready to tell his story, and if he'd come out of the silence of death to warn his family about something terrible on Pale Peak.

Chapter 12

Numi's yipping heralded their arrival at Mudhole. She dashed toward the copse of trees, excited by the barking coming from within. Onwé jogged after her and discovered Tiwé sitting on a log beside his friend Angela. Zeus thundered up to Onwé to issue a salvo of curious sniffs, then raced around the pond a few times with Numi at his heels. The dogs only saw each other every few months, and Onwé sometimes tried to use the fact as a pretext to arrange hangouts with Tiwé.

"Hi, son," Onwé said, not sure whether it was safe to go in for a hug.

Tiwé stood up and greeted his dad but did not approach him for an embrace. Instead, he looked to his friend.

"Angie, you remember my father?"

"Hi, Mr. Lopez," she said, popping her hand up for a meek wave. Angela was thirteen now, two years older than Tiwé, but her small stature made her look even younger than him. Her bright green eyes were a peculiarity on the reservation, made brighter still by the crow-black mane that framed her face.

"I remember you, pretty lady," Onwé said, offering a warm smile. "You keepin' this kid out of trouble? I need both of those emeralds on him at all times."

Angela replied with a bashful shrug.

Tíwé rolled his eyes. "I don't do anything Mom would get mad about. I don't need anyone looking out for me."

"Wish I'd been that smart," Onwé said, recalling the many conflicts he'd had with Tíwé's mother. "Glad to see you're still wearing it long, by the way." He reached out to pat his son's head, but Tíwé dodged the attempt and took a step back.

Onwé was used to his son's coldness, but it still wounded him each time the boy refused affection. For years he'd sought to make amends for treating Tíwé and his mother poorly, but neither of them seemed interested in rekindling the relationship. Now, Luke's harsh words from earlier in the day rang in Onwé's thoughts, reminding him that without his family, he was an incomplete man.

"Hey, uh," Onwé said, trying a different approach at a connection, "you still out exploring all the time?"

"Of course," Tíwé replied, smiling at Angela. "We're making a map of all the cool spots we find in the woods."

"No mines, right?" Onwé asked.

"No mines," they both replied.

"No caves, no tunnels, no holes in the earth," Onwé added, all too aware of his son's tendency to disobey him by technicality.

Two years ago, Tíwé had snuck out with his friends to explore a shuttered mine at the foot of the mountain. When they removed the wooden barrier to enter, a rockfall broke Tíwé's collarbone and knocked him unconscious. The ordeal had resulted in his mother becoming even more protective. Thankfully, Tíwé seemed genuinely uninterested in spelunking after the accident.

"Do you remember Mr. Ortega?" Onwé asked. "The man

who lives next to Moya?"

Both kids replied with vacant stares.

"Well anyway, I saw him today, and he was making a staff for his daughter, kind of like mine. I realized...why don't I make one for you? They're great for adventuring. I bring mine everywhere."

Tíwé caught Numi as she trotted by and gave her a big hug. She relished in his attention and looked up at Onwé as if to rub it in.

"No offense, Dad," he said, "but I never got that prayer necklace you said you were making a while ago. Or the sage pouch before that. And you didn't even show up for my spring ceremony."

The truth stung. Onwé had sobered up three years ago, but when the addiction had passed, an ugly remorse took its place. Like a long winter storm, sadness had blurred the months together, causing him to miss a few milestones on his son's journey to Nauktí manhood. Onwé abandoned the effort and changed the subject.

For the next half-hour, Tíwé and Angela brought him up to speed on life in Lake Namarjo. They talked about the local school; it was still run by the church association, but had begun to incorporate classes designed by the tribal council. They talked about hardship; every person on the rez knew someone who struggled with poverty or drugs or despair. But mostly, they talked about exploring Pale Peak, which filled Onwé with dread.

The wanderlust that ran so strongly through Ashthenôví's bloodline had possessed Tíwé since childhood. The boy, like his father, loved nothing more than following the call of the wild into Pale Peak's vast woodlands. But Tíwé was eleven now—the same age as Akántha had been when he'd vanished—and this fact caused a superstitious anxiety in Onwé.

"You remember the hiker's code, right?" Onwé asked, interrupting Tíwé's story about a mutilated elk he and Angela had found.

"Yes, Dad," Tíwé replied, releasing a petulant sigh.

"What's the code?" Onwé pressed.

Tíwé shot a look at Angela as if to say, *time for some half-assed fathering*. The hiker's code was a set of rules outlined by his dad after the incident in the mine, and Onwé made him recite it every time he sensed Tíwé's want for adventure.

"Stay. In groups. On trails. Out of caves."

"And?" Onwé pointed a finger at the nearby pond. Zeus and Numi lay near it, covered in mud and adoring each other's company.

"On the hills, off the mountain," Angela said, speaking in a motherly voice to Tíwé, who replied with a resentful glare.

"That's right," Onwé said. "You want to go any farther up than Mudhole, you tell me. I'm fine with you rompin' around down here, but I don't want you anywhere near the big woods up near Autumn Ridge. Not unless I'm with you."

"But you go all the time, Dad," Tíwé protested. "You afraid I'm gonna go missing?"

Tíwé dropped his gaze when he saw the look on his father's face. He knew his dad had lost a friend to these woods long ago, but didn't seem to understand how much it still haunted him. In fact, Onwé had never really opened up to his son about Akántha.

"Sorry, Dad," Tíwé said at last.

"It's alright," Onwé replied. "You'll understand when you're older."

He reached out and rubbed the hair on Tíwé's head to annoy him, and this time, his son didn't duck. Then Onwé called Numi over and prepared to leave.

"Looks like rain's coming," he said. "You guys want me to walk you home?"

"That's okay, Mr. Lopez," Angela replied, pointing to the massive German shepherd. "We've got him."

The retort satisfied Onwé. Zeus was naturally protective and wouldn't let anything happen to his people without a fight.

"Okay. You be safe, then. *Ád'nab táwi kōsú'ké yániith.*"

Tíwé glanced at Angela, knowing she'd understood what his father had said.

"He says, *'Get home before dark,'* stupid."

"Ah, right," Tíwé replied with embarrassment.

"Aren't you practicing with your mother?" Onwé asked, surprised at his son's lack of comprehension. Onwé had spoken Nauktí around the house for years, but after the separation, the effort to raise Tíwé bilingually had apparently ended.

"I try with him," Angela said, batting playfully at Tíwé. "But he's pretty dense. *Te'anoi nakhan!*"

"It's that goddamn school of yours," Onwé said, feeling anger welling up inside as images of Voth swirled in his mind.

The forgetting of Native languages was not just a byproduct of federal schools—for decades, it was official policy to ban their speaking. Thirty years ago, little Angela would have been beaten by adult missionaries for daring to speak Nauktí.

"Keep up with it, son," Onwé said, pulling his hiking staff from its resting place against a nearby tree. "Keep the language. For your old man."

Tíwé nodded dutifully and called Zeus to his side.

"Good seeing you, Dad," he said hesitantly. It was more an admission than an assertion.

"You too, bud. Maybe we can do it again soon."

Zeus led the two kids away. As they walked, Onwé called out, "Love you, son." But Tíwé didn't look back.

Chapter 13

On his walk home, Onwé could not shake the fear of his son disappearing on the mountain. People went missing all the time in Cold Valley, and he'd lived on the rez long enough to know the vanished never returned.

Luke and Onwé had been just boys when it happened to Akántha. They couldn't understand the gravity of the situation the way their parents had. But as they grew up, their confusion festered into darker feelings. Both men harbored a deep and unresolved pain, and ultimately, they began to treat it with substances. It was a calamitous cycle with which many Native communities struggled: the tendency of a people who, upon having their culture and land and their very tongues stolen, turned to drugs as a means of self-medicating. This destruction gave the federal government and its missionaries cause to "save the poor Indians."

As Onwé trudged against the wet wind toward Autumn Ridge, he thought about Luke's journey out of the darkness. As much as he hated to admit it, Onwé respected his friend for transforming himself from a roaring alcoholic into a sober man of God—even if that god was not the one of his people. Luke had found his absolution, and his belief that he'd been made whole through Christ seemed to lift him out of the torment he'd known since childhood.

Onwé had found no such clarity. Although he'd managed to get himself off the drugs, no gods or fellowships had swept in to repair the wreckage of his soul. Akántha had taken a big piece of him when he'd left, and Tíwé another; it would require more than a church to make Onwé whole again. Sobriety had left him alone in a dark house, worlds apart from his wife and son, with only his regrets to keep him company. Regrets, and a mouthy dog.

The thought drew Onwé's attention to Numi. She stood a few yards ahead, peering worriedly into the nearby woods. The intermittent drizzle swelled to cascades of rain, and the wind lashed at the pines, hissing as it filtered through a mane of countless needles.

Something rustled beyond the tree line. A chorus of animal cries rang out from all directions. Onwé approached the dog, who had begun whimpering at the eerie bleating that echoed around them.

"It's okay, girl," he said, patting her side.

A herd of bighorn sheep exploded from the forest, rushing past the two where they huddled on the trail. Several ewes shrieked in terror as they bolted past, dashing northward toward the high fields. They were followed by a large, limping ram, who'd no doubt stayed behind to protect his family from the threat. The great spiral of horns crowning his head had cracked, and dark blood ran down his face, soaking his white muzzle. Even in the gloom, the wideness of his eyes told of what he'd seen. The ram paused momentarily to regard the wandering human and his dog, assessing whether they too deserved a battering, but decided to limp around them in pursuit of the other sheep.

After the ram was gone, something remained in the forest behind him, screaming in fright and unable to escape whatever had seized it. The cries weakened to a death rattle, and after a long moment, the woods fell silent.

"Mountain lion," Onwé said to Numi. "Probably nabbed one of the lambs."

She looked up at him and shivered. Over the course of her life, Numi had seen her share of black bears and elk in the Rockies. She'd heard the screeching of pikas as they fell into the claws of a bobcat or an eagle. Numi had even heard the mating calls of pumas, which tingled the spines of even the most hardened mountain folk. But never had she shaken and cried in Onwé's arms until today.

"You big baby," he said, rubbing her ears. When she refused to continue up the trail, Onwé hoisted the dog to his chest and carried her. But after a few steps, a new sound arose behind them: a wet, gurgling groan.

The cry wavered, seeping from some trembling maw, tightening into a lazy imitation of the lamb's screams. It repeated two or three more times until it reached a near-perfect mimicry, and then it rang out over the valley with great confidence. Lightning arced across the angry sky, and its flash momentarily revealed a large figure in the woods.

Onwé's mind ran amok trying to assign an animal to the hunched form.

"Mowwwt...mowt-en...liii–onnn..." the thing in the woods stammered, its voice crackling through a clot of blood and phlegm.

Onwé's body froze. Numi wriggled her way out of his arms and flopped to the ground, trying to put distance between herself and the animal that made such hideous sounds.

"Biiiig...baaaaaby..." it croaked, wheezing slow breaths of air between words.

The realization that this creature had listened to him and was now practicing his speech shook Onwé from his stupor.

He took off running up the trail, wishing he could move as fast as the bighorns, and commanded the dog to flee.

"Home, Numi!" he shouted into the rain. "*Té'nak'yani!*"

"*Youuuu...*" the thing called out behind them. Its voice dropped low and guttural, then rose to the timbre of a young child. *"One of...the lambs... One of the laaaambs..."*

Chapter 14

The two arrived back in Autumn Ridge at nightfall, having raced the entire way home. The town had apparently suffered another blackout, as it often did in the stormy season, and was now just a dark smudge on the mountain. Even the church was shuttered. Only the faint twinkle of wood fires glowed from house windows. As they passed the vacant police station, Onwé prayed Tíwé and Angela had made it home without incident. Tomorrow he'd return to the station to call his son.

Rain and the sweat of terror soaked Onwé to the bone. He took the dog inside and lit a fire, and they both shivered before it until the grip of fright had loosened. The warm glow of candles Onwé had placed around the house calmed his nerves, and soon, he found himself sinking into his father's armchair, trying to remember the legends Old N'wenthāil had told him as a boy.

He faintly recalled the story of a child who had encountered a creature that spoke in his grandmother's voice, but the details escaped Onwé, and the harder he tried to conjure the tale, the heavier his eyelids grew. Onwé drifted in and out of sleep to the rhythms of rain and Numi's breathing, and caught glimpses of strange things lurking in the forests of his dreams.

Hours later, Onwé awoke to the scrape of Numi's paw against his shin. She gazed up at him with needful blue eyes and nudged him with her snout, indicating she wanted to go outside to pee.

"Good idea, little one," he said, feeling the urge himself. Onwé pushed open the back door and stepped into the soggy night, recalling the experience they'd had earlier in the shadow of the pines. Both man and dog fearfully surveyed the area before walking further. Onwé squinted at the army of ponderosa and spruce bordering his property, and Numi swiveled her ears in all directions to capture the movements of hidden things. Satisfied there was no danger, she bolted to the nearby tree line to relieve herself, and Onwé clambered into the outhouse that stood a few yards away.

As he drained himself into the composting vat, he thought of Karl Ortega, and pitied him for the responsibility of managing outhouse waste throughout the town. The work was even less glamorous than that of an under-supplied handyman, and at least Onwé never had to get his hands *that* dirty. He listened to the patter of drizzle on the wooden roof of the structure, and to the nearby crunch of Numi's paws against the twig-laden ground.

The dog began to growl.

At first, Onwé could hear no cause for it but the incessant *hoo-oo* of the owls, but when he left the outhouse, he heard the distinct laughter of a child somewhere in the woods.

"Lalala... Laaaalala..." it sang robotically, as if practicing a song with one note. The child burst into laughter at its own singing, then continued the effort in different pitches.

Onwé shuddered, knowing full well that no child should be wandering the dark at such an hour. Numi sniffed frantically at the air, sensing things her master could not, and whatever she smelled seemed to raise her hackles even more.

Onwé approached the dog. She held a defensive position against the wall of trees. The moon intermittently pierced the clouds and made shafts of silver light in the woods, but they weren't bright enough to illuminate the source of the noise.

"Ahh soul me aahh doo... Soul me aaaahh doooo... I'm a...naked souuul..." the child sang, unable to stay on-key.

Onwé recognized the words immediately: Warren, the transportation safety investigator, had mentioned he'd sung them on their ill-fated camping trip to search for the downed plane. The melody, on the other hand, he recognized from somewhere else, but in his fear he could not place it.

"It followed us home," Onwé whispered to the dog, tearing his gaze out of the blackness and shooting a glance at the house behind him. Even though the door was only a few steps away, he felt he'd never make it if he ran.

"Get inside, girl. Go."

As Numi relented and backed away from the tree line, the child unleashed a wail that thundered across the forest. It washed through the air in streams of gibberish: a mixture of random English and Naukti words, few of which were correctly pronounced, all of it incoherent. And though they were nonsensical as a statement, the sharpness of their enunciation sounded like a threat.

Long-buried memories rushed up in Onwé, dragged from the depths by the familiar voice. The tone, the language, the unmistakable laugh—all of it converged upon him to extract a question he feared to ask:

"...Akántha?"

A chorus of terrible voices swelled up throughout the forest, singing the lamentation in unison. Beneath the mournful song rang out the cries of dozens of children.

"I wanna go home!" one sobbed.

"When do we go insiiiiiide? When do we go insiiiiiide?"

another said.

"*Mā'én'in nathwél!*" someone shouted: "Down in the hole!"

Numi appeared to catch sight of something past the trees and nearly tripped over herself as she scurried back inside. Onwé's instincts commanded him to flee to the house with her, but a morbid curiosity seized him, and he stood for just a moment longer.

As he stared out into the gloom, a ray of moonlight slipped through the rolling clouds and illuminated the tree line. A figure stood there, wreathed in shadow, towering two feet or more above Onwé's height. Its arms reached skyward in a gesture of worship, unnaturally still as if frozen by the icy wind, and its fingers jutted in painful directions. The head, obscured by angular shoulders and a mess of black hair, swiveled back and forth on its crooked neck, as if the twisted figure was unable to bear the revelations it received, and motioned: *No more, please, no more.*

The image of a conductor passionately leading a choir formed in Onwé's mind, and he staggered back toward the house in fright. The clouds moved once more over the moon, and the figure vanished, along with the mournful voices.

Onwé found Numi cowering under the bed upstairs. He climbed underneath with her and wrapped his arms around her body, meanwhile eyeing the old rifle that leaned in the corner of the room. The two lay together through the wee hours, straining to hear anything more over the rain.

A million thoughts ran through Onwé's head—some of his father, some of Akántha, and some of the federal agents he'd camped with. He recalled Warren's story about a shadowy being hypnotizing him with a song and leading him through the woods. The thought caused Onwé to tighten his hug around Numi. The warmth of her body and the thump of her heart brought him some semblance of calm, but he could not stop asking himself over and over:

What the fuck was that?

Eventually, the rain abated, and the night crept by in silence. Just as dawn's light began to bleed into the room, a loud knock echoed from downstairs. Someone was at the door.

Onwé remained still, wondering if the thing in the woods had come to drag him out. Then he heard someone speak:

"It's me. You awake?"

Onwé crawled out from under the bed. He recognized Luke's voice, but was suspicious of whose mouth it had come from. Numi followed sheepishly to the top of the stairs. She waited there, casting a wary gaze at the door.

"When were you baptized?" he asked.

"Three years ago," Luke replied. "Think it was August. Why?"

Onwé pulled the door open. Luke's appearance almost made him gasp. Dark rings drooped beneath his sunken, bloodshot eyes, and deep lines of worry framed his cracked lips. His short hair poked every which way, uncombed after a fitful sleep. He gazed through Onwé with the same thousand-yard stare he'd worn in the church the previous night.

"Jesus, man," Onwé said, looking his friend up and down. "Thought I had a bad night."

"Couldn't sleep," Luke replied, lurching into the house like a wandering corpse.

Numi descended the stairs and cautiously approached Luke as he dropped onto the armchair. Onwé seated himself nearby and watched the dog regard her old friend with suspicion. She sniffed at him a few times, then slinked away as if she'd never met him before and disapproved of his intrusion. Luke glanced at her briefly, but in similar form, did not seem to recognize her.

"Something you wanna talk about, brother?" Onwé asked, unable to quit his study of Luke's ghastly state.

"Yes," he breathed. Luke's gaze fell to his trembling hands. He picked at his nails. "I think I'm ready."

"For what?" Onwé said.

Luke swallowed hard.

"I'm ready to tell you what happened that night."

Chapter 15

Luke had not been himself since the expedition into the nameless place. Over the years, Onwé had seen his friend undergo significant change—from traditionalist to Christian, drinker to teetotaller, boy to man—and yet something had always remained constant about Luke's identity. But ever since the camping trip and his midnight journey to the cave, Luke had become unfamiliar in a truly eerie way. Something inside him was missing, stolen by whatever he'd been through.

"It wasn't just black I saw," Luke mumbled, his attention drifting inward. "It was a house."

The look on his face reminded Onwé of Warren—those pensive, horrified eyes too bewitched to look away from whatever he saw in his memory. Luke stared into the ashes of the fireplace as if the mysterious house stood within them.

"A house in the woods?" Onwé asked.

"*Óknóth-úden,*" Luke replied in Nauktí.

"The Briar House?" Onwé repeated with confusion.

"I heard a voice in the trees," Luke went on. "I was cold, but following it kept me warm. And the warmth made me unafraid."

"Whose voice did you hear?" Onwé asked.

"My mother's."

Both Luke and Onwé had lost their parents in years past, which had drawn them closer to each other and to Moya. But Luke never spoke of his mother and father; the pain had always seemed too much to bear.

"Old N'wenthāil used to tell us to ignore the voices when we played in the woods," Onwé said, more to himself than to Luke. "I never really took the warnings literally."

"I couldn't help it," Luke said. "It felt...*right*. I followed the voice for a long time. It led me up a hill overlooking the woods, and the house was there. The moon was so bright I could see dirt caked on the windows, and branches on the roof. It was like the whole thing had just risen up out of the ground."

"Out of the ground?" Onwé said.

"Like a mushroom," Luke replied. "The door was unlocked. Inside, it felt like home. Like I'd lived there my whole life. My mother's voice told me to look for her in the cellar out back, and down there I found this door..."

"Did you open it?" Onwé asked, equally fascinated and disturbed by the scenes his mind conjured to match the story.

"Yes," Luke said, "I watched myself open it."

"Where'd it lead?"

"Stairs," he whispered, as if confessing a secret. "*Thousands* of them, vanishing into the dark. I followed her voice all the way down into the mountain. I felt years...*centuries* pass while I walked deeper and deeper. I saw my body age and wither and die as I walked. But the stairs kept going, so I did too.

"They ended at a sunlit beach. Above the water, I saw a city of white stone. Old ships floated through the sky, ferrying people across. It looked like Heaven."

Luke appeared withdrawn into the tale he now related, such that his eyes unfocused into featureless black pits. Onwé did not speak. He just studied his friend while the man drifted from one bizarre memory to another.

"My mother told me we'd go over the water and into the city, where I could be with her. But then I started to feel cold...so cold I woke up. I found myself in a long tunnel, with cold air blowing from one direction and warm from the other. It smelled like the earth, the way the caves smelled when we were kids. Clay and soil and moss, that kind of smell. And then my mother's voice started to change."

Luke paused, disturbed by the images behind his eyes. His breath quickened.

"The voice wasn't my mother's anymore. It was *him.*"

Luke pointed at Onwé's hiking staff. The sickly orange light pouring in from the windows gave the thing a malevolent aspect. His eyes locked onto the old bracelet that fastened the little cross to the wood. Akántha had made it a few weeks before he vanished.

"You heard his voice?" Onwé blurted out. "Are you sure?"

"It was him," Luke repeated. His jaw clenched rhythmically, trying to force the words from a mouth that feared to speak them. "He knew everything about me, Onwé. He knew my parents. My problems. He called me 'Líkōté'. I'm sure it was Akántha. But the way he spoke—it wasn't like how a person talks."

Luke shuddered and looked away, rejecting the sounds that echoed in his mind. Onwé guessed the voice was like the one he'd heard in the woods.

"What did he want?" Onwé pressed, recalling the multitude of dreams in which Akántha had tried to show him something.

"He asked me about his mother. Told me to bring her down to him. He talked about a choir, and how he'd teach us to sing."

"Teach us to sing?" Onwé repeated. A familiar nausea

washed through his guts.

"Yes," Luke shifted nervously in the armchair. "He said all we'd need to do is follow him down to a black wall and pass through a great door. But at that point, I was awake enough to know I was in danger, so I ran. I followed the cold air out of the tunnels. That's where Numi found me."

Onwé got up and paced the room, grappling with the madness of the story. He wanted to dispute it as an elaborate nightmare, but after his own experiences earlier, he felt called to accept his friend's words.

"I believe you, Luke," Onwé said with a hopeless sigh. "There's something outside... It followed me home. Old N'wenthāil was right about this mountain. The spirits. The *things*. I saw it with my own eyes. I never much believed until now."

"My dreams," Luke went on, ignoring Onwé's admission, "ever since that night... They're...infested. Rotting me inside. Hollowing me out."

Luke reached over and pulled Onwé's hiking staff from its spot near the mantle. He poked at the little cross that dangled from it.

"The light of my faith is flickering," he said. "I feel my doubt rising. When I close my eyes, all I see are those stairs. I see myself descending."

"You're scared, Luke," Onwé said gently, trying to reassure his friend. "I'd be scared shitless if that happened to me."

"It's worse," Luke replied, voice tightening with emotion. "I feel my soul imperiled. I feel the mountain's shadow on me, even at night."

Onwé didn't know what to say, so he put his arms around Luke and gave him a hug. It took a long while, but eventually, Luke hugged him back.

"I have something to confess," Luke said, pulling away

from the embrace. "Something I've kept from you since we were kids."

"What is it?" Onwé asked, feeling his stomach climb into his throat. Given the nature of the conversation already, he prepared for the worst.

"The nameless place," Luke said, "I told you I'd been there before."

"Yes. You said you went there with Akántha."

Luke nodded.

"He came to me and said he'd found a house out there. He wanted to show it to me."

"That can't be true," Onwé said, refusing to believe the boy was that stupid. "That place is miles away from the rez. Akántha would never go that far out alone. He was the biggest coward of the three of us."

"You're not wrong," Luke replied, putting the staff back in its place. "Akántha had never been out there before. He said he knew the house was there because he saw it in a dream. He already knew the way."

"So did you find the house?"

"No," Luke said. "We made it a little ways into the forest, but I got scared and made us turn back. Akántha was furious. The next morning, he was gone."

Onwé considered the revelation for a while and stared out the nearby window. From here he could see the outhouse and the wall of trees behind it.

"Why did you hide this from me?" he asked, his voice becoming accusatory. "Does Moya know? Did the police ever search those woods?"

Luke answered the questions with a hesitant stare.

"Do you realize this might have helped us find him!" Onwé said, now seized with anger. He found himself standing over his friend.

Luke rose to his feet and stared into Onwé's eyes.

91

"Moya knew. The BIA knew. Your father helped organize the search party."

"Then everyone knew but me," Onwé replied, hurt by the admission. "Why?"

"They thought you'd blame me. You've always been kind of a prick. No offense."

With that, Luke headed for the door.

"I need to sleep," he said, "but I'm afraid. I'll talk to you later."

"Óknóth-úden," Onwé replied, his mind returning to the eerie house Luke had described. "What's behind the black wall?"

Luke glanced up at Numi, who had returned to her place at the top of the stairs. She watched him timidly and backed away further as his eyes pierced into hers.

"I hope I never find out."

Part II:

BONDS

Chapter 16

A wet week slogged by. The winds brought a deep chill from the north to settle over the valley, and an ominous quiet accompanied it. Snow had not yet come to the rez, but the night air bit hard enough to clear the streets after dusk, and now smoke belched from the chimneys of every house in Autumn Ridge. Onwé found himself in the chair beside the fire, lost in one of his father's old books, Numi snoring at his feet. Somewhere between the pages, he began to drift.

"Help! Somebody help us!"

Onwé awoke to distant cries and the *thunk* of his book flopping onto the floor. For a moment, he didn't know where he was, having been ripped from the depths of a dreamless slumber.

"God, can anyone hear me?!"

When his senses gathered, Onwé recognized the dim shapes of his living room in the glow of the dying fire, and the dog's form racing from window to window. He realized the voice was coming from outside, and suspected that whatever had visited his yard the previous week had returned for an encore of its horrid nightsongs.

A baby shrieked somewhere on the dirt road in front of

Onwé's home, reinforcing his suspicion. Then a chorus of familiar voices began to ring out. He peeked through the curtains and saw neighbors throwing their doors open and emerging from their homes.

The old wall clock read 2:10 a.m. Onwé wrapped himself in a tattered blanket and poked his head outside. He spotted a group of figures up the road, holding flashlights and gathering around a hunched person. Numi slipped between his legs and bolted up the road, curious about the commotion, and Onwé hesitantly followed.

"What happened?" people asked over the weakening sobs of the baby. "Are you hurt?"

Onwé nudged his way into the throng and found a short, pudgy white man in shredded clothing, swaddling a terrified infant with his jacket. A pair of thick glasses sat crookedly on his face, its cracks and scratches obscuring his eyes. Fine cuts on his cheeks implied he'd bushwhacked through the wilderness without a light.

"My God," a woman gasped, examining the baby. The child couldn't have been older than six months, and its lips had blued in the mountain air.

"I'll get Dr. Farmer," a teenage boy said, taking off toward the medical center in town.

People all around the disheveled visitor began ripping off their coats and wrapping him and the child. The man tried to explain himself, but his teeth chattered so hard they shredded his words:

"P-p-plane, went down... Other s-side of the m-mountain... I- I s-saw the lights. F-followed here. Pilot was...m-mad..."

The man handed the child to the woman nearest him, took two steps forward, and collapsed into Onwé's arms. Onwé set the man gently on the cold gravel and rubbed his arm in a vain effort to keep him awake.

"What's your name, buddy?" he asked, trying to keep the man's attention long enough to extract a bit more of the story.

Numi nudged her way through the small crowd and tried to help by licking the man's face. He seemed relieved by the presence of a dog—or perhaps just the warmth of her tongue—and moved a trembling hand through her soft fur. She responded by lying against him, instinctively sharing her warmth, as she had for Onwé years ago when he'd smacked his head on a tree branch.

"Is...the kid...okay?" the man asked dizzily, teetering on the edge of consciousness.

"Hopin' so," Onwé replied, watching his neighbors as they whisked the child into the warmth of their home. "Doctor's gonna take good care of her when he gets here."

"Him," the man said breathlessly. "It's a b-boy. Name's Stefan. F-father...dead. Mom too, m-most likely."

"How long have you been out here?" Onwé asked.

He considered the possibility that this man could be a survivor of the crash he and Warren had investigated. It seemed unlikely, however, that someone so out of shape could survive ten days on the mountain, especially in these clothes. And how could a baby have endured the brutal cold for that long?

It was more likely this man was referring to a second incident. The notion that two planes might have collided with Pale Peak in the span of a few weeks sent chills rippling through Onwé's body, and he dared to wonder the cause of such strange events on the mountain.

Just then, Police Chief Steve Winépo appeared with two officers at his side and Magnus Farmer a ways behind. Most of the men were dressed in evening wear, having been summoned unexpectedly from the quiet of their homes, and looked baffled at the arrival of a stranger from the forest.

Dr. Farmer knelt beside Numi to examine the visitor. He peeled the man's eyelids open and shined a small light upon them, then palpated the man's head and throat.

"Get him down to medical as fast as you can," he said over his shoulder to the officers.

They hoisted the man into a canvas stretcher and headed downhill toward the only lit part of town.

"Doc, he had a baby with him too." Onwé pointed at a nearby house. "Chris and Wendy are thawin' him out."

"A baby?" Dr. Farmer repeated with surprise. "Good Lord. Bring him along then, quickly." He hurried after the deputies while muttering to himself about this godforsaken mountain.

It took some convincing, but Onwé was able to get the couple to take the baby to the medical center. He shouldered open the building's heavy doors and barreled down a hall, leading Wendy and Chris as they clutched each other and the child. They waded through the hall, fearful and suspicious. Health care in Cold Valley, like many other federal services in Indian country, had a legacy of cruelty: Chris's grandparents had endured the humiliating examinations and unethical experiments of the pre-war era, and Wendy's cousin had been sterilized without her consent. Everyone on the rez knew not to trust the doctors, even when an honorable one like Magnus Farmer ran the center.

The four of them arrived in a dim room lined with beds, and as soon as they entered, the nurse lifted the whimpering baby from Wendy's arms and disappeared behind a door. The mysterious man lay half-conscious in a bed surrounded by clamoring police, while Dr. Farmer scurried to and fro, checking vitals and repeatedly telling his new patient to stop fiddling with his clothes.

"I already belong to a church," the man said hesitantly, as if refusing a demand. "No, no, I don't want to."

Brown, thinning hair clung to his forehead, weighed down by the grit acquired on his trek. An oily glaze covered his skin, no doubt the product of sweat, dripped and dried and unwashed for days.

"Moderate hypothermia," Dr. Farmer said to Steve, who nodded in agreement. "If he gets worse, you'll need to call for an evac to Namarjo."

"You gotta make it through tonight, pal," Steve said, wincing as he watched the doctor rig an IV to the man's arm. "Nobody's comin' up that road to save you 'til morning."

The man began to sob.

"I don't want to," he wept. "Please...don't let him take me down in the hole."

The doctor threw a set of heavy blankets over the man and squinted into the fluid bag.

"They usually snap out of it when the body temperature rises to about ninety-six degrees," he said, pushing a handful of salt-and-pepper hair from his brow.

The nurse emerged from the back room with the baby in a small gurney, surrounded with layers of water-filled heat pads. The child's cries had strengthened, giving relief to Chris and Wendy, who stood anxiously in a corner. They looked so fraught with worry they might have passed as his birth parents.

"Thasss a good sound," the strange man said lethargically, seeming to regain some of his awareness. "Right, doc?"

"That's right," Dr. Farmer replied, giving the man a brief smile and pulling a lab coat over his pajamas to warm himself. Then he nodded at Steve and his officers and said, "You can try your hand at a few questions, but he's gonna fall asleep in a minute. He'll be ready for you boys in a couple hours."

"How far did you have to walk to get here?" one officer asked.

"Do you remember which direction you came from?" said the other.

"Are there any other survivors?" Steve asked, leaning over the man to search his eyes for awareness.

The man's head lolled to the side. His attention fell on Onwé, who waited quietly beside Numi in the shadows a few feet away.

"Whatsh your name there?" he asked in slurry speech.

"Me? Uh, I'm Onwé."

"An' the dog?"

"Oh, this is Numi."

She wagged her tail in salutation.

The man's eyes closed, his body giving in to exhaustion. He let out a deep sigh.

"S'better than a cave," he mumbled. "Warmer."

Dr. Farmer fished through the man's jacket and retrieved an ID card, then handed it to Steve.

"Gaylen Poor," the police chief said.

"Mm," the man grunted in affirmation. His eyes remained shut, and his expression reflected the warmth now creeping through his body.

"You carried this child across the mountain by yourself?"

"Mm."

"In the dark?"

"M'hm."

Onwé stepped forward and looked over the man and the baby, unable to comprehend the sheer will it must have taken to survive such a trek in this cold.

"You're braver than you look, Gaylen Poor," he said, resting a hand on the man's shoulder.

Gaylen's eyes cracked open just for a moment. He looked up at Onwé, then drifted off to a hard-earned slumber.

Chapter 17

Fitful dreams plagued Onwé's sleep through the small hours. He got out of bed just after dawn, unable to bear the thoughts of plane crashes and missing people in the wilderness. He fed Numi and set out to Moya's house to weather-strip the door.

The cold air sank its teeth into his skin the moment Onwé stepped outside, but the morning light filled him with some sense of relief. Few days this month had the sky been clear, but now a brilliant sun crested over the mountains to the east, bathing the town in a golden hue.

Onwé saw the young Samuel Cotter pulling bundles of firewood out of a truck and lugging them up to Moya's porch, where he stacked them with great care. The front door opened, and Moya's scowling face emerged to examine Samuel's work.

"Not here, Mr. Cotter," she said, throwing a rickety thumb over her shoulder. "The shed's around back."

Samuel nodded, unable to catch his breath enough for a response, and hoisted one of the bundles back up into his scrawny arms. He shuffled to the side of the house, catching sight of Onwé watching him from the road.

"And, uh, come inside when you're done," Moya added in a milder tone. "We'll get you fed."

Surprised at Moya's emergent tolerance of Samuel, Onwé decided to come back later and let the two work things out between them. He turned to head into town for some breakfast, but nearly leaped out of his skin when he came face-to-face with Luke, who'd been standing mere inches behind him.

"Shit, man!" Onwé said, shocked both by Luke's proximity and his worsened appearance.

Luke's face was sunken and weary, with prominent dark rings encircling his eyes. Usually, he was one of the best-manicured men in town, and prided himself on his shift to a clean-cut neophyte of the church. Now his uncombed hair matted to his head in clumps, and what little facial hair he could grow stuck out in random patches.

"Walk with me, brother," he said in a low voice, gazing through Onwé as if through a ghost.

"Are you sleeping at all, man?" Onwé asked. "Think it's about time you go talk to Dr. Farmer."

"I don't need anyone's help," Luke snapped. But then he seemed to regret his tone, and his speech softened. "Heard about Gaylen Poor. Quite a story."

"Quite a story indeed."

The two men set off toward the town square, Onwé glancing at the police station as they passed. It was early enough that most folks were still asleep—including the police, apparently—but Onwé expected another swarm of BIA investigators would soon arrive in town.

"Have you eaten?" Onwé asked, taking in more of Luke's disheveled state. The man's skin seemed to hang a bit.

"Not hungry," Luke said flatly. "I need to talk to Pastor Burke."

"What about?"

Luke ignored the question.

The two friends carried on across the town and followed the church road. Onwé talked a bit about Gaylen's arrival on the rez, and he tried to broach the idea of a second plane having crashed on the mountain. Luke avoided the subject entirely and grimaced as if the conversation caused him physical pain.

"Let Steve and his boys handle it," he said. "My hiking days are over."

As they approached the church, Onwé noticed three congregants huddled together, examining something near the building's entrance. The group chattered worriedly among themselves, disturbed by whatever they were seeing. They swatted each other's hands away any time one of them tried to touch it.

"Good morning, friends," Luke said, his voice still flat with exhaustion. "Have you seen Pastor—"

Luke's words vanished from his mouth when the congregants stepped aside, revealing a large, crafted object above the front door. The hideous thing dangled from the awning, twirling slowly in the breeze on strands of long, raven-black hair. A ring of twigs enclosed a web of bloody twine, throughout which small bones had been woven. A mess of flattened roadkill had been tied to its center, and the feathers harvested from the corpse now jutted prominently from the hoop. The whole structure creaked as it swayed, weighed down at the bottom by the desiccated skull of some long-dead animal. Blood had run the length of the object and spattered onto the front door, tarnishing its fresh white paint and the visage of purity the church sought to display.

"Lord Jesus," a weathered voice blurted nearby.

Onwé whirled around to find Burke Voth standing nearby, holding a box of supplies. The pastor bulldozed

103

through Luke and Onwé and pushed one of the women aside to get a better view of the thing, shoving the box into her arms as he did.

"What in God's name is going on here?" he demanded, turning on his congregants. "Who's responsible for this...this blasphemy?"

When no one responded to the questions, Voth's attention snapped to Luke.

"What is the Second Commandment?" he said, each heaving breath filling him with more hot air.

"Uh, graven images," Luke replied, unable to rip his gaze from the object.

Savage idols, Onwé thought. Suddenly, he knew exactly who would have constructed such a thing. A surge of laughter rushed up from inside, and he barely caught it behind his teeth.

"Is this your petty revenge?" Voth said, leering at Onwé. "You and that godless friend of yours?" He ran a finger through the streak of blood on the door and held it up for all to see.

"Onwé didn't do this," Luke interjected, stepping in front of Voth. "He was with me the whole time."

"Show me your hands," Voth demanded, ignoring Luke. "All of you. Hands out!"

The congregants obeyed and presented their hands to the pastor. He circled the group, looking for evidence of mischief, and examined Onwé from a distance.

"Our hands are clean," Onwé said, wholly amused with the drama unfolding on church grounds. "Are yours?"

"Don't give me that crap," Voth growled. "This is an egregious violation of the Code of Indian Offenses, and I know some of you keep busy with your *arts and crafts.*"

"Our people don't make these things," Luke said, daring to challenge the pastor. "None of the tribes in Cold Valley do."

Voth scoffed in anger and yanked the object down. It plummeted to the ground and broke into pieces, reminding Onwé of Karl's shattered warding staff. Not satisfied with its destruction, Voth scooped up the knot of wood and bone and ripped its web apart, then jammed the mess into the box the woman held. He paused, noticing something about the skull, and pulled it back out.

One of the incisors was missing. Voth ran his bloodstained finger over the pocket that had once housed the tooth, and then he began scanning the ground. When he failed to locate the tooth, he seemed to have an epiphany and shoved his way through the group.

He bounded down the stairs and headed across the field toward his living quarters—an austere house that had been home to every pastor before him since the church's foundation.

The congregants trailed behind Voth. Luke and Onwé followed at a distance. They arrived at a small grave behind the house and found the makeshift headstone kicked aside. Someone had disinterred the remains, and now a ribcage and other bones lay strewn about in the dirt. The skull had been taken.

"Oh my God," Voth said, falling to his knees. He touched the bones with a trembling hand and began sobbing. "How could you?"

Onwé had nearly forgotten that once upon a time, Burke Voth had owned a dog. It was many years ago now, long before Onwé had gotten started on the drugs. Using had damaged his memories of those times, but he faintly recalled Voth milling about the town with the old retriever.

Come to think of it, he was less of an asshole back then, Onwé thought.

"We'll help you bury her," Luke said, gently patting Voth's shoulder.

"Merciless savages," Voth hissed through a cascade of sobs. "Godless heathens, curse them."

He rose to his feet and wiped his eyes before turning to face Onwé.

"If I can prove you and Ortega are responsible for this, I'll have you both before a Bureau tribunal. I swear before God, you'll see the inside of a jail cell."

Voth then turned to Luke and the others, who waited timidly at his side.

"Tell no one about this. Do you understand? One word uttered and I'll cast the lot of you out of this congregation and you can burn in the lake of *fire.*"

The group stood in silence, frightened by Voth's rage.

"Clear out," he said, yanking the tangle of feathers and twigs from the box and disentangling the bones. "And Onwé, get that door repainted. *Now.*"

Voth returned his attention to the remains and began placing them back into the plot. The congregants dispersed, and Luke and Onwé walked together across the field.

"You ever notice how everyone keeps telling us to keep our mouths shut?" Onwé said, remembering the BIA's admonition to stay mum on the plane crash.

"If you had anything to do with this, you've got to tell me," Luke said quietly, trying not to draw the pastor's attention. "Things could get serious. He's not gonna let this one go."

"Let him squirm," Onwé said. "I didn't do a damn thing. And he got what he deserved."

"How can you be so callous?" Luke retorted. "What if that was Numi? How would you feel?"

Onwé laughed, causing Luke to glance nervously over his shoulder.

"You know why nobody's ever dug up any of *my* pets?" he asked. When Luke failed to respond, he said, "Because I don't go around breaking other people's shit."

Onwé hadn't told Luke about the incident at Karl's house, and didn't bother now. He knew Luke would just deflect on behalf of his beloved pastor and probably quote some Bible passage about the futility of revenge.

"Shame on you," Luke said, shaking his head in disgust. "Sometimes I can't believe what a jerk you've become."

"You're one to talk, buddy." Onwé shoved Luke away from him as they walked. "You've been a real fuckin' handful ever since you dreamed about Akántha."

"Stop," Luke said.

"Why don't you just take some sleeping pills and get your ass back to normal? I doubt praying will do you any good."

"Stop," Luke said, with threatening finality. "You have no idea what I've been through. Just *stop.*"

"Voth isn't gonna help you," Onwé said, risking pushing Luke over the edge. "That man's not as decent as you think. And he won't believe your weird story about a disappearing house, that's for damn sure. The other church folk will call you a lunatic."

In a burst of rage, Luke rushed at Onwé and shoved him with all his strength. Onwé staggered a half dozen steps and recovered his balance just in time to avoid falling. He steadied himself against the surge of fear and adrenaline now coursing down his limbs.

"Keep your mouth shut about my church and my faith," Luke said, squaring off and awaiting Onwé's next move. "If you don't, I'll shut it for you."

Onwé saw the righteous indignation on Luke's face and decided not to engage. Instead, he waved a hand dismissively and kept walking. Luke stood his ground and glared at Onwé with ghastly, bloodshot eyes, watching him head back toward the church.

At the far edge of the field, in the woods beside the cliff,

Onwé noticed the shadows turning. A memory of the twisted figure lurking behind his house came to him, and he wondered if the hulking thing often watched the town from afar. He squinted into the trees, hoping it was the rising sun causing their shadows to bend—but he couldn't shake the feeling of hungry eyes upon him.

Chapter 18

As much as Onwé hated obeying Burke Voth, he knew he had to repaint the door. Much of his income came from odd jobs around the church, or from the needs of its congregants. Voth sometimes referred his congregants to Onwé for work on their houses, and in exchange, Onwé grudgingly withdrew his many protests against the congregation's activities on the rez. He deeply resented his relationship of dependency on the church, but he had to make a living. The rations provided by the BIA and the Valley Commission were enough to sustain him, but supplies and medicine—especially for Moya—cost money.

To be sure, the expense of fixing Moya's home each year after the brutal winter was enough to justify the work. But if Ashthenôví were still alive, Onwé knew it would be impossible to explain himself to him. His father would have been outraged to witness his son sprucing up the church that had come to Indian land without right or invitation. In fact, he'd even once referred to the church members painting a fence white as "the artists of colonialism."

Onwé bickered with a phantasm of his disappointed father as he finished cleaning the blood from the door and repainting it. All the while, he watched a flock of congregants march up the hill and stream into the building, smiling at him as they passed. Scores of people—*his* people—strolled gaily into the place Onwé conceived of as the slaughterhouse of their traditions. They smiled and laughed and hugged each other along the way, never fearful their conversion had taken something Indigenous away from them. In fact, as Luke had put it once, they appeared more whole as *Indians in Christ* than they ever were before.

Onwé despised the ugly mixture of revulsion and loneliness their cheer stirred within him. He sealed up the paint bucket and set off to return it to the shed out back, passing Luke on the steps as he did. Although they nearly touched each other, Luke refused to acknowledge Onwé or look at him at all. He simply brushed by, dour-faced and glassy-eyed, and walked into the embrace of an older man inside the church who called out, "Brother!"

Onwé snorted and locked up the supplies, then made his way back down the hill alone.

Near the town square, young Samuel rushed past Onwé without so much as a nod, probably fearful of how Voth might react if he were late for service.

"How was breakfast?" Onwé called out, but received nothing beyond a quick "Sorry, Mr. Lopez!"

He chuckled and headed for Moya's place to get the weather stripping done. She was inside, wrapped in an old sweater, shuffling between the table and the washing basin with a handful of dishes. The fireplace roared and filled the small living room with its heat, but little of it ever traveled to the back of the house, where Moya's bed sat unused. She'd mostly slept on the battered old couch since Akántha vanished, and Onwé imagined it was not just the warmth that drove her there. Being as close to the door as possible meant Moya could snatch up her son in a desperate hug a few moments sooner, if ever he walked through it.

"Must have been some feast," Onwé joked, heading to the basin to wash plates.

"Nothing special," Moya said, not looking up from her work.

"Hell of a blaze," he added. "Did Samuel build this fire?"

Moya set down a plate a little too hard in the basin. The clatter echoed across the house and wiped the smile from Onwé's face. She sighed and took a gulp of tea from one of the cups.

"Luke's right, after all," she said. "I could go a bit easier on him."

"Oh?" Onwé replied, trying to conceal his surprise. "I thought he drove you nuts?"

Moya smiled, a rare enough thing that Onwé cherished it each time.

"He's a good kid. Stupid, but a good kid."

Onwé didn't press the point. Samuel bugged him, but the young man was always willing to help Moya. As she aged and as her sight failed, she'd need all the help she could get.

"You know, Moya, we could do this every day," he said, dabbing her arm with a soapy sponge. "I'd be honored to share my home. And if my father were here, he'd insist."

"You know I need to be here," she replied, squeezing his arm lovingly.

"But eventually..." Onwé said, looking into her eyes.

Moya nodded, conceding the point.

"It's not enough that I'm going blind," she said. "Ash would have harped on me until I went deaf. Stubborn mule, always braying over what's best for me."

Moya dried the last of the dishes and gazed out the window. Onwé watched her focus on the trees, losing herself in reverie. He dared to wonder how she'd react if her son popped out of them, as he should have done years ago.

"I miss Ash almost as much as I miss my boy," she said.

"You don't need to be alone in the dark, *Néthédi.*" Onwé put his arm around her. "You still have family here. Move in with me."

Moya hugged him back.

"Don't worry about me. I've been in the dark for twenty-four years. I have to be here."

She receded from his embrace and drifted over to the couch.

"But why?" Onwé pressed. "Akántha would be able to find you anywhere. Especially at my place." He took a seat next to Moya and scooped up a blanket from the floor.

"Your mother could hear the spirits," she explained, pulling the blanket over both of their laps. "Your grandmother even more so. Old N'wenthāil could sometimes see them as they passed. But in all the years I've spent listening, I've never once heard my son. There is no song of welcome from the other worlds. All I have is silence."

"That's why you should leave this place," Onwé said.

"I never got to send him off," Moya replied, referring to the Nauktí tradition of singing a guiding hymn to the spirit during the funeral ceremony. "I don't know where he is. I don't know if he's lost. But I feel him here, in these walls. In this fire. I know you don't understand, Onwé. But I have to be here."

Onwé took in Moya's words without protest. He saw the frailness of her body as she sat shivering beneath the blanket, and felt the brittleness of her resolve in the way she spoke. He knew this rickety old hovel was the only thing left anchoring Moya to her son. The only piece of Akántha that remained.

"He visits my dreams, *Néthédi,*" he said. "Luke's too. I think he's still here... I think he wants to show us something."

Onwé took Moya's hand. Upon it he felt the coldness of a person near death, and worried her spirit might not be willing to bear another lonely winter on Pale Peak.

"Whatever it is," Moya said, glancing at the door on the off-chance Luke might come barging in, "it's got Líkōté scared half to death."

Chapter 19

Within days of Gaylen Poor's arrival, another troop of BIA agents descended on the reservation to peck around. The town stirred with unease at their presence, knowing they only showed up during times of sorrow and strife to intervene on behalf of the federal government. Everyone regarded the furtive men as heralds of dark times, but few knew they'd come in search of answers about a second plane crash on Pale Peak.

The six agents made their way around Autumn Ridge over the course of two days, interviewing residents who'd met Mr. Poor on the fateful night he'd emerged from the woods. They took special interest in baby Stefan and barred curious neighbors from visiting Wendy's home. Dr. Farmer scuttled back and forth between the Miller house and the medical center, often with an agent on his heels, muttering to himself like he always did.

By the time the agents arrived at Onwé's home, their welcome seemed to have worn thin even among the tribal police, and now only Burke Voth looked enthusiastic about their presence. Onwé opened the door in the early morning to the pastor and two BIA men, and saw the gravity of their expressions. Steve Winépo stood a dozen yards back, keeping an eye on the situation but distancing himself from the conversation.

"Mr. Lopez," Voth said with restrained contempt, "these gentlemen are here from the Bureau with a few questions about Gaylen Poor."

"Fellas," Onwé said, ignoring Voth.

The men introduced themselves, but Onwé didn't catch either of their names. Instead, his mind wandered across the mountain, out into the nameless place, where he imagined the second plane had gone down. He recalled the corpses he and Warren had found and wondered how long anyone could survive out there in this cold. The snow would be here any day, and would surely kill any passengers who remained out there.

"Where's Vince and Paul?" Onwé asked, interrupting the pleasantries one of the agents had begun to babble. "They were your boys, right? They make it home okay?"

"Well, Vince took thirty-some-odd stitches and a course of antibiotics," the taller agent said, glancing at the other for a corroborating nod. "And Paul, he—he's moved on from the Bureau."

"Mountain air seemed to disagree with him," the shorter man added.

Onwé couldn't tell if the comment was an attempt at a joke.

"What about Warren?" he asked, "from the uh...the National Board of Plane Crashes or whatever."

The men exchanged another look, but this time, it was a disquieted one.

"Not sure about him," the taller man said, "but we did see some of his...photography."

The short agent shook his head at his colleague and

quickly changed the subject.

"Mr. Lopez," he said, "would you mind telling us what Mr. Poor told you when he arrived on the rez?"

"He was delirious," Onwé replied, catching Numi as she tried to bolt out the door to meet the strangers. "He didn't say much of anything, except that his plane went down. You guys find anything yet?"

"Are you sure that's all he said to you?" the shorter man asked, ignoring Onwé's question. "We understand you were present with him at the medical center."

"If you know that," Onwé replied, "don't you already know what he said? Dr. Farmer was there. Steve too."

The police chief looked off down the road, pretending not to listen to the conversation.

"We're just trying to get the full picture here, Mr. Lopez," the taller agent said. "It's a little plane and a lot of woods. If you remember anything, track one of us down, alright?"

"Got it," Onwé said, knowing already he had no intention of seeking these men out.

"And Mr. Lopez," the shorter agent added, "if it's all the same to you, please keep our chat to yourself. We're trying not to start a panic in the community."

Onwé snorted, resentful that government spooks from far away kept coming to his town and telling him not to speak.

"Be a shame if there was a panic," he said, leering at Voth. "Panicky folks aren't calm. Harder to keep under the federal thumb."

Steve turned around to hush Onwé, but the shorter agent silenced him with a hand.

"I assure you it's not about that," he said with a smile. The man spoke as if he'd been briefed on Onwé's disdain for the BIA, and used a friendly tone that came off a bit oversold. "We're just asking for a bit of discretion during an ongoing investigation. I promise you, we have the community's best interest in mind at all times."

"Best interest," Onwé repeated flatly.

"Believe it or not, Mr. Lopez," said the taller agent, "the Bureau really does work toward the prosperity of all Indians. That's why we're here—figure out what's going on, and ensure nobody on the rez gets hurt."

"Is that why you guys keep rejecting our request for running water and flushing toilets?" Onwé snapped. "For the prosperity of all Indians? There's a tribal elder up that road there who gets to shit in a freezing outhouse every day."

Both agents reacted to the comment with quiet exasperation. Steve risked a quick glance and looked away, and Voth rolled his eyes in exhaustion. At last, the shorter agent went for broke and tried to meet Onwé halfway.

"You're right," he said. "We're not perfect, and we know the struggles of your people. But we really do want to help."

Onwé gripped the door knob so hard he thought it might crumple in his hand.

"Help?" he repeated. "You *helped* us by banning our language in school when I was a kid. Now half of us can't even understand our own grandparents. You helped my dad by fining him for trying to teach our songs to kids. You banned hunting in our forests and poisoned our rivers—very helpful there. Now we have to beg *this* jackass for food." Onwé shot a cold glare at Voth. "And after all that, my friend and I still tried to help the BIA search for the plane, and we almost fucking died. To hell with you."

He slammed the door and leaned against it, instantly remorseful for his outburst. At the same time, he was haunted by the image of his father, who'd have chastised him for going too easy on the agents. Ash was known to haul off and throw a few agents around in his day. It was a miracle they hadn't shot him.

"Welp, this has been productive," Onwé heard Voth quip.

117

"Let's move along, gentlemen. Leave Mr. Lopez to his... philosophies."

A half-hour later, there came another knock. Onwé opened the door to find a disappointed police chief and a furious lead pastor. Behind them loomed John Tall Rock, probably summoned by Voth to ensure Onwé would listen to whatever they had to say.

"Believe me, I get it," Steve said with his hands up in an effort to pre-emptively calm Onwé, "but that wasn't the way to handle things. Right now, we've got bigger fish to fry."

Onwé felt the urge to apologize for his temper, but when he tried to speak, Voth cut him off.

"Your petty grievances are an embarrassment," the pastor said. "Those men are just trying to do their jobs. Do you even care if there are survivors out there? Do you care that you're humiliating the council?"

Onwé felt the steam rise inside him again. He wanted to slap the condescending look right off Voth's face, but he feared he'd kill the old man with one blow.

"Don't talk," John said sternly, "just listen, Onwé. The council has called a meeting. We will hear testimony from Gaylen Poor about the crash. Since you were present during his arrival, we're inviting you to join us. But I'm warning you, if you act out in there, I can't see you getting another invitation."

It was no secret Onwé wanted to become a member of the tribal council someday. Not only would it be a personal honor for him, but Onwé believed he could more effectively advocate for his people if he were legitimized through its membership. He nodded in agreement.

"Our cooperation right now takes precedence over our

problems with the BIA," Steve added. "Lives could be at stake."

He and John turned and headed for the road, but Voth lingered behind just for a moment.

"Don't screw this up," the pastor said in a low voice, leaning into Onwé's personal space. "Don't shame Ashthenôví in front of the elders."

The words set off explosions inside Onwé's head. Burke Voth didn't give a shit about Ash's legacy, and simply hearing him utter the great man's name caused Onwé to tremble with rage. He found himself wondering what it would feel like to stare into Voth's eyes while choking the life out of him. Instead, he settled on a quieter form of resistance: he would bring his father's hiking staff to the council meeting, and Voth would recall his recent lesson in *savage idols* any time he looked over.

Chapter 20

However remote its offices were from Pale Peak, the Bureau of Indian Affairs was the ultimate authority over the reservation, and it demanded full reporting on crimes and catastrophes that occurred in Indian Country. This included the occasional trespass into tribal council meetings, and today, the team of BIA agents stood aligned on the wall opposite the elders' table, as if to illustrate the opposing forces in the room.

John Tall Rock, Moya River Stone, and the other tribal leaders sat together, listening patiently as they'd been trained to do over the decades, while the senior agent enumerated a list of actions and restrictions to be carried out on the reservation: no talk of the investigations, no interfering, and no travel off the rez for any resident until further notice. As usual, Indian silence was of utmost importance.

Onwé was not offered a seat. He stood awkwardly in a corner in full view of Luke, who had likely been invited by Burke Voth and Steve Winépo to answer questions about the first crash. The three of them loomed in the back, watching the meeting unfold. Though the gloom of the hall obscured most of Luke's face, Onwé could still feel his burning stare.

"Folks, there's been a second incident on the mountain," the senior agent announced. "Another private plane, this time on the north face. We don't think anyone survived the first crash out west, but this one's different. Two survivors made it to Autumn Ridge a few days ago. We expect there could be more."

"I understand that Mr. Poor is well enough to speak with us today," John said, rising from his seat and giving a *come-hither* gesture to Dr. Farmer, who had just poked his head into the room.

The doctor led a hobbling Gaylen Poor to the center of the hall and chaired him between the two parties.

"What is Mr. Poor's condition?" Elder Tavshíí asked.

"A sprained wrist, some bruised ribs, a few spots of frostnip, and a mild concussion," Dr. Farmer replied. "Miraculous, really. Considering..."

"Mr. Poor," Voth said, filling the hall with his sermonizing voice, "the tribal council and the Bureau of Indian Affairs have invited you here today to listen to the story of your arrival in Autumn Ridge. We ask that you tell us, to the best of your recollection, how exactly you came to be here."

Gaylen studied the faces around the room and nodded timidly. He was a small man, and looked even smaller under the withering gazes of elders, feds, and a brooding minister.

"This is a federal investigation," Voth added. "It would behoove you to tell the truth at all times."

Gaylen nodded again. He took a deep breath that was abruptly halted by the pain in his ribcage, then began with the disclaimer: "I understand if you don't believe what I'm about to say."

"You'd be surprised what we believe," Onwé said from across the room, hoping the interjection did not violate some behavioral expectation of the council. He recalled Luke's terrible story of the Briar House and wondered if Gaylen had also encountered strange things on the mountain.

"We flew out of Salt Lake City," Gaylen said. "My company's negotiating a merger with a firm there. A few of their guys were coming back to Dallas with us. One of them was a Norwegian guy with a wife and baby... I don't know why they were there."

"Transportation Board says there were sixteen passengers on the flight," one of the agents said. "That seem right to you?"

"...I think so," Gaylen replied after a moment. He took a long drink from a glass of water Dr. Farmer had handed to him, then winced when he tried to set it down on the floor. "We had a delay due to weather over the Rockies, so we took off just at sunset. The plane hit turbulence halfway across the mountains, and the Norwegian lady started crying. Everyone was scared, but this lady...she lost it. Babbling like crazy in some weird language."

"Norwegian?" the agent proposed.

"Maybe, but I don't think so," Gaylen said with a doubtful expression. "Her husband looked like he couldn't understand what the hell she was talking about. It sounded so...*weird*."

"Did it sound like a prayer?" Voth asked from the far end of the room.

"Come to think of it, Reverend," Gaylen said between labored breaths, "it sounded a bit like singing."

Luke seemed to shift uncomfortably where he stood.

"We heard someone yelling in the cockpit," Gaylen went on, "and the stewardess rushed up there. Then everything went crazy. The plane dove. Stuff was flying everywhere. People were on the ceiling. The screaming was so wild, it sounded like...like a symphony. And I realized I was part of it. Then I blacked out.

"When I woke up, I couldn't feel anything at all. I saw

broken trees and pieces of the plane everywhere. The sky was black. I realized we'd come swooping right down through the woods, like it was a runway."

"How many survived?" the agent asked.

"Seven of us made it out—eight, I guess, counting the baby. The stewardess and one pilot got out. The Norwegian guy was dead, but his wife survived. Three other guys from my company made it too. We grabbed what we could, and they helped carry me out. Blankets, a couple of flashlights, whatever luggage we could find."

"Did the pilot tell you what happened?" Moya asked from the elders' table. "What brought the plane down?"

Gaylen hesitated.

"Remember how I said you won't believe me?" he said.

Moya nodded.

"It was the copilot who survived," Gaylen said. "He said the captain was staring out the window, down into the dark, like he could see something no one else could. Whatever it was, the guy never moved that whole period of turbulence. He just stared. Then, all of a sudden he grabbed the controls and performed an emergency descent. The pressure dropped in the cabin and we all blacked out. When we woke up, we saw a tree had come through the windshield and went right through the captain's chest. I looked at him when we grabbed the flashlights. That face... He looked...*relieved.*"

The tribal elders looked at each other in disbelief.

"We wandered for a little while," Gaylen went on. "Tried to get our bearings. Took shelter in a cave beside a little river, and eventually we got a fire going. But then it started raining and we had to move deeper inside. It was so damn cold."

One of the agents flipped through a notepad and cleared his throat.

"The plane was due in Dallas two days before you showed up here. What happened during that time?"

Gaylen's expression became even more grave. He searched the room, unsure of the words he knew were about to leave his mouth.

"By morning, the pilot had fallen ill," he finally said. "He developed a fever, and it just kept getting worse. He said he was hearing voices deeper in the cave. Told us he saw lights back there too.

"Then the others began acting strange. The Norwegian lady—Nora, I think—took ill. She kept waking up screaming. She said there was something else in the cave, sitting in a stone chair at the very bottom of the tunnel. She said it asked her about her baby, and told her it wanted to hold him."

People throughout the hall shifted in their seats and exchanged unsettled looks. Even Voth, whose face was fixed in a near-permanent grimace, seemed rattled by the tale.

"When the pilot heard Nora's dream," Gaylen continued, "all of a sudden, his fever broke. He became alert and cheery and asked Nora a whole bunch of questions. He told her he'd had a dream too, that this mountain sits upon a hidden church buried deep down in the earth. He said within its walls, a choir of angels sings perpetually. That's why everyone was hearing voices."

"Cave gasses," the first agent said dismissively. "They can make people hallucinate. The crash alone was probably enough to cause these nightmares. Any traumatic event will do it, really. We see it all the time."

"Let him speak," said Pélō'é, the only Pozi elder on the council. She pointed a brittle finger at the agent who'd interrupted Gaylen. "Maybe in your world, dreams are just dreams. But to my people, they are meaningful. Mr. Poor, please continue."

"Yes, ma'am," he replied, wiping the sweat that had begun to collect on his face. His breath quickened at the thoughts racing through his mind, causing him to wince in pain. "It wasn't his dreams that frightened me. It was his enthusiasm. The pilot had that look in his face, that lunatic smile, like he knew we'd all be going to Heaven any minute and he couldn't wait a second longer. He kept telling us we had nothing to fear, and that we should follow him down to the church. He said he knew the way.

"That night, I woke up to a bunch of hellish noise. There was screaming and laughing coming from farther back in the tunnels. I never would have followed it, but when I looked around, I saw that the pilot and Nora were missing—and the baby. I feared he'd done something terrible, so I grabbed the flashlight and went searching."

"Where were the other survivors in all this?" John asked.

"My colleague was next to me, practically catatonic," Gaylen replied. "The other two men were gone. One of them had been wearing a brown suit on the plane, and I found his clothes on the ground at the mouth of the cave. It was like he'd stripped down and run off into the forest. I found the other one a few hundred yards into the tunnels, crumpled up with some kind of wound to his abdomen. Blood everywhere. He pointed further down the tunnel, toward the screaming."

"Who was screaming?" Moya asked. "The woman?"

"No," Gaylen said in a dreary voice. "It was the baby. The woman was laughing. She laughed so hard she could barely breathe. I followed their voices until I came to a set of stairs, and—"

"Stairs?" the agent interrupted.

"Yes. Hundreds of them. Broad and steep. Carved right into the stone with a sort of...*elegance*. I wanted to run away, but I couldn't ignore the baby's screaming. So I went looking for him."

Luke abruptly pushed himself off the wall and made for a nearby refreshment table. He gulped down two glasses of water, and in the better light, Onwé could see the panic on his face. Luke's eyes looked at once exhausted and frantic, reflective of a sleepless terror that had plagued him since the camping trip. There seemed to be no end to his turmoil, and Gaylen Poor's story only deepened it.

"The stairs went on and on," Gaylen continued. "They made me dizzy. I thought I saw the cave walls covered in these…dripping pustules. The whole tunnel writhed and quivered like I was walking through a giant stomach. Then I found myself in some kind of big cavern, and at the far end was Nora. She was laying on the ground, pointing up at the pilot, who was sitting in this huge stone chair that looked like…like something a king would sit in. His face had been torn out. Skull and brains and all. Just a giant hole for a head. In his arms was Stefan."

"God save us," Voth blurted out in disgust.

Other people around the hall recoiled at the image, and the agents began muttering incredulously to each other.

"I'm telling the truth," Gaylen asserted. "I know it sounds crazy, but this is what I saw."

He scanned the room until his gaze fell on Luke, whose panic betrayed that he believed the story.

"I grabbed the baby and ran for my life," Gaylen said. "Nora started screaming and tried to follow me, but she didn't have a light. As I ran up the stairs, her voice changed. All of a sudden, I heard my kids calling out to me."

Upon hearing this detail, Luke headed for the exit. He shrugged off Voth's attempt to intercept him and threw open the door, causing its knob to ping against the wall outside. Samuel had been waiting dutifully out there and followed Luke as he brushed past. In a rare display of informality, Voth hurried after the two and left the council meeting without pardon.

When the room settled, John bade Gaylen continue.

"I was so scared." Gaylen wrapped himself in a protective hug and recoiled at the pain it caused in his ribs. "I walked for hours. There was a house high up on a ridge, but I couldn't get to it. Then I saw lights in the distance, so I headed for them."

"And that brought you here," Tavshií said.

Gaylen nodded.

"I didn't think there were any houses on that part of the mountain," Pélō'é said with a confused look.

"I know what I saw," Gaylen replied. "The lights were on. Someone was home."

"I must say," Moya interjected, "assuming you've told us the truth today, you've exhibited bravery worthy of merit. What do you make of all this, John?"

John Tall Rock considered Gaylen's tale and returned a baffled expression.

"It's beyond me," he said in defeat. "I've heard legends, but nothing like this."

"I'm reminded of an ancient story my people used to tell," said the old man sitting beside Pélō'é. It was Emmanuel, Karl Ortega's father, one of the two Ineho elders on the council. "Some of them believed that the *Lōbsh'á'loth* are found on a mountain here in the Rockies. In English, the word means something like 'the mouths of Hell.' At night, children would rise from their beds and sleepwalk into them, following the songs of children who went before. I believe Mr. Poor's story. My grandfather said even worse things about these caves."

"Hideous," Moya grumbled.

Nănk, the other Ineho elder, looked to the BIA agents along the far wall and projected his voice to them. "That's why it was such an insult for us to be corralled onto this reservation, gentlemen. It's why so many of our people chose to die instead. They believed this place sits on top of Hell."

"If only Ashthenôví were here to guide us," Tavshií said from across the table.

127

The other elders nodded, even Moya, and Onwé felt a little sting from the comment. Ash was gone, and he'd left behind a son who seemed unfit to carry his father's torch through the coming darkness.

Chapter 21

Despite their recent tiff, Onwé knew he had to find Luke. He stayed at the council meeting just long enough to hear the closing statements: Gaylen would convalesce in Autumn Ridge until he was no longer needed for the investigation, and would then be evacuated to Denver. Baby Stefan would remain in the care of Wendy Miller until the government identified his next of kin. John Tall Rock sanctioned Wendy's request to look after the child, and Burke Voth seconded the motion due to her membership in the church.

Onwé slipped out of the meeting hall before he could be roped into a stale conversation between the elders and feds. He knew where to find Luke before even thinking about it and hiked up the church road, staff in hand, lost in thought about the house on the ridge from Gaylen's story. Could Mr. Poor have discovered *Óknóth-úden*—Luke's "Briar House"?

The church gleamed a haunting white against a backdrop of departing storm clouds, and the **Jesus is Lord in Cold Valley** sign creaked on its hinges in the breeze. The surrounding grounds were desolate; no church folk scurried about like they usually did, preparing for one of their many cheery events.

Two girls passed by the windows inside and came out the

front door as Onwé approached. To his surprise, it was little Angela, followed closely by Hannah Miller, Chris and Wendy's teenage daughter.

"What are you doing here, sweetie?" Onwé asked, befuddled by Angela's presence in Autumn Ridge without her father. "How'd you get up here?"

"Hi, Mr. Lopez," she said in her mousy voice. "I walked. Just wanted to visit my friend."

Hannah clutched a Bible and a stack of papers to her chest but managed a half-wave at Onwé. He nodded back.

"That's almost eight miles, Angela," he said, trying to hide the worry in his voice. He remembered the bloodied ram and the terrifying voice that had called out to him on that road. "You didn't do that alone, did you?"

"No," she replied, smiling. Her big green eyes moved to the massive German shepherd sitting quietly at the end of the porch. "Tíwé let me borrow him. He's a good bodyguard."

Zeus sat at attention a dozen feet away, studying Onwé carefully. Onwé was shocked he hadn't noticed the dog when he'd walked up to the church. In that moment, he wondered how many cougars and bears he'd unwittingly trotted past on his hikes.

"Oh," he said. "Well, I still don't like the idea of you coming up here without Tíwé. You tell that boy to look after his own. Better yet, don't make that trip without an adult. It's too dangerous."

Angela nodded, and an awkward pause fell over the conversation.

"So, when are you heading back?" Onwé asked. "I'll walk you home."

"That's okay, Mr. Lopez," Hannah said, hoisting the stack of papers a little higher to her chest. "Angie's staying over at my house tonight and helping me with Bible study."

Chris and Wendy had converted two years ago, much at

Luke's behest, but their daughter Sonya had refused to follow in their footsteps. A rift had grown in the family, but with time and pressure, she eventually joined the church and adopted the name Hannah.

"Oh? That's very nice of you," Onwé said to Angela, trying his best not to sound disappointed.

Angela's parents had also converted, and had similarly forced a new name on their daughter. It pained Onwé to watch his friends and neighbors leave the Old Way, and he feared that if Angela took up the new faith, she might pressure Tíwé to do so as well. The boy liked Angela so much he'd probably take the dunk if she asked.

The mere thought of Tíwé joining the church instantly caused a spark of rage to flare in Onwé's chest. Onwé rarely lashed out at new converts, but his increasing sense of abandonment fueled his hatred for Burke Voth, whose personal mission seemed to be to kill Indian culture and bury it under the mountain.

"Well, we've got to be going," Hannah said, appearing to sense Onwé's mood. "I want Angie to meet little Stefan!"

"Okay, girls," Onwé said, "have a nice time. Angie, I'll walk you home tomorrow."

"Kanákshî natáj'né," Angela said with a wink as she passed. *We will meet again.*

Onwé interpreted the salutation as a secret message: *Don't worry. I won't convert.*

Zeus bounded up to Onwé, gave him a perfunctory lick, and followed the girls off the porch.

For just a moment, Onwé stared at the church door and examined his recent paint job.

Looked better with the blood streaks, he thought.

He pushed the door open. Luke was sitting once again in the pews, head in his hands, flanked by Voth and young Samuel. The men spoke in low voices and fell silent when they noticed Onwé looming in the entryway.

"Came to check on you, brother," Onwé said in a conciliatory voice. "You doing alright? You looked upset at the council meeting."

"You shouldn't be here," Luke replied flatly. He lifted his head but did not turn around to see his friend.

"What do you mean?" Onwé asked.

"All this sorrow…" Luke said, facing the empty lectern from which Voth delivered his sermons. "You ever wonder why so many bad things happen in Autumn Ridge?"

"The answers could fill books," Onwé said, not following where Luke was going with the question.

"I wonder if I've been too forgiving," Luke went on, "of myself and others. I try to walk with Christ. But maybe I focus too much on God's mercy, and not enough on His justice."

"What are you saying?"

Onwé stepped inside the church and leaned the hiking staff against the wall. Voth and Samuel looked over their shoulders at him. He couldn't help but wonder what they'd been saying to Luke behind closed doors.

"I'm saying, God is trying to shine His light onto the rez, and maybe the people who won't accept that light are keeping us all in darkness." Luke stood and turned around, leering into Onwé with dead eyes. "I'm saying, what if it's *you?*"

The accusation hurt. None of the converts had accused Onwé of doing harm to the people by fighting to keep the Old Way, but their occasional stares told him how they really felt.

"You're scared," Onwé replied. "I am too. But I'm here for you."

Luke snorted.

"You're here to drag me away from my community," he

said, anger rising in his voice.

Voth nodded, and Samuel moved to another pew, evidently afraid the conversation might come to blows.

"Your community is out *there*," Onwé replied sharply. "Not in here with this gargoyle telling people that without God, they're already dead."

Voth bristled at the insult and rose to rebuke Onwé, but Luke cut him off.

"But you *are* dead," Luke said. "All of you who refuse the gift of Christ have brought a curse on our land. Now strangers show up in our town with tales of demons. Sin is a beacon for wicked things, Onwé. The church is our only hope for keeping the darkness at bay."

"Unbelievable," Onwé said, shaking his head in disgust. "In case you don't remember, all those heathens out there are *your* people. *Your* family. This church seems more like a cult hideout than a sanctuary."

"Dead," Luke repeated. "But thanks to the Baptists, we are born again, and we live new life in Christ. Some of us, anyway."

"Oh, please," Onwé spat, helpless not to be drawn into the same tired debate that had plagued their friendship since Luke's conversion. "Look around, man. Has anything really changed? The tribes are still broken. The people are still poor. Drug use and suicide are on the rise. For God's sake, three people in town killed themselves this year!"

"Those things are why we need the church!" Luke bellowed, startling both Samuel and Voth. "Tradition isn't going to save us. *This* is the answer." He opened his arms, gesturing at the room they stood in. His pallid eyes darted around as if following a presence no one else could see.

"Look at yourself," Onwé said. "You look like death, man. You need to see the doctor, not huddle in this place and wait for salvation."

"Fuck you," Luke snapped. "You have no idea what I need."

"Take it outside, boys," Voth commanded. *"Now."*

Luke obeyed and barreled down the nave toward the door. Onwé had to dodge him or else get run down. He glared at Voth and then followed Luke outside.

"I can't be like them," Luke said, halting in the gravel lot that overlooked the town. "All the unsaved down there... Just a bunch of miserable husks waiting around for the end."

"We have good reasons to be unhappy, you jackass," Onwé snapped. "Just because you ignore those people and make-believe everything's fine up here with your congregation doesn't mean we don't suffer."

"You all suffer because you reject the truth," Luke said, turning to Onwé. For all the zealous anger in his eyes, there was still something eerily vacant about them. "You choose not to come to Christ with me, and your choice opens a doorway for...whatever's out there on the mountain. We *need* salvation, Onwé. All of us."

"We suffer because of what men like Voth did to us!" Onwé shouted, outraged at the thought that his people were to blame for the dreadful things happening on Pale Peak. "You abandoned us, Luke! You abandoned me and Moya and everyone who loves you so you could join a cult!"

Onwé found himself squared off with Luke, whose large form was blurred in the haze of rage. Luke towered over him, unmoved by the fiery accusation, and stared into Onwé's eyes with intense scorn.

"I needed to feel something other than despair," he said, sharpening his words into knives. "Maybe being pissed off all the time is good enough for you, but I'm *done* with it, and I'm done with you—until you're ready to admit your faults and accept the truth of God."

"What do you mean, done with me?" Onwé snapped. "You're making all this nonsense up because you're sick, man.

And Voth's making it worse with all the bullshit he whispers in your ear."

Luke balled his fists, obviously battling within himself not to lash out and slug Onwé.

"You've never been able to respect my decision," he said through gritted teeth. "I won't listen to your whining about the Old Way anymore. I don't want to live the rest of my life scraping by on false hope with a bunch of fucking *moon-worshippers!*"

"Fine, then." Onwé threw his hands up in defeat. "Go climb up your damn cross. You think you're some bigshot with your fancy new name and your stupid haircut. Voth knows you're just like me—another hopeless Indian. And he preys on hopelessness, *Likóté.*"

"My name is *Luke,*" he growled, ramming his chest into Onwé's and sending him staggering backward. "And I'm not hopeless. You're just an asshole with no one left to bully. You've chased everyone else away who ever meant something to you."

"Don't you fucking dare," Onwé snarled, knowing exactly where this was heading.

"That's right," Luke taunted. "I know your pain. I know the anger. We both fell apart over the years. But I never put that hurt on anybody else. Can't say the same for you, can I?"

"Likóté, I swear on my father's grave," Onwé said, trembling with murderous rage. His stomach dropped at the words he knew were coming. His ego would not suffer the insult to pass.

"Remind me, Onwé, what did you do?" Luke asked in a mocking tone. "Oh, *I remember!* You got high, attacked your wife, and shattered Tíwé's arm when he tried to stop you. Do I have that right? And now he hates your guts. Your only son, and he despises you. Paragon of the Old Way right here, ladies and gentlemen."

"You son of a bitch!" Onwé screamed.

He charged at Luke, swinging wildly, but Luke dodged the blows and landed a lightning-fast counterpunch to Onwé's jaw. The impact sent Onwé to the ground in a heap, where he found himself blinking up at a swirling sky. The taste of iron flooded his mouth, and after a moment, Luke's blurry form came into focus. Onwé spat blood at him defiantly and pulled himself to his feet, but the world danced around him. He went right back to the ground.

Luke sank to a crouch and peered into Onwé's rolling eyes. Satisfied the fight was over, he smirked.

"Not a warrior. Not a wise man. Not a leader," he said with disappointment. "Some son of Ashthenôví *you* are."

Chapter 22

Onwé finally clambered to his feet after a few minutes on the ground. By the time he was able to stand, he found himself alone in the gravel lot. Luke had long since returned to the church, and Voth and Samuel spoke near the window, occasionally glancing outside with concern. Humiliation and resentment innervated Onwé's limbs, and he steadied himself enough to walk back up to the door, where Voth tried to intercept him.

"That's enough," Voth commanded, trying to usher Onwé back outside.

Onwé slapped the pastor's hands away and ripped the hiking staff from its place against the wall. He trudged up to Luke, who'd returned to the pews and was now bowed in prayer.

Without a word, Onwé tore the metal cross from the staff and hurled it to the floor beside Luke. The *ting* sound it made echoed across the church, drawing Luke's attention away from his prayers. He opened his eyes and studied the object, then gazed up at Onwé as if he'd been stabbed in the heart.

Onwé turned away and headed for the door, knowing

he'd just done something that could never be taken back. On the day of Luke's baptism a few years ago, he'd given the cross to Onwé and told him, "If ever you decide to join me in Christ, give this to someone else who needs it."

Despite his hostility to Christianity and the pain it had wrought on Natives, Onwé kept the trinket as a gesture of respect for Luke, and had placed it on the hiking staff among a collection of other meaningful objects. Now, the bond it signified was broken.

Rain began to fall on the lonely walk down the hill. It reminded Onwé of the coldness that had rooted its way into his heart over the long years without his family. He *was* miserable and hopeless, and the truth of it stung. He knew none of Luke's hurtful words were lies: Onwé was not worthy of the respect accorded to his father, Ash, and he was incapable of maintaining relationships with the people who mattered to him most. Like so many others on the rez, he would grow older and more bitter with the passage of time, and then finally, a dark winter would take what was left of him. In a sense, he *was* already dead.

But the worst of it was a truth even Luke could not accept: Onwé rejected the idea of absolution. Onwé believed that by harming his family he'd betrayed his most sacred charge, and for this, he could never be forgiven—not even by a god. He viewed his soul as permanently stained, unable to come clean, no matter how much he begged a higher power. For this reason, he resented the church for selling forgiveness to his people.

On the evening of the following day, Onwé stood at the window facing the woods behind his home. He watched the individual trees blend into a black mass in the gathering dark, and wondered if Nora, the other survivor Gaylen Poor had mentioned, was still out there. Onwé drew the curtains and lit a fire, intent on remaining out of the public eye until the swelling of his jaw had reduced. Tonight, he hugged Numi more than usual, and she licked him profusely, aware of his dour mood. His face still throbbed a little, each pulse reminding him of all the dreadful things he and Luke had said to each other.

"Stupid fuck," Onwé grumbled, resentful toward Luke and alarmed by his recent change in personality. Something had happened in that cave. Something had gotten inside him, and now, Luke's faith seemed unable to purge it.

As Onwé stared into the flames, his thoughts drifted to Akántha, and to the plane crashes. He imagined the so-called Briar House rising from dark soil, and stairs vanishing into the mountain. He wondered about the ghoulish figure that had appeared in his yard, and if it would return. The dreams, the voices, the dreary singing—all of it swirled in Onwé's mind, suffocating him with thoughts of death and torment.

In times like these, Old N'wenthäil and Moya would have prayed together, listening for signs from the spirits. There before the crackling fire, Onwé considered praying for Luke—both to the First Spirit and to Jesus Christ—but the idea was quickly doused by the realization that no help ever seemed to come to Autumn Ridge from the next world. A century of Nauktí prayers had not stopped the destruction of his community, nor had they returned his people to their rightful homeland. And the Christians, for all their zeal, had been unable to save the Indians. Onwé wondered if any gods were listening at all, or if all magic had gone out of the world and taken hope with it.

A gentle knock on the door pulled Onwé out of his brooding. He recognized the knock's pattern and immediately knew who it was. He hesitated, unsure if Luke had returned to hit him again. At the same time, an even grimmer thought arose in his mind: the shambling corpse of Akántha—the only other person who knew the *secret knock*—arisen from the dead to drag Onwé into the woods.

"Who is it?" Onwé called out.

"Just a pilgrim in the night," Luke replied through the door. His voice came out raspy, spoken with vocal cords frayed by hours of screaming. "May I...come in?"

"What do you want?"

Onwé looked over at Numi, who did not rush to the door as she normally did whenever she heard Luke approach. Instead, she sat upright, frozen with the same hesitation seizing Onwé.

"Thought I'd stop by and let you know I'm alright," Luke replied. "Finally got some rest."

Onwé approached the door and cracked it open a few inches. As soon as he did, Numi issued an uneasy growl. She cowered in her place beside the fire, peeking around the side of Onwé's chair.

"That's... that's good to hear," Onwé said, caught off guard by Luke's appearance. He expected his friend to look a bit healthier, but instead, Luke's appearance was so ghastly it made Onwé take a step back.

The moonlight cast the man's skin in a deathly pallor, and the haunted vacancy of his gaze seemed to betray the absence of a soul. The circles beneath his eyes had deepened to bruise-like stains, scoured upon his face by a dozen sleepless nights. Luke had not changed clothes in days, and wore his jacket unzipped, as if unaware of the gnawing cold.

"I don't know how long I slept," Luke said, grinning madly, "but I've never felt better. I dreamed beautiful things, brother. Unimaginable things. We were kids again. Akántha was there. He taught us all the secrets of the Old Way... How to make fire in our hands. How to see in the dark, where the spirits go."

Luke fell silent and turned his head to the side, as if listening to a voice over his shoulder.

"Buddy," Onwé said, realizing how dire Luke's situation had become, "why don't you walk me down to Dr. Farmer's house? I've, uh... I've got to pick up Moya's medicine."

"When I woke up, I prayed," Luke said, ignoring Onwé's request. He took a step forward and stood in the threshold of the door, causing Numi to growl louder. The fireplace threw its dancing light across Luke's face. He looked like a bloated corpse dragged from a river.

Onwé searched Luke's eyes for anything familiar but saw only a terrifying emptiness. The man seemed gone now, having left behind a hollow body animated by madness.

"I'm ready for my pilgrimage," he whispered.

"Your...what?" Onwé replied.

"Walk with me, brother," Luke said, unable to contain the wild grin spreading once more across his face. "Akántha's waiting. He's answered my prayers."

Numi took a few cautious steps forward, baring her teeth and snarling at Luke.

"I already know the way," he continued, regarding the dog with disdain. "Come find me when you're ready."

With that, Luke turned and headed out into the darkness of the road.

"Luke!" Onwé called. He walked out onto the porch but was sent back indoors by the blistering wind. "Luke!"

His friend ignored him and carried on westward up the dirt road, humming a strange song as he moved.

"Likōté!" Onwé shouted.

Luke turned and looked back at Onwé for a long moment—then sprinted off into the night.

Chapter 23

In the distant past, the Nauktí had looked to the stars to track the seasons. The positions of their constellations dictated the arrival of winter, and thus they could prepare in advance. The Ineho, however, who had lived in the great mountains to the north, steeled their people for winters by way of *Yōktha*— a great feast and bonfire that occurred at sight of the first blizzard.

Yōktha was, by its nature, a sudden and spontaneous affair, thrown together in a rush and disbanded just as quickly. As such, the people had little notice to prepare and would abandon their regular responsibilities for the day. The frantic holiday was so thrilling to outsiders that when the federal government relocated the Ineho onto the reservation, the Nauktí and Pozi peoples quickly adopted the tradition. In time, *Yōktha* came to symbolize not just the coming of a new year, but also a shared Native identity in Cold Valley.

This year, *Yōktha* was announced by the Ineho elders twenty-four hours in advance. The whole of Autumn Ridge was abustle. Townspeople scurried about with more cheer in their faces than usual, hauling supplies to and fro and dragging hundreds of tables and chairs into the square.

Families streamed in from Lake Namarjo to see relatives, while John Tall Rock and Steve Winépo directed the event as best they could.

High up on Pale Peak, the BIA team frantically searched for the wreckage of Gaylen's plane before the snow began to fall.

Onwé spent the day baking bread with Moya and Tíwé, but he could not shake the worry from his mind about Luke's frightening behavior. A week had passed since the night of Luke's mysterious "pilgrimage," and Onwé hadn't heard from him since. Luke had holed himself up in his home on the other side of town, loathe to see anyone, claiming to be catching up on badly needed sleep. Onwé had tried to visit him once with John and Dr. Farmer, but Luke refused to open the door and told them he was nursing a fever.

Onwé also harbored a deep anxiety that the unspeakable thing in the woods might return for another visit. He hadn't yet told Moya about it, for fear she might bring it up with Tíwé. If the boy and his mother heard of Onwé being visited by ghouls and spirits, they'd think he was back on drugs.

"Be social," Moya said, poking Onwé in the back and pulling him out of his gloomy thoughts. He'd been staring out the kitchen window, barely noticing Zeus and Numi, who chased each other around in the little clearing that made up Moya's yard.

"Sorry," he replied, turning his attention to Tíwé, who sat on the tattered couch in the living room. "Where's your girlfriend, bud?"

"She's *not* my girlfriend," Tíwé replied, shaking his head in embarrassment.

"But you like her," Moya teased, kneading a hunk of dough in a wooden bowl. "Eyes bare the soul, they say."

"Even if I did, I don't know how to get her to like me back."

Onwé beheld his son from across the room, quietly noticing the things a father tends to notice all at once: kids grow up too fast. Tíwé wasn't very tall for his age, but he seemed twice as big as he was when he and his mother had left Autumn Ridge. His ponytail was long and crow-black, and his big brown eyes studied everything they fell on, betraying the curiosity of his age.

Now, he was beginning to notice girls. Onwé had missed so much, and feared to miss another day.

"All the women in town chased your grandfather," Moya said with a giddy smile. "Give it time."

"Give it eleven more years," Onwé added in a stern voice. Teen pregnancies were common on the reservation, and Tíwé didn't have much in the way of a male role model.

"Now they all chase Luke," Tíwé said, flexing his arms and laughing. "Mom's friends are crazy about him. Will he be there tomorrow, Dad?"

Onwé hesitated, desperate to avoid a conversation about Luke. He feared upsetting Tíwé with the details of Luke's condition, but not as much as he feared divulging something creepy that would entice Tíwé and his friends on a quest up the mountain. Onwé shot an urgent look at Moya, trying to signal her not to mention any details.

"Not sure on that one, son," he said. "Luke's sick right now. But he told me to tell you hello."

"Lots of people getting sick right now," Tíwé mused. "Lots of weird stuff going on. Some kids at school said there were lights over the mountain. They say a UFO crashed into it. That's why there's government guys around, and that's why people are getting sick."

"The BIA's been down in Namarjo too?" Onwé replied, feeding a new tray into the oven.

"The what?" Tíwé asked.

"Uh, I think they're dealing with some kind of

contaminant up at Mirror Lake," Moya said. She knew the boy's penchant for disobedience and had caught Onwé's message.

"Contaminant?" Tíwé repeated with skepticism.

"Dreadful boring business," Moya replied. "Having to hear about it at the council meetings puts me right to sleep."

Tíwé seemed satisfied with the explanation and appeared to lose interest in the topic. Onwé breathed a sigh of relief, happy to know the news had not yet spread across the reservation. Cold Valley was a small place, and the truth would come out eventually, even from behind the doors of the tribal council building—but for now, he hoped his son's attention would remain east of the mountain and out of its mysterious caves.

"So," Onwé said, tossing a hot piece of bread to Tíwé, "will Angie be there tomorrow?"

"Probably," he said. "She's staying with Hannah. But they mostly ignore me. That girl's a vampire or something."

"What makes you say that?"

"Angela just acts different around her. Weirder. I dunno. Moya, do you remember any stories about the bad spirits in the mountains?"

Moya's eyes darted to Onwé, then back to the boy.

"Well, they're all pretty much the same," she said dismissively. "The moral of the story is always *stay out of the woods* or *don't listen to strange voices.*"

"Angela told me about *the cold people*," Tíwé said, moving from the couch to the table to be closer to Moya. "You know, the ones who can only walk on snow."

"Those are from Ineho legend," Moya said, washing flour and bits of dough from her hands. "You'd have to ask Karl next door."

"She also told me about the *Hollow One*," he went on. "*The Impostor.* Right, Dad? They learn people's voices and then call you into the woods. How do you say it? *At'an-A'ano...*"

Onwé was struck with a memory of the shadowy figure from his backyard: arms stiffly raised, head bowed in prayer, moonlight slinking over its bulky form. He tried to hide his discomfort at the thought, not wanting to pique his son's curiosity.

"Where'd Angela hear this stuff?" Onwé asked, forcing a dismissive tone. "You guys aren't reading those damn ghost books anymore, right?"

Onwé was referring to a series of pop-history books called *Haunted and Forgotten* that Tíwé had gotten his hands on years ago. It was an entry in one of those books that had driven Tíwé and his friends to explore the old mines, nearly getting the boy killed in the process.

"No, Dad," Tíwé said with annoyance. "Angie just reads a lot about history."

"That creature is *not* part of our history," said Moya. She removed her cooking apron and tossed it over her shoulder.

"It's creepy, though," Tíwé replied. "It reminds me of the *Diné* and their skin-walkers."

"Older than the skin-walkers," Moya grumbled. "Older than any belief, older than our species."

"Hm," Tíwé said, regarding her words.

"I don't care if Elvis himself calls out your name," Onwé said, shooting a stern look at his son. "You stay on the damn trails. You hear me? There's all kinds of shit that'll kill you on this mountain. No need for ghosts and monsters."

Before Tíwé could protest, Onwé poked a finger into Moya's ribs and lightened up his tone.

"So what about you, young lady? Is your boyfriend gonna be there?"

"Don't even," Moya snapped, threatening him with a wooden mixing spoon.

146

"You've got a boyfriend, *Néthédi?*" Tíwé gasped.

"Heck yeah, she does," Onwé replied, laughing while he fended off hard *whacks* from her spoon. "A distinguished man of the cloth, in fact!"

"I thought you hated that guy," Tíwé said, cracking up at the little duel playing out before him.

Moya sighed deeply and lowered herself onto one of the chairs at the kitchen table.

"I don't *hate* him," she admitted. "I hate why he's here and the cult that sent him. But he's a decent kid."

Tíwé studied Moya, appearing to sense the conflict in her heart.

"It doesn't help that he's so damn cheerful," she went on. "Reminds me a lot of my boy."

"I've noticed it too," Onwé said, rubbing Moya's shoulder. "Akántha lit up every room he ever walked into. And he wasn't trying to sell anything."

A while later, Tíwé set out to deliver a few bags of bread to the festival coordinators. Onwé and Moya remained inside, relaxing by a fire. They exchanged the same old stories about Akántha they always traded when Moya felt up to talking about him, and Onwé wondered if she ever got tired of the cycle. He wondered about the wicked spirits Tíwé had mentioned, and nearly asked Moya the question looming in his mind: did she believe they were responsible for Akántha's disappearance?

At last, he decided against it. The deep lines on Moya's face affirmed she'd considered the possibility over thousands of lonely nights.

Chapter 24

Onwé refused to allow Tíwé to walk back to Lake Namarjo by himself. He also feared hiking back up the mountain alone in the dark, and so he convinced his son to stay the night. It was the first time Tíwé had slept in his father's house since the separation, and the occasion left Onwé feeling so overwhelmed, he tossed and turned for hours. More than anything in the world, he wanted to put his family back together, and having Tíwé home ripped open the old wounds Onwé had inflicted on himself. He reasoned that all he could do was move at Tíwé's pace, and perhaps in time, the boy would learn to love him again.

By late afternoon the following day, *Yōktha* had begun. All of Autumn Ridge gathered in the town square, shivering beneath a roiling gray sky. They laughed and traded stories, making their way through a buffet line staffed by John Tall Rock, Steve Winépo, and a few volunteers. Onwé and Tíwé stood in line, chatting with folks who'd scarcely seen the boy in years, and loaded paper plates with as much food as they could fit. Zeus and Numi begged at their feet, driven wild by all the delicious smells wafting in the frigid air.

Even Voth's congregation participated in the festivities.

The Valley Commission had concluded years ago that *Yōktha* should not be regarded as an idolatrous ceremony to be suppressed, but rather as an opportunity for the Baptists to mingle with the masses and warm them up to the faith. Congregants plodded down the church road in groups, hugging people as they arrived, and Voth himself worked the drink station with a rare smile on his face.

"Lady of the hour." Onwé nudged his son with an elbow and nodded toward a nearby table. There sat Angela, talking excitedly with Hannah and two teenage boys. "Go hang out with her!"

"I think she likes older guys, Dad," Tíwé said with defeat.

"Nonsense," said Onwé, giving him a little push. "Don't you pay attention at all? Angie likes brains. Those are Doug's kids. Complete dumbasses."

"In case you haven't noticed, I'm not exactly a genius myself," Tíwé said. "My teachers think I'm an idiot."

"I bet Angie would tutor you if you asked," Onwé replied. "My teachers hated me too. And your grandfather. Boy, did they fuckin' hate him." He patted his son's back and sent him off.

Zeus trotted after Tíwé, locked onto the plate of food he carried.

As Onwé moved toward the drink station, he crossed paths with Dr. Farmer and Gaylen Poor, who chatted like old friends. Gaylen looked to be feeling a bit better and informed Onwé of his imminent departure from the reservation. A hundred questions ran through Onwé's mind about Gaylen's terrifying ordeal on the mountain, but there were too many people around, and the man finally seemed to be having a good day, so Onwé held his tongue. Instead, he asked Dr. Farmer if he'd seen Luke, and learned the doctor had tried to check in on him earlier. Just as before, Luke had refused to open the door.

It was unlike Luke to miss *Yōktha*. Onwé decided he'd head to Luke's house and try to coax him out with a plate of food. Onwé stopped when he heard a deep voice call his name.

He knew it was Voth before he turned around. The man loomed hesitantly nearby, having left his drink station duties to the junior pastor. In an effort to preserve the spirit of the day, Onwé softened the guarded posture that normally seized him whenever Voth was around, and attempted a half-smile. Numi received the pastor with a few cheerful licks.

"Thanks for helping out," Onwé said, looking out at the gathering crowd. "Must be eight hundred people here."

"They're my neighbors too, you know," Voth replied, taking in the scene before them. The genuine smile he'd worn minutes earlier had faded, and his eyes betrayed the contempt he felt for the son of Ashthenôví. After a moment, he cleared his throat and came to the reason he'd stopped Onwé. "I assume you haven't spoken to Luke in the past few days, have you? He hasn't shown up at church."

"He's holed up at home." Onwé nodded across the field to a row of houses that lined the river. "Says he's got the flu and won't come out."

"Pity," Voth said. He surveyed the nearby tables, searching their occupants until he found Karl Ortega sitting with his twenty-year-old daughter, Shay.

The two laughed and joked with family, and Shay wrapped her arms around her father and leaned into him. She had always been close with her dad, especially after her mother's disappearance nine years ago.

Onwé studied Voth for a while, guessing at the inscrutable man's thoughts. The wind kicked up briefly, sending empty plates flying off of tables, and a blast of distant thunder reminded Onwé of the transience of *Yōktha*.

"So, uh, I was gonna walk some food over to Luke's place…" he offered, trying to excuse himself from the interaction.

150

Voth didn't respond. His gaze remained fixed on Karl, his face bereft of its typical scowl when observing traditionalists. Instead, he looked upon the Ortegas as if watching a distant, happy memory play out. He looked strangely vulnerable then, and for a moment, Onwé saw him as just a lonely old man. Somewhere deep inside, the pastor must have known what he'd done to Karl was shameful. Onwé seized the opportunity to appeal to Voth's humanity.

"You know," he said, moving shoulder to shoulder with the pastor and looking out at Karl, "I've hurt a lot of people in my life. Started taking responsibility only a few years ago. I used to think apologizing was for the weak, but now I realize, it makes you strong. It's a thing worth doing, even when the other person won't listen."

Voth seemed to consider the words, but then scoffed and walked away. Onwé looked down at Numi, who regarded her master curiously. He shrugged at her, wondering if dogs could detect which people were rotten all the way to the core.

As the two ambled through the party, Onwé noticed Gaylen Poor had bumped into Chris and Wendy Miller. Little Stefan lay swaddled against Wendy's chest, looking up at Gaylen and grasping at the man's fingers. The delight on Gaylen's face warmed Onwé, causing him to forget his disdain for the snobby pastor.

Onwé stopped in his tracks and nearly dropped the plate when he saw Moya a few yards behind Gaylen. She walked slowly, assisted by Samuel Cotter, who'd lent his arm to her for support. Moya clutched him like an old friend and laughed heartily as they made their way toward the buffet line. The two were deeply engaged in conversation, pausing only to greet other members of the community as they moved through the crowd.

"I'll be damned," Onwé muttered. He couldn't help but laugh, recalling all the times Moya had snipped at young Samuel for his juvenile ignorance.

Even Numi appeared dumbfounded by the odd pair.

Then, a strange noise erupted on the mountain.

A loud *boom* echoed over Pale Peak, mixing with peals of thunder and the snarl of stormy wind. The sound took many forms in Onwé's mind: the snapping of great trees, the cracking of lake ice, the splitting of boulders as they plummeted from the cliffs during an avalanche. But then, when people nearby began to scream, the sound took a new shape: the explosion of a rifle blast.

Another shot rang out, but the way it echoed across the jagged landscape made it difficult for Onwé to locate the source.

"*Moya!*" a raspy voice called out.

All around, people began to panic, bumping into each other and scrambling to identify the danger.

"*Moooyaaaaa!*" it shrieked again.

Onwé turned around the moment another blast went off, this time much closer to him. Party-goers scattered in terror when Steve Winépo fell to the ground, clutching a gruesome wound on his shoulder. The shot nearly took the police chief's arm off, and his blood spattered across the faces of those standing next to him.

"You'll go up in the trees," the voice rang out gleefully.

A dozen yards away, a shirtless Luke emerged from the chaos, gripping an old hand-me-down Krag rifle and smiling hideously. His wild eyes almost glowed from the blackened pits around them, and spit dribbled down his chin from screaming and panting. He giggled and scanned the area, chambering another round for his next victim. The thick muscles in his torso twitched frenetically, as if animated by a powerful electric current.

"You'll go up in the trees!" Luke shouted through uncontrollable fits of laughter. "All of you! But for His Elect, I'll bring you down to *Him!*"

He raised the rifle and fired—and Karl Ortega's head detonated in a flash of gore. Before his daughter could open her mouth to scream, another round lanced through her chest, and she slumped over her father's corpse. Family and friends around them trampled over her body as they fled for their lives.

Onwé sank to the ground and froze, immobilized by a terror he'd never known. Thoughts of Tiwé arose in his mind. He tried to call to his son, but the shock silenced him. Numi cowered beside Onwé, shaking intensely and flinching each time Luke cried out.

"Moya!" Luke yelled again, his tone oscillating between hateful and hysterical. "Akántha waits for you! He cries out for you in the dark! Come with me, and you'll be together again!"

"Ti...Tiwé," Onwé gasped, trying to regain his wits. He stared at the people running and colliding around him, but couldn't locate his son.

Luke strode across the party grounds, ignoring people who were too elderly to flee and passing those who hid beneath tables. He came upon Wendy Miller, who made a shell around little Stefan with her embrace. Chris shielded them both with his body and begged Luke for mercy.

"The child..." Luke said in a mournful voice, "...he goes down in the hole. He is chosen!"

Luke then fell silent and gazed off into the distance, listening to something no one else could hear. He mumbled to himself and nodded, as if obeying commands from the voices in his head.

Gaylen Poor, who huddled beside Wendy and Chris, noticed the opportunity and rushed at Luke. He threw all his weight into the crazed man and tried to wrestle the gun from him, but Gaylen was small and had scarcely exercised a day in his life. Luke easily overpowered him and landed a massive punch to Gaylen's injured ribs, sending him to the ground, where he moaned in agony.

"Down in the hole," Luke said, becoming overwhelmed with emotion. "Poor Gaylen. You've seen it before, haven't you? You remember. It's so deep, deep down... You could crawl forever."

Luke wiped the tears from his face with a dirty hand—and then fired point-blank into Gaylen's abdomen. The force of the blast soaked Luke in blood, and now he truly looked like a demon from one of Voth's stories of Revelation. He leered over Wendy and her family while thumbing a new round into the gun, but then, Luke's eyes darted to the pack of residents fleeing out of the square onto the river road.

"Moya!" he bellowed, noticing the woman trying to make her escape on arthritic knees.

Samuel held Moya by the waist and arm, trying desperately to assist her, but when he heard the recognition in Luke's voice, he shoved her to the ground. Just before she hit the gravel road, an explosion echoed over the mountain, and Samuel's chest burst open in a fountain of blood. His body tumbled over Moya's, and she grabbed him in a horrified embrace. She squeezed the dying boy as if she believed she could keep his spirit trapped in his body—but he bled out in seconds.

At the sight of Samuel's death, Onwé found his voice. Luke cycled the bolt of the rifle, readying another attempt on Moya's life.

"Líkōté, stop!" Onwé cried out. "For Christ's sake, *stop!*"

Luke's head snapped toward Onwé. As the familiarity gathered in his eyes, he smiled a wide smile and growled, *"The son of Ashthenôví lives."*

Luke wheezed huge, panicky breaths and pointed the rifle

154

at Onwé's face—an act which sent Numi into a frenzy. The dog dashed at Luke with a ferocity she'd never shown before and sank her teeth into his forearm, causing the shot to go wide. The blast stunned Numi, giving Luke a chance to free himself from her jaws and club her with the butt of the rifle. As she fell to the ground, Luke stood over her and leveled the barrel at her head.

"The Black Wall could use a guard," he said, his voice low and morose.

Luke tried to work the bolt of the rifle, but the round jammed in the chamber. He became enraged and uttered a curse in a language Onwé could not begin to discern, then deftly cleared the jam with a whip of his arm. The large round spun through the air, whirling like the wings of a dragonfly until it plinked onto the ground. As he fished into his pockets for more ammunition, another voice called out nearby.

"Likōté," it said with conviction.

Two loud *cracks* ripped through the air, and Luke's belly and chest erupted in ribbons of blood. He staggered forward and tripped over the dog, falling face down into the dirt, where he remained motionless.

Onwé turned and saw John Tall Rock. The large man stood over Steve, holding the police chief's revolver with a trembling hand. Tears poured freely from his unblinking eyes, and his chest heaved with terrified gasps.

The world spun around Onwé. People wandered and screamed and held each other. Some ran, others stood frozen, and many lay on the ground, too afraid to move. All of them were trapped in the same dreamlike stupor that had arrested Onwé, preventing him from making sense of what had just happened.

He saw a bloodsoaked Moya still cradling Samuel's body like a mother holding her child. Through loud sobs, she chanted an old Nauktí prayer used but once in a person's life to ward off death. Her broken cries haunted Onwé; the flood of pain reminded him of the sounds she'd made two decades ago, when the police called off their search for Akántha. It was a sound he'd hoped never to hear again as long as he lived.

In the swarm of people, Onwé spotted Tíwé and Angela trying to make their way toward him. Zeus dutifully pressured them backward, using his body to nudge them as far away from Luke as possible. Chris and Wendy rushed toward their daughter, Hannah, checking her for injuries and hugging each other frantically.

Nearby, Numi stirred to consciousness and trotted over to Onwé, who threw his arms around her and began to cry. She had warned her master of danger before, but today, she'd directly intervened to save his life. As he held onto her, Onwé became overwhelmed with gratitude for the loyalty of dogs. He kissed her face and told her "Thank you," knowing with certainty she understood. The bullet meant for Numi lay on the ground beside them, and Onwé picked it up, possessed by an unexplainable feeling that he should keep it.

The sounds of coughing and sputtering arose a few yards away. It was Gaylen. He remained flat on his back, gently holding his abdomen with both hands. In all the chaos, no one had yet noticed Gaylen was alive. Onwé found his legs and stumbled over to the man.

"Mr. Lopez," he gurgled, recognizing Onwé.

"It's okay, buddy," Onwé said, inspecting the horrendous wound. "Don't talk, alright? Just breathe. I'm gonna get Dr. Farmer, and we're gonna get you fixed up." He shouted at a nearby woman to find the doctor.

People began to collect around the two men, gasping at the sight of the wound. The ground ran red beneath him, and Onwé knew Gaylen had only a few minutes before he bled out.

"Is...the kid...okay?" Gaylen asked. Blood dribbled from his lips and slurred his words.

"He's okay," Onwé replied, placing his hands over Gaylen's in a vain attempt to staunch the bleeding. "Wendy's got him."

"It's a boy," Gaylen said with a dizzy grin. His eyes unfocused, and the color ran from his face.

"That's right." Onwé gave his hand a little squeeze. "And you saved him. Twice. You're a hero, pal. Just hold on, okay? Just… Just wait for the doctor."

Gaylen smiled once more, and his breathing slowed.

"It's good here," he whispered, closing his eyes. "Right here. S'better than a cave."

Gaylen's body went slack, and he sighed into stillness.

Dr. Farmer appeared and knelt beside Onwé, but it was too late. When he determined there was nothing to be done, the doctor scurried over to Moya to check if she'd been hit.

Onwé remained with Gaylen for a long while, feeling the warmth go out of his hand while he held it. He recited two prayers—one he'd learned from Old N'wenthāil, the other he'd learned in boarding school.

Onwé placed his hand over the dead man's heart and said, "You're braver than you look, Gaylen Poor."

Wendy approached with little Stefan, both crying furiously. She sank to her knees and touched Gaylen's forehead. She thanked him in Nauktí, then retreated to her husband's arms and left the scene with her family.

As Onwé gazed down upon Gaylen's face one last time, he watched a few snowflakes land on the man's brow and melt away.

Winter had finally arrived.

Part III:
PRAYERS

Chapter 25

Snow, like madness, sometimes arrives with little warning. It can accumulate while a man lies dreaming in his bed, and when he awakens, he steps into a world cold and changed. Pale Peak separated the people of Cold Valley from half their sky, which gave cover to oncoming storms, and likewise, it separated them from the rest of the world, which made the descent into madness a little steeper.

Not a soul wandered Autumn Ridge that night. The streets were empty and the people huddled in their locked homes, reeling from a massacre perpetrated by a beloved member of the community. The Cold Valley Baptist Church stood dark and empty, now but a gray smudge against a black sky, unable to offer solace to anyone. And high above the storm loomed the dreaded mountain, indifferent to the suffering below.

Hours earlier, the BIA team had finished recovering corpses from the two plane crashes, only to find more bodies waiting for them in town. They worked with Steve Winépo's men to document and clean up the scene, but were unable to orchestrate a full intervention from Denver on account of the blizzard. Steve lay in the medical center, attended by Dr.

Farmer, who was woefully under-supplied to perform surgery on such grievous wounds.

A few beds away, hidden behind a wall of standing curtains, was Luke. He lay unconscious, slowly dying of his injuries. The doctor and his nurse muttered quietly with investigators, who flanked Luke with their clipboards and cameras and monitored his condition for hours. No help would come from Lake Namarjo for the time being; the only road into Autumn Ridge was treacherous and covered in snow.

In the morgue behind the medical center lay the ruined bodies of Luke's victims: Samuel Cotter, Gaylen Poor, Karl and Shay Ortega, and two Pozi women who'd been walking from the church down to the square for *Yŏktha*. Twelve other corpses populated the little storage room also, each of them a mangled, burnt, and decomposing husk retrieved from the crash sites. Whispers of other tragedies on the mountain began spreading through the town.

Onwé had seen Luke and Steve briefly in their hospital beds, but was sent away when the agents started their work. Now, the medical center looked like a twinkling star from Moya's porch; no one would have guessed from this distance that a madman dreamed darkly within its walls. Onwé had seen Luke's eyes darting rapidly beneath closed lids while he lay comatose, and he wondered what horrific things they must be watching. Rage and despair and confusion swirled within Onwé, fomenting a desire to grab his own rifle and put a final end to Luke's insanity. He shook off the thought and opened the door.

Inside, Tíwé tended to Moya, scrubbing dried blood from her arms and neck. She sat on the floor in silence, completely vanished into herself. Her wiry hair dangled in front of her face, obscuring her eyes and granting her a little privacy as she processed what had happened. In her hands she clutched a book Samuel had kept in his jacket. It was too small for a Bible, but its well-worn cover implied it must have been of some personal significance to him.

Nearby, Zeus attempted to console Numi, who was so distraught she ignored Onwé when he entered the house. Instead, she gazed listlessly at the wall, as if she could see through it and down to the place where the people had been slaughtered. Over the past few weeks, Numi had watched one of her favorite people turn into something unrecognizable, and now she lay hopeless on the floor, unable to comprehend why such terrible things had happened.

"Dad," Tïwé said in a shaky voice. He dropped the blood-soaked rag onto the floor and looked up at his father. "Why?"

Onwé had no clue how to answer the question. He hadn't told his son about the plane crashes, nor about Luke's dreadful story of hidden places in the mountain. He felt Tïwé deserved an explanation, but conveying such an unfathomable tale to an eleven-year-old boy proved difficult.

"Luke was sick," he offered, aware it was a paltry thing to say. "He got sick a little while ago on our camping trip. Something happened to his mind."

"He tried to kill Moya," Tïwé said, bursting into tears. *"Look* at her."

The pain Onwé felt when looking upon the poor old woman reminded him of the long years he'd spent without Akántha, and later without his wife and son. Loss was common in Cold Valley, but its sting never dulled for anyone. A certain absence had now gathered over Moya, as if she'd collapsed into a black hole right there in the living room of her old house, the rift swallowing everything around it. Onwé could hug and console her all he wanted, but nothing would ever fill the void today's rampage had left in her. She'd lost her new friend—a friend she desperately needed—and she'd also lost Luke. The mountain had taken even more from a woman

163

who'd already given everything.

"I don't think he was in control anymore," Onwé said, sinking against the door and thumping to the ground. "I don't think that was Luke at all."

"What happened to him?" Tíwé demanded.

"We went too far out," Onwé said. "There was an accident. Those men came from the city to investigate. Luke found a cave and went inside, and when he came out, he was just...different."

Tíwé's expression betrayed that he now understood Onwé's admonitions to stay on the trails.

"What was in the cave?" he asked.

"I don't know," Onwé replied. It was a half-truth; he wasn't sure he believed the things Luke and Gaylen claimed to have seen in the tunnels. He wanted to believe they'd hallucinated it. "Maybe he breathed some poison gas or something. But when he came out, he was sick, and it got worse and worse."

"Násh'thawén édī," Moya grumbled: *Bad air? Bullshit.*

Onwé and Tíwé cleaned and dressed Moya and put her in the bed. Then they retired to the couch with the dogs and sat there before the crackling fire. They whispered about the terrible event and what would become of the town, but they never spoke the names of Luke's victims.

Every Nauktí in Cold Valley, even the secular ones, respected the tradition of allowing time to pass before naming the recent dead. Their people believed the soul's journey into the next world was a difficult one, and its success depended upon the silence of the ones they'd left behind. In time, a loved one would sing a hymn whose words offered guidance to the traveling soul, but until that day, the dead were left to rest.

Long after Moya had fallen asleep, a tiny knock occurred at the door. It was Angela, who'd spent the evening with Hannah and Stefan, and now she'd come to check on Tíwé.

When Onwé opened the door, she practically fell into his arms, a frightened child who'd seen things even men at war could not bear. Onwé threw his arms around her and cried with her, and when she calmed down, she hugged Tíwé and the dogs and told them all, *"Áyynä´fé'ná'vī"—Thank you for protecting me.*

The three eventually fell asleep there in Moya's living room—first the kids, and then Onwé. He lay on a pile of blankets, listening to wind batter the house. Luke's frantic screams echoed in his mind. Onwé dared to wonder about Luke's hideous promise to Moya: that Akántha was alive, waiting for her to join him in the darkness. He wanted to believe Luke had lost his mind, and there was no truth to his deranged prophecies. But the totality of everything that had happened on Autumn Ridge convinced him otherwise.

A sinister presence—the stuff of dark legend—lurked on Pale Peak.

Onwé fell asleep to a memory of the wounded ram. It stared into his eyes with the terror of a prey item, breathing raggedly through its flared snout. Then it turned and limped off into the black space beyond consciousness.

In his dreams, Onwé followed the ram to a strange house in the forest, wreathed in vines, sitting ominously in the distance beyond a row of trees. The snow beneath his feet glowed eerily as if moonlit, but the pines springing from it vanished into a sky as black as the innards of a cave. Only a faint red star clung in the void, barely visible through a maze of branches.

The ram wandered just ahead. Its limp worsened until the animal could walk no more. It collapsed into the snow, and after a moment, a man rose up from its place.

165

Gaylen Poor.

He was nude, and as pallid as a rotting corpse. The wound that had killed him was now a mass of root-like scars snaking across his midsection. He made his way toward the house and studied the forest as he walked, enthralled with its spectral stillness. A morose song wafted in the air, sung by unseen children, drawing the dead man in with hypnotic allure.

When Gaylen passed the nearest tree, he looked back at Onwé with eyes that glimmered a sinister yellow and smiled a knowing smile. He motioned for Onwé to follow.

Onwé looked down at himself and saw that he too was decaying. Old, tattered flesh had begun to slough from his arms. The ponytail that had constantly brushed his shoulders was now missing; his hair had been cut short in a poor imitation of the style worn by the men of Voth's church.

The unnatural song rose in intensity, its many singers folding their voices into impossible harmonies over scales Onwé had never heard before. The music sickened him and drove him to seek the shelter of the weird house. Onwé rushed toward the front door, a tide of nausea swelling in his gut.

He opened his eyes.

Onwé found himself standing beside Moya's bed, peering out the window that faced the woods behind her home. Zeus and Numi flanked him, leaning against the windowsill and watching something he could not see. The voices still rang out from across the little field but receded into the trees as Onwé fully awakened.

Zeus, normally brave and protective of his family, looked like he might flee at any second. His nose twitched at the hints of an unfamiliar scent, and his eyes moved to and fro, glued to something lurking in the dark. Growling at shadows was a pastime for both dogs, but now, neither one made a sound.

"Ha'an'tué," a voice rasped behind them.

Onwé, Zeus, and Numi jumped at the noise. They looked

166

back to find Moya sitting upright in bed, stiff-spined, mouth agape in disbelief. Her eyes were closed, but her attention was fixed out the window upon whatever the dogs had been watching. She leaned forward as if to clamber out of bed, but Onwé caught her and laid her back down, where she protested for a moment, then went slack.

"He's here," she said quietly. *"Ha'an'tué."*

Onwé had not heard that word in twenty-four years, and its utterance lifted the hairs across the back of his neck. It was Moya's nickname for Akántha: *My Light.*

"He's come back," she whispered. A smile spread across her sleeping face. "He's come to sing for me."

Chapter 26

Four days passed, and in that time, Moya fell ill. A fever kept her bedridden, and her vision seemed to worsen inexplicably. She slept most of the time, and when she was awake, she remained withdrawn and reluctant to speak. The pain of so much loss had taken its toll, and Onwé grew increasingly worried about her.

Dr. Farmer visited while making his way down a list of people who'd been involved in the shooting. He deduced Moya's condition was trauma-related and left instructions for her care, explaining that many folks in Autumn Ridge were displaying symptoms of "gross stress reaction" and "survivor syndrome."

Onwé was unfamiliar with these terms, but he took them to mean that with the proper care, Moya's health and sight would recover. He set about making her comfortable and fetching her medicine in Samuel's stead, occasionally reminded of the boy's absence by the dearth of early morning knocks at the door.

Dr. Farmer also informed Onwé that the police had released the bodies from the morgue. Those who'd died in the shooting would receive their burials, and the corpses of the crash victims would go with the BIA agents to Namarjo, now that the snow plows were running. Steve and Luke would be moved to the little hospital down there, where they would undergo surgeries they'd needed days earlier. The doctor expected Steve to recover, but warned Luke was likely too far gone to be saved.

Upon hearing of Luke's grave condition, a mixture of anguish and rage swept over Onwé, driving him out onto Moya's porch for air. His head spun and his eyes watered in the stinging cold. What Luke had done was unforgivable, and Onwé felt in his heart the killer deserved to die. But the thought of losing him, of turning him into yet another ghost on the mountain, ripped Onwé apart.

A heavy blanket of snow covered the town before him, darkening its buildings by contrast. The sheer amount of it was baffling for the first storm of the season, and now the ramshackle houses of Autumn Ridge jutted from a bed of white, like the tombstones of a wintery graveyard. Their frosted roofs sagged under the weight of fresh powder, and their windows, glazed with ice, scattered the dying firelight pouring out of them.

Few people moved between the dreary homes, and those who did walked solemnly, reminding Onwé of *the cold people*—wraithlike beings of Ineho legend whose feet would burn on any surface but snow.

Onwé wanted to cry. He mourned his fellow townspeople and their odious deaths, and he despaired for Moya's loss. Her life of suffering and her resulting frailty weighed on him like an anchor around his neck. His teeth ground behind trembling lips, and his jaw ached under the knot of screams dammed in his mouth. Onwé's thoughts turned as dark as the churning sky, and a shadow crept over his soul. It was the shadow that lurked in the deepest part of him, unresponsive to prayer and only temporarily pacified by healthy habits.

Now, the shadow imparted a clear message: *Let's get high. Just this once.*

Onwé had fought with his shadow before. In the past, he'd lost many battles. On those days, he'd found himself making the short walk to visit his dealer, who lived just two doors down from Luke. A few years ago, he'd finally won the war and gotten sober, and although the shadow still occasionally fell on him, it passed quickly if he ignored it.

Today felt different.

The cravings plagued Onwé's brain and dried his mouth, compelling him to pilfer his savings tin and take that short walk. But he would not give in. He asked Tiwé to look after Moya, then stopped at home to grab supplies and headed straight for Ash Hill. With him, he brought his rifle, his hunting knife, and his hiking staff, as well as both dogs.

Onwé feared the unspeakable voices in the woods and the horrible thing commanding them, but even more, he feared giving in to the cravings and having his son discover him in that state. If Tiwé ever caught his father on drugs again, the brittle relationship would go up in flames, and Onwé would spend the rest of his life alone in his creaky old house on Pale Peak.

Thick snow covered the earth and obscured the trails, but Onwé knew them by heart. The trio passed through white forests and fields, hopping over ice-covered logs and gushing streams. In the trees above, squirrels shivered in their dreys, and crows watched silently as Numi and Zeus trespassed in their lands. Big snowflakes danced on the wind, but the storm had mostly passed, leaving a silence behind it unique to mountain winters.

The frigid beauty would have stirred him on any other day, but Onwé could not focus on the world around him. Instead, his mind replayed cruel visions of his friends' last moments at *Yōktha*. He saw Karl's head burst open and Shay's chest bloom like a red rose as she fell to the ground. Onwé saw a bloodsoaked Moya lying on the road, weeping over Samuel's corpse. He saw Gaylen's bluing lips. The brutality of their murders ripped through him, and the hole it left filled up with the shadow, causing in him a hunger no food could sate.

Nothing dulled sorrow like the junk sold on the rez. Onwé knew it could not bring his friends back, just as it could not heal the wounds inflicted by Akántha's disappearance all those years ago. But it did offer a sort of friendship: the drug was a warm hand on Onwé's shoulder in times of loneliness, an embrace he could fall into when there was no one around to hold him. It quieted the thoughts of loss and failure, and delivered him far away from Cold Valley into the serenity of dreams. Now, the shadow promised to steal away the visions of death—if only he gave in.

Onwé ignored the empty promises. He cursed the temptation and filled himself with breaths of frosty air. The bitter cold soothed his rage, and beneath the fiery anger hid a purer emotion: sadness. He allowed himself to break down while he summited Ash Hill, occasionally falling to his knees and leaning weakly into the snow. The dogs circled and sniffed at him, aware of his state of mind. They licked at his face, encouraging him to complete the journey.

The view at the top pulled Onwé out of his grim reflections. He looked out across the nameless place, now a dale of snow-draped pines vanishing into an icy fog. Above it, soaring mountaintops poked through the clouds, glimmering in the late sun. The blanket of snow that had tucked in the world last night now deadened the sounds of nature, casting Onwé in a dizzying silence.

He sat on the same old log he used to share with his father and watched the dogs mill around in the snow. They inspected the clumps of it that sloughed off the aching branches and chomped at dripping icicles. Zeus charged around, begging

Numi to chase him, and vigorously shook away the frost that rimed his coat every few minutes.

Here on the hill, Onwé always felt connected to his dad, and now he was flooded with bittersweet memories of him. He closed his eyes and ran his fingers over the carvings on the hiking staff, and Elder Tavshii's words echoed in his mind: *If only Ashthenôví were here to guide us.*

Ash had always seemed to know what to do in times of crisis. He'd been a bull-headed and unrepentant man, but not foolishly so, having gathered his wisdom and conviction from a vast collection of old books provided by universities. After years of hoarding them, he fought successfully for a grant to build a small library in Autumn Ridge, and donated his collection to it. Ash believed his people's independence would come from an understanding of the wider world, and the vehicle for that understanding was literacy. He always said that if the government was willing to provide money and books that could lead Natives to self-determination, then federal assistance was a good thing, and the ends would justify the means.

This was how Ash had come into the seat of tribal leadership. He'd deftly won concessions from Washington and its churches, all while protecting the rez from the worst of their influences. At the time of his death, the Indians of Cold Valley had more funding for their schools and more latitude in their religious practices, and Ash had become something of a small-time legend in Indian country. But his final project, a grant request to relocate the entire population of Autumn Ridge down to Namarjo, was refused a dozen times by the BIA. Onwé always wondered if the rejection had broken his father's heart.

The Bureau of Indian Affairs never expressed interest in the strange death of Ashthenôví Lopez. There on the freezing log, Onwé recalled the last months of his father's life, during which Ash had withdrawn from his responsibilities to his people and spent the dreary days of winter in solitude on the mountain. He no longer took the boys fishing or hunting, and instead admonished them to stay close to home, all the while scouring Pale Peak for something he would never discuss with his family.

Then one day, a pair of local fishermen discovered Ash's broken corpse near the trail to Mirror Lake. He'd fallen from a cliff he had no business standing on and landed just in front of the cave that had always haunted young Onwé's dreams. The tribal police had concluded the death was self-inflicted, but Onwé struggled to accept their findings. If Ash truly had ended his own life, maybe it was because he felt he'd let his people down. Or maybe it had something to do with whatever he'd been looking for on his lonely travels across Pale Peak.

In a few short years, Tíwé would be the age Onwé had been when Ash died. Onwé remembered that painful distance between himself and his father before the end, and now felt it with Tíwé. He worried he and the boy would never be close again. Onwé worried the shadow would take him away from his son once and for all, and that Tíwé would grow up without a father, just as Onwé had.

Numi approached Onwé and rested her chin in his lap. He examined the snow that caked her fur and beheld the purity of its color. Immediately, his mind's eye blemished it with spatters of Karl's blood, and he pushed her away and stood up. Numi followed her master down the hill, while Zeus brought up the rear, dragging behind him a large stick he'd dug out of the snow. When Onwé saw it, he picked it up. It was chin-height, the perfect base for Tíwé's hiking staff.

"Good boy," he said, patting Zeus's back.

He checked the knife at his side, adjusted the rifle on his shoulder, and took a staff in each hand for the journey home.

The dogs trotted off ahead, leaving Onwé to lug the many objects that bound him to his family.

Chapter 27

A few days ago, the town of Autumn Ridge had been bustling with folks excited to put on a feast. For the first time in a year, the air had felt electric, both with the spirit of *Yōktha* and with the approach of a vengeful winter. But in six brief minutes, the rare exuberance had been shattered, and the town seemed to die in its lonely seat on the mountain.

Now the town stirred once more, but this time like a graveyard full of wandering spirits. People came out of their homes and into the streets, shuffling wordlessly into small groups and heading to the east side of town. In silent processions they drifted up the church road, staring out into the square where the unspeakable tragedy had occurred. Heavy snow covered the area now, concealing the remnants of gore that had stained the earth there—but it did nothing to hide the memory of it from the survivors. Each of them looked on the place as if the killer still lurked there with his rifle, screaming raggedly about the dreadful things "down in the hole."

Four Christians had died by Luke's hand: Samuel Cotter, Gaylen Poor, Abigail Skye, and Faith Sommers. The two Pozi women had been his first victims. He'd gone to the church, perhaps intent on slaying Burke Voth, but found it empty, and headed toward the feast. He met Faith and Skye along the road, who'd likely greeted him with smiles, having known Luke their whole lives.

The church now held a service for them. Voth led the surviving families inside at the head of the line and filled the remaining pews with townsfolk. So many people crowded the building that some stood in the back of the house, and others listened from outside in the cold. Even a few federal agents came to pay their respects.

Inside, Voth delivered a prayer of comfort. He related stories of each deceased person's virtues and, at times, did so laboriously, his voice freighted with ill-concealed anguish. While eulogizing Samuel, by far the youngest of Luke's victims, his practiced elocution broke to candid remarks about the tragedy of it all. Eventually, Voth fell silent, overcome with grief. Brother Duncan finished for him.

Onwé did not know the etiquette for Baptist funerals. He didn't know the words to their hymns, nor had he ever heard their sacred music. Nonetheless, he felt compelled to honor the Christians in the Christian way, as he had so often called them to honor the traditionalists in the Old Way. He prayed for the souls of the dead and hoped his father would forgive him for engaging in the rituals of the colonists. In that moment, for the first time since he could remember, he felt like a part of the group, rather than an outsider looking in.

Onwé had asked Moya if she wanted to attend the service to honor Samuel, but she'd seemed unable to bring herself to face the permanence of his death by ceremonially acknowledging it. So he'd left her at home with Tíwé, who took great pride in caring for an elder of his people during her time of need.

But as Faith's husband delivered his speech to the congregation, a truck pulled up outside, and Moya entered the church with Tíwé and John Tall Rock. The speaker went quiet, and the congregants murmured to each other, shocked to see the staunchest traditionalist on the rez set foot in the Cold Valley Baptist Church. Moya's hatred of the Baptists was legendary; in five and a half decades, she'd never even been up the church road, even when the smell of their backyard barbecues wafted over the hungry town.

She stood in the nave, clutching Samuel's book and waiting patiently for Faith's husband to finish his statement. Brother Duncan approached and shook John's hand, then whispered with Moya a bit. A short line of speakers delivered their remarks, and then Duncan approached Voth and said something that made his eyebrows jump.

"A non-member has asked permission to say a few words," Voth said, looking directly at Faith and Skye's families in the front rows. "If it's alright with you."

They regarded Moya with surprise, each of them probably recalling a separate time in which she'd cursed their religion or insulted their god. But she looked old and frail today, the angry fire that once burned in her now thoroughly doused.

"If she's here to honor them, she's welcome," Faith's husband said after a pause.

A few others nodded in agreement.

As Moya shuffled toward the lectern, Luke's words echoed in Onwé's mind: *Thank God Ash isn't here to see this.* Dozens of people stared at her as she passed, most of them wearing hesitant and morbidly curious expressions. One in particular looked up at her with uncommon warmth: Angela. The girl sat beside her father, who'd come up from Lake Namarjo to attend the service, and now kept his arm wrapped defensively around his daughter's shoulder. Angie's mother was likely still at home, where she'd been fighting a losing battle against lymphoma. On Angela's other side sat Hannah, her parents, and baby Stefan.

Moya stood awkwardly beside the lectern and nodded at Voth. She gazed down at the closed book in her hand as if drawing courage from it, then spoke. For the first time in days, her voice had life in it.

"I realize I'm breaking a few rules here," Moya said, loud enough for Onwé to hear clearly from the back of the room. "People of my faith don't set foot in this building. And we don't say the names of the dead who haven't completed their journey. But Samuel was a man of Christ, and this is where he liked to be. He recently told me that he'd lost his parents a few years back, and it got me thinking. At this service, he's a son without a mother. I thought it would be fitting that a mother without a son should stand in for his family."

The congregation murmured in approval, and so Moya opened the book and flipped through its pages.

"I got to know Mr. Cotter a little better over these past few weeks," she went on, showing the book to her audience, "but I never knew he enjoyed poetry until...until after he was gone. This here's a collection of works by old Christian poets, and one of them has stuck with me these past few days. This one's by a Puritan woman named Anne Bradstreet, written all the way back in 1665—a hundred years before the first Indian reservation in the country. It seems Mrs. Bradstreet knew loss even better than I do."

Moya held the book up near her face and cleared her throat:

> *"With troubled heart and trembling hand I write,*
> *The Heavens have changed to sorrow my delight.*
> *How oft with disappointment have I met,*
> *When I on fading things my hopes have set.*
> *Experience might 'fore this have made me wise,*
> *To value things according to their price.*
> *Was ever stable joy yet found below?*
> *Or perfect bliss without mixture of woe?*

I knew she was but as a withering flower,
That's here today, perhaps gone in an hour;
Like as a bubble, or the brittle glass,
Or like a shadow turning as it was.
More fool then I to look on that was lent,
As if mine own, when thus impermanent."

Moya closed the book and lowered it, but continued speaking with her eyes squeezed shut:

"Farewell, dear child, thou never shall come to me.
But yet a while—and I shall go to thee.
Meantime my throbbing heart's cheered up with this:
Thou with thy Saviour art in endless bliss."

A few members of the victims' families were moved to tears by the poem, but Moya remained stoic. They might have thought of her as cold, but Onwé knew she simply had no more tears to shed after despairing in her home the past four days. After all she'd been through, he was simply glad she was alive.

"My son was never baptized," Moya went on, "but if somehow in the afterlife he crosses paths with Samuel Cotter, I know he'd be in good company. Samuel was a good man." She paused for a moment and regarded the book, then added, "And I was hardly nice to him."

And with that, Moya walked back to John and Tíwé. A few hands reached out to comfort her as she passed, and a woman stood up and embraced her. One of the men got out of his seat and offered it to Moya, which she graciously accepted. Wendy Miller assumed the lectern and honored Gaylen Poor for his bravery in saving her life and the life of baby Stefan, who sat cradled against her chest as he had during the massacre.

179

After the closing prayers, the church emptied, and Onwé gathered with his friends and family out in the snow. He and Moya greeted Angela's father and wished her mother well, though everyone knew the outlook was quite grim. Angie's dad tried to convince her to come home, but she begged to stay over at Hannah's a few more days. Chris and Wendy assured her dad they loved having Angie over, and that she'd been reading the Bible with Hannah on a nightly basis.

Angela shot a glance at Onwé during the exchange that seemed to imply she was uncommitted to the practice. Her father obliged, but only until the schools reopened. They'd shut down for the week because of the tragedy.

"Maybe I could come hang out with you sometime," Tíwé said to the girls nervously. "I love reading too!"

They nodded warmly, but did not extend an invitation.

That evening, in the field across the river on the other side of town, Elder Emmanuel led a traditional ceremony for his son and granddaughter. Karl and Shay were laid to rest in Autumn Ridge's cemetery alongside three generations of their family, and the surviving relatives gathered in mourning. Adults wept and held each other, and children stood in strange silence, faintly aware of the depth of this tragedy but unable to process why it had occurred.

Unlike their Nauktí neighbors, the Ineho did not fear to call out to those who'd passed on. Emmanuel set bundles of herbs aflame and wafted them in the air, invoking ancestral spirits to ferry the souls of the dead into the afterlife. The people sang and cried out in their ancient tongue.

In any other circumstance, their wailing would have drawn the ire of Burke Voth. But today, none of the Baptists dared interfere with the ceremony, even if it did violate the

Code of Indian Offenses. Karl's relatives carried on proudly in their tradition, federal law be damned.

A group of Naukti and Pozi also attended the ceremony, offering comfort to the living and prayers for the dead. To Onwé, who watched the funeral from a distance, the intercultural expression of sorrow felt like a grim variant of *Yōktha*.

Because he'd chosen to attend the Christian service, Onwé was a bit late for this one and decided not to interrupt it. He watched from afar, leaning against the wooden fence that separated the shuttered library from the river.

The snow glowed faintly orange in the late sun. Soon, darkness would rise from the east to eat away at the sky. The distant people shuffled to and fro, performing obscure rituals in the dying light, but they moved sluggishly, arrested by the biting cold and the weight of sadness. A woman collapsed to her knees and cried out in despair, but was quickly lifted back up by her family. Onwé didn't speak a word of Ineho, but he knew she'd cursed Luke and the gods for taking away her loved ones.

Burke Voth rounded the corner of the library. He paused for a moment, surprised to see Onwé there, and then slowly approached.

Voth was still in his church attire. He leaned against the old wooden fence beside Onwé and brushed a clump of snow off the top rail. He looked out across the field at the mourners, observing them with heavy eyes, and occasionally rubbed his face as if trying to wake himself up from a nightmare. The two men shared the long moment in silence, exchanging only a brief glance devoid of their mutual hostility.

Onwé had never seen Voth in such a state. The man was disheveled, deflated, and unshaven. He looked as pitiful as Luke had the night he'd confessed to Onwé about the cave and the Briar House. Perhaps this tragedy had shaken the faith of

Cold Valley's most eminent pastor.

Eventually, the ceremony came to an end, and the mourners dispersed. Both Onwé and Voth remained in their places along the fence, watching the sun creep toward Pale Peak to cover the valley once more in freezing darkness. When Voth finally turned to leave, he paused and looked back at Onwé.

"I'm sorry," he said quietly.

Before Onwé could respond, the pastor walked away.

Onwé followed, intent on checking in with Moya and Tíwé back at her home. Two men came sprinting down the hill in the distance, shouting Voth's name across the town square.

"Mr. Voth!" they called out. "Come with us!"

The men reached him the same time Onwé did—two federal agents clutching rifles in their hands.

"What's the meaning of this?" Voth demanded, shaken by the sight of weapons at the ready.

"Town leadership is gathering at the tribal council building," one of them said. "Need you to report there right away."

"What's going on?" Onwé asked, approaching the trio.

"Get inside, folks!" the agent shouted at some people walking nearby. "Everybody inside until further notice."

Voth looked at Onwé with concern, clearly not ready for any more bad news. Onwé returned the expression.

"It's your buddy, Luke," the other agent said, scanning the area behind Onwé like a hawk searching for a rabbit. "His bed's empty at the medical center. He's gone."

A deathly chill arced across Onwé's body. He tried to speak, but a frigid wind came screaming off the mountain and stole his breath away.

Chapter 28

When Voth and Onwé reached the tribal council building, they came upon a group of lawmen arguing out front. Nearby, John Tall Rock, Chris Miller, Dr. Farmer, and a few elders looked on worriedly.

"How is it even possible you could have fucked this up so badly!" the Special Agent in Charge shouted at two members of the tribal police.

The nearby BIA team and a few task force members from Denver joined in their superior's withering stare. Clouds of hot breath issued from the SAC's mouth while he bristled. Gobs of his spittle fell like a tiny rainstorm on the heads of those who'd failed him.

"I uncuffed him so the nurse could change his clothes," one of the policemen replied meekly. "She was preppin' him for evac. They took Chief Winépo first."

"He...he *was* comatose, sir," the other officer said.

"Was he now?" the SAC replied. "Well, because of you two chuckleheads, I've got a mass murderer on the loose, and a nurse who's gonna need plastic surgery. When this manhunt is over, I'll see to it you're both out of a goddamn job."

"What the hell did he do to the nurse?" Onwé demanded,

invading the group and stepping up to the SAC. He searched the officers for an explanation, but neither of them dared to speak.

"Ask him." The SAC jabbed a finger toward Dr. Farmer.

The doctor shuffled over hesitantly, afraid to provoke the agent's ire. A few specks of blood tinged the white of his medical jacket, and more of it darkened his fingers.

"I can't explain it," he said, his mouth hanging open in exasperation between words. "He-he just grabbed her when she leaned over...looked into her eyes. She started screaming, and he-he whispered to her."

"What did he say?" Onwé asked. He drew closer to the doctor so the nearby elders couldn't hear.

Dr. Farmer simply gazed off past the houses and into the distant woods, distracted by something out there.

"Magnus," Onwé whispered.

"Something about her dead father," he finally said. "Something he couldn't have known."

"Then the son of a bitch smashed a window and climbed out," the SAC added. "She took a piece of glass to her own face. She'll live, if you call that living. And *these dipshits* here lost our man in the fracas."

The officers lowered their gazes, trained over a lifetime in the art of tolerating the abuse of federal employees. They nodded silently while the SAC instructed them to patrol the streets of Autumn Ridge, keeping folks indoors and looking out for Luke.

"Rest of you," he said in a commanding voice, "I want you paired up and sweeping these woods. John and I'll run trucks down the road to Namarjo, and I want two men on those elders at all times. Nobody in or out of the council building. I don't know if he's comin' back for more."

Onwé realized Luke might go after Moya to finish what he'd started at the feast. The man's bloodcurdling shrieks replayed in Onwé's mind—the way he'd smiled and cried while screaming her name, the promises he'd made, the murder in his voice.

"Oh fuck," Onwé said, nearly toppling over as his legs turned to icicles. *"Moya."*

"Easy now," John Tall Rock said, advancing on Onwé just in time to prevent him from collapsing. "She was the first one we went for. We've got her over at the station. Tíwé too. Nobody's getting in there."

A flood of relief swept through Onwé's body. John gave him a good shake to revive his senses.

"What about the gun?" Onwé asked, pulling in a shaky breath.

"In lockup," John replied. "They tossed his house. Took his knives too."

"You're the friend, right?" the Special Agent in Charge said, laying a single knuckle into Onwé's chest. "You either help us find him, or get your ass to shelter and don't say a word to nobody. That goes for you too, Elders! No talk, no panic! You understand?"

The elders nodded, and John led them back inside the building. Chris approached Onwé and greeted the agents stiffly.

"Son of a bitch pointed a gun at my wife," he said, clenching his jaw. "I'll help you find him. It's the least I could do for Gaylen."

Chris, like Luke, had chopped his hair off when he'd gotten baptized. He looked young and energetic, but lacked the strength of the man who'd tried to kill him. It would take Chris and Onwé both to overpower Luke if they found him. If Luke had a weapon, all bets were off.

"Fine," the SAC said, motioning at one of the nearby BIA men. "Becker, squad up with these guys. If you find the perp and he's armed, shoot to kill."

Agent Becker grunted through his prominent mustache and followed Chris and Onwé up the road, away from the council building.

A river of dark thoughts rushed through Onwé's mind as the group made their way to his house. He half expected to find Luke sitting in his chair beside a fire, enraptured by the carvings on the hiking staff. When Onwé fetched his rifle from its place near the bed, he wondered if he would be the one to put Luke in the ground. He glanced out the window to the tree line and imagined some ghastly creature watching him, gleeful at the chaos plaguing the town.

"I think he's been fuckin' around in the woods," Onwé said, throwing the rifle over his shoulder as he stepped back outside. "I know his favorite trails. *Híneshé,* Numi. Come, Zeus."

Onwé picked the trail that led upriver and snaked right past the cave where Ashthenôví died. Chris followed behind, unarmed but eager for a fight, and Becker brought up the rear, resting a heavy hand on the revolver at his hip.

Only a sliver of sun poked over the mountain now, the rest of it hidden by a wall of rock and ice. Twilight would cover the eastern slope within a few minutes, which was more time than Onwé wanted to spend in the woods tonight. He walked carefully, afraid Luke was behind every tree, staring back at him with predatory eyes. Owls began to hoot, and the deep chill of night rolled through the forest.

Judging by the paths carved through the powder, someone had walked the trail recently, but the falling snow made it difficult to tell who it might have been. In the fading light, the footprints almost looked like they'd been made by kids. Onwé remembered the horrible, off-key sound of children singing in the dark. He shuddered at the thought and pulled his rifle from his shoulder, praying he wouldn't need to use it.

The mess of tracks weaved a few dozen yards up the familiar trail, but then broke off to the left. He, Chris, and Agent Becker walked a few hundred steps to a place where the trees began to thin, giving way to a small clearing. At its center rested a huge snow-caked log, and upon it sat a crooked figure in dark clothing.

"There," Onwé whispered, gripping his rifle with shaking hands. He wondered if he possessed the courage to fire it. It'd been years since he and Luke had hunted, and he'd never pointed a gun at a person before. He remembered the ease with which Luke had fired upon his own people, and knew he had nothing like that kind of resolve within himself.

Chris and Becker fanned out, widening their approach to the figure. In the gloom, it looked like a man with asymmetrical limbs and shoulders, sitting in repose and awaiting the moon's arrival. But as Onwé and the dogs drew closer, he saw the figure was actually two girls clad in dark winter coats, leaning into each other for support. One of them had been resting her head on the other girl's shoulder, but then looked up at her. The other girl brushed her friend's hair aside and kissed her lips.

"Hannah?" Chris blurted out nearby.

The girls quickly pulled away from each other. One of them leaped to her feet.

"Dad?" she replied, regarding the three men with shock.

"Angie?" Onwé called out, shouldering the rifle and motioning for Becker to lower his weapon.

"Uh, hi," she replied in her mousy voice. She clasped her mittened hands together nervously.

Numi darted up to Angela, oblivious to the awkwardness of the moment.

187

"What the hell are you doing out here?" Chris bellowed, anger rising in his voice as he realized his daughter had been sneaking around. He pointed a finger back and forth at both girls, barely able to enunciate his thoughts. "And what in God's name is this?"

Hannah's eyes brimmed with shame. Her lips pursed for a moment, and she tried to hold back her emotions. The dam broke when her father approached her and she burst into tears.

"I'm sorry, Dad," she sobbed.

"Is this where you are when you're at 'Bible study'?" Chris snapped, eyes darting around the grove.

It was peaceful, spare the deathly cold of it, and Onwé noticed its similarity to Ash Hill: a quiet place to be alone with one's thoughts, or with a lover.

Hannah's big wet eyes searched Onwé and Becker for their reactions. Angie's remained downcast.

"You're fifteen years old, for God's sake!" Chris said in exasperation. "What will your mother think? And Pastor Burke? Do you realize this could humiliate our family in the eyes of the church!"

"Look," Onwé said calmly, "let's just get them home, alright? They're kids, Chris. Voth doesn't need to know about this."

"How long has this been going on?" Chris demanded, ignoring the suggestion.

"Not long," Angie replied. She spoke softly, but by the plumes of breath rushing from her mouth, Onwé could tell she was panicked. "We come out here to get away from all the sad stuff in town."

Onwé approached Angela and put his arm around her. She looked up at him with an expression that reminded him of the heartbreak permanently etched on Moya's face.

"It's okay," he said. "Let's go get a fire going. It's freezing out here, isn't it?"

She nodded and wiped tears from her eyes. They held hands on the walk back.

Angie wasn't particularly well liked at school, owing to her bookish timidness, and her parents had never been overly nice to her. Onwé supposed she didn't have anyone who was kind to her besides Tíwé, and so it made sense that she reveled in Hannah's attention. The girl was older, taller, prettier, and maybe even smarter than Angie—and loved spending time with her.

But even if it was a passing thing, as many teens are wont to experience, this sort of crush would not go unpunished on the rez. The church might have tolerated some Indian customs on its best days, but homosexuality was patently unacceptable, as evidenced by Chris's grumbling about "raising a dyke" and "inviting sin into the house."

Hannah walked beside her father in silence, risking only a quick look back at Angie while the group tramped down the snowy trail. The Millers disappeared into their home without a word to Agent Becker, who'd smartly kept his mouth shut throughout the whole affair.

Onwé, Angela, and the dogs gathered with Moya and Tíwé down at the police station, where they'd been given a small conference room to themselves. It didn't take long for Moya and Tíwé to notice Angie's distressed state. Onwé deflected questions about what had happened, but Angie eventually told them she'd gotten Hannah in trouble by going off into the woods without permission.

Tíwé, preternaturally adept at sensing a person's inner feelings, gave Angie a hug and said, "I like hiking with my special friend too."

The look she returned to him revealed Angela had

189

realized in that moment how dear a friend Tíwé really was.

"Don't let those cunts tell you who you can love," Moya said, eviscerating the gentle moment with her sharp tongue. "They tried to tell me once. But the heart wants what it wants, doesn't it?"

Angie returned a surprised look, probably wondering how Moya had figured out her secret.

"I think there's room in mine for anyone," she replied sheepishly. "It's not about boys or girls."

Onwé looked at Tíwé and covertly tapped himself on the head, mouthing the word *brains*. Tíwé replied with a vague nod.

"Did they find Luke?" Moya asked, regarding her surroundings with a discomforted expression.

"Not as far as I know," Onwé said, heading for the door. "But I'll see about getting us out of here. Maybe they can post a guard at your house. I won't have you sleeping in a jail with no beds." Before Onwé walked out into the hall, he looked at Angela and said, "I guess I have to repeat myself because you kids never listen."

"The hiker's code?" Tíwé replied.

"Damn right," he said. "*Stay*. In groups. On trails. Out of caves. On the hills, off the mountain."

"We know," Tíwé sighed.

"But you broke the code, didn't you?" Onwé said.

Angie nodded in embarrassment.

"You went off the trail, and you went on the mountain. And you didn't leave enough light to get home."

"I know," she said. "It was dumb."

"But you're not dumb, are you? Tíwé, is Angie dumb?"

Tíwé shook his head.

"Smartest girl I know," he replied, smiling at her.

"So don't do dumb things, alright?" Onwé said.

Angie's gaze remained in her lap. Numi approached and

shoved her snout into the girl's hands.

"Do you think Hannah's in a lot of trouble?" Angie asked timidly. Tears began to roll down her cheeks.

"Don't worry, sweetheart," Onwé replied. "I'll work on her dad. He can be reasoned with."

Onwé lingered in the doorway for a moment, studying the kids and wishing they wouldn't grow up so damned fast. He sighed deeply and knocked a fist against the door frame to break the heavy silence.

"Did you and Hannah ever see any weird shit out there?"

"No," she replied, wringing her hands, "but we heard weird noises once. Hannah's been having bad dreams ever since."

"Bad dreams?" Onwé asked. "What about?"

Angela looked up at Onwé with worry in her eyes.

"She dreamed of taking Stefan out of his crib in the middle of the night. Took him to a creepy house in the woods."

Chapter 29

John Tall Rock and the Special Agent in Charge were just pulling up to the station when Onwé stepped outside. The night's cold assailed him, and the headlights on John's old truck illuminated the snowflakes that danced in the air. John got out of the truck and checked in with the agents, then approached Onwé. After a brief conversation, both men agreed John would drive Tíwé, Angie, and Zeus home to Namarjo on his next patrol. The snow was light enough, and Luke was nowhere to be found.

"If he's outside all night," John said, "I reckon he's dead by dawn."

The SAC agreed to release Moya into Onwé's protection on condition they remain in her home and permit an officer to search the house. Onwé agreed, and a tribal police officer searched every nook and cranny of the house until he was satisfied Luke wasn't hiding in there.

Moya slept in her bed, and Onwé rested on the couch with his rifle in his lap. Numi lay at his feet, saddened by Zeus's absence.

———•◎•———

Onwé pulled the rifle up near his chest when he heard a knock at the door. Morning light spilled in through the old windows, illuminating Moya's sleeping form, and he felt relieved they'd survived the night. He peeked through the curtain and saw John Tall Rock on the porch, holding a brown folder under his arm.

"You find him?" Onwé asked before he even finished pulling the door open.

John answered the question with a worried look and shook his head.

"More bad news, I'm afraid," he said in a grave voice. "Hannah Miller's gone."

"Oh, Jesus," Onwé said, lamenting that he didn't report the dream Angela had told him about. "Let me guess, the baby's gone too?"

"How'd you know?" John asked with surprise.

"Fuck!" Onwé shouted.

Moya stirred and looked over at the two men.

"It was some time in the night," John went on. "She picked him up and walked right out the front door. Left it unlocked. Chris and Wendy didn't notice a thing until this morning."

Onwé leaned his rifle against the wall and stepped onto the porch.

"I suppose you know what happened, then?" he said, looking out across the neighborhood. The day was bright and clear, but the whipping wind stung every uncovered inch of Onwé's skin.

"Chris told me everything," John replied, brushing aside the locks of long hair that fluttered across his face.

"Did he tell you he yelled at her and gave her the church talk?"

John let out a sigh of resignation. In his time as leader of the tribal council, he'd seen more than his share of families torn apart by conflicting moral values. If nothing else, the church always managed to complicate things.

"I was hoping you'd remember anything she said that might tell us where she's gone."

A terrible feeling washed over Onwé, the same mixture of fear and nausea he'd endured when Luke had told him about the Briar House.

"You remember Gaylen's story at the council meeting?" he said, shuddering at the thought.

"I do."

"He said he saw a strange house on the mountain while he was carrying the baby."

"I remember," John said. "But there aren't any houses out there. He was turned around."

"No," Onwé said, glancing back through the window to ensure Moya was still in bed. "Luke saw it too. Said it could move. He called it *Óknóth-ûden.*"

"House of…thorns?" John said.

"Something like that," Onwé replied. "Luke found it when he and I took the investigators on that little camping trip."

"Did you see it too?"

"No. But I think he was telling the truth. He said a voice led him to it."

"Luke was out of his mind," John said, dismissing the uncomfortable thought. John was a far more spiritual man than Onwé, and was probably so frightened by Gaylen's story, he didn't want to accept it.

"That was the day all this started," Onwé replied. "After Luke found the house. And last night, Angela told me that Hannah dreamed about a house just like it. She dreamed of taking the baby there."

Moya emerged from her house wrapped in a thick blanket. She looked over the two men with bleary eyes.

194

"Come inside, you fools," she grumbled. "It's fuckin' freezing out here."

"What did you think of Gaylen Poor's story?" Onwé asked her. "Did you believe him?"

Moya studied Onwé for a long moment, then looked at John, realizing something had gone terribly wrong...again. She instinctively looked over her shoulder to the window beside the bed, as if remembering the dream of Akántha's frozen body.

"I've never seen the things Gaylen talked about," she said, tightening the blanket around her skeletal form, "but I believe some of the old legends. There's things out there I don't ever want to meet."

John, like the other elders, regarded Moya's opinions with great respect. The fact that she didn't flatly deny the truth of Gaylen's story seemed to bother him a great deal. He shook his head as if to free his mind of dark thoughts.

"We've got our hands full with the manhunt right now," he said to Onwé. "BIA's got more guys comin' up from Denver in the next day or two. But their priority is finding Luke before he hurts anyone else. I'll see if the tribal police can spare a man or two to go check out this house you're talking about. Until then, give us a hand and ask around town for Hannah. She probably took the baby and crashed at a friend's place to get back at her dad."

"What if you're wrong, John?" Onwé said. "What if she's out there right now, freezing to death with a baby in her arms? You really want to risk Hannah Miller becoming just another *vanished Indian?*"

John tossed a hand up in frustration.

"Who's gonna protect the town if I send a posse up the mountain and then Luke shows up here?" he said. "I want every door knocked before we go sending our boys on a wild goose chase. I know Steve would agree if he was here."

John nodded respectfully at Moya and turned to leave. As he did, he handed the brown folder to Onwé.

"I need this back," he whispered.

Onwé examined the folder and then watched the tribal leader walk off into the snow. He knew John Tall Rock was not a stubborn man, and didn't blame him for not circling the wagons for Hannah. Both men had seen too many times how the Bureau of Indian Affairs dragged its feet on missing persons cases in Cold Valley. When they weren't hunting mass murderers, they hardly poked around at all before concluding the person—almost always a young woman—had "run off to the city for a better life."

John was probably a feather's weight from breaking. He'd put two bullets in a man he considered a son, and as far as Onwé knew, no one had asked him how he was doing. Since Ash's death, John had selflessly acted as a father to his people, and the job was almost entirely a thankless one.

"I have to go," Onwé said to Moya. "Come, Numi."

The dog leaped to her feet and dashed outside, happy to be anywhere but trapped indoors.

"Where are you going?" Moya asked, scowling at the cold weather.

"They're looking in the wrong place," Onwé replied. "I'm gonna find Hannah."

Chapter 30

It took a bit of convincing, but Onwé was able to get Moya to agree to stay at the tribal council building while he was gone. He stopped by his home with Numi and opened John's folder, recognizing its contents were meant to be a secret. Inside was a collection of photographs.

At first, Onwé didn't recognize the blurry shots. But as he flipped through the stack, he saw Warren's overlit face glistening with drool and snot. The man's eyes looked black and demonic, and his smile stretched wider than his lips should have allowed.

Onwé sifted through a dozen photos of the wrecked campsite, of Numi peering into the trees, and of himself standing rigidly, gazing up at the moon like a bewitched scarecrow. He saw artfully angled shots of Paul eating boreal toads from the mud and feasting on the corpse of a rabbit.

The last photos were of Vince prostrating himself near the fire and examining a glimmering knife. Behind him, just beyond the reach of the firelight, was the dusky shape of a boy.

Onwé didn't know what to make of the photos. He knew something paranormal had occurred that night to sicken the group, and now his mind wandered to dark and terrible places.

He remembered the strange figure in the yard, and imagined the corpse of Akántha walking listlessly between the trees. For now, he tried to push the thoughts away.

Find Hannah. Bring her home.

Onwé hid the photos and suited up for the long trek. He strapped his knife to his waist and grabbed more rifle rounds. He considered bringing the hiking staff along, but reasoned he should be unburdened in case he needed to fight or flee.

"Let's go, Numi," he said.

Then the two were off.

Chapter 31

It was too dangerous to venture into the nameless place alone, but Onwé knew of a ridge high above Ash Hill that would give him a view of the whole region. If this so-called "Briar House" existed, he would be able to see it. First, he and Numi headed up to the grove where they'd found the girls the day before. Onwé hoped Hannah would be there and spare him the long journey westward.

The pines had been eerily still last night, but today, they creaked and groaned and thrashed about in a roaring wind. Numi looked overwhelmed by the noise, her ears swiveling wildly and her head cocking in a different direction every few seconds.

Onwé's heart sank when they arrived in the grove and found it empty. In the sunlight, the little clearing looked as perfect as a gift shop painting of the Colorado wilderness. He followed Numi to the log where the girls had been seated and leaned against it, catching his breath.

While Numi sniffed her way around the tree line, Onwé thought about Luke and the days when they used to hike the nearby trail up to Mirror Lake. He ached for those times, and felt overwhelmed with anger and sadness for what his lifelong friend had become.

Numi suddenly veered into the trees, following a curious scent.

"Whatcha find, girl?" Onwé called out.

When Numi didn't return with a stick or the bone-picked remains of some little animal, he pushed himself off the log and walked over to her.

"Forget about the chipmunks," he said. "Look for Hannah and Stefan." He patted her side and looked down at what she'd found.

Tracks.

A lone person, maybe a small woman, had been here recently. The footprints came from nowhere; they almost looked like someone had climbed down from the nearby tree and leaped into the snow. Whoever had made them seemed disoriented. She'd wandered aimlessly a few dozen paces, then abruptly headed northwest. Judging by the distance between each footprint, she must have been running.

"Hannah!" Onwé shouted. He took off after her, weaving between trees and trampling half-buried shrubs.

Numi rushed out ahead, easily springing through the snow. They followed the footprints until Numi halted at a discarded winter coat on the ground. Onwé picked it up and found it torn down the middle and covered in blood, as if the person wearing it had frantically cut the jacket off instead of just unbuttoning it. He held it to his chest for size and concluded it belonged to a woman.

"Hannah!" he shouted again.

Numi ran on, following a trail of scent to another article of clothing—a pair of jeans draped over a tree branch a dozen feet off the ground. Onwé could not imagine why they'd be up so high, but when he spotted them, his concern grew to panic. Was the girl suicidal? Without winter gear, she'd be dead before the hour.

The pair raced across the landscape. The trees thickened,

and soon it was difficult to see more than a few feet ahead. Onwé ran past a long-sleeve shirt and tripped over a boot. Numi found a pair of underwear and a bloodsoaked bra. The dog stopped dead in her tracks, her gaze locked on something just ahead. Onwé slid to a stop beside her, and as he did, a rolling cackle spilled through the forest.

"Hannah?" he called out.

Onwé could see her wandering behind the trees, laughing madly and muttering to herself. It wasn't clear whether she was carrying the baby, and Onwé had the morbid thought she'd buried him somewhere in the snow.

Numi slinked away, flanking Hannah from one side while Onwé moved to the other. But when a woman with straw-gold hair and pale skin came into view, Onwé froze.

"Have you seen him?" the woman asked in a strange accent. She was completely nude and stood rigidly, facing away from Onwé and looking down at something in her hands. If it was Stefan, he wasn't making any noise.

Onwé hesitated. He thought of the creature in his yard, and wondered now if this was a person standing before him— or something else entirely. Her limbs twitched, and she loosed terrible, hacking coughs. Small, bloody gashes pocked the skin all over her body, likely caused by her reckless dash through the wilderness. Dried blood caked much of her arms. She cocked her head painfully to one side upon sensing Onwé's presence but then trained on a sound he couldn't hear.

"Jesus Christ," he said, beholding the woman's monstrous state. Onwé quietly unslung the rifle from his shoulder and held it at low-ready.

The woman whirled around, bones crunching like river ice beneath her frost-tightened skin. She stared into Onwé with black and bloodied sockets, her ruined eyes now a mess of gore draping down her face. The woman raised her ghost-white hands near her chest in a defensive posture, clutching a small, jagged object in one of them she'd no doubt used to mutilate herself. Her jaw trembled, teeth clattering through the words she spoke, and her eyebrows jumped as if she could see Onwé— and recognized him.

"I hear him calling to me," she said, her thick accent spilling out of lips as blue as the winter sky. "But I c-can't..."

"My God... *Nora?*" Onwé said. "Is that you? Are you... Stefan's mother?"

"Stefan!" she cried out, taking a big step toward Onwé and holding the object out in front of her like a knife.

Numi, who watched from behind the woman, began to snarl.

"He's alive!" Onwé said, taking a step back. "He's okay. Just calm down, alright? I need you to drop that thing and put your clothes back on. You don't want to die out here, okay? You're losing heat real fast."

"I'll take you to him!" Nora replied, resuming her eerie cackling. "I-I can see the way!"

Onwé tried to protest, but Nora raised the object in her hand and carved some kind of symbol on her forehead, laughing as she made the cuts. She looked down at the dog and spoke something in another language.

"This way!" she screamed, spitting out the blood that dripped from the wound onto her lips. She looked back at Onwé with a gore-smeared grin. "And *you* bring the baby to us. And-and the mother! Yes, the *weeping mother!*"

With that, Nora took off running through the trees, singing as she went.

It took a moment for Onwé's brain to process the horrific scene that had unfolded before him, but he soon realized Numi had run off in pursuit of the woman.

"*Numi!*" he cried, afraid Nora might try to hurt the dog. He ran after her, rifle in hand, hoping he wouldn't have to pull the trigger.

With each frantic step, Nora moved further away from

her clothes, and thus any chance of survival on the frozen mountain. Her path intercepted the trail that snaked up to Mirror Lake, and suddenly, Onwé knew exactly where he was.

The mouth of a great cave came into view. A feeling of otherworldly mystery washed over Onwé as he moved toward it. Its visage stirred long-forgotten memories of dreams that had plagued his childhood. He'd seen this cave from a distance countless times with his father while they'd hiked up to Mirror Lake, but never had he come this close to it.

This was the place where Ashthenôvi had died.

Onwé watched, fright-frozen, as Nora bolted into the cave. Numi darted after her, unable to control her curiosity. The maw of darkness swallowed them up, and Onwé wailed in fear, begging the dog to come back. A lightning bolt of terror struck through him, innervating his limbs with the will to do the unthinkable. He couldn't leave Numi. He couldn't lose anyone else.

Against all his father's warnings, Onwé rushed inside.

"Goddamn Huskies!" he shouted. "Numi, get back here!" His voice died away in the depths of the tunnel, but after a moment, it bounced back to him in distorted and menacing tones. After only a dozen paces in, the darkness became all-consuming, as if Onwé had fallen into a black hole in the forgotten space between galaxies.

The dog's yipping echoed strangely through the tunnel. Each bark seemed to recede deeper into the fathomless dark, and Nora's singing wafted with it on the dank cave air. Onwé crept forward, following the jagged walls with his hands and cursing himself for not having brought his flashlight. He stumbled over the grooves of the stone floor, fearful in each step that he'd plummet into the bottomless chasm of his childhood nightmares. Every admonition he'd given Tíwé now cycled through his mind, each one making him a hypocrite. But in that moment, Onwé would rather die in the cave than live the rest of his life knowing he'd abandoned his dog to it.

Onwé's hands slid over things his brain could not identify. The textured stone gave way to glassy surfaces adorned in places with elaborate carvings. He fumbled his way around statues whose geometry he could not comprehend, and staggered through doorways whose height he could not reach with his hands. The ground smoothed into a flat plane, and the tunnel broadened until he could no longer touch both sides with his arms extended.

"Where are you?" Onwé called out. He screamed for Numi and tried to follow the echo of her cries, but they seemed to come to him from every direction at once.

Then, other voices began to seep through the tunnel from deeper places.

"Did you see it!" an old woman shouted. "Up in the trees!"

"No, no, no, he goes down in the hole!" a man replied enthusiastically.

The tunnels bent and warped their voices until they sounded nearly inhuman.

"I'm lost! I'm lost!" several children cried out at once. They shrieked and whimpered in fear, then laughed hideously when Onwé spun around, seeking the source of their calls.

The darkness had no depth at all; it was as if Onwé wore a black bag over his head. He stumbled around, shaking terribly and trying to follow Numi's barks, but he was no longer sure which way was forward and which was back. Even if he found the dog, he worried they'd never get out.

A high-pitched yelp pierced through the din and struck Onwé at the level of his soul.

Numi had been injured.

She screamed farther down in the tunnels, filling the air with bone-chilling yelps that silenced the other voices.

"If you touch my dog, you're fuckin' *dead*, lady!" Onwé

screamed into the blackness. His threat returned to him as a hideous mockery of itself.

Onwé's courage gathered all at once, propelling him blindly in Numi's direction. He fell to the ground and moved toward the noise on all fours, swatting at the gloom in front of him every few paces. He called to Numi, and she to him, until at last his hand met her form.

"What happened, baby? What happened?" he said, pulling her into his arms. He ran his fingers over her bloodsoaked fur until they arrived at a large gash.

Numi jolted in pain at Onwé's discovery. She licked his face when he hoisted her up and began to carry her through the dark.

"This is why we don't run off, you goddamn idiot," he said, tears welling up in his eyes.

The cut was bad, but thankfully, it was on her haunch and probably wasn't lethal. Nonetheless, the feeling of her warm blood covering his arm filled Onwé with a sort of terror the voices could not—the fear a parent experiences when their child is in danger.

Onwé leaned against the tunnel walls and pressed on, holding Numi tightly to his chest. She buried her snout against him, crying in pain and fright. Nora begged them both to follow her, but Onwé moved in the opposite direction of her voice, following instead a passage whose air felt slightly cooler than the others.

As they moved further away from Nora, a chorus of children's voices filled the tunnel once more.

"Ahh soul me…ahhhh soouul mee… Ahh dooo…"

"Na-naked…naked souuuul…"

"Lalala…lalalalaaaa…"

One of the children cried out only a few feet from Onwé, causing him to nearly drop Numi as she squirmed in terror:

"When do we go insiiiiiiide? When do we go insiiiiiiide?"

"When mother and child are one," a man with a deep voice replied. *"Then we go down in the hole...aaallll the way down to the bottom!"*

Sharp pains began to radiate up Onwé's neck and around his head, throbbing each time one of the voices rang out. He'd suffered migraines as a boy, and the one incubating in his skull now threatened to turn his legs to rubber. Gray static appeared around the edges of his vision, framing the darkness before him and slowly encroaching toward the center. Whenever he blinked, he perceived ineffable forms shambling about in the distortion, but they vanished as quickly as they appeared.

I'm gonna pass out, he thought to himself, realizing both he and Numi were doomed if that happened. But he pressed on, motivated by the dog's crying, until the pitch-black of the tunnel shifted to a midnight purple. The air felt cooler and drier, and soon, it moved over his skin in gusts.

"You bring them down to us!" Nora screeched once more.

The sheer malevolence in her voice pushed Onwé the last few steps out of the cave. He collapsed into the snow in a sunlit forest, dropping Numi and the rifle in the process. Blue birds sang overhead, and the sound of bristling pine needles flooded him with relief.

After a few moments, the migraine dissipated, and Onwé's vision returned to normal. He gathered the dog and the gun and risked a look back at the cave. The entrance was a little hole set into a rocky slope, barely two shoulder-lengths wide and shrouded by shrubs and branches. Onwé had never seen this cave before.

"Let's get the fuck out of here," he said.

Numi winced at the anger in her master's voice, and again buried her face in his chest.

Chapter 32

"It's okay, it's okay." Onwé nuzzled his forehead against Numi's and tried to control his panic.

The cut on her body was long and jagged, but not deep enough to have nicked an artery. He was hopeful the dog would live, but she'd need stitches, and Onwé had very little cash for the expense. The idea of borrowing money from the church crossed his mind, but he spat at the thought.

Onwé carried Numi downhill until he emerged from the woods into a great clearing. He surveyed the area with exasperation. They'd somehow exited the tunnels on the open ridge above Ash Hill, where he'd originally planned to go in search of the Briar House. But this ridge was more than an hour away from town on a day without snow. Today, it should have taken him two hours to get here.

"How?" Onwé said breathlessly, halting near the edge of a cliff.

He and Numi looked out over a vast gorge whose river fed the nameless place to the west. In the distance, craggy peaks rose toward the sky, forming the boundary of the world he knew.

Onwé looked back at the woods leading up to the cave.

By his best estimation, he and Numi had only been inside the mountain for fifteen minutes. He assured himself the experience had simply shaken his wits, but a deeper part of him believed there was something wicked about the tunnels beneath Pale Peak. He remembered the unfathomable shapes of rock his hands had found there in the darkness, and thanked God he'd been unable to see them.

As Onwé searched the ridge for a way down to Ash Hill, he noticed a huge trough in the ground. It looked as if something big had been excavated from the earth here. The hole appeared manmade, owing to its square borders, and might have been the foundation of a cellar. Onwé imagined a stone giant from old Nauktí legend plucking a cabin right off the ground and chewing it up, leaving its base exposed.

Night had fallen by the time Onwé stepped into his house. Fiery pain seared his back from carrying Numi, and the rest of him felt like he'd been dipped in the icy river. He lowered the dog onto her blanket and, with his last ounce of strength, cleaned and covered her wound. Then he collapsed into his armchair, too tired to set up the fireplace or even peel off his jacket, which was now a mosaic of blood and fur. The town was quiet, and the Valley Commission had forbidden Dr. Farmer to waste precious medical supplies treating animals. No help would come until tomorrow.

Some hours later, Onwé awoke in frigid darkness to the tics and scrapes of Numi's nails across the old wooden floors. The dog was ambling around the house, groaning as she moved.

"Numi?" he whispered.

The dog replied with a string of distressed grumbles and continued moving around the living room. Onwé stood up on wobbly legs and went for the lights, but when his hand found the switch, a nightmare resurfaced in his mind: a dream of dogs eating people and people eating dogs in an orgy of violence in the forest. The cave mouth smiled wide upon the scene from nearby.

Light flooded the room when Onwé flicked the switch, chasing the ugly scene from his mind but illuminating another before him. Numi sat by the window, facing Onwé and trembling. She tried to lie down, then sat up abruptly, then tried again, then stood up and walked a few steps, looked out the window, and repeated the motion. The dog grumbled the entire time, like an old man arguing with himself under his breath. Numi had bled through her makeshift bandage, and the bloody prints all over the living room indicated she'd been at this for hours.

"Sweetheart..."

Onwé dropped to his knees and pulled the dog in for a hug. Numi recoiled in fear and issued a little growl, then looked up at the ceiling in confusion.

She might have a fever, Onwé thought. *Can dogs get fevers?*

He reasoned that if the wound had become infected, Numi's behavior might be strange until he could get her some antibiotics. There was no veterinarian on the rez, but there were a few people who had drugs and could stitch up animals. Poverty was the mother of innovation in Cold Valley, and Onwé had a guy for almost everything.

"What did she cut you with, baby?" he asked, his voice tightening with sadness. He recalled the small object in Nora's bloodied hand, and surmised it was some kind of stone.

The dog paced back and forth between windows, staring out at the black woods and sniffing erratically. She looked through him when he spoke, barely recognizing her daddy at all, as if a ghost had called to her from afar.

The night was long and restless. Onwé lit a fire to banish

the gloom and warm the house, but it did little to comfort Numi. As the hours passed, he noticed her eyes had begun to bulge and yellow. They darted in every direction, perceiving things in the house and outside that Onwé could not see. She groaned and yelped and grumbled, and any time Onwé approached her, she snarled and bared her teeth.

Onwé's heart broke at the sight of Numi's discomfort. Her wretched state only worsened as the hours crept past, and soon he began to worry she might not survive the night. Numi became more jittery each time she looked outside, until finally she collapsed onto her bed, shaking and whimpering. Onwé was finally able to wrap his arms around her and attempt to comfort her, but when he did, big tufts of fur came loose and stuck to him. She refused food and water and would not allow him to check the wound again.

Somewhere in the small hours, Numi began to yowl.

Her voice came out lower and more gravelly than even Zeus's monstrous barks, rattling the windows and filling Onwé with fright. Numi was no longer herself, and with each passing minute, he felt more afraid to be near her. Still, he cradled the dog between her restless wanderings. During the rare and fitful sleep she got, Numi twitched violently and emitted ghastly, half-lunged howls in dissonant melodies like the voices on the mountain. And each time, she jolted awake and looked around wide-eyed, as if beholding nightmares that had spilled over into reality. Onwé wondered if she'd dreamed of eating people too.

At last, Onwé began to nod off. His mind wandered to wicked places. Stress and exhaustion warped his surroundings, and disturbing memories of the tunnels and the massacre plagued his thoughts.

When Numi jumped awake and looked around, her eyes were missing, and knots of pale worms writhed in the sockets. But then, when Onwé flipped on the light, the dog's eyes were restored and pierced through him with a mixture of fear and fascination. He could no longer tell if he was awake or asleep, and imagined himself trapped in a perpetual twilight of consciousness. The night wind carried faint and mournful lullabies from the woods into the house, but Onwé tried to convince himself he was only dreaming.

Numi jolted awake once more, rousing Onwé too, and began convulsing. Foam seeped from her mouth and nostrils, and her reddening eyes rolled back in her head. Onwé held her tightly, stricken with terror that these were her final moments.

"Please...no," he cried, rocking her back and forth in his arms. "Please don't leave me, girl. Don't go."

Numi was the last tether between Onwé and his old life. Akántha had been the first to leave, and then his father, his wife, his son, and now Luke. Onwé imagined himself growing old in the house all alone, waiting around like Moya for someone to come walking through the door to take the pain away. The thought made him want to die.

Onwé placed his hand over the dog's wound and prayed in the old language, loud and confident, as Old N'wentháil had taught him. He invoked his ancestors and the medicine spirits of Nauktí tradition. He called upon Náhnako, guide of souls, to encourage Numi to remain in her body.

But the dog stopped breathing.

Onwé ran out of prayers, and found himself begging Jesus Christ to intervene and save her life. In his desperation, he pledged his soul to the God of the Christians, if only Numi would overcome her illness. He vowed to accept baptism and cease his resistance to the church. He swore on his life to take up the faith.

But no miracle came.

Numi's muscles went slack, and she passed quietly in Onwé's arms. He burst into tears and clutched the dog to his chest. Onwé screamed into her fur, loud enough to be heard across the void between worlds, and begged her to come back. After several minutes of this, he laid her down and covered her with her favorite blanket.

"*Yed'yén yathī nafíí,*" he said to her. *I'll love you forever.*

Then, he retreated to his bedroom to escape the agony of her stillness.

Chapter 33

The silence of the house devoured Onwé like vultures on a carcass. For nearly a decade, he'd slept to the rhythm of Numi's breathing and had awakened to the touch of her snout. Now, only the hateful weather of the mountain made any sound.

Onwé lay in his bed, staring up at the ceiling, wishing this day was just another bad dream. He remained motionless until red light seeped in through the window, unable to do anything but watch a flood of memories drift past. He remembered Numi's first winter, how much she'd loved rooting beneath the snow.

A familiar noise interrupted his reminiscing.

Scraping. Groaning.

Mumbling.

Something coughed—a very human cough.

Something slowly climbed the staircase—and then quickly lurched back down.

Labored breathing filled the air, wet and gurgling, a sound that reminded Onwé of Old N'wenthāil's death rattle. He rose from his bed and crept to the bedroom door. Through it, he could hear movement downstairs.

"Numi?" he whispered.

Onwé pulled the door open slowly.

White and gray fur lined the stairs in big clumps, and a bloody mark streaked the wall beside them.

"Numi?" he said a little louder. He made his way down the stairs, careful to avoid stepping on the chunks of fur, but his foot connected with something wet and slippery.

Skin.

A large patch of pinkish, reddish flesh squished beneath Onwé's toes. He lifted his foot and peeled off the object, regarding it with disgust.

A loud, ghoulish yowl filled the house, followed by more sputtering coughs. Onwé reached the bottom of the staircase and looked out over the shadowy living room. At its far end, he saw a dark figure shuffling near the window, backlit in an aura of red. It stood about five feet in height and moved stiffly, as if awoken from a slumber of centuries.

"...Is that you, girl?"

The figure's head whipped toward Onwé when it perceived his voice. As it did, Onwé saw the profile of its snout. It was Numi—but she was walking upright on her hind legs.

Onwé flicked the nearby lightswitch, bathing himself and the staircase in yellow light. Its weak glow reached the living room enough to illuminate the dog a bit more. Most of her fur had sloughed off, along with large portions of her skin. Her limbs had become hideously elongated, and now she stood on two legs of unequal length, the feet gnarled into club-like extremities. One of her forelegs remained mostly canine, while the other extended down past her waist, twitching and writhing.

Numi let out a gasp of excitement, recognizing Onwé in the light, and began staggering toward him with her mouth wide open. Additional rows of teeth had sprouted from her gums, filling her jaw with a fan of rotten daggers. A bloodied

214

tongue slithered across them hungrily.

"What the fuck!" Onwé said, his breath catching in his throat. "S-stay back!"

The dog wheezed violently as she came toward him. Onwé circled the armchair to avoid her, but she never ceased her approach. She tripped and fell to the floor, but lifted herself back up and continued onward, gurgling and chattering with each step. Numi's eyes, now faintly glowing, bored into Onwé with the same predatory stare Luke had worn when he cut down his friends at *Yōktha*. Her mumbling took on new urgency, and she spoke with an articulation not unlike human speech.

The dog repeated whatever she was trying to say over and over as if reciting some dark prayer, her voice tightening to a higher pitch and alternating between different notes.

She was *singing*, Onwé realized.

"Numi, please stop," he begged, yanking the rifle from its place against the wall.

He backed another circle around the room, but the dog ignored his pleas. She snarled at him between the verses of her song, and the melody reignited the sharp pain in Onwé's head. The more she spoke, the fuzzier his vision became, until his field of sight became a wall of haze and static.

Onwé fell against the staircase and fled up the steps on all fours, dragging the rifle by its muzzle. The dog charged, sliding across the wood floor on her misshapen limbs and lumbering up the stairs. Onwé slammed the bedroom door on her horrid body, trapping her head against the frame.

"Numi, stop!" he cried.

But the dog—or whatever she was now—seemed to revel in his fright. Numi sang and groaned and snarled, pushing desperately to get inside the bedroom. Onwé pressed against the door with all his weight, and as the wood inched deeper against the dog's throat, her singing only grew louder and more shrill. Their eyes caught momentarily in the chaos, and Numi's face appeared stretched into a malevolent smile. He fired his rifle into the ceiling, hoping the blast would scare her off, but she didn't react.

Onwé knew he could not hold out much longer. The dog raged against the door with such unnatural force, he would have believed a bear had broken into his house. Her hot, vile breath poured over his arm, her countless teeth mere inches from his flesh. His ears rang from the deafening blast, but the dog's wicked singing pierced through, antagonizing his migraine. Onwé fumbled with the rifle, realizing he'd left the box of rounds downstairs on the table.

His eyes fell on the bullet he'd picked up from the ground after Luke's rampage. It stood on the corner of the nearby dresser, hiding in the shadow of a framed photo of Tíwé. Onwé hadn't yet decided whether he should get rid of the thing; he'd held onto it to ponder its significance some other time. But now, this bullet was the only chance he had to save his own life. He kicked the dresser, sending the round clattering to the wooden floor, and pulled it nearer with his foot.

"Awah!" Numi shrieked. *"Onwah! Onnnwaah!"*

The hideous voice, its near-human timbre, its gleeful urgency—everything about it filled Onwé's skull with ice. His thoughts froze. His movements slowed. His fingers refused to obey. The dog finally threw the door open and sent him crashing into the wooden bedframe.

For a second, he could only watch Numi regard him with a ravening stare. But when she lunged, his senses gathered just enough to coordinate a wild thrust of the rifle butt. It collided with Numi's head, knocking her to the floor and stunning her.

Onwé leaped to his feet and flipped the rifle around, loading it with trembling hands. As he aimed it at Numi, he recalled the moment Luke had done the same thing.

"Please stop," Onwé said breathlessly. His tears blurred everything in the room to simple shapes, but Numi's hairless, patchy body stood out like a gruesome beacon.

She issued a long gurgle that grew to a melody, and rose once more to her hind legs.

Luke's words echoed in Onwé's mind.

The Black Wall could use a guard.

Numi charged.

Onwé pulled the trigger.

The blast ripped through the morning air, deafening him. The muzzle flash blinded him. But in the image burned into his retinas, Onwé saw Numi's chest explode. The round had hit its target and lanced clean through the bedroom door. The dog dropped to the floor and remained motionless for a long moment.

As the ringing in Onwé's ears subsided, he heard Numi exhale her final breath—and it sounded like a sigh of relief. The eldritch glimmer in her eyes faded, and a deathly silence fell over the house.

Chapter 34

The sun rose, but Onwé scarcely noticed. He was alone now.

He sat in the stillness of his home, averting his eyes from the few photos of everyone he'd lost on this wretched mountain. The house had once felt like a tiny prison he'd been born into, but now it was a vast expanse, void of any warmth and much too big for one man. For the first time in eight years, the air went undisturbed by Numi's rhythmic breathing. Today the squirrels would descend from the trees out back and find no dog to chase them.

Onwé spent the hours drifting around his home, haunting the rooms like a restless ghost. Chris Miller stopped by, but when he approached, Onwé drew the curtains. It was cold, colder than any time he could remember in this house, but he preferred the numbness. He chose not to build a fire for fear of waking up in its light and searching the floor for Numi, momentarily forgetting she'd never sleep there again. The only sounds he heard now came from the snarling wind outside. It battered the windows as if to remind him that death would soon return to claim one final soul.

It wasn't always like this.

In the days of Onwé's great-grandparents, the Nauktí lived in multi-family dwellings. When someone died, the survivors were never alone, and could always seek comfort in the presence of kin. It was the federal government that ended this way of life when they passed the Dawes Act and forced the Nauktí into single-family allotments. They built houses for the Indians of Cold Valley, but in doing so, they took something away from them. Now, Onwé sat alone in his empty home. It stood in a row of other houses concealing other lonely people.

Near the end of the day, Onwé mustered the strength to go upstairs and collect Numi's body. He wrapped her misshapen form in the old blue quilt she'd loved so much and carried her out back. Winter had hardened the ground, so he worked through dusk to dig her resting place. Then he lowered Numi into the earth and shoveled frozen dirt over her. He said no prayers at all.

By nightfall, Onwé couldn't bear the cold any longer. He lay in bed, far away from Numi's favorite place near the hearth, plagued with thoughts unbidden. The photos he'd avoided throughout the day now flickered in his mind to the crackle of the dying fire. The loved ones he'd lost or driven away leered over his bed, cloaked in shadows, dancing to his misery and the faint songs on the mountain. He stared at the rifle he'd used to end Numi's life, fearing its power and the little voice that whispered, *"Do it."*

Heavy knocking on the door stirred Onwé from his shock. It was John Tall Rock and Chris Miller, muttering worriedly to each other. The sun blinded Onwé when he stepped outside. It was past noon.

"You okay?" John asked, obviously aware that something was wrong.

"No," Onwé replied curtly. "Gaylen was right."

"What do you mean?"

Onwé hesitated. He wanted to tell John about the woman he'd seen, but he didn't want anyone to get hurt or lost in the tunnels.

"Just make sure everyone stays out of the caves," he said. "Any news on Hannah?"

"We found the baby," Chris offered.

"Oh, thank God," Onwé said with relief.

"Hannah dropped him off at a friend's house," John added. "Told 'em Chris here was drunk and punchy."

"I *wasn't*, for the record," Chris said. "I don't even drink."

"Where'd she go?" Onwé asked.

John gave Chris a reassuring nod.

"We haven't found her yet," he said, "but we're lookin'. Oh, Tíwé called the station. Wanted to check in on you."

"He did?" The simple thought allayed Onwé's grief for just a moment.

"You bet," John replied. "Told him I'd drag you down to the phone."

Onwé followed the men down to the station, where he met a swarm of BIA agents buzzing around outside. Backup had arrived, and by the looks of it, they'd just returned from another search for Luke.

Inside the front office sat one of the two telephones in Autumn Ridge. Onwé dialed Tíwé's mother's number, momentarily bitter that half the people down in Namarjo had phones in their houses. The resentment vanished when his wife answered.

"Hello?"

"Bel?" he replied, caught off guard. She never answered the phone. Onwé couldn't remember the last time they'd spoken, and now, the softness of her voice made his heart crumple.

"He's been crying," she said. "Everyone here... The whole

town is broken. I don't know what to do."

"I'm so sorry," Onwé said. "No one ever thought—"

"Let me get him," she interrupted.

"No, wait," Onwé said, glancing around the office to ensure he was alone. "It's good to hear you, Bel. Are you—"

Tíwé's voice poured through the phone.

"Dad?" he said. "You there?"

"Yeah, it's me. How are you?"

"I dunno," he replied. "Angela told me I should check on you."

"That's nice of her."

Onwé tried to hold the pain down inside, but it forced its way up. Tears welled in his eyes, and a lump in his throat tightened the vocal cords.

"Tíwé, about what happened… There's some things a kid should never have to see. When everything settles down, I'll come down there and talk with you."

"It's crazy down here," Tíwé said. "There's cops everywhere. Mom won't let me out. Everyone's scared."

"It's the same up here," Onwé replied. "Just chaos."

"I'm having nightmares, Dad," Tíwé said, his voice becoming shaky the more he spoke. "Ever since… Ever since Luke…my dreams have been ugly."

Onwé recalled his own hideous dreams of late, and those of Luke and Hannah. A new fear struck him: had Tíwé been exposed to whatever was causing this madness?

"What have you been dreaming about, son?"

"All those people dying," he replied. "The screams. Moya, with all that blood on her."

"Anything else?" Onwé asked, fearful that Tíwé might start talking about a house.

"No. Just that."

"I'm so sorry this happened," Onwé said. "I still can't wrap my head around it."

"Angie thinks we should be up there with you," Tíwé said. "She wants to look for Hannah. But Mom wont let me go. I told her Zeus would protect us, and he'd kill Luke. But she just won't listen."

"I don't want you coming up here at all," Onwé said, glancing out the nearby window at all the cops and agents. "Either of you. You stay down there until I tell you, you hear me?"

"Yes, Dad," he replied. "At least you've got Moya and Numi."

Onwé's brief pause was enough to draw Tíwé's notice. The kid was unusually perceptive for his age and always seemed to sense what others were feeling.

"Dad? You alright?" Tíwé pressed.

Onwé leaned into the counter on which the telephone sat, overcome by grief once more. He couldn't hold the tears back any longer.

"Numi's gone, son."

"What?" Tíwé said, his voice rising with emotion. *"How?"*

"She-she got sick," Onwé said, unsure how to explain it any further. "There was nothing I could do. I buried her last night." He saw flashes of the dog's hideously transformed body, and a wave of goosebumps rolled up his arms.

Tíwé began to cry. He'd lived down in Namarjo for a few years, but he and the dog had been friends long before he'd moved away. Onwé looked up for a moment to see John Tall Rock standing nearby, holding a few cups of coffee. He averted his eyes quickly and walked off, but he'd certainly heard about the dog.

"I need to come up there, Dad," Tíwé said through tears.

"No." Onwé's tone was harsher than he'd intended. "Not right now. It's not safe."

"But—"

"I need you to swear to me you'll stay put," Onwé commanded.

"I'll stay put," Tíwé repeated.

"You tell me the truth," Onwé said. "Right now. Have you and Angie gone into any caves? Any mines?"

"No, Dad," Tíwé said. "I swear. Not since my collarbone."

Memories of the tunnel invaded Onwé's mind: the stone, the dark, the earthen must of the air. He could almost hear Numi's horrified yelps and the laughter of the crazed woman. Onwé imagined Akántha, lost and wandering underground, crying out for help.

"You have to swear you'll never go inside those fuckin' things again," Onwé said. *"Ever."*

"I keep telling you I won't," Tíwé said. "Why're you so worried about it all of a sudden?"

"I'll tell you someday," Onwé replied. "I know I've broken a lot of promises to you, son. I have no right to ask you to promise me anything. But I need you to make this one...and keep it."

"Dad," Tíwé said, "I learned my lesson, okay? If you ever find me in one of those caves, it's 'cause I was dragged in there, kicking and screaming."

Chapter 35

In the coming days, Onwé languished in the silence of his home. The loneliness, the cold, the bruises he'd sustained in the cave—the ache of it all was blunted, like the sensation of pinching a sleeping limb. Although he breathed and wept and even ate a little, Onwé didn't feel like he was living so much as taking up a bit of the infinite space within the house. And in that vacuum, the shadow returned to tell him how to fill it.

The cravings began on the second day. They started as a thought between fitful naps and grew to a feverish lust by evening. Onwé argued within himself, half convinced of his own worthlessness and abandonment, the other half still clinging to the belief that sobriety would someday reunite him with Tíwé and Bel. Nonetheless, the urge persisted, amplified by the deafening quiet and the dropping temperature. More snow had fallen, and now it thickly caked the windows and obscured the outside world. He felt a thousand miles away from the nearest soul, marooned on a spiteful mountain that wanted him dead.

Onwé found no rest. Despite his lack of appetite, he repeatedly investigated the empty pantry. He tried reading some of the books his father hadn't donated to the library, but his eyes unfocused each time after a few dozen words. No matter what he did to distract himself, his thoughts always returned to the hunger in his veins. The shadow loomed behind Onwé, throwing even more cold upon him, the sort a cozy fire could not chase away. Instead, he craved a different kind of warmth, and the only place he could find it was in a crumbling house near Luke's.

"Fuck it," Onwé grumbled just after sunset. He grabbed the savings tin and pulled out a wad of crinkled bills and coins.

The power of junk always took Onwé by surprise. On more than one occasion, he'd begun to fantasize about it while at work or while resting at home, only to find himself on his dealer's doorstep. The cravings were that powerful. They stole his time, and put him in places and situations he couldn't remember arriving at.

Onwé pulled the front door open, fumbling with his coat as he did—and jumped at the sight of a group of people gathering on his porch.

"Hello, Onwé," Voth said, standing in the middle of a crowd of eight of his congregants.

The people had various looks of sympathy and sadness on their faces, and the pastor himself spoke in a gentle, almost weepy tone. Each of them held a paper bag or covered dish or other object in their hands.

"Uh...hi," Onwé replied, studying the crowd and hoping they didn't notice his bedraggled appearance.

Voth took a meek step forward and swept a hand through the air, introducing his friends.

"We heard of your recent loss," he said, "and now we've come to help you bear the burden. Kristen here brought her famous apple muffins, and Eva made her stew. Joseph has a pot roast... Heck, you won't need to cook for days."

The shock of their generosity seized Onwé, and he was unable to respond for a moment, so Voth filled the pause with more introductions.

"Ah, you may recall Diana's artwork hanging in the library and the police station," he said.

A young woman stepped forward, holding a blanket-covered canvas. Voth uncovered it, revealing a painting of Numi lovingly gazing up at Onwé as he patted her head. The colors were striking, and the liveliness of the dog's eyes stole Onwé's breath.

Tears dripped down Onwé's face while he studied the picture. He reached for it unconsciously, like a child reaching for his mother, and then looked up at Diana.

"I'm so sorry, Mr. Lopez," she offered. "We're all animal lovers too."

"Blessed are those who mourn," Voth added, "for they shall be comforted. May we help you with these? We'd be happy to leave them on the table."

Onwé nodded and stepped aside, allowing Voth and a few others to enter his home and place their gifts on the kitchen table. Two or three of the church folk gave hugs to Onwé as they left his porch, and soon everyone was gone, except Voth, who lingered behind for a moment.

"The muffins really are a treat," the pastor said awkwardly. He seemed shorter now, stooped by the recent tragedies he'd witnessed, and hunched a bit as if lugging a weight around his neck. His face looked even older now, bleached with a deathly pallor and pitted with grief-sunken eyes.

"Thank you," Onwé said, wiping the tears from his face before they froze. "It's been hard."

"I know something of it." Voth opened his wallet and retrieved a tattered sketch of a golden retriever. "Her name was Daisy. She loved eating flowers. Even the ones that made her sick. I don't think I've slept a full night in all the years she's been gone. I still wake up early to let her out."

Onwé leaned against the front door, exhausted by sorrow.

"That's what I'm afraid of," he said. "I don't have a schedule anymore."

Voth sighed and looked out at his congregants, who were still tromping their way to the town square in the distance. He risked a quick glance into Onwé's eyes, then dropped his gaze to his feet.

"I've been thinking about what you told me at the feast," he said.

Images of Moya clutching Samuel's lifeless body flashed through Onwé's mind, blocking out the memories of idle conversation that had taken place before the massacre.

"I don't recall much from that day," Onwé replied.

"About apologies," he said. "Even if you think the other person won't accept it."

"Oh...that," Onwé said.

Voth balled his fists tightly, then opened them and examined his palms, letting go of something unseen.

"My pride kept me from approaching Karl," he said with defeat. "I should have told him I was sorry."

Onwé felt a flicker of rage at hearing Voth speak Karl's name. He hadn't forgotten the senseless act of violence, nor the racist dig about a "nice quilt," which Onwé had interpreted as a reference to smallpox-infected blankets. But all of that seemed like ancient history now, forced into the darkness of time by the recent tragedies on Pale Peak.

"It wouldn't have mattered," Onwé said in a grim voice. "He'd still be dead."

Voth grimaced.

"I set a poor example of those who labor in Christ's name," he said.

"If it makes you feel any better," Onwé said, "you're not the first."

Voth let out another deep sigh and rubbed his hands

together. He was too old to go without gloves in this weather. Onwé wondered how much longer the pastor could bear to stand there on the porch. He certainly was trying to reach out, and Onwé couldn't deny it.

"I owe you an apology as well," Voth added. "When I saw that grave disturbed, when I saw poor Daisy, I spoke some words that have been used to hurt Indians for centuries. My nightly reflections have revealed the depth of my shame to me."

Onwé looked at Voth and saw the sincerity in his weary eyes.

"Just remember going forward," Onwé said, "there's no point trying to hurt people who're already numb. That's what generations of pain does to Natives. Or else they find ways to numb it themselves, like me and Luke."

Onwé felt the shape of the savings tin under his arm. He held it tight so as not to jingle the change inside. Voth nodded at his words, perhaps approaching an awareness that respect went a great distance with the Nauktí.

"You think if I prayed, he'd hear me?" Voth asked after a long pause. "Karl, I mean."

"My people would say he's making the long journey," Onwé replied. "It takes time. We don't call out to them for a while. Then again, he was Ineho. Death for them is a bit different."

"Maybe later, then," Voth said. "It can wait."

Onwé was touched by the pastor's effort to respect the Old Way, but he couldn't let go of his hatred for the man who'd spent years opposing Ashthenôví and manipulating the tribal council. The best he could do was hold his tongue and search for common ground with a fellow dog lover.

"Bet Numi would've liked Daisy," he offered.

"I reckon," Voth replied. "Two goofballs in the snow."

"Please thank your congregation for me." Onwé wanted

228

to go inside and collapse into the armchair. The shadow had passed, and the cravings had subsided. The thought of those apple muffins now seemed more appealing than the junk.

"I'm sure they'd prefer to hear it from you," Voth said. "You're welcome at the church, you know. Not just to work on the grounds, I mean."

Voth gave Onwé the lightest of taps on the arm and stepped off the porch.

"Maybe," Onwé said under his breath, watching the old man disappear into a wall of icy fog.

A sinister breeze began to kick up, and the buildings in the distance vanished, one by one, until the world shrank down to the size of Onwé's house.

Back inside, Onwé put the painting of Numi in a closet, knowing he wasn't ready to look at it. He placed the savings tin up on the highest shelf in the kitchen and gave it an extra nudge to ensure it was out of reach. Then he stuffed one of the muffins into his mouth and looked out the window. The outhouse was barely visible in the flurry, and the woods behind it were entirely conquered by darkness.

But then Onwé noticed something else: fresh dirt scattered atop the snow. He set the muffin and kettle down and approached the window near the fireplace—the one Numi had stared out fearfully on the night she'd fallen ill. Onwé gasped and ran to the back door, throwing it open so hard it crashed into the wall.

"*Numi.*"

The grave Onwé had spent hours digging was now a hole once more. Dirt lay scattered over a wide area between the back of the house and the woods.

Numi's remains were gone.

229

Onwé whirled around, frantically searching for an explanation, and found a set of tracks in the snow. He followed them as they meandered senselessly between the trees and the outhouse and the grave and the kitchen window, over and over, as if someone on drugs had cased the yard. But on closer inspection, the steps were too wide, and the feet were too big. It couldn't have been a person. He tried to convince himself a bear had dug up the dog and run off with it, but he knew deep down that probably wasn't true.

Numi's death had shattered Onwé's heart into a thousand pieces, and now the sight of her defiled grave set those pieces on fire. A dangerous mix of agony and rage overcame him, and he thought about grabbing his rifle and heading off into the woods. Luke's words outside the church returned to humiliate him:

What if that was Numi? How would you feel?

A wave of guilt washed over Onwé as he remembered gleefully watching Voth sob over Daisy's grave.

Shame on you.

Onwé walked to the edge of the woods and peered into the foggy abyss. Luke's voice echoed in his memory:

The Black Wall could use a guard.

A voice seeped through the forest, as if responding to the one in Onwé's head.

"I'll go with you," it croaked, brittle and freighted with sadness. "Please don't leave me. Don't leave me here again."

Onwé strained to listen and squinted into the gloom. The icy fog stung his eyes, and the whispering wind played tricks on his ears—but he was certain he recognized the voice.

"Wait for me," it pleaded.

It was a woman.

"Where are you? I don't know the way..."

"Moya?" Onwé blurted out.

He caught himself a few steps into the tree line,

wondering if he was being lured by the same creature that had called out to him on the road back from Mudhole. Moya was too frail to be wandering around in the snow at night. It *couldn't* be her.

"I've waited so long," she said, bursting into tears. "Nine thousand lonely nights. No more. Please, no more."

The pain in her voice was unmistakable. Onwé remembered it from the night the tribal police had called off the search for Akántha and, more recently, when Samuel Cotter died.

"Moya!" he shouted.

Onwé dashed into the trees, barely able to make out the shapes before him in the faint light glinting off the snow. He called to Moya over and over, following her voice as it grew more desperate. Finally, he beheld a petite figure lurching across the wintry landscape. She clutched herself and shivered, her head hanging low near her shoulders as if she'd been drugged.

"Moya, what are you doing!" Onwé cried out. He ran over and threw his arms around the woman to prevent her from pressing deeper into the forest.

She yelped with surprise and looked frantically in every direction.

"Where am I?" she asked, panting. "Is that you, *Ha'an'tué?*"

"No, Moya," he replied. "It's just me... It's Onwé."

"Where is he?" she asked, nearly collapsing in his arms.

Onwé examined Moya and saw she wore only a heavy nightgown and slippers. He realized all at once what had happened: she was sleepwalking. She'd been lured outside.

"He was just here," she said, sobbing once more. "I saw him... I saw my son."

A large figure stepped out from behind a tree. Onwé and Moya froze, watching it rise from the height of a boy to that of a tall man. Although veiled in shadow, Onwé could see the figure studying them back for a moment—and then it teetered and fell into the snow, catching itself at the last moment on its limbs and rushing away into the dark. It howled in the distance, the pitch wavering from guttural depths to soaring whines. Then, a wet cackle flooded the woods.

Moya clutched Onwé in terror. Both of them remained rooted to the ground, trying to comprehend what they'd seen.

But then, the creature returned.

It rushed toward them from out of the darkness and loped in a wide circle around the pair, keeping just behind the nearest trees and snarling hideously. It skittered like a giant spider, transferring its weight fluidly from one indiscernible limb to another. As it moved, its ghoulish head bobbed around on a crooked neck, studying everything—or nothing at all—as the trees and snow rushed past.

"*At'an-A'anotogkua,*" Moya gasped, clawing at Onwé's jacket like a frightened animal.

Impostor.

"*One...of the laaaaambs...*" the creature groaned, tapping on tree trunks and clawing at logs as it moved. It slid to a stop and froze in place for a few seconds, bewitched by something up in the featureless canopy.

The clouds shifted above, and a ray of moonlight filtered through. The beam fell upon the creature, illuminating its putrid face for the briefest of moments. The thing peered up into the glow with lidless, screaming eyes, as if witness to something even more ghastly than itself.

"*Have you ssssseeeen him?*" it hissed.

Then, it rose up once more and ran off into the gloom on two legs, laughing as it went.

"*At'an-A'anotogkua,*" Moya said again, shaking violently. "*At'an-A'anotogkua.*"

232

Chapter 36

"I thought I believed in the elder spirits of the mountains," Moya said, clutching the sage pouch around her neck. "That's how I was raised. My grandmother's grandmother knew all about them up north. But seeing one now... It makes you wonder if your faith is just a story you take for granted."

Onwé emerged from the little kitchen and handed Moya a steaming mug of tea. The stubborn woman had refused to go to the medical center to be checked out by Dr. Farmer, insisting she just needed to warm up at home. Onwé convinced her to come to his house, where he felt better-equipped to protect her. Moya now rested in the old armchair by the fire, still trembling from the horror of their encounter with the thing in the forest. She tightened the heavy blanket around her body and shook her head in revulsion.

"It knew my son," she went on. "Knew his voice. Knew he was a little boy. I wonder if he spoke to it all those years ago."

Her unblinking eyes never moved while she talked; they remained fixed on the window facing the woods.

"What did it say to you?" Onwé asked.

Moya inhaled sharply and held her breath.

"Tell me," Onwé prodded.

She shook her head.

"That thing's been following me around," he said, dragging a chair from the nearby table and sitting beside her. "I think it waits out there at night."

"I've seen it in my nightmares," said Moya. "I've felt it watching me while I sleep. It wants me to follow it."

"I know," Onwé said, remembering Nora's words in the tunnel. The crazed woman had demanded he bring Moya and baby Stefan into the caves.

"I dreamed Akántha was leading me somewhere," Moya said. "Something about a church, I think. It felt just like him, Onwé. I wasn't afraid until you woke me up."

"What did he tell you about this church?"

Moya sighed and looked at Onwé with guilty eyes.

"He told me your father was there, waiting to pray with me for our people."

Onwé's heart went berserk in his chest. Could this creature have been responsible for Ashthenôví's death? If it was clever enough to fool the smartest man on the rez, surely his unremarkable son didn't stand a chance.

"I have a confession to make," Moya said, putting her hands on his. They hadn't warmed at all in two hours. Her touch was cold as death.

"What is it, *Néthédi?*"

Moya gazed around the room, examining every permutation of whatever she needed to admit. She sighed again, probably realizing some truths cannot be blunted.

"Loneliness can make a fool of anyone," she said, her expression betraying a deep shame. "Times were hard back then. You were just a baby. I was so desperate to escape, and Ash was my only friend."

Onwé studied Moya quietly. He waited for her confession,

not realizing he'd already heard it. Moya watched stiffly, allowing him to piece the truth together.

"You mean..." He studied her back.

"Ash was a good man," she said in a reassuring voice. "He loved your mother with all his heart. That was clear to me."

"Oh my God," Onwé said. It felt so plainly obvious, he wondered how he'd never realized it before.

Moya wiped a tear as it dripped down her weathered face.

"Akántha was your brother."

A million thoughts rushed through Onwé. Feelings of anger and confusion swirled inside him, compelling him to get up and pace around the tiny living room. He'd grown up an only child, and all that time, his sibling had lived just down the road.

"I never told a soul, Onwé," Moya continued. "Not in thirty-six years. Everyone just assumed my boyfriend knocked me up before he overdosed."

Moya stood with great effort and intercepted Onwé. She held his arm and stilled him, and they both looked out the window into the night.

"Somehow, this creature knew anyway," she said. "I don't know how it learned the secret."

"Why didn't you tell me before?" he asked, trying to keep the anger out of his voice. Onwé wondered if he'd have treated Akántha any differently when he was alive if he'd known. Maybe he'd have been more protective of his little brother.

"I didn't want you to be upset with your father," Moya said, pulling Onwé back to his seat beside the armchair. "I didn't want to be a homewrecker. If it makes any difference, I never told Akántha either. I thought the secret would die with me."

"It almost did," Onwé snapped. "What if you're wrong about this *Impostor?* What if it intended to hurt you? If I hadn't shown up when I did..."

"Maybe," she said, unconvinced. "When I was young,

235

some Ineho girls told me a story about a being called the Night Shepherd. They said it looks for special people and feasts on their nightmares. It coaxes them out of their beds and takes them away to the woods. I always figured it was just a story to frighten kids."

"How does it choose its prey?" Onwé asked.

"Hell if I know," Moya replied. "That story doesn't really belong to the Ineho. It's a borrowed legend. The Impostor, the Hollow One, the Night Shepherd—this creature doesn't come out of the tradition of any tribes in Cold Valley. But my grandmother respected the earth spirits, even if they were foreign to our people."

"Old N'wenthāil taught me the same," Onwé admitted. "She once told me about a spirit of the woods that called out to people in familiar voices. Do you think Akántha…"

He didn't need to finish his sentence.

"I've spent all these years wondering just that," she replied. "Sometimes, it was a bear. Sometimes, it was a rockslide. And sometimes…the forest just swallowed him up. If this Impostor is real, then so are any number of bad spirits known to our people. I guess the truth wouldn't bring him back anyway."

Onwé nodded. He couldn't imagine the agony of losing Tíwé to the mountain, nor the torment of wondering for decades how it had happened. The night of Akántha's disappearance rushed into his mind, bringing a flood of old memories Onwé had tried for years to forget.

"I've been afraid to bring this up with you," he said, "but Luke told me that Akántha once tried to get him to look for a house in the woods. Apparently, he'd seen it in a dream."

Moya nodded slowly, recalling the terrible night.

"Yes," she said, "the search team scoured that area for days. They found nothing."

"Well," Onwé said, "that's where the first plane went

down. We took those BIA guys to look for it, and that's when Luke started acting strange."

"Dreadful," Moya replied.

"Something weird happened to all of us that night at camp," Onwé continued. "Some of us got sick. Luke went missing. We found him sitting in front of a cave."

Moya's breath quickened, and she wrung her hands in her lap.

"A few days later," Onwé continued, "he admitted what had happened that night. He told me a voice led him to a house. He found a tunnel beneath it, and followed the voice into the mountain. When he realized who was speaking to him, he ran like hell."

"My son?" Moya asked.

Onwé nodded.

"He instructed Luke to bring you down into the mountain. Something out there is pretending to be Akántha, and it wants to take you somewhere. It's been trying to coax me out too."

Moya froze in the armchair, seized by the horrible images her mind must have painted to Onwé's words. Her lips barely moved when she spoke.

"At *Yōktha,* Luke said something about going down in the hole. He said Akántha waits for me there."

"Néthédi, " Onwé said, rubbing her arm, "did Akántha say anything unusual before he disappeared?"

Moya's eyes softened as she waded into the old memories of her boy. In her best times, she seemed to live in the moment, unburdened by the ghosts in her head. At her worst, those memories carried her deep into the past, leaving only a husk in the present. Onwé watched her drift away into the dark place, and was reminded that his addiction did the same thing to him.

"He was out playing with Líkōté one day," she mumbled. "That night, he got sick and talked in his sleep. I woke up and saw him standing by the window. He was looking at something outside. He told me someone was waiting for him out there. I thought it was just a fever dream, so we prayed together, and then he fell asleep. Two days later, he was gone."

Onwé looked over at the place on the floor where Numi used to sleep.

"The other night, when Numi got sick," he said, "she kept staring out the windows too. It was like there was somewhere she knew she had to be, but she was afraid to—"

Onwé's words piled up in his mouth as he turned to face Moya.

A figure loomed just behind her, peering in from the window beside the front door. It was tall and masculine, with broad shoulders and muscular arms. Upon noticing it had captured Onwé's attention, the figure leaned closer to the glass, and the firelight illuminated a face tightened into a frantic smile.

Luke.

"Holy shit," Onwé blurted out, "it's *him!*"

Moya hadn't even looked over her shoulder before Onwé was halfway up the stairs to the bedroom. He snatched the rifle from its place beside the bed and thundered back downstairs.

"Who?" Moya said, looking over her shoulder.

"Luke!" he yelled.

The figure had vanished, but when Onwé threw the front door open, he saw fresh prints in the snow leading off the porch. He threw on his jacket, barely able to jam his flailing arms through it, and stuffed his feet into his old boots. Then he grabbed a handful of rifle rounds from the table.

"Stay here and lock yourself in," he growled. "I'm gonna kill this son of a bitch."

Chapter 37

Luke moved with inhuman speed. By the time Onwé had stumbled out into the night, the man was gone, but the direction he'd fled in was clear. The tracks headed to the end of the road, past the houses, where Old Cemetery Hill rose up against the mountain on the west side of town.

Onwé trudged through a foot of snow. Blistering cold assailed him as the powder crunched into the openings of his untied boots. He didn't care; the rest of him burned with the fires of rage. It blazed down his arms, into his fingers, urging him to put a round straight through his best friend's skull. He marched up the little hill toward the old cemetery, which lay in disrepair after having filled up decades ago. The new one stood closer to the church, and Onwé fantasized it would soon be home to another grave.

At the crest of the hill, beneath a spray of stars, was Luke—bewitched by the pale moon and stiff as a frozen corpse. He kept perfectly still as Onwé approached, bowing his head and holding an eerie vigil over the town below.

"Turn around, you son of a bitch," Onwé snarled. He kept the rifle trained on Luke, but the closer he got, the less confident he felt about pulling the trigger. His hands shook so hard the barrel danced around its target.

Luke didn't respond. He remained motionless, even breathless, and continued his silent meditation. He still wore a hospital gown, but now it was shredded and covered in unspeakable stains.

Impossible, Onwé thought. He knew no one could survive this cold without winter gear.

"I said face me!" he shouted. "Look at me, Luke."

Again, Luke ignored the command. He clasped his hands together in prayer and slowly raised the gesture over his head, pointing it at the night sky. A strange red star blazed there.

"*Likōté!*" Onwé screamed. His voice echoed over the valley and returned a few times.

"Ah, yes," Luke said, dropping his arms to his sides. "I remember the old names." He finally whipped around, revealing the smile still plastered on his waxen face. "But I've abandoned them, and the false gods they honor."

"How could you do this!" Onwé said. "How could you do something so heinous? Your friends... Your family! You've broken us all. You've ruined *everything!*"

The flood of emotion blurred Onwé's sight, but he could vaguely perceive the two bullet wounds on Luke's torso through a large tear in the gown. The skin had rotted there, leaving hardened knobs of flesh that looked like putrefied roses.

"Walk with me, brother," Luke said, taking a few steps forward. "I'll explain everything."

"Don't you fucking move," Onwé commanded, steadying the rifle. He doubted it could hurt Luke any more than Steve Winépo's gun had, but in his fear he didn't know what else to do.

Luke halted in his tracks and issued a sinister laugh. His eyes glimmered faintly with eldritch light. They moved over Onwé's body, penetrating to his frightened core.

"You look terrible," Luke crooned in a sympathetic voice, but the wolfish grin never left his face. He spoke in a manner too formal for him, as if he now possessed an unholy intellect. "Riven heart, rent soul. I see you now, wandering in the dark of your misery. Join us in the underlight, brother! Down there, it's brighter than you think. We see by the glow of the pale angels."

Snow crunched somewhere nearby. Onwé risked a glance over his shoulder and beheld a huge form lurking back and forth behind the nearest trees. The creature had returned.

"What the fuck is that thing, Líkōté?" he whispered.

Luke's expression softened. He stared at the lumbering shadow.

"Another pilgrim in the night," he said in a low voice.

The creature growled in response, filling the air with guttural chanting.

"Wachu...wachu...wole my...wole my..."

"It went after Moya," said Onwé. "What does it want with her?"

"Same thing I want," Luke replied. He took another step forward, causing Onwé to brace the rifle once more. "To save you both. To reunite you with all the ones we've lost."

"All the ones you've murdered," Onwé snapped.

"Alllll the waaaans...youuuf...mm-muuurted..." the thing in the woods croaked.

"The son of Ashthenôví lives," Luke said. A rapturous smile spread across his face. "He *lives,* brother."

Onwé remembered the statement. Luke had said it before, while cutting down his neighbors at *Yōktha.* At that time, Onwé had thought Luke was talking about him, but after hearing Moya's confession tonight, he knew it referred to someone else.

"You've seen Akántha, haven't you?" Onwé said.

Luke closed his eyes and nodded, like a worshiper

receiving the Gospel.

"I have," he crooned. "I saw him adorned in radiant white robes. The pale angels gave him a crown of stars."

"Where is he, Líkōté?" Onwé asked, lost in the fantastical nonsense of Luke's words. "Do you know what happened to him?"

"I wondered all my life," Luke said, "and now my prayers are finally answered. My heart is whole again. Akántha joined the deathless congregation. He sings at the head of the choir. I've visited him, brother. Heard his sweet voice. I've seen the kingdoms in his eyes—*numberless* kingdoms beneath the earth."

"The what?" Onwé took a step back. The icy pain in his feet had begun to climb up his legs. "Where is this place?"

"Here," Luke said, his eyes aflame with the knowledge of forgotten mysteries. He held his palms out over the ground. "It's *here*. You should see it, brother. More beautiful than all the cathedrals of old Europe."

"You've never been to Europe," Onwé said, backing up another step. "I'm pretty sure you've never even left the rez in your life."

"I've traveled farther than you can imagine," Luke replied, gazing through Onwé to some place beyond the world. "I've walked the hidden road. Descended the endless stair. I've crossed beyond the Black Wall... And I've brought something back for you."

Luke reached into the rip in his hospital gown and exposed a festering wound in his side. From it, he tore a small, black object.

"You should try wearing this." He extended his hand. On it lay a jagged stone that glinted in the moonlight.

A wave of nausea hit Onwé the second he laid eyes on the shard. It looked just like the object Nora had used to cut herself, like the stone protruding from the head of the corpse he and

Warren had found in the nameless place.

"What the hell is that?" Onwé said. Though it made him feel sick, he couldn't tear his eyes away from it.

"A gift," Luke said, "from the Bishop."

"Voth isn't a bishop," Onwé muttered, spellbound by the faint lights he'd begun to perceive in the shard. He took a step toward Luke, suddenly unafraid of his friend's ghoulish appearance.

"*Voth,*" Luke spat, as if uttering an ancient curse. "The false prophet. His time will come. He'll go up in the trees."

"Or down in the hole," Onwé added vacantly, his mind now flooding with a myriad of visions. He saw unfamiliar landscapes and strange constellations, all of them falling away into the mouth of a large cave.

"*Down...in...the hoooole,*" the creature growled nearby.

"No, brother," Luke said, holding the shard even closer to Onwé. "Only the Elect go down there. All the way down to the Black Wall."

Onwé's visions turned wicked. He heard the roar of engines and the screams of terrified passengers. Numi staggered through his mind, wobbling on her hind legs and moaning quasi-human speech. The wound on her haunch bled profusely, and Onwé wondered if she'd been cut with a black shard like the one Luke now offered. The nausea overpowered the shard's allure, and Onwé fell to his knees and vomited in the snow.

"Get that thing away from me," he sputtered.

"I'll hold onto it for you," Luke replied, jamming the shard into his own neck. He didn't wince at the pain, and his eyes never left their deathless trance, not even to blink. "When you're ready, the Night Shepherd will bring you to us. Moya too. We'll all be with Akántha again."

Luke lunged at Onwé and pulled him to his feet with terrifying strength. Onwé realized that if he wanted to, Luke could drag him into the tunnels with ease.

"You stay away from Moya," Onwé said, finding his courage, "or God as my witness, I'll blow your fuckin' head off." He tried to lift the rifle once more, but Luke snatched it from his hands and snapped it in half like a desiccated tree branch.

"Men cannot reconcile with the power of the elder spirits," Luke said, tossing the pieces of the rifle away. "You will have Akántha—and the Bishop will have you. The great door is open to us, brother. Tell our people. Tell the congregation. Find me at the Black Wall...*and bring Moya.*"

A spiritual anguish fell over Onwé as he stared up at Luke's face. He'd known this man all his life. He remembered the brave and precocious boy called *Líkōté*, and the man named Luke he'd grown up to be. He remembered their friendship through loss, through addiction, and through conversion. All at once, he remembered the bad times and the good, the winters and the springs, the dreadful passage of time and all the changes it had foisted upon their lives. But now, as Onwé looked into the eyes of his lifelong friend, he detected nothing like a human soul behind them.

Luke stood before him, but he was no longer a person. Was this the ultimate fate of the people of Autumn Ridge? Had the spirits condemned them to haunt the woods and lonely caverns of Pale Peak?

"What have they done to you, Líkōté?" Onwé asked in a defeated voice. "Who are you?"

Luke's hands came together in another gesture of prayer, and he gazed up at the red star.

"I am washed in the river of darkness," he said, "born again in the fathomless deep. A witness to the wonders to come—from beyond the Black Wall."

"What's behind the Black Wall, Líkōté?" Onwé asked.

Weeks ago, Luke had responded to this question with

fearful ignorance, but now he wore a zealous expression on his face.

"The Bishop of the Mountain," he proclaimed, "in His Church Beneath the Roots."

The thing in the forest wailed hideously, and the crunch of twigs and snow announced its approach. Onwé turned around to see the hulking form step out into the clearing. Luke's cold hands fell onto Onwé's shoulders from behind, holding him stiffly in place as the creature bounded toward them.

"The Night Shepherd," Luke whispered. "It searches for those who possess something the Bishop wants. It takes them, dead or alive. Out there in the nameless place, it looked inside of you and found something. So it followed you home."

"Followed you home," the creature said in Onwé's own voice.

"You are one of the Elect, my brother," Luke continued. "The Bishop prefers you come willingly...and that you bring the others with you."

Luke released Onwé from his clutches and shoved him toward the creature, who was now only a few dozen yards away. It twitched and groaned and wheezed as it came at him, hungering for something unfathomable.

Onwé didn't hesitate. The moment he regained his balance, he took off like one of the sheep at Mudhole. In response, a score of ghastly voices rose in the forest, injecting fresh terror into Onwé's muscles. He barrelled down Old Cemetery Hill and practically flew through the snow, losing a boot in the process and grating his foot on icy pebbles. He ran as if Luke and the monster were upon him, and imagined each second he'd feel those hands on his shoulders again, dragging him backward into the tunnels.

But the moment never came.

Onwé burst into his home, nearly giving Moya a heart attack in her seat. He looked at her, breathless, wordless, unable to correlate the things he'd seen and heard into

245

anything like a sensible train of thought. The monster's words flooded his mind, repeating themselves over and over:

Followed you home... Followed you home...

And while he looked down at Moya, trying desperately to speak, Onwé realized why Luke had held such a long conversation with him.

He was helping the monster learn Onwé's voice.

Part IV:
DOORS

Chapter 38

Onwé shifted restlessly in the armchair. He'd fallen asleep there a thousand times before, but tonight, he could not slow his racing mind. The silence, no longer broken by the snores of a dog, amplified the nervous thumping of Onwé's heart against his chest. Moya slept in the upstairs bedroom, exhausted by the hard talk they'd had earlier, and by the creeping terror of knowing Luke was still lurking somewhere outside.

Onwé didn't bother to report the encounter. He knew the feds would never believe a story so ridiculous and full of "Indian magic." It was no longer a mystery how Luke had evaded the BIA search teams; he'd likely vanished into the tunnels any time he heard agents approach.

Hours passed. Onwé gripped his hiking staff, waiting to bludgeon anyone who tried to enter the house. He stared out the nearby window, trying to remember the appearance of the Impostor. It was a strange thing, as curious as it was frightening, a hulking giant of a man that could move like any number of animals in the forest. Its locomotion was sometimes human, other times feline or even arachnoid. Its voice—that *repulsive* voice—seemed to change with the wind.

He wondered about its nature, and remembered something Moya had told him earlier: *I've seen it in my nightmares. I've felt it watching me while I sleep.*

The creature seemed to loom near houses at night. What if it could see into a person's dreams, and even influence them? Onwé, Luke, and Moya had all recently dreamed of Akántha and of other unspeakable things. What if the monster could sift through their sleeping minds, churning their dreams into nightmares to extract information?

The dreadful thoughts eventually began to weigh down Onwé's eyelids as heavily as they did his mind, and he sank into a fitful sleep. He floated there for hours, sweating coldly under a thick blanket, drifting farther and farther away.

Onwé cracked open his eyes and found himself blinded by the morning sun, whose milky light flooded into the house from every window. It was cold, but not bitterly so, and a chorus of birds sang jubilantly outside.

Onwé hoisted himself up from the old chair and noticed he felt unusually refreshed. He heard no sounds from upstairs and reasoned Moya was still asleep, so he went to the back door to let Numi out to pee.

"Gorgeous day," he said to himself, taken aback by the radiance of the blue sky above the woods. It felt like he'd slept through winter entirely and had awoken just in time for spring. When he pulled open the door, a gust of cold air rushed over him, invigorating his spirit and filling him with a hopefulness he thought he'd lost.

Numi didn't dash between his legs as she normally did every morning. Onwé looked over and saw her empty bed. In the same moment, he heard her cheerful yipping outside. Out back, the dog frantically circled a big tree, begging a pair of squirrels to come down just a little closer.

Onwé felt possessed by the desire to spend the day outdoors. He layered on his clothes, laced up his boots, and grabbed the old hiking staff, which had toppled to the floor while he'd slept. The birdsongs wafting in the air grew louder, conveying such exultation that Onwé felt almost physically pulled by them into the yard. There, he called to Numi, but she continued her pursuit of the acrobatic squirrels as they vaulted across the trees. For the first time in a while, Onwé found himself laughing, and happily followed the dog farther into the woods.

He felt strangely unburdened. No worries about money plagued him while he pushed through mounds of snow; no anger toward the church heated his blood. His attention gathered on the feeling of reverence that imbued him as he took in the wintery landscape. Pines creaked and swayed in the breeze, and sunlight gleamed in every icicle and clump of snow. It didn't bother Onwé how misshapen the squirrels looked from below, nor how unusually tall the trees seemed as he pressed deeper into their embrace.

Numi barked up ahead, but always kept far enough away that Onwé couldn't lay eyes on her squarely. She seemed to lead him in a westerly direction, probably sniffing out a new path to Ash Hill. Today, Onwé didn't really care where the trails took him. His only thought was to follow his feet. Once in a while, he became aware that the lovely birdsongs were unfamiliar to him—but each time his focus came to a point, their volume swelled, and his body thrummed with the ecstasy felt only by lovers of music.

He moved effortlessly up the slopes, never stopping or feeling tired, meandering with the dog beneath the snowy canopy in a state of remarkable bliss. But the further he wandered, the colder he became, until at some points he had conscious thoughts about it—but the dog or the birds or the wind always drew his attention back to the painterly landscape.

Thoughts of Moya began to flicker in Onwé's mind. Flashes of her standing in the dark appeared in the most distant part of his memory. He began to wonder where exactly he was and how he'd come to be here, unable to recall how long he'd been walking or where he'd been before. Numi persisted in her cheerful yipping, nagging her master to follow her just a bit deeper into the forest.

When Onwé arrived in a little clearing, he was struck with the uncanny sense he'd been there before, and it was not a comforting feeling. The wind kicked up a bit, stirring the sleepy trees ahead and bristling a million needles all around him. His skin ached from the cold, and he worried the weather might turn. He noticed something dangling from a tree branch up ahead but could not seem to focus his sight upon it.

Suddenly, the image of a frightened boy appeared in Onwé's mind. The child stood there in the snow, pointing at the swaying object, or perhaps at the dark space behind the trees.

Akántha.

The pieces fell together.

Onwé had found the place from his recurring dream.

The various birdsongs abruptly flowed into each other, layering their melodies like the sections of an orchestra. But the effect of the music had worn off, and an unsettling feeling swept over Onwé as he stared at the swinging object. The brilliant light of day began to fade.

Out of the corner of his eye, he caught sight of the dog loping into the darkening woods on contorted limbs.

"...Numi?" Onwé whispered, spellbound by the thing in the tree.

He moved through the clearing slowly, rubbing the blur from his tired eyes. He saw a gnarled circle of twigs and branches encrusted with ice and glinting in a beam of pale light. A shimmering metal trinket had been woven into its center, and something big—perhaps a stone—was suspended just below it. As he approached, gloom devoured the trees around him until hardly anything existed but the weird object just ahead.

Onwé's vision gathered, and his senses soon followed.

He'd been sleepwalking in the dead of night.

There in the middle of the field, he gazed up at the sky and saw the moon in its lonely place over the mountain. Beyond it gleamed a ribbon of stars arranged into the nameless constellations he'd seen in Luke's black shard. One star blazed a deep red, and by its light and the others, Onwé was reminded of a silver crown encrusted with a large ruby. He remembered this star glimmering above Old Cemetery Hill, and wondered if it had been summoned from beyond by Luke's wicked prayers.

The cold of winter's midnight stung him now. Icy wind lashed at the nearby trees, ripping Onwé's attention back to the strange object. When he came within reach of it, fear rippled up his body in freezing waves.

Savage idols.

It was a dreamcatcher, not unlike the one fashioned by Karl Ortega to torment Voth. But Karl was dead, and this idol was hidden far too deep in the mountain's backcountry to conceivably be a practical joke. The object had been woven with black hair and strips of sinew, adorned with feathers, and smeared with gore. A leather necklace clung to the center of its web, the pendant slung upon it immediately recognizable.

Luke's cross.

Onwé hadn't seen it since he'd thrown it at Luke inside the church. He studied the cross for a moment, ruing the fight they'd had that day, but then his eyes were drawn to the large shape just beneath it:

A skull.

Unlike the one Karl had affixed to his dreamcatcher, this skull was fresh. It glimmered in the moonlight as if slightly wet, and its bold white color indicated the animal had been healthy when it died.

Onwé tapped it with his hiking staff. His heart froze in his chest. He realized the skull belonged to a dog. Extra rows of teeth protruded unnaturally from the jaw.

Images of Numi's desecrated grave came flooding in, and the truth of her passing roared back in a wave of despair. Onwé finally remembered he'd been at home with Moya.

And just like her, he must have sleepwalked into the night.

Numi—or the thing that *looked* like her—yowled from the woods behind him. The sound rose and fell like the birdsongs from earlier, but the voice was desiccated and off-key. It wavered between grumbles and yips and attempts at human speech.

Onwé whirled around to see a shadowy form appear between the trees. It lumbered on all fours, then rose and staggered toward him on two legs.

"Mommmma?" it called. *"Mommommommy? Mommomma?"*

The voice shifted rapidly between textures, accents, and pitches, and finally settled on the timbre of a young woman.

"Momomomomomumum… Moymoy… Mooooyaaa? Moya?"

The figure stepped into the field, where the moon revealed hints of its features. Onwé's knees locked. He could only stand and watch the ghastly stalker of the tunnels approach him while mumbling its curses.

As it drew near, the creature towered over Onwé, dwarfing him by nearly two feet. Tattered rags clung to its massive torso, its broad shoulders blocking the view of the woods from which it had emerged. The pale light now illuminated a gruesome but familiar face.

Hannah Miller.

"Oh, God," Onwé muttered, bursting into tears at the idea that Chris's daughter was dead.

The girl's youthful features were unmistakable—even when stretched hideously over a head far too big. The eyes, once delicate, now bulged with the terror of death. The lips were stretched bloody over a maw of dagger-like teeth. A dark-purple worm of a tongue flicked in and out of the mouth with the creature's ragged wheezing, but no *numi* swirled in the icy fog. Its long arms bore the complexion of a Naukti girl, but the skin had frayed to gory tatters over the unnatural muscles beneath it. Hannah's body had been turned into a sort of costume.

"Ha'an'tué," it rasped. *"Is...that...youuu?"*

It extended a gnarled hand to Onwé and held deathly still, animated by some force beyond biological life that made its movements almost mechanical.

Onwé stumbled backward and felt the icy touch of the dreamcatcher upon his neck. He yelped in surprise and dropped the hiking staff in the snow, flailing his arms over his head to disentangle himself from the disgusting web.

"I crossssed...the chasm of eternity...for youuu, Onwé..." the creature growled in many voices.

Onwé turned and ran for his life, pulling the object from the tree in the process. Numi's skull, fastened to the catcher by a rope of hair, battered his shoulder as he sprinted toward the tree line. He screamed and tried to pull the gore-slathered pieces from his body, tearing at wood and string and sinew. In the process, his hand met with Luke's cross, and he instinctively yanked it free.

"Oh God, help me," he begged. "Lord Jesus, help me!"

"Beee baaack-k-k...before daaaark-k-k-k..." the creature called out.

In the distance behind him, Onwé could hear his father's old hiking staff being snapped to pieces.

Chapter 39

As Onwé trampled his way through a curtain of thick pines, his dream returned to him once more: Akántha tugged at his arm with one hand and gestured at the cruel idol. Behind it was a belt of trees obscuring a large, dark shape.

Now, that shape took substance before his eyes.

Onwé perceived a strange, tall house at the center of a moonlit field. It looked like a beacon in the harsh landscape, its edifice covered in warmly glowing windows that poured firelight over the snow around it. An old cobblestone wall wrapped around the building in ruined segments, ending at a group of weird statues, each as big as the Impostor itself.

Óknóth-ûden, Onwé recalled in Luke's voice.

The Briar House.

He had come to the great ridge above Ash Hill, where he'd emerged from the tunnels with an injured Numi. But on that day, no house had been here—only a hole in the earth. He remembered Luke saying the house appeared to have risen out of the ground. Onwé could see a crust of fresh soil upon its roof, black like that of the recently churned dirt over Numi's grave.

Before Onwé could conjure an explanation for this

mystery, he heard the crackle of tree branches behind him.

"Wachu...wachu...wole my...wole my..." the Impostor growled. It burst forth from the woods, barreling toward him at tremendous speed with a frightfully crooked gait.

The primal fear of death struck through Onwé's body like a bolt of lightning. He took off toward the house, plowing through drifts of snow and leaping over the jagged rocks that dotted the field. His pursuer followed, cackling gutturally at the challenge of a motivated target. Onwé sailed over the low wall and made for the front door, nearly tripping over a thick, thorny vine as he passed. He launched his full weight at the door and turned the knob simultaneously, praying it was unlocked—and crashed to the floor inside. He slammed the door shut and threw the heavy lock, expecting the Impostor to break through it with ease.

But no attack came.

Instead, a symphony of voices erupted on the mountain, perhaps celebrating Onwé's arrival at the strange house. Outside, the creature marched in a circle around the property, sucking in huge gasps of air and howling in forgotten languages. How many centuries had it wandered the Rockies? How many time-lost tribes had it studied and feasted upon?

Onwé crept low through the room, peeking out the windows to get a better look at the monster. The house brooded over a yard choked with thorny weeds and the eerie statues they'd conquered.

Five sculptures of humanoid *things,* not so different from the Impostor, protruded from the snow. One looked like a woman crossed with a spider. Another was a man whose head was stretched into ribbed protrusions. Their elongated arms clawed at the sky for redemption, but were ensnared by greedy vines that seemed to thrive even in the deepest cold. Onwé faintly recalled statues like these from his father's books on historical architecture, and imagined they served as grotesque

258

monuments, but to what, he couldn't guess.

The creature lurked among the statues now, occasionally freezing in place and mimicking their poses, or else studying their faces with hypnotic reverence. Hannah Miller's face had vanished from the Impostor's skull, and now its features were amorphous and bloody, as if awaiting the application of new skin. As it meandered between the carven ghouls, the creature almost seemed to forget about Onwé and the Briar House. It eventually made a solemn walk back to the forest and vanished into the night.

Onwé breathed a sigh of relief and collapsed against the wall. He examined his surroundings and beheld an inviting home, lightly furnished, with a chair sitting before a hearth. A fire burned gently there, warming the air to a temperature that could seduce even a frightened man to sleep. Nearby, a short flight of stairs led up to the second level.

Onwé dragged the chair in front of the door to brace it, then warmed himself before the fire. He wished Numi were still alive and imagined holding onto her.

I'll wait until dawn, he thought, *then make a break for it back to town.*

The night was unnaturally long. Over time, Onwé began to recall its events. He remembered discovering Moya wandering in the woods at dusk, and the conversation they'd had in his living room. Onwé saw Luke's anemic face in his mind and instinctively looked to the windows to make sure the deranged man hadn't returned. He recalled chasing Luke up to Old Cemetery Hill, remembered his story of the hidden church under the mountain.

The memories were interrupted by a rhythmic tapping on the front door—the *secret knock*—performed with what

259

sounded like the tip of a claw.

Onwé's anxiety skyrocketed. He scanned the room for a weapon and found a fire poker, but when he grabbed it, he knew it wouldn't protect him. He sank into a corner and fished around in his jacket for the cross necklace he'd torn from the dreamcatcher.

"Hello?" Onwé heard his own voice call from outside.

The knocking continued, this time in the rhythm of a quickening heartbeat.

Tic tic. Tic tic. Tic tic. Ticticticticatic.

"Hello?" it repeated, this time in Luke's voice. "May I...come in? Just a pilgrim... the night...in the night, in the night."

Onwé buried his face in his arms and began to sob. The weight of the world had always pressed on him, but this monster and the horrors it had wrought in his life were unbearable. For a moment, he no longer cared if he lived or died.

"Ssssome ssson of Ashhhhthenôví *you* aaaare..." the voice hissed.

"Fuck you!" Onwé shouted.

"May I...come in?" it repeated. "Walk with me, brother. Down in the hooooole."

"I'll *never* go with you," Onwé said. "You'll have to kill me first."

The monster snarled with frustration and began coughing and hacking. By the time it finished, its voice had changed to an old woman's—a poor imitation of Moya.

"Ak-k-k-kántha...followed..." it rasped. "You could crawl forever."

"Go back to Hell!" Onwé screamed. He threw the fire poker at the door and watched it bounce harmlessly to the ground. Then he slung the necklace over his head and held the cross tightly beneath his chin. He tried to pray, but the words escaped him.

"What did you dream?" the monster said, reverting to Onwé's voice. "He's renur- reten-returned...to my dreams as well, *Néthédi.*"

The Impostor seemed to be trying to impart a message to him: *I've been watching you a long time.* He cringed at the thought of all the lonely hikes he'd taken through the wilderness of Pale Peak, and dared to wonder how many times those deathly eyes had studied him from nearby.

Tictictictictictic.

Suddenly, fragments of an old prayer came into Onwé's mind from his years in boarding school.

"Hear my prayer, O Lord," he said. "Listen to my cry for mercy! My enemies are chasing me. They made me live in darkness, like those long dead."

"What if it's *youuuu?*" the creature said in an accusing tone.

A wet cackling noise echoed through the door and filled the house. The fire flickered intensely, as if whipped by a bitter wind.

"Begone, monster," Onwé said forcefully, trying to conjure vague memories of the things he'd heard Voth shout over the years. "The Lord Jesus Christ is my armor. Even the demons believe—and shudder!"

The wicked laughter morphed into the crying of a child, and soon a young voice mumbled indecipherable things outside. Onwé continued forming prayers out of the bits of quotes he remembered from his Christian schooling, and after a while, the muttering seemed to fade away.

Onwé risked a glance out the window once more and saw the petite figure of a boy standing just beyond the cobblestone wall. At this distance its features weren't discernable, but he knew exactly who the child was meant to resemble. It raised a frigid arm and pointed up at the house, just as Akántha had in the dream.

"Lōnán!" it called. *"Lōnán!"*

Father.

Then, the figure bent over backward and scrambled off into the forest, its bones shifting and reconfiguring as it loped.

Chapter 40

Old N'wenthāil's stories were true after all. The *At'an-A'anotogkua* had returned to the mountain out of generations in myth.

Any doubt Onwé had about the creature's ability to enter his mind was swept away when it spoke the word *"Lōnán."* That word, paired with the voice and gesture, was a clear message that this monster had awareness of Onwé's nightmares. There, it had learned the voices of Onwé's dead relatives and other secrets of the grave to use against him. Had it done the same to Akántha?

And this "Bishop." Could that be who Akántha was calling to in the dream? The "father" in his church beneath the roots? Onwé wondered if Akántha wasn't trying to show him the mysterious house, but rather to warn him not to enter it.

He scooped up the fire poker and climbed the staircase to the only bedroom in the house. A candle burned within it, throwing just enough light upon the small room to make it feel like a cozy hideaway. Stacks of books covered the nightstand and filled the corners of the room, and a heavy door with a lock walled out the sound of the embers popping downstairs. Tonight, Onwé would wait out the darkness and the lurking things it gave cover to. He crawled onto the bed and, with his last ounce of strength, peeked out the window just above it.

Outside in the field, a tall man stood in knee-deep snow. He was completely nude and faced away from the house, holding unnaturally still with his arms wide and palms open. His head was tilted on a craned neck, gazing up at the moon as it hung over the western mountains. Two thick braids of black hair draped down his back, seamed with brilliant white strings, denoting the prestige of a Nauktí spirit-warrior.

"Dad?" Onwé gasped.

He knew it couldn't be, but in the moment, the sight stole his breath. Ashthenóví had been the only man in Autumn Ridge who wore his hair as if prepared for battle, and for years, it had drawn the ire of church officials and their federal cronies. In fact, it was an open secret he did it just to piss them off.

Onwé was thirteen the last time he saw his father. His heart compelled him to go outside for a closer look, but he fought the urge and remained in the bedroom, trying to convince himself it was an illusion. Ash remained as rigid as the statues in the yard, welcoming the moonlight and snowflakes that fell gently upon him.

"Lōnán'ath fén'íí mákwénd," he reassured himself: *My father is dead.*

Onwé clutched Luke's cross and mumbled prayers to his father and to Christ for help. The longer he held it, the more he felt imbued with an inner fire that could protect him from the elder spirits. He wondered if this magic truly came from the god of the Christians, or if it was just the power of his own desire for divine intervention. Maybe this was how Luke had felt after his baptism. Maybe this was why Voth's congregants seemed so hopeful in such a hopeless place.

Sleep finally came—but Onwé suffered nightmares of Numi screaming in the tunnels.

"Bad dreams?" a familiar voice asked from nearby.

"I think so," Onwé mumbled. He rubbed his eyes and saw the candle had burned out. Pale spears of moonlight thrust in through the window, revealing the room itself had inexplicably grown larger.

"You know," the voice said, "good sleep only comes to those with a clear conscience."

"Some things never wash off," Onwé replied. He sat up against the old pillows and gazed around the room. It seemed to have stretched, and more books tottered around him in higher stacks than before.

In the shadows where the moonlight couldn't reach was a pair of softly glowing eyes set into the black silhouette of a man. He was seated in a chair Onwé couldn't be sure had been there earlier.

"You can't wait this one out," the man said. "It wants you to stay here."

Onwé looked over his shoulder at the window, assuming the man referred to the creature outside. It was still there, frozen in the same place, though its head had changed direction to follow the path of the moon through the sky. The window itself was now partially covered by a massive vine whose thorns ticked and scraped against the glass as it slid.

"I know the way out," the man continued. "A hidden road back to town...and to other places."

Onwé's awareness gathered enough to recognize the voice, and a chill rippled up his body.

"Lōnán?" he said in disbelief.

"Piith'tué," the man responded: *My son.*

"How?" Onwé asked, stirring in the bed. He felt his mouth go dry with fear. "It can't be."

"You called out to me," the man said, his eyes flickering in the gloom. "I heard you across the dark."

"Why'd you leave us, Dad?" Onwé demanded, his vision blurring with tears. "Why'd you leave me so young?"

"Why do any of us leave?" he said gently. "We spend our lives searching for joy. Sometimes we find it in faraway places. Your brother showed me the way. Now let me show you."

"Is Akántha alive?" Onwé pleaded.

The figure raised from the chair and stepped into the pale light. He was a handsome, dark-complected man of athletic build who stood a few inches taller than Onwé. A thick, black braid rested on either of his shoulders, framing a face of strong Nauktí features. The man studied Onwé with a hawk-like stare, then smiled gently in approval.

Onwé's heart crumpled. This was Ashthenôví. It had to be.

He sat down on the bed, close enough that Onwé could see the youthfulness of his face. In all the years he'd been gone, Ash hadn't aged a day.

"Yes, my son," he said. "Akántha lives. But he needs you now...and his mother."

Moya's mention rattled something in Onwé's mind. He glanced around the room once more, regarding the strangeness of it with new suspicion.

"I think I should leave," Onwé said, pulling the old blanket off himself.

"You'll freeze to death out there," Ash said, nodding at the window. "Or that *thing* will find you. There's another way. Trust me, son."

Ash placed his hand on Onwé's shoulder.

The warmth of his father's touch, a feeling he'd longed

266

for all these years, made Onwé close his eyes for a just moment.

"I've missed you so much, Dad." He leaned in to hug Ash, but closed his arms around empty air.

Onwé opened his eyes and found himself in another place—darker and much colder than the bedroom. Moonlight filtered through the cracks of a door somewhere above and fell upon a flight of moldering wooden steps. He felt damp cement beneath his feet and a stone wall beside him. A dank, earthy odor invaded his nostrils, signaling to Onwé that he was underground.

The cellar, he thought.

Luke had mentioned this place. Now, Onwé tried to recall what he'd said about it. He squinted in the dark, trying to discern the details of the room. A few old bookcases stood against the walls, lined with what appeared to be jars of various sizes, some glass, others porcelain. Onwé examined them and found hair and teeth, apparently human, and some even contained scraps of putrid flesh.

Something gleamed behind one of the jars. It thrummed faintly with the color of starlight, flickering like a tiny campfire on the nearest shelf. It drew Onwé toward it, enticing him with its eerie beauty. He rubbed the sleep from his eyes and yanked on his own hair to ensure he wasn't dreaming. Then he reached behind the jar and scooped up the object.

The warmth of total relief flooded through Onwé's body, washing away every fear and anxiety he'd carried with him all his life. His eyes rolled back in his head, and his body went slack, unable to withstand what felt like an orgasm of the soul.

But soon, otherworldly voices poured into his mind. They chattered and shrieked and sang like the ones in the forest, but these came from deep within, and they filled Onwé with incomprehensible feelings and visions. He watched in wonder as a ghostly Native man descended the stairs and picked up a glittering object from the same shelf. Onwé could see it more clearly now: a black shard, identical to the one Luke had offered him on Old Cemetery Hill. The man used the shard to ritually cut his own braid off, then placed the braid in one of the jars while muttering what sounded like a prayer. Finally, he walked straight through the wall and vanished, crying as he went.

Moments later, a ghostly white woman descended the stairs and laid herself upon the floor, listening with her ear pressed against it.

"Please," she begged, "please bring her back."

She repeated the request several times. After a long pause, the woman nodded obediently, then grabbed the shard and cut her wrists. She chose a jar from the shelf and drained her blood into it. A white man, perhaps her husband, rushed down the stairs and dragged her out of the cellar, shouting the name "Jennifer" over and over.

Onwé let go of the shard and watched it clatter to the floor. He looked upon it and felt as if he were looking up into the night sky, the way he and his father used to do on Ash Hill. Its beauty ensorcelled him with frightening ease, and he guessed Luke might have come into contact with this shard in the same way.

It took every ounce of Onwé's strength to pry his gaze from the stone. When he did, he noticed a faint red light behind him. He turned toward it and saw a shape that had been invisible minutes prior—a huge door outlined with glowing, red inlays. The magical lines depicted not only the door itself, but an elaborate arch above it, adorned with runes of an old and sinister aspect.

It was the door through which the weeping man had passed.

Onwé grabbed the cross dangling around his neck, but

this time, it did nothing to allay the dread now coursing through him.

An ear-splitting howl shattered the silence. The sound came from outside, and Onwé didn't have to guess what it was. Something huge bashed against the cellar door at the top of the stairs, as if a horse had reared up and stomped upon it. The creature outside ripped at the door with all its strength, its onslaught halted only by the fire poker, which had been jammed between the handles from the inside.

The door began to splinter. It wouldn't hold long.

Onwé frantically searched the cellar for another way out, but he already knew there was only one way: *the hidden road.* He sucked in a huge breath, praying that the entity that had spoken to him in his dreams was indeed Ashthenôví and not some ghoulish pretender. Onwé shuddered at the wailing outside, and at the thought the monster was herding him into the mountain. He imagined the Briar House as a lure on the forehead of a great anglerfish and, by stepping through the red door, he would fall into its maw.

Onwé's guts writhed inside him. His mind went numb. He drifted through the glowing door like a spirit, feeling no resistance at all. On the other side, he found himself standing at the top of a flight of stone steps that vanished into the dark.

Chapter 41

Onwé had known darkness all his life: the constant power outages in Autumn Ridge, the oppressive storms, the moonless nights of winter. He'd grown up far away from the lights of big cities, and had made his home in a wilderness behind a wall of mountains. But the dark of the tunnels beneath Pale Peak was beyond comprehension. It filled the space like black liquid, concealing the details of his surroundings as it must have across numberless centuries. It soaked him up entirely, siphoning away the last remaining drops of faith and confidence he'd carried beyond the glowing door. The dark took something from him—something he wasn't sure he could ever get back.

Onwé lurched down countless stairs, keeping one hand against the wet wall beside him. He felt the muscles behind his eyes flexing erratically to focus on anything. At one point, he stepped away from the wall to determine the width of the staircase and found it was unfathomably wide. He gave up trying to find the other end.

Onwé continued ever downward, his mind projecting hints of restless *things* upon his field of vision. The steps were not only wide, but tall, too tall to be easily climbed by humans, and he dared to wonder who or what had carved them. Pale Peak was old, and the places beneath it were perhaps even older. Could this be the entrance to *Knûth-Sōkáān*, that fabled void between worlds the first tribes had spoken of?

"Yes," someone whispered from further down the stairs. "Many souls wander here, lost forever. The unguided cannot find the way. Follow my voice, son. Follow me."

"Father?" Onwé whispered, not daring to speak any louder. He remembered the terrible sounds he'd heard in the tunnels with Numi and feared attracting attention to himself.

"Don't be afraid," Ash replied, his voice echoing unnaturally. "Come to me, and we'll walk the hidden road together."

The presence of his father here in the tunnels violated everything Onwé knew about Nauktí spiritual tradition. His people believed that when a person died, their spirit journeyed so far away it could not speak into our world. When the Nauktí prayed to their departed loved ones, they hoped for signs in the weather and harvest and in the changing of fate—not for the appearances of ghosts.

"How do I know it's you?" Onwé asked.

"You'll know it in my embrace," the voice replied, "and in the faces of your family when you come to us. They wait for you."

The more the voice spoke, and the longer Onwé walked down the seemingly endless stairs, the more relaxed he became. A hypnotic peace fell upon him as it had in the bedroom of the Briar House. His father spoke to him more and more, drawing him further into the depths of the mountain, but he could not remember each phrase by the time it was finished. Eventually, Onwé consigned himself to the pleasure of the dreamlike stupor he'd sunken into.

The dank air moistened his skin, and the cold of it bit down hard, but an inner warmth kept the discomfort at bay.

After a while, Onwé felt like he was floating in a raft down a river of darkness, and above him he perceived the twinkling of faint stars. He dreamed with his eyes open of reuniting with Ash and Akántha and the others he'd lost, all of them collecting in the doorway of a sprawling cathedral hewn into a great cavern.

Whisper-filled hours drifted by. The stars around him whorled in kaleidoscopic patterns. A single red star remained fixed in place.

At long last, Onwé's feet touched flat ground, and he found no more stairs to descend. The change in direction stirred him from his reverie, and a gust of warm air melted away the visions of his family. He stumbled into a rocky wall at the bottom of the staircase. The warm air blew from his left and howled up the tunnel to his right, as if escaping far off into the open sky.

"I knew you'd come," another voice said. It whispered so gently, Onwé could scarcely hear it.

"Who's there?" Onwé said. New anxiety wrapped itself around his windpipe, and fragments of Luke's confession about his journey into the caves surfaced in Onwé's mind.

"It's been so long," the voice went on. "I never thought we'd speak again."

A word rose from the pit of Onwé's stomach like a tide of vomit. It spilled out of his mouth in a horrified whisper:

"Akántha?"

Distant singing seeped through the tunnel on a gust of hot air. Dozens of voices swelled in rhapsody, then fell away to low and eerie chanting. One by one, they wove together, folding into each other until a single voice replied:

"It's me."

The pounding of Onwé's heart against his chest reminded him of the creature bashing on the cellar door.

"Come to me, brother," it said. "It's not too much further.

I have so much to tell you of my travels."

The voice indeed belonged to a boy the same age as Tíwé, or as Akántha when he'd gone missing in 1944. But the sharpness of its enunciation and the urgency of its request seemed unusual for Akántha's personality.

"Follow my voice until you see the underlight," it said.

Onwé froze in place. Every hair on his body stood on end; every inch of his skin tingled in fright. His senses told him to run as fast as he could up the other end of the tunnel, but something deeper inside enticed him to follow the voice.

"What happened to you, Akántha?" Onwé asked, his indecision anchoring him to the ground. "What happened all those years ago?"

"I dreamed of the house and the hidden road," the voice said. "And then I found them. But some secrets can't be kept. I came back to show our father the way. Now let me show you."

"Let me show you," Ashthenôví's voice repeated.

Onwé's hypnotic state faded quickly, and with each unnatural word, he became more aware of how much danger he must be in. He began to back up through the tunnel, moving with the warm air instead of following the voices against it.

"No," Akántha beckoned. "You're so close. Come to me."

"I...I have to check on Moya," Onwé sputtered. "She'll want to know we spoke."

The chanting swelled in distant caverns once more at her mention.

"Yesssss..." it replied. "Tell her that I've heard her cries... Tell her where to find me."

More hot air blew through the tunnel, carrying the incessant chanting with it. Onwé's eyes watered from the heat, and he turned and began blindly dashing away from Akántha's voice.

"Tell them all!" it shrieked after him, deepening in pitch until the voice sounded demonic. "Tell them to find me down in the hole."

Onwé tripped over a large rock and slammed into the ground. He clambered to his feet and kept running, scraping his hands along the tunnel walls to find his way.

"Brother!" the voice bellowed, now unrecognizable. "Gather the ones who believe—*and find me at the Black Wall.*"

As he ran, the black shard gleamed in Onwé's mind. Countless emotions and memories and physical sensations shot through him until he could no longer follow a train of thought. Only the shard lingered in his vision, its inner light radiating from countless stars.

After an unknown period of time, Onwé exploded from the tunnels into the icy woods. He toppled into a mound of fresh snow and lay there, catching his breath. The light of early morning glinted off the trees around him, and when he sat up, he beheld the cave where his father's body had been recovered in 1945. Hellish voices poured out of it, chanting words that sounded guttural and ancient:

"Geptré! Gorleth! Aurokkné! Magroloth! Ûrdn!"

Onwé couldn't fathom their meaning, and had no desire to. Instead, he mustered what little strength remained in his body and limped into town, freezing, dehydrated, and sick. All the while he fought to clear his mind of the black shard, which turned ceaselessly behind his eyes. The stone had opened a door into the mountain, and Onwé worried it had also opened a door into himself, through which monstrous things could pass.

Chapter 42

The days following Onwé's journey through the tunnels melted together. Upon his return to Autumn Ridge, he'd found a panicked Moya waiting in his house, and learned he'd somehow been missing for two nights. She had informed the tribal council of Luke's reappearance, but the federal agents had refused to form another search party, owing to the worsening conditions on the mountain.

Onwé avoided questions concerning his whereabouts. Instead, he asked John Tall Rock to look after Moya for a few days, saying only that she wasn't safe in her home. John obliged, seeing the anguish in his eyes, and offered an old Nauktí prayer of strength.

"I'll tell you what happened," Onwé promised to both elders as they left his home. "I just need some time."

Something had changed inside him. A part of Onwé had not yet escaped the tunnels, and his mind still wandered their endless depths. Awful memories lingered with him: the smell of clay and caverns, the sound of his feet upon the stairs, the tormenting visions...and that singing. That damned, infernal singing.

As the hours slithered past, Onwé felt the black shard in

his hand where there was none, and felt its malady burrowing into his core. He worried he'd been infected with the madness that had possessed Luke at *Yōktha*. Touching the shard had revealed to Onwé a hidden door in the cellar. Had it also revealed something in him to this "Bishop" under the mountain?

The dreamcatcher lingered in his thoughts as well. The idol danced on a wicked wind in his memory, swaying and swirling and dripping and creaking. The cross upon it glinted in the pale light of the moon, and that skull—poor Numi's skull—stared at him through cave-like pits. What if in destroying the dreamcatcher, he'd granted some kind of dark permission to the Impostor? What if the cross he'd salvaged from it now opened him up to the intrusions of bad spirits?

Onwé found no safety in his father's house. The creature outside didn't need to break down the door and come lumbering in to grab him; it was already here, invading every quiet moment. Prayers felt meaningless, both to Christ and to the Naukti spirits, and the few psalms he remembered rang hollow. The only words that seemed true now were those which had been uttered by Luke:

"I feel my soul imperiled. I feel the mountain's shadow on me, even at night."

That dread ran through Onwé like electricity, making it impossible to sit still. Wicked energy thrummed beneath his skin, across his veins, and in the pit of his brain. It gathered into the corrupting force he knew so well. It promised him sleep. It promised to rid him of the terrible thoughts. It told him the same thing it always told him:

You need to get high.

Eventually, the quiet urge grew into a ravenous hunger, and Onwé couldn't starve for another minute. He grabbed the stick he'd intended to craft into a hiking staff for Tiwé and used it to knock the savings tin from its place on the high shelf.

As he scooped up the tin, someone called his name from outside. He opened the front door and found Burke Voth looming there on the porch, more grim-faced and pallid than usual.

"I'm sorry to trouble you," Voth said, his gaze fixed on the floor.

To Onwé's surprise, the urge abated slightly in the presence of company. A bit of relief washed through his veins.

"Believe it or not," he replied, "I'm glad to see you. You really do have perfect timing."

For the second time in a week, Voth had intercepted Onwé on his path to self-destruction. Onwé considered the possibility it could be a sign from God, and bade the pastor come in.

Onwé pulled a rickety chair from the nearby table for himself and motioned for Voth to sit in the armchair by the fire. As Voth took in the austere surroundings, Onwé saw he looked particularly disheveled. The man hadn't bothered to brush his hair in days, and the unshaved skin of his face hung loosely from the bones. His eyes, barely open, looked swollen with sorrow.

"We're holding a prayer vigil for Hannah tomorrow night," Voth said in a deflated voice. "I wanted to let you know you're welcome to come. I'm sure it would mean a lot to Chris and Wendy."

A sudden wave of nausea crashed over Onwé at the mention of Hannah's name. He imagined them agonizing in the privacy of their home, hoping every day they'd wake up to their daughter coming through the door. Little did they know, Chris and Wendy had just begun the long and hopeless journey Moya had been on for decades. But Onwé could not bring himself to divulge Hannah's fate. Even after all they'd been through, he was not confident the couple—or anyone—would believe what he'd seen: their dead daughter, butchered and worn like old rags by a hulking ghoul.

"That's kind of you," Onwé replied after swallowing back the urge to vomit. "I'll be there."

"I'm struggling to advise them." Voth shifted his lanky legs and wrung his hands together. "May I tell you something in confidence?"

"Of course," Onwé said. He could plainly see the pastor's discomfort, and was reminded of Luke's uncharacteristic fidgeting in the weeks after he'd given up alcohol. He wondered if Voth drank privately in his little house behind the church.

"I don't think she's coming home," he blurted out. The admission seemed to cause him physical pain, and he squeezed his eyes shut. "My heart tells me she's gone. And I feel like I'm lying to her parents when I reassure them."

The nausea swept back over Onwé. Sweat beaded on his face.

Maybe getting high isn't such a bad idea after all.

"I feel the same," he admitted.

"I've prayed every night for Hannah's return," Voth continued, "and for guidance. But I feel…unanswered. Ignored, even."

Onwé knew the feeling well. He recalled his final moments with Numi, and how no gods or spirits had intervened in his most desperate time. In fact, he remembered many times throughout his life in which his prayers had gone unanswered.

"We Nauktí have no angels to advise us," Onwé said. "Nor do our ancestors speak to us the way Christ does to the Christians. We have the First Spirit and its many forms. But they reveal things in such subtle ways that most people never listen."

"What do they tell you?" Voth asked.

Onwé gazed out the nearby window. His eyes fell on the woods.

"Nothing," he said. "Nothing at all."

"In my twilight years," Voth said, "I believe I've entered my dark night of the soul." He got up from the chair and walked to the window Onwé stared through. For a long moment, he peered into the woods. "Are you familiar with that expression?"

Onwé shook his head.

"It's a process of spiritual cleansing," he replied, his breath fogging the window. "Very painful. I feel the Lord's hands upon me, breaking me down and molding my spirit into His instrument. All these years at the head of the Valley Commission, I thought I was righteous, but now I see my delusions for what they were. God commands that I atone, and I have to do it alone. He won't speak to me until the work is done."

"Burke," Onwé said in a gentle voice, "you've devoted your life to your faith. What do you need to atone for? Aside from being an asshole, I mean."

The pastor turned back to Onwé, his eyes brimming with resurfaced guilt.

"A great number of things," he said, "that I'm only now beginning to see. God has pried open my eyes and blinded me with the truth of my actions."

He wiped away tears before they could roll down his cheeks. Onwé felt taken aback at the vulnerability Burke Voth now displayed and didn't know how to respond to it.

"Someday, I'll beg for your forgiveness," Voth said in a trembling voice. "Yours, and so many others'."

The pastor apologized once more for the intrusion. He excused himself, eyes downcast, and headed for the door. As he passed Onwé he paused and said, "That which I have done unto the least of my brethren, I have also done unto Christ."

Chapter 43

That night, Onwé picked Moya up from John's place, where he learned she'd talked in her sleep—and even wandered around in the dark. The two walked home in the deepening cold, trading stories about how unwell they both felt.

"Something's wrong with me," said Moya, huddling beneath a pile of blankets on her couch. "My body moves against my will. My mouth speaks words I'm not thinking. Dr. Farmer would say I'm crazy, and Old N'wenthāil would say I'm inhabited by strange spirits."

"You're not crazy," Onwé replied, checking each door and window to ensure they were secured. "It's that thing in the woods. It wants us both. It wants to take us into the mountain."

"To my son," Moya corrected. "He was a sleepwalker too, toward the end."

The two exchanged grave looks. Neither of them accepted Akántha was behind all this. Still, a morbid curiosity nagged at Onwé. He needed to know what had happened to his friend all those years ago, as much as he needed his own son.

Onwé grabbed Moya's frigid hands and sank down in

front of her. She was mostly blind now, and her eyes remained unfocused, as they did whenever she ruminated about her child.

"*Néthédi,*" he said, "did this creature ever give something to you? Something it wanted you to keep?"

Moya shook her head and pulled her hands away.

"*At'an-A'anotogkua nēmwési tōth'tolhó... Sásh'óu'yannen.*" *The Impostor does not give. It only takes.*

"I didn't want to scare you before," Onwé said, "but I think that's what happened to Luke. I think he touched something he shouldn't have, and it made him sick. The same thing just happened to me, *Néthédi.* I let the darkness in."

"Was it a little black stone?" Moya asked, her gaze still vacant.

"How did you know?" said Onwé.

Moya remained still for a long moment.

"I think you should have another chat with Mr. Voth," she said at last.

With that, Moya leaned back and buried herself under the blankets.

Onwé lay down on the empty bed and kept watch out the nearby window. The longer he waited the more tired he became, and soon, he realized his insomnia was diminishing. He drifted into the space between consciousness and sleep, carried there by the gentle rhythm of Moya's breathing.

As he sank into darkness, Luke's voice echoed in his mind, zealously sermonizing about the one he'd called "the Bishop." Like a magic spell, the words conjured an image that swirled together in parts: a dark tunnel, a great cavern, a stalagmite throne. A shadow fell upon the chair, and from it emerged some vile abomination whose gnarled hands beckoned him further into the dark. The river of Onwé's thoughts had been poisoned, and in his sleep, it flowed into deep chasms of insanity.

In his dreams, Onwé found himself wandering through Autumn Ridge, whose gravel streets meandered between ruined houses and vanished into caves. Its people, now starving and emaciated, walked beside him under a darkened sky that snowed only ash. They wept and cried, their faces full of fear, and babbled in languages seemingly ancestral to the ones he knew. The people marched in rowdy throngs up the mountain, beating themselves with sticks or lashing themselves with cords, some of them ritually carving their own skin with knives or glass.

A man whispered something into the ear of a little girl as he passed her on the road, and upon hearing his words, she began screaming and tearing at her own hair and skin. Seas of naked, mortified flesh washed around Onwé, and he couldn't help but think of Dark Age Flagellants embarking on a pilgrimage.

Onwé followed the mob of his hopeless neighbors past corpses and fires and destroyed buildings. He watched them disappear into the throat of a great cave, and as they stepped into the blackness, they broke out in songs and prayers—and desperate, violent screams. The cries of children rang out most severe, changing over time into monotonous humming or gruesome choking noises.

The sounds terrified Onwé so much he leaped out of bed and vomited on the floor. With puke still dripping from his lips, a grim revelation dawned on him. Onwé realized at that moment *why* the voices had demanded he tell Moya about the Black Wall. He knew why they begged him to speak of their house of worship to the people in Autumn Ridge. The Church Beneath the Roots was evangelical, much like the Baptist churches of Cold Valley, and its power depended upon recruiting new souls.

Onwé called out to Moya, wanting to share his new theory with her—but when he looked at the couch where she slept, he found it empty. The blankets lay strewn on the floor, and upon them was an old sage pouch necklace Akántha had made for her. In all the years since his disappearance, she'd never taken it off.

"Oh *fuck,*" he said.

Onwé instinctively ran to the back door and found it unlocked. When he tore it open, a flurry of frosty wind pummeled him. Some time in the night, a new storm had arrived to bury the mountain once more in heaps of choking snow. In the tree nearest the kitchen window, a crude dreamcatcher swung.

"Fuck!" Onwé shouted. His curse was drowned in the icy din.

Chapter 44

John Tall Rock wasted little time combing the town for the missing elder. Before eight o' clock that morning, three tribal officers and ten civilians wandered Autumn Ridge, knocking on doors and shouting Moya's name. The BIA had ended its investigations and declared Luke and Hannah presumed dead. The two agents who remained said Moya stood no chance in this weather.

So much powder had fallen, the town was almost erased from sight. The snow-capped roofs of houses blended into the white landscape, and most people remained shivering indoors, unable to face any more bad news on the mountain. Even the church, which had once gazed proudly over the rez from the eastern slope, was now a frozen artifact to be excavated in some distant day. The building, like the mountain itself, seemed abandoned by God and condemned to an icy fate.

Burke Voth's little hovel peeked out from an ocean of snow. Onwé had trudged up the unplowed church road with great effort, powered by his terror for Moya and the anger of knowing the pastor might be hiding something. He clomped over the drifts that had formed a barrier at the front of the house and pounded a fist on the door. A haggard Voth answered.

"Moya's gone," Onwé said, panting. "Walked right out the door in the middle of the night. John told me she's been sleepwalking."

Voth's eyes didn't widen at the news. His sallow face barely seemed to react at all, as if he'd somehow known this day would come.

"Come in, then," he said, barely above a whisper.

The two gathered in his tiny living room, and in that moment Onwé realized that for all his power and influence, Voth lived no better than anyone else on the mountain. The place was cramped and austere, and only a few pieces of old furniture filled the house. Upon them lay dozens of open books and papers covered in notes that must have been scrawled over decades. Though Onwé knew him to be dishonest, the pastor did seem earnest in his faith.

"She told me to ask you about Akántha." Onwé bored into Voth with an accusing stare.

"Yes," he said plainly. "I thought she might."

Voth bade his guest sit at the little breakfast table. Then he scooped up what looked like an old diary and dropped down into the other chair.

"I came here in nineteen thirty-seven," Voth said. "Took my father's place at the church. I was sure I knew the path the Lord had chosen for me: to break down centuries of false gods and myths. Save Indian souls. Do you know where I'm from?"

Onwé shook his head.

"Karl had it wrong," Voth said. "It's Virginia, not Alabama. Grew up in a real old-fashioned church community there. My father had already made a name for himself before he'd come out here. I followed him, and by the time I arrived in Autumn Ridge, I was obsessed with living up to his reputation. If I could run my own church association, I'd really be doing the Lord's work, and make my father proud. I found power as leader of the Commission—but I did horrible things to attain it."

"Tell me what you did," Onwé demanded, his impatience tightening the muscles all over his body.

Voth set the diary on the table and locked eyes with Onwé.

"Your father never told you?" he asked. "It was why he hated me."

Onwé pondered the question. He'd never considered there might be a specific reason why Ash detested Voth. A rage of centuries flowed through the veins of every Native; the reasons were numberless.

"My father hated all the missionaries," Onwé said. "The pastors, the Commission. Anyone trying to destroy our way of life on behalf of the government."

"It's true," Voth replied, dropping his gaze in shame. "He had no love for any of us. But that man wanted me dead."

"Why?" Onwé asked.

Voth shifted uncomfortably in his chair.

"It's a small town," he said. "I saw the way he checked in on Moya and her boy. They tried to keep it a secret from your mother. So I threatened him. Told him to quit opposing the church. Give up all the rituals and his nonsense about the Old Way—or else I'd humiliate them all.

"He was quiet after that. Couple years went by without him stirring up any trouble. We won over a lot of converts during that time. But then one day, he came to me with his request for relocation, saying his people had suffered enough. I didn't listen. I certainly wasn't going to move down to Namarjo and be forced into a junior position in one of their churches."

Onwé's body ignited with vengeful heat.

"You blackmailed my father and kept us all here so you could keep your stupid church job? You hung our people out to dry for *that?*"

"Yes," he murmured.

"People literally freeze to death up here, you fucking *asshole!*" Onwé shouted.

"I live with my guilt every day," Voth replied. "I assure you, it is the oubliette of the soul."

Onwé wanted to bludgeon Voth with his own diary. He forced back his violent urge, trying to focus on more pressing matters.

"Burke, this is important. Do you know where Moya is?" he said, his voice breaking with emotion. Each passing minute could have been her last, and Onwé wasn't ready to lose another loved one.

"No," Voth replied, "but her boy..."

"Tell me," Onwé said. "You owe me *at least* that."

Voth nodded and kept his gaze on his lap.

"Akántha met my Daisy once," he said. "She was just a pup. Loved kids. He and I got to talking a bit that day in the town square. Told me he'd been having bad dreams. He wouldn't say what about.

"Then one night, I was walking home from a prayer group. It was dark. Too dark for kids to be out alone. And I saw a little boy standing at the tree line, just looking up at the moon."

"Akántha?"

"Sure enough," Voth replied. "He was sleepwalking. Feverish. He'd have frozen to death being out there much longer. He confessed to going off into the woods to places he shouldn't have. Said something about a rock he'd found. Scared him to death. He thought there was something out there—some kind of monster calling to him. Even in his dreams."

Onwé realized his hands had formed a deathgrip on the arms of the chair. He let go and instantly felt pain arcing up his wrists.

"I took the kid home," Voth went on. "Told his mother to get him checked out by Dr. Farmer. She refused, as you

Indians tend to do. The next thing I heard, he was gone."

Onwé considered the story and searched Voth's face for dishonesty.

"Did you tell my father about this?" he asked.

Voth squeezed his eyes shut, forcing out the words he'd held in for decades.

"Yes," he whispered, "and I helped organize the search effort...but I kept the Bureau out of it. I made sure there was never a federal investigation into the disappearance of Akántha River Stone."

"You *what?*" Onwé snapped, jumping to his feet. "How could you do such a thing?"

"Autumn Ridge has the highest rates of disappearance and suicide in Cold Valley," said Voth. "It was my job to lead the people here to salvation. Kids going missing wasn't a good look. The BIA put pressure on us to get things sorted up here, and the Commission began rumbling about new leadership. Everyone was worried about our funding."

The dam broke inside Onwé. Justice had to be done upon someone guilty of so many offenses. He lunged at the pastor with all his strength and caught Voth by the throat. The two careened to the hard floor.

"Well, you got what you wanted, you son of a bitch!" Onwé shouted. "Are you happy now?"

Voth clawed at Onwé's hands. Choking noises filled the room.

"They might have found him!" Onwé shrieked, droplets of spit flying out of his mouth. "He might still be alive! Do you realize what you've done!"

He let go of Voth when the man's eyes began to bulge from their sockets. As much as Onwé despised him, he couldn't bring himself to commit murder. The two lay on the floor beside each other, one shaking with rage and the other gasping for air.

"How many people...go missing every year...on reservations?" Voth sputtered. "Women are kidnapped. People vanish. The bodies rarely turn up. The BIA wouldn't have done much, I swear. They only care about high-profile cases that could make them look bad—like your friend Luke."

Onwé wiped the tears off his face. The truth of Voth's words stung him; the government rarely put boots on the ground for missing persons cases on the rez. Still, maybe Ash could have convinced them, had Voth filed the report.

"I was wrong," the pastor went on, struggling to sit up. "I was wrong to ignore what Akántha told me. Months later, I heard voices calling out from the woods. They were people from town who'd passed away. Some of them I'd baptized myself over the years."

"*At'an-A'anotogkua*," Onwé said, rubbing his face with trembling hands. "Luke called it the Night Shepherd."

"A demon," Voth replied, "disguising itself as a loved one. That's how the Devil comes to us. Akántha was a smart kid, though. He knew not to trust the voices. He called them *'stolen tongues.'*"

"That's why it comes to people while they sleep," Onwé said.

Voth rubbed his neck. Bruises had already begun to form.

"He wasn't just sleepwalking that night," he said. "His movements, his speech. He was articulate. He seemed almost hypnotized...possessed, even."

The pastor's words corroborated Moya's claims about losing control over her body and mind. Onwé had even experienced it himself. The creature was infiltrating its victims' dreams—and then their bodies.

"You knew something was hunting people in Autumn Ridge," Onwé said, "and you did *nothing*."

"I thought our faith would protect the town," Voth replied. "I truly believed if we all came together in the Lord... I've written it all here." He pointed at the book, which now lay open on the floor.

Onwé shook his head, unwilling to accept Voth's rationalizations.

"And my father searched for him after everyone else had given up," he said.

"Yes."

"He learned the truth," Onwé said. "And that's why he's dead."

"Yes," Voth admitted. "...I could have prevented all of this."

In all his life, Onwé had never been so overwhelmed with hatred and disgust. He climbed to his feet and went to leave, done forever with Pastor Burke Voth.

"So much blood on your hands," he said as he ripped the door open. "*You* are the monster, Burke. Truly, you are the Demon of Cold Valley."

Chapter 45

"I can't believe it. I can't believe this is happening."

The heartache in Tíwé's voice was more than Onwé could bear. Even through the phone, he could feel his son's anguish. The boy was only eleven and had already witnessed more death and despair than most people would in their lives—and now his father had to deliver the news that Moya had gone missing.

"We have to find her, Dad," Tíwé implored. "Let me come up there. I can help."

Onwé believed him. There was no doubt in his mind Tíwé would scour the entire mountain five times over and freeze to death before giving up on Moya. She'd always been a beloved grandmother to him, the wisest elder in his life.

"You stay put," Onwé replied, "and keep your eyes open down there. I'm heading out with a search team today. I think I know where to look."

"But Dad," Tíwé protested, "I can bring Zeus—"

"I've gotta go, son," Onwé said, glancing out the window of the police station. "Just stay put. I love you."

He paused for a moment before hanging up, hoping Tíwé would say it back. Instead, the boy offered, "Be careful, Dad."

Onwé exited the building and noticed a group of people gathering in the town square. John Tall Rock and Chris Miller were speaking with Kai, a tribal police officer in a black cowboy hat. Two young men Onwé vaguely knew from the church, cousins Eric and Isaac, chatted beside them in matching blue coats. All of the men spoke to each other with grim expressions and busied themselves with the supplies they carried. When they saw Onwé, their conversations ceased.

"Everyone ready?" Onwé asked, checking the leather sheath that held his knife.

"I'm here for my daughter as much as I am for Moya," Chris said. "We're bringing them both home today, God willing."

The others nodded. As they shook hands with Onwé, Voth appeared behind him, covered in bruises from their recent encounter. Onwé was instantly furious at the idea the pastor might try to halt their quest, but then he saw Voth was dressed in layers of winter gear.

"Kai here told me you all were heading out," he said, nodding at the tribal officer. "I'd like to help with the effort, if I may."

Onwé regarded the pastor for a moment and saw the shame in his eyes.

"No skin off my back," he replied. "Try not to have a heart attack on the way up."

The party headed northwest up the slopes, wading through the snowdrifts and rocky terrain. Pale Peak seemed to react to their intrusion with hostility. Inky clouds gathered as they hiked, and the temperature plummeted. A ferocious mountain wind swept through the valleys and lashed their faces, and the woods seemed more shadow-haunted than usual. Their destination was the high cliff Onwé had begun to call "Numi's Ridge," but he didn't waste his breath explaining why they needed to go there.

"There's no way...that woman...could've made it this far," Isaac gasped. He and his cousin Eric were brave men, but they were not fit for mountaineering. Even Burke Voth outpaced them, surprising everyone with his endurance.

"No," Onwé said without looking back. "Not by herself."

Eventually, the party arrived at Numi's Ridge. Onwé stopped in his tracks, surprised by what he saw: a wide, white field sprawling up to the woods on its eastern side, and ending abruptly at a cliff to the west.

The Briar House had vanished.

The men clomped through the snow, and Onwé surveyed the place where the house should have been. They found the skeletal remains of a low stone wall, and a deep trench that should have been a cellar—but no wood, no frame, no cement remained. Just as Luke had said, it appeared the house had sunken into the ground. Onwé imagined a tarantula dragging a lizard into its burrow, and wondered if the Briar House had "received" Moya in the same way it had welcomed him.

John and Voth expressed befuddlement that some kind of construction had been done here on the ridge. Onwé ignored them and continued toward the nearby woods. The cave he'd carried Numi out of waited there, and he had a grim feeling their true destination could be accessed through any of Pale Peak's tunnels.

All paths lead to the hidden road, he thought in Akántha's voice, *and the hidden road leads to the Church.*

The men pressed on between the trees. As the narrow cave came into view, Onwé couldn't help but to see the thing as a yawning, black maw awaiting his arrival. The mountain was eager to lure him into its belly. He wondered just how deep its tunnels delved.

Chris caught up with Onwé as he walked, pulling him out of his grisly thoughts.

"You think we'll find Hannah too?" he asked.

The anguished hope in his expression ripped through Onwé, reminding him acutely of Moya in the days after Akántha had gone missing. Onwé tried to soften his pessimism as he recalled the creature wearing the poor girl's face.

"My heart tells me we won't," he said gently, "and I hope to God it's wrong."

Of all the terrible things Onwé had ever said in his life, discouraging Chris was the worst, and in that moment he'd have died to return Hannah to her dad. The broken man buckled under the weight of Onwé's reply, but then he took a deep breath and straightened up a bit.

"My hope is in our Heavenly Father," Chris said with conviction. "He'll protect my daughter."

"Let us pray for her soul," Voth said, approaching the two. "And for Moya's."

Chris and the other church members bowed their heads while the pastor spoke. As Onwé waited for them to finish, he felt a distinct pressure in his hand, as if he were still holding the black shard he'd found in the cellar. He retrieved Moya's sage pouch from his jacket and placed it around his neck, where it tangled awkwardly with Luke's cross. Then he joined in the prayer, speaking "Amen" at its finish.

When he opened his eyes, he saw John and Kai—both devoted traditionalists—regarding him with shock. He avoided their stares and walked between them.

"I have to warn you," Onwé said, squeezing into the tight cave entrance, "you might see some things in here that I can't explain."

Chapter 46

The group passed into the cave single file. A soft, unceasing wind rolled through it—a breath exhaled perpetually since the mountain was young. The air was thick with moisture, and carried on it the odor of roots and mushrooms and wet, crumbling stone.

Onwé had felt an old horror in this place with Numi, an ancestral fear passed on to him through generations of his people. The same feeling seized him now as he waded through the tunnel, reminding him there must be some truth in every grim legend about Pale Peak. He'd traversed these caverns twice before, but never actually saw their innards. This time, he'd brought a flashlight.

The men clicked on their lights and pointed the beams down the black throat ahead: a granite passage, occasionally buttressed with shale and pillowy sandstone. Manes of crystals seamed the walls, and big, drooping stalactites blocked some of the path. The men moved between them wordlessly.

As they passed through a few intersecting tunnels, Onwé began to feel disoriented and could no longer remember the way out. He was lost in a labyrinth of shadows, whose impossibly angled turns confounded his mind and sense of balance. The way seemed hewn intentionally to play tricks on the eyes, and he could feel his companions growing more and more afraid as they trod onward.

Onwé led them down sloping paths of rock, guided only by his inner feelings and occasional whispers his friends could not hear. The black shard had connected him to the elder spirits; he felt their presence now behind the stone walls and beneath his feet, leading him ever downward. The deeper the group plodded into the mountain, the wider and taller its tunnels grew, until they became more like large rooms. Occasionally, the men weaved between stalagmite pillars jutting from the ground, some of them finely sanded to glass-like textures. Carved upon their surfaces in fine lettering were strings of characters whose origin seemed ancient.

"Don't," Eric warned Chris, who was about to run a finger over the script. "This looks demonic."

"Holy *shit,*" said John, his voice echoing all around them. "Guys, get over here."

The men hurried to the far end of the chamber.

"My God in Heaven," Voth gasped, beholding what John had found.

The room came to an abrupt cliff overlooking a sea of darkness. A long, narrow staircase descended away from them into a chasm so enormous its depth swallowed the flashlights' beams. No walls, no ceiling, no floor were visible—only the stone steps floating in oblivion.

"What... What *is* this place?" Chris said in a trembling voice.

"The hidden road," Onwé replied grimly. "Come."

He began the steep descent.

The passage of time was incalculable under the mountain. It was impossible for Onwé to tell if it had been an hour or a day since they'd found the staircase. Each step brought him deeper into a dreamlike state, and his awareness came only in flashes between long gulfs of mental vacancy. He recalled only pieces of the things his light revealed: crumbling stairways above and below him, overlapping each other and vanishing into darkness in both directions. Some were wide and some were narrow, and all of them had decayed under the lapse of lightless centuries. He wondered fleetingly if they led up to other places on the mountain—other mysterious houses—to carry the "Elect" down to the Church.

At some point in their seemingly eternal march, Onwé and his companions found themselves on a stone floor at the bottom of the chasm. Each of them looked dazed, as if they'd just awoken from a bout of sleepwalking.

"Rest here," he said, dropping to the floor and opening his pack.

The men sat in a circle and drank from their canteens. John produced a few large candles from his satchel and lit them, encouraging the others to save their flashlights. Batteries were hard to come by on the rez, but due to frequent power outages, there was always an abundance of candles. John had brought enough to light a house through a dreadful night.

"Moya can't have made it all the way down here," Isaac said, shuddering with fear. "Not in her condition. It's impossible." He'd begun to lose his nerve and kept looking back to the stairs that had brought the party this far.

"Even if she had," Eric said, "we'll never find her. There's way too much ground to cover, and we're running out of light. We should go back, you guys. *Now.*"

Onwé understood their fear. He too felt the dread of wandering the abyssal depths of the mountain, of journeying past the boundaries of where humanity should never cross. The ancestors of the Cold Valley Indians had warned of this place, and of the poor souls lost in it—but Onwé knew he was already doomed. Whether or not he entered the caves, he had touched the black shard and could now feel a presence within himself originating from down here in the hopeless dark. It drew him further and further into the bowels of the earth, and even in his home on Autumn Ridge, he'd felt its pull.

"I won't abandon Moya," he said. "I can't go back."

"Neither can I," said Chris. "Not without my daughter." The sweat of terror glistened on his face in the candlelight, and the certainty of death haunted his stare. But Chris had to be strong for his little girl. His love for her had gotten him this far.

The cousins implored Voth to reason with Onwé, but the pastor shook his head.

"My fate is bound to Moya's," he said gravely, looking over at John and Onwé. "I'm meant to be here."

"Then let's pray again," Isaac said with a quivering voice. He pressed his hands together with conviction, steeling himself for the journey ahead.

Onwé gazed off into the infinite blackness around them. A hideous feeling told him they were far too deep for Heaven to hear their cries. He joined the men in prayer, but inside, he believed he was now orphaned from the gods.

Chapter 47

They marched on, candles glimmering faintly in their hands. As the men stumbled through the featureless void, the chasm closed in around them, and they found themselves creeping through a series of dizzyingly symmetrical hallways. These rectangular passages looked built for things much taller than people, and their lengths were segmented by ornate stone doors that swung on iron hinges. When Onwé examined the elaborate carvings upon one of the doors, he saw the work had been committed with a mastery almost beyond comprehension.

"How do you know the way?" John whispered to Onwé at the head of the line.

Onwé stopped in his tracks and listened to the silence.

"I can hear Akántha's voice," he whispered.

John returned a dreadful expression.

Onwé moved through halls so desolate he doubted even ghosts would haunt them. An ancient stillness hung in the air, and even gentle footsteps sounded blasphemous in the quiet. He clutched the dripping candle, mesmerized by the eldritch shadows it threw down the hall, which took the form of strange shambling things lurking in the gloom. When he looked over his shoulder to his friends, Onwé imagined a procession of elder beings drifting through these halls millennia prior, on their way to carry out forgotten rituals. He recalled Old N'wenthāil's stories of the first tribes on Pale Peak and their fear of *Knûth-Sōkáān,* that dreadful emptiness between our world and the next.

The dank air suddenly began to warm.

"This way," Onwé called, quickening his pace.

The men passed through the door at the end of the hall and poured out onto a field of granite hills. The path beneath them snaked across the open space, weaving between the stoney mounds and vanishing into a plot of strange ruins in the distance.

On every hill stood hundreds of moldering headstones crushing slowly against each other, like a mouth overcrowded with teeth. Bits of tottering walls jutted from the cavern floor here and there, much like the wall that had encircled the Briar House far above.

"A graveyard," Voth said breathlessly.

"No," Isaac choked out. "No, no, no... This is wrong. We shouldn't be here. We have to leave *right now!*" He tried to run back toward the hall but was intercepted by Kai, who wrapped the frightened man in a bear hug.

"You can't go alone," he said as Isaac struggled against his grip. "We need to stay together. Everyone needs to decide: should we go back?"

"Get off me!" Isaac screamed. "I'm not gonna die down here!"

He slipped out of Kai's grasp and fled back up the hallway into the maze of other passages.

"Isaac!" his cousin yelled. "Don't!"

The group watched Isaac recede into the hall, where the flame of his candle flickered out. His footsteps and haunted cries returned to them for a short while—then vanished with him into the darkness. Eric and Kai went after him but were quickly discouraged by the impossible gloom. Kai returned a weeping Eric to the group.

Onwé, now sick with fear and guilt, bade the remaining men keep going. A shouting match broke out over whether to search more for Isaac, but Eric could not persuade the others to turn back. He howled up the passage at his lost cousin until his voice went hoarse and then tearfully rejoined his companions, cursing this wretched place beneath the mountain.

They pressed on through the graveyard in their little bubble of candlelight, following the road past countless headstones and obelisks of inscrutable purpose. Whoever was buried down here had lived long ago when the mountains were young. As Onwé trod over their ancient resting place, he felt as if he'd shattered an accursed silence.

"Look," Kai said, pointing at a chunk of metal lying on the ground.

"Impossible," Voth said. He lowered his candle near the object to examine it. "It's from one of the planes."

He strode toward the nearby hill and revealed hundreds of pieces of debris. A pair of seats, an engine, and a broken wing lay strewn about. The men fanned out and searched for human remains, but found nothing.

"How could these get down here?" John asked, holding his candle up near Onwé's face.

"I told you," Onwé replied, "there are things down here I can't explain."

The cemetery gave way to a sort of charnel town filled with elaborate humanoid statues and monuments of abstract forms. Chiseled upon their plaques was the same obscure language the men had seen in the higher tunnels, and Onwé wondered if any of these words were the ones he'd heard screamed in the tunnels on his last visit:

Geptré! Gorleth! Aurokkné! Magroloth! Ûrdn!

301

Standing among the other ruins were leering charnel houses, most of them strangled by thick, overnourished vines. These were the same wicked plants that grew on the Briar House, and Onwé guessed they were the reason that building was able to move. He imagined houses springing up throughout the Rockies, luring people down to *Knûth-Sōkáān*. He wondered how many forgotten places waited in the ground, buried in histories beyond mortal recollection.

"How can anything grow down here?" Kai kicked one of the vines snaking over the path. It twitched in response, causing the officer to leap back in fright.

There in the necropolis, one building stood out in particular—a large, crooked pyramid fashioned from rock as pale as bone. The building was set into a hill and leaned menacingly toward the group, as if poised to devour them. Its front doors sat wide open like eager arms, and the old road led straight into it.

"Humble yourself," Akántha whispered.

"This way," Onwé said. The hair stood up on his neck as they drew near.

A warm wind sighed from its entrance, extinguishing the candles when they stepped inside. The group fumbled for their lights, terrified to remain in the horrific blackness for more than a few seconds.

"We're running low," John said, stuffing his candle into his pack. "I don't think we have enough for the journey out." He shot a look of hopelessness at the group.

"Jesus Christ, help us," Eric babbled through a new volley of tears. "You've led us here to die, Onwé."

"Two flashlights at a time," Onwé replied, motioning for everyone but Kai to switch their lights off. "Make them last." He remembered Luke babbling about the "underlight" and wondered how much longer they'd be in the dark.

The beam of Onwé's flashlight revealed a hexagonal

room whose bookshelf-walls stretched upward infinitely. Countless books towered over the men, occupying an impossible space for the size of the building. They filled the air with the stink of old parchment and leather.

"It looks like ours," John said, referring to the little library Ashthenôví had helped build in town. That building was also hexagonal with wide double doors, but its bookcases stood only a foot over Onwé's head.

"Something tells me it's not a coincidence," Voth replied.

A single tome lay on the floor, curiously free of the ancient dust encrusting everything else in the building. Kai stooped down to grab it, but Voth intervened, slapping the heavy thing from his hand and sending it flopping back to the ground. The smack of its weight upon the stone floor echoed on through the endless dark above them.

"For God's sake, man," Voth whispered. "Some books should go unread."

Kai shined his flashlight upon the floor where the book had landed—and noticed a narrow passage at the base of one of the bookcases. The men looked worriedly at each other while Onwé inspected it, then scoffed in disbelief at his words:

"Time to be humbled."

He dropped to his stomach and slid into the passage, kicking up plumes of white dust as he forced his body through. Voth cursed under his breath and squatted on weathered knees, dutifully following Onwé. One by one the others joined, until all six companions slithered down a tunnel no wider than a laundry chute. A hot breeze rushed through it, burning their eyes as they crawled.

"I can't breathe," John croaked, panicking at the back of the line. "I can't fuckin' breathe. I gotta get out!"

"The way out is through," Onwé called, repeating the sinister voice he'd just heard. "Keep going, John."

They squeezed through winding natural caverns that became narrower and narrower. Onwé dragged himself over sharp rocks and sticky, foul-smelling growths. He slithered over the long bones of some dark-dwelling creature but refused to examine them, terrified to learn of the unspeakable things that had once lived beneath the Rocky Mountains.

The air became even hotter. A chorus of ghoulish voices rolled through the tunnel, wailing a song that distantly resembled Baptist hymns.

"Jesus Christ!" said Chris, bursting into tears.

"Don't listen!" Voth shouted over the cacophony. "Don't listen to it!"

"Hurry!" Onwé screamed, pulling himself forward with all his strength against the whipping heat. He fought for every inch, grating his body across the jagged stone as he crawled.

At last, he reached the tunnel's end. Onwé plummeted to the ground a few feet below and watched his flashlight roll out in front of him.

But he didn't need the light to see the cavern. Huge clusters of glowing mushrooms illuminated the scene: a dark, mirror-like surface stretching enormously over the far end of the chamber.

They had arrived at the Black Wall.

Chapter 48

The men found themselves in a cathedral-like room so large the entire town of Autumn Ridge could have fit inside it. On one side was a gigantic staircase wide enough to march a hundred people up shoulder to shoulder. Its steps descended from the dark recesses of the mountain and stopped near Onwé, where he remained fright-frozen as his friends wriggled out of the cramped tunnel.

On the opposite side of the chamber stood a vast, imposing wall as high as a castle rampart. Its featureless surface gleamed with a barely visible luster, as if a thin layer of glass contained the darkness beyond it. Onwé swayed dizzily in its presence, reminded of the way he'd felt looking at the black shard.

The men approached the wall, bewitched by its haunting beauty. Some of them started babbling nonsense, but Onwé couldn't focus long enough to discern who was talking. An insidious warmth flooded him, soothing his aching muscles while at the same time triggering the warnings of his soul. He noticed a few chips in the wall's surface, and once again, he felt the weight of the black shard in his hand.

"So beautiful…" he heard himself mumble.

As his eyes unfocused into the wall, an endless cosmos appeared. Waves of stars washed over the void before him, swirling and dancing hypnotically. Onwé felt gravity pulling him forward. He plunged into oblivion. Celestial bodies blurred past him in tremendous glowing streaks, and he traveled to the most distant reaches of the universe, where a single red star burned at the center of an empty expanse. It slowly took the form of a colossal, burning eye watching him intensely. It looked downward, imploring Onwé to look too, and there he saw thousands of people and other *things* huddled together before the Black Wall. They clutched religious idols and shouted prayers for salvation. Through the wall he could see a massive church complex—and the ruins of even older civilizations upon which it had been built.

The visions sickened Onwé, gnawing at the fraying tethers which had once held his sanity intact. His screams vanished into the din of hopeless prayers.

"Onwé!" a familiar voice cried out, piercing through the cacophony of shrieks. The sound broke the wall's hold over him and ripped him back to reality.

Moya.

The woman sat propped against the far edge of the Black Wall, clutching something in her arms. Somehow, he and the others had missed her entirely. Even Chris, who stood only a few yards from her, didn't seem to be aware of her at all.

"Moya!" Onwé shouted. "Guys! She's here!"

John, Voth, Chris, Eric, and Kai remained fixated on the wall, each of them standing a few inches from it and peering lifelessly into its depths. Onwé rushed past them and slid to a crouch beside Moya.

"Are you alright?" he asked frantically. "How the hell did you get down here?"

The frail woman looked up from the ragged bundle she held. Her eyes glowed faintly, conveying the horror of having learned things no human should know.

"Someone helped me," she said. "I...I thought it was you."

Onwé knew then why the Impostor had been impersonating his voice.

"Did you go inside?" he asked, squeezing her arm. "What did you see?"

"I found him," Moya replied, hugging the bundle to her chest. "I've got my son."

Onwé looked closer and saw a tangle of old bones protruding from a tattered red coat. He stared at it in disbelief. It was Akántha's jacket.

"It can't be..." he said. His heart nearly died in his chest.

"I've got my son," Moya repeated, her voice trembling with emotion.

Nearby, Chris began to scream, reacting to something in the wall. He stumbled backward and collapsed onto the stone floor.

At the same time, John Tall Rock threw up on himself and staggered away from the wall, choking on his own sick. Eric clutched his head in pain and wailed an old Ineho song. Burke Voth remained still. He nodded tearfully and looked down at his feet, as if enduring a brutal shaming.

Kai gazed longingly at his own reflection, ensorcelled by the warped figure staring back at him. He smiled and touched his own face—then pulled on his lips and yanked his hair, seemingly testing whether his body was real. After a moment, he ripped out his eyelashes and jammed fingers into his eyes. His reflection mimicked his actions but stretched and elongated hideously with each tortured groan.

"Moya," John gasped, finally noticing her. He hurried over and examined her for injuries.

"Let me in!" Kai begged. *"I must see Him!"*

The tribal officer dug his fingers into his ruined eyes and tore them from their sockets. Then he smashed them against the Black Wall and smeared their pulp across its surface.

The wall reacted to Kai's touch. Crimson lines began to appear in it, coming together to form an arched rectangle. They glowed so fiercely the entire chamber took on a bloody hue. Kai now stood before a cruel-looking door, much like the one that had appeared to Onwé in the cellar—but triple its size.

Upon seeing this, Eric approached the door in wonderment. He studied it for a moment, then resumed bellowing his ancient song. As he did, he smashed his face into the door a half dozen times and dropped dead onto the ground.

"Get her out of here," Onwé commanded John.

The elder nodded and pulled Moya to her feet.

"I can see now." She pointed at the grand staircase at the far end of the chamber. "I know the way out."

The two hurried toward it, Moya jogging with unnatural agility.

"Guys!" Onwé yelled to the other men. "We got her! Let's get the hell out of here!"

He shook Chris vigorously until the man quit screaming, then grabbed Voth and yanked him toward the stairs.

"No," the pastor said, fighting against Onwé's grip. "I need to hear this."

A deep rumbling echoed through the cavern, the sound of rock scraping against rock.

The great door slid open.

"Yes!" Kai shrieked in ecstasy. "Praise Him, our loving Master! His door is open to us, and he's found Isaac!"

He ran through the door without hesitation and disappeared from sight—but then screamed the screams of a man falling into an eternity of torment. His cries bent into dark melodies and were joined by a chorus of other voices. Soon the music of incomprehensible terror filled the chamber outside the Black Wall.

As Onwé directed his remaining companions, a figure emerged from the darkness beyond the door. It paused at the threshold, keeping an inorganic stillness that reminded Onwé of the statues outside the Briar House.

"Brother," it said, "your family is waiting."

Chapter 49

Even in the swirl of terror and chaos, Onwé recognized that voice.

"*Likōté,*" he gasped.

The man in the doorway nodded. Just enough light fell upon him to illuminate his revolting features—a body contorted as if stuffed by a blind taxidermist, and a face exsanguinated from an unspeakable death. His eyes blazed brightly now, full of knowledge of the elder spirits, but his dead gaze remained in the air just over Onwé's head. A foul, black ichor dribbled from his lips. He smiled placidly.

Another form appeared out of the blackness: a shaggy four-legged animal with limbs of unequal length and an oddly misshapen head.

"Numi?" Onwé said, nearly retching at the sight of her.

The dog looked more monster than animal. She sat impatiently beside Luke, stiff-spined and ready to lunge. The fur remaining on her body had darkened with dried blood, and her desiccated lips peeled away to bare a patchwork of mismatched teeth.

"Even in the dark," Luke said, patting Numi, "she helps the chosen find their way. But you found us on your own, didn't you? I can sense it... You've finally accepted the Bishop's gift."

Onwé felt the black shard in his palm once more, and at the same time, sensed the heaviness of his eyelids. Voices whispered in his mind, urging him to walk through the great door.

Luke extended a hand to Onwé and left it in the air, holding it impossibly still.

"Walk with me, brother," he crooned. "Come and see the splendor of the Church Beneath the Roots. Everyone is waiting for you."

"I've already got who I came for," Onwé replied in a defiant tone. "And I'll see to it the government buries you fuckers down here forever."

He turned and headed toward Chris and Voth, who had backed halfway across the chamber in terror of Luke.

"It's true," Luke said, "the Bishop has returned Akántha to his mother. It is a gesture of His infinite grace. But there are still others you can see again."

Ashhhhthenôví, a thousand voices whispered in Onwé's head.

"*Lōnán!*" Akántha's voice shrieked from beyond the great door.

Onwé spun around to face Luke. Hatred and sorrow washed through his veins, and though he doubted his father was beyond the Black Wall, his heart still cried out to take the chance.

"Tell me what really happened to my brother and my dad," Onwé said. "After everything you've taken, at least give me that."

Little black tentacles slid out of Luke's mouth, stretching his lips into a grin-like scream. He choked out something between a laugh and a death rattle, and then the appendages receded, and his expression went blank.

311

"I think you know," he said.

"I need to hear it," Onwé replied, balling his fists so tightly he felt his fingers popping.

"Once in a great while," Luke said, "when the stars are just right, the Church opens its doors to the Elect. Your brother accepted his baptism and joined the deathless congregation. Ash lost his nerve. Now's your chance to prove you are braver than your father."

The myriad voices babbling in Onwé's head swelled with the choir singing beyond the door, their screams harmonizing in a sickly beautiful way. Beneath them, an impossibly deep voice growled commands in an unknown language—but Onwé understood it nonetheless.

Come in.

Onwé felt his limbs compelled by an unnatural force. He lurched toward Luke and the door, feeling the world melt into a fever dream.

"No," he said breathlessly, trying to stay awake. Visions of Akántha came into his mind, sleepwalking through the icy woods beneath a waning moon.

"Whether you accept the gift of the shard," Luke said, "or the call of the Night Shepherd, you *will* join us. The Master has deemed it so."

"Tell your master to go to hell!" Voth yelled.

The pastor's arms slid around Onwé's chest and tugged him backward. Chris joined in, dragging their dazed friend toward the grand staircase at the back of the chamber.

"It is His will!" Luke screamed, his voice suddenly dropping in pitch. "The Bishop of the Mountain will have you, Onwé Lopez! *And the weeping mother!*"

As the men pulled him away, Onwé saw the darkness shift behind Luke, and shined the flashlight at him. Luke had not been standing in the doorway at all. Instead, he floated a few inches above the ground. Luke's body slumped forward like a discarded puppet, revealing a gigantic arm protruding from the dark.

Sickeningly long fingers with too many segments writhed behind Luke's corpse, causing it to twitch and twist unnaturally. The skin of the hand was pallid, leathery, and covered in patches of phosphorescent lichen. Thorny vines coiled tightly around every bit of the arm, imprisoning the flesh in a stinging vise that reminded Onwé of the crown of thorns worn by Jesus Christ. Oily ichor dripped from the many wounds, as it had from Luke's mouth, its color as lightless as the wall itself.

"Don't look at it!" Voth commanded.

But Onwé did.

Two obsidian eyes glinted in the flashlight's cone, each the size of a man's head. They locked with Onwé's, their shocking visage stealing the breath from his lungs. A feeling invaded him, something akin to the sickest he'd ever felt as a child in the harsh winters, and all his muscles went slack. He imagined his soul leaving his body, drawn into the gnarled hands of the massive ghoul in the doorway.

Onwé vanished into a memory that did not belong to him.

He galloped through a long, dark tunnel on all fours, his wet limbs smacking the freezing stone. Though it was a lightless place, he could see the spectral outline of every rock and mushroom, and could peer through the ground into the infinite caverns below. Up ahead, a man crawled desperately toward a blinding light in the distance. Onwé caught up with him easily, crazed with a violent hunger that ached in his corpse-like body. He loomed over the man, watching his pitiful attempt to escape, but felt no sympathy for him.

The man reached the light—the mouth of a cave.

He looked back at Onwé.

Lōnán.

Though Onwé looked through inhuman eyes, and possessed sight that pierced flesh and bone, he instantly recognized his father.

"*Ashhhhthenóví,*" he snarled.

Ash roared in defiance. With a burst of strength, he clambered to his feet and squared off with Onwé. He produced a hunting knife from his coat and clutched it at his side, too exhausted to raise it any higher. Between ragged breaths, he shouted prayers Onwé recognized from the old warding rituals of his people. A brilliant purple light blazed within his chest—the color of a warrior's soul in Nauktí legend.

Onwé lunged at Ash, seizing him by the throat with a gruesome hand. He lifted his father off the ground and stared into his eyes. Ash growled hatefully and drove the blade into Onwé's chest, again and again. Shrieking pain radiated across Onwé's torso, and he howled in a thousand voices at once. He clamped down on Ash's throat and twisted, snapping the man's neck and ending his resistance. Then he slammed Ash's body onto the doorstep of the cave with such force the bones snapped.

Onwé heard the voices of two men in the woods and loped back down the tunnel. A few dozen yards in, he scooped up the broken body of the child Ash had been carrying—and began practicing the boy's screams.

"Run!" Voth shouted into Onwé's ear, summoning him back from the vision. "For God's sake, *run!*"

Chris and Voth lifted Onwé to his feet and dashed for the staircase. Onwé followed but paused at its first step, still

314

fighting for what remained of his hollowed mind.

A hideous crackling of bone echoed through the chamber as Numi rose up on her hind legs. Her limbs jerked violently, twisting and unfolding into new shapes until she became taller than a man. Her shoulders snapped and broadened. Her head splintered and reformed into the shape of a human's. She howled in miserable pain, then cackled wetly.

Impostor.

From out of the darkness came another colossal arm. Now two ghastly hands clutched Luke's body from behind the wall, and began pulling and ripping it until the corpse spread thinly across the door like a spider's web. The Impostor bounded through the gorey mass, absorbing Luke's visage into itself, and rushed at the men on the staircase.

"Down in the hoooole," it growled, *"sooo deeeeep dooooown..."*

The men raced up the stairs. Even Voth moved with impressive speed as the hellish voice called after him. Onwé kept the light on the steps ahead so everyone could see, not daring to turn it back on their monstrous pursuer. He could hear the creature snarling a few dozen steps behind.

"Daddy!" it begged in Hannah's voice. *"Daddy. I'm sorry, Dad. I'm sorry. Dad. I'm sorry, Dad. Dad. Sorry Dad. Dadadadadadadad..."*

The impersonation was too much for Chris. He stumbled and fell, bursting into tears as his daughter's cries reverberated through the tunnel. Onwé tried to help him to his feet, but the creature was on him in a flash. It dragged him into the darkness with little effort. Chris Miller screamed all the way down, until his voice faded beyond the Black Wall.

A few steps ahead, Onwé found Voth slumped over, trying to catch his breath. After hundreds of steps, his body had finally given out.

"Go," he wheezed, pointing up the stairs.

"Let me help you," Onwé replied, grabbing Voth's arm.

315

The pastor swatted his hand away. He looked down into the ancient gloom behind them, and a hopeless expression came over his face.

"Get Moya the hell out of here," he said, "and *never* come back." He climbed to his feet and turned to head back down the stairs.

The creature bayed hungrily, bounding through the blackness toward them.

"No, Burke!" Onwé protested. "Are you out of your mind?"

"I have been," he replied calmly. "Now I see the light."

Voth wiped tears from his eyes and took a deep breath.

"I pray the Lord God will forgive me for what I've done," he said, looking back at Onwé. "I hope someday you'll forgive me too."

With that, Burke Voth marched down the stairs beyond the glow of Onwé's flashlight, intent on slowing the creature.

Onwé fled up the tremendous stairs. He searched for John and Moya, trying to focus on his movements as the pastor's voice filled the tunnels. Voth commanded the wicked presence beneath Pale Peak to obey the power of Christ. He shouted prayers like war cries. For a moment, Onwé almost believed the man would put up a fight against the monster. But soon, Voth's powerful baritone collapsed to fearful babble before tightening into blood-curdling screams.

Onwé stumbled up the endless stair, weighed down by the loss of his friends. Behind him, the mad cackles of the Impostor rattled through the darkness. It laughed and wheezed and bent its voice until suddenly, Ashthenôví was calling out from the depths.

"Bad dreamssss?" it said. *"Ssssome things never washhh off..."*

Onwé tried to ignore the voice, but each word felt like a dagger to the ribs. He grabbed at the tangle of things on his necklace—Luke's cross and Moya's sage pouch. He fumbled with the pouch until it opened and then scooped out a wad of sage. He retrieved his lighter from his coat pocket.

In the jumble of movements, Onwé dropped his flashlight. It bounced down the stairs, throwing its beam in every direction, leaving him blind in the murk before him. He kept running.

"Onwé!" John bellowed from somewhere high above. "Follow my voice!"

Onwé felt a rush of cool air on his skin. New hope surged through his limbs.

"I heard you acrosssss the daaaaark," the Impostor called in Ash's voice.

The terrain abruptly changed. The stairs disappeared from beneath Onwé's feet. He fell forward and collided with the ground, and heard his lighter skitter across it.

"Fuck!" he screamed.

Onwé frantically swept his hand around as he crawled. The Impostor's uneven footfalls echoed closer and closer. It cried out with glee, eager to take its prize back to its master behind the wall.

But then, Onwé's hand fell upon the lighter. He scooped it up and placed the sage on the ground at the top of the stairs—and set it on fire.

The tiny blaze illuminated the area. Onwé had made it to the upper tunnels, where a frigid breeze rolled through. Although the flame was small, it produced a pungent odor that wafted down the stairs on the wind. The creature shrieked and hissed, and the chorus of wicked voices rose in horror.

From out of the darkness came a grotesquely mangled Luke. His rotten skin hung off the bones of a thing beyond Native myth. The teeth protruding from his minced lips could amputate a leg. His height dwarfed even John Tall Rock. The certainty of imminent death swept over Onwé.

The closer the Impostor drew, the more it reacted to the smoke. It coughed and sputtered and fell to one knee, thrashing about in frustration. The sage burned out, leaving man and monster in the gloom of sunless eternities.

Onwé knew he had but one chance. He tore his knife from its sheath and leaped upon the creature, stabbing it repeatedly as it flailed about on the ground. He drove the blade into its neck, where it became stuck.

"For my family," he said through frightened sobs.

Then he shoved himself off the monster and ran against the cold breeze.

"Waaalk with meeee, brotherrr," it croaked. *"Whaaat's behind the Black Waaaaall..."*

Onwé didn't stop to listen. He had no faith the sage would protect him for long. He bolted up the tunnel, following John's voice and calling out to him through a cascade of tears.

At long last, Onwé turned a corner and saw a circle of blinding light. He dashed toward it at full speed, barreling into the embrace of John Tall Rock.

They stood at the entrance to the cave where Ash had died. It was late morning, and the snow gleamed brightly on the sundrenched mountain. Moya sat beneath a tree a little ways away, still holding the tattered jacket and its contents against her chest. She looked up at the blue sky as if seeing it for the first time.

"Let's get her home," Onwé said, trying to catch his breath. "It's not safe here. It'll never be safe here."

John nodded. He looked back at the cave for a long moment. He knew the others weren't coming back.

Chapter 50

For the Nauktí, death was the beginning of a long journey to the next world, part of the chain of nine realms through which all souls must pass.

The death of a child was of particular spiritual significance. Centuries ago, Moya's people would have placed Akántha's remains on a wooden pyre and set it aflame. They'd have sung emphatic paeans to the spirits as the wind carried his ashes over the valley. The elders would have acted out stories of Nauktí legend, and loud expressions of grief would have echoed across the mountain long after the fire burned out.

However, the death rituals of Cold Valley's tribes had changed with time and pressure. A Nauktí funeral now resembled something more familiar to most Americans, something more palatable to the clergy. Today, the people of Autumn Ridge stood in a huge circle and watched, at long last, as an old woman buried her child.

Moya wrapped Akántha's bones in the blanket she'd knitted with his grandmother long ago, and lowered the bundle into a hole in the cemetery. She sat on her knees and covered the hole with dirt, then used some of it to mark her own face—

the symbol of a parent in mourning. Near the rock she'd chosen for the headstone, Moya placed a few sheets of paper—her final prayers for him—and burned them. She remained there in the snow, whispering the goodbyes she'd held inside for twenty-four years.

John Tall Rock delivered the hymn. He beat a drum slow and heavy, singing as loud as he could. The song contained instructions to the soul for the long journey into the next world:

"Anahi'ké sōl…"	*Follow the wind*
"Sól'mé al'dúl."	*and the song adrift in it.*
"Anahiné sōle'i…"	*Follow the voices*
"Ité'hí tenákó."	*that call you home.*
"Aman'éka sōl…"	*Find the world beyond*
"Sól'mési a'nún."	*and the music within.*

The other mourners repeated John's words:

"Aman'éka sōl… Sól'mé al'dúl."

Onwé recognized the words and melody. Warren had sung an Anglicized version of it on their trip into the nameless place. Decades had passed since Onwé had heard the music recited in his own language, and now it moved the deepest part of him until he could barely stand.

He tightened his hug around Tiwé and Angela, who'd come to support Moya on the most important day of her life. They looked up at Onwé, their eyes full of questions, but the only time they spoke was to join in the hymns. Tiwé seemed to have been practicing the language, and enunciated the prayers well enough.

Onwé studied Angie for a moment. In her eyes, he saw a quiet hopelessness and knew she'd lost someone more dear to her than a friend. Hannah and her father had been declared deceased, and this evening, their funerals would be held alongside Burke Voth's and the others' who'd given their lives to bring Moya home. Onwé pitied Angie for knowing so much death at such a young age. He stroked her hair and prayed she'd find solace in her friendship with his son.

There was a freedom in the chanting of old Nauktí. The hymn swept away all the horrible visions cluttering Onwé's mind, at least for now, and he turned inward to bid farewell to his long-lost brother. Like everyone else at the ceremony, he could feel the relief and sorrow radiating from Moya, and joined with her in unfettered weeping for the long winter she'd endured—a winter that was finally ending. The pain expressed by hundreds of people in that moment affirmed to him that Moya was not alone. He was sure Akántha could hear them.

Onwé looked at Tíwé and knew he could never tell him the truth. The boy would spend his life wondering what had happened on Pale Peak—why hundreds of people had vanished over the decades, and why death had descended so violently this season on Autumn Ridge. Tíwé would grow up believing the lies of the federal government about runaways. And perhaps deep down, he would sense the terrible presence still looming beneath the ground.

But Onwé knew the Bishop *wanted* him to talk about the church inside the mountain. It *wanted* him to tell his son of the elder spirits lurking beneath the rez. Perhaps belief in them was enough to open a person up to their whispers, as belief in God awakens a person to His signs.

Onwé wondered if Ashthenôví had arrived at the same conclusion years before. If the vision of Ash's death was true, then he'd sacrificed himself in a final act of bravery for his people. What if Ash had chosen to die to protect the very secret John and Onwé now kept?

In that moment, there beside the grave of Akántha River Stone, Onwé vowed to never put Tíwé's soul at risk by invoking the hateful beings of Pale Peak. To do so could be as dangerous as putting the black shard in the boy's hand. He would warn his son only to avoid the caves and odious voices on the mountain, for the Nauktí people believed forbidden knowledge was animate, and desired to be learned.

John Tall Rock had arrived at the same conclusion. A day later, as the tribal council convened, he stopped Onwé outside the building and made known his desire to keep the details of Moya's rescue private.

"They wouldn't believe a word of it anyway," John said, referring to the Bureau of Indian Affairs. "They'll call it 'Indian superstition' and use it against us. It's what they've always done."

Onwé handed the folder of Warren's photos back to John and simply nodded. He had no intention of being made to look crazy by the government and the Valley Commission.

The two entered the hall, relieved to see that Moya was absent. She was probably still at home, resting in her own bed. Moya no longer waited on the old couch for her son to walk through the door. Perhaps she slept and even dreamed of pleasant things.

At the long table sat Elders Tavshií, Emmanuel, Nǎnk, and Pélō'é. Across from them stood Pastor Duncan Campbell, who would no doubt inherit Voth's leadership of the church. Two BIA agents flanked him, alongside four members of the Valley Commission. One of the agents cleared his throat and called the meeting to order.

"We understand the remains of a missing person have been recovered," he said, "but that it cost the lives of a few residents here in Autumn Ridge. Mr. Tall Rock, Mr. Lopez, we'll be taking your statements regarding the matter at the conclusion of this meeting. And be assured, if either of you were involved in these incidents in any unlawful capacity, justice will be swift."

Both men seated themselves at the table and did not offer a reply.

The agent eyed them suspiciously, then continued his announcements.

"Mr. Tall Rock has suggested to this team that the bodies in question are unrecoverable due to collapses in the tunnels. If we determine this to be true, I'm sorry to say, there won't be an excavation. I'm hearing from Washington that they'd sooner dynamite all caves and mines on the mountain as a safety precaution."

"This council strongly recommends that solution," John said. "No one should ever have access to those tunnels again."

"We'll keep you informed," the agent responded. "Come spring, I'd expect the work to begin."

"It needs to be done immediately," Onwé said. "We won't risk another life lost to those caves."

The elders nodded in unity.

"I'll see if I can push it through," the agent replied.

Onwé knew the BIA wouldn't risk its own men to sweep the caves for bodies, and had faith the agent would keep his word.

The second of the two federal agents stepped forward while the other backed away.

"We realize this might not be an appropriate time to make this announcement," he said, "but the Bureau must inform you that the western part of the mountain has been approved for private sale. Development would take place well outside of the reservation's border, and these things take years. I can assure you it won't affect your community."

Pélō'é, the only Pozi elder on the tribal council, cursed under her breath. Her ancestors had lived on that land, and had been forcibly removed to Cold Valley a century ago.

"You're damn lucky Ashthenôví isn't here," she said, thumping her fist down on the table. "You're damn lucky."

Onwé nodded in solidarity. His father wasn't Pozi, but the man had spent years petitioning the government to return that land to its previous owners. Now, luxury cabins and paved roads would be built in the nameless place and along the cliffs of Numi's Ridge. The tourists of Orchid Valley would never know the dark history of that region, and like so much of Indian history, those secrets would be buried for the pursuit of profit.

A member of the Valley Commission approached the elders' table.

"Speaking of Ashthenôví," the man said, "Onwé, I've got something you'll want to see."

He removed a folded letter from his jacket and set it on the table.

"This here's an official request from Burke Voth to the Commission, imploring us to revive your father's bid for relocation assistance. I received it this morning."

Onwé looked down at the letter, incredulous. His brain could barely register what he was hearing.

"Considering the strength of Pastor Burke's endorsement," the man went on, "the Commission has agreed to stand behind it. We'll be coordinating with the Bureau on the details in the coming weeks."

"But…" Onwé mumbled, staggered by the development.

"I can't speak on behalf of my superiors," said one of the BIA agents, "but I can tell you there's appetite for it at the Bureau. After all you folks have been through."

A silence fell over the elders. None of them could believe what they'd just heard, Onwé least of all. They'd fought for decades to relocate the population of Autumn Ridge to the valley, and now, with a simple handwritten letter, the powers that be would make it so. In Lake Namarjo, residents would have access to a real hospital, to flushing toilets, and to paved roads. There were more telephones, more schools, more *people.*

Tears welled up in Onwé's eyes, and a large hand fell on his back. For just a moment, he imagined it was his father returning to hold him, but when he looked, Onwé saw John smiling back at him.

"Gentlemen," the agent said, interrupting the gentle moment, "we'll see you at the police station."

As the BIA and Valley Commission cleared out of the building, the elders lingered behind to talk amongst themselves. John hesitantly shared some of the story of what had happened in the tunnels, but gave few details of the horrors they'd witnessed. The other elders seemed to detect the reason for his brevity and did not press for more. Though they came from different tribes with different spiritual traditions, each of them had some awareness of the fact that Pale Peak was a site of ancient evil.

"How can we advise our people?" Emmanuel asked. "What happened to my son and granddaughter—it can never happen again."

"You're right," Onwé said. "Do you remember what their killer said at *Yōktha?* He spoke like a pastor. This presence on the mountain...it's like a disease. We spread it through our stories. If we tell anyone, we bring attention to"—Onwé glanced at John—"to the spirits that mean to harm us. And they'll *notice.*"

Tavshii nodded and took stock of the others.

"We don't name our recent dead," she said in a frayed voice, "and for the same reason, we won't name the elder spirits. We must not call out to them."

Pélō'é, Emmanuel, and Nănk agreed.

"Yes," Onwé replied. "This presence must be forgotten."

"Let it pass into myth," said Nănk, "and may its curses die with it in the caves."

Chapter 51

Back home on the porch, Onwé searched for the red star Luke had beheld at the cemetery, but it was nowhere to be found. He hoped its absence meant the wicked things on the mountain would vanish with it.

He joined Tíwé inside, where they sat on the living room floor. They gazed up at the old photos above the crackling fire, reflecting upon all their loved ones who had gone out of the world. Onwé's eyes remained fixed on a grainy picture of himself, Luke, and Akántha standing in front of the woods. He fished through his memories, trying to recall what sort of adventure they'd had on that day. But the shadows dancing over the walls distracted Onwé and took life of their own, forming wicked shapes in the corners of his vision. No matter how hard he tried, he could not escape the prison of his poisoned mind.

"Wish Numi was here," Tíwé said softly. "I really miss her. Zeus does too."

The name brought back a flood of tender memories, momentarily weakening the intrusive thoughts. Onwé looked at the bullet hole in the wall from that fateful night when he'd ended the dog's life. He got up and opened the closet, retrieving the painting of Numi that one of the church women had given him.

"Wow," Tíwé said, mesmerized by the art. "Who made that?"

"A friend," Onwé replied, wondering if he'd ever held a real conversation with Diana. He fetched a hammer and nail from a nearby drawer and hung the painting over the bullet hole. The two regarded it for a long while in silence, lost in the nostalgia of better times.

"Is that for me?" Tíwé finally asked, nodding at the undecorated stick leaning in the corner of the room. "You said you were gonna make me one."

Onwé sighed, knowing he'd let his son down once more. He hadn't worked on the hiking staff at all. The thing was still just a dirty tree branch.

"Yeah, I, uh, I just haven't been able—"

"It's perfect, Dad," Tíwé replied, hugging his father. "Yours looked ridiculous with all that crap tied to it. I like this one the way it is."

Onwé chuckled and returned the hug.

"Oh, and I've got something else for you," he said, removing the empty sage pouch from around his neck. "It belonged to Moya, but she doesn't need it anymore."

Tíwé sniffed the pouch and instantly knew what it was.

"For protection," he said, putting it on. "Does it really work?"

Onwé considered the question. He saw the Impostor's shadow weaving between the trees in his mind, and heard the hellish songs of the dead belching from caves on the mountain. Mountain sagebrush was a sacred herb in his culture, but Onwé had little confidence left in the spiritual power of his people. Nothing seemed to ward off the Bishop and his demons for long.

"I hope so," he offered grimly. "Keep it. Just in case."

As the night deepened, Onwé sank further into his private gloom. Something tugged at him from beyond the world, and he felt his mind inextricably connected to the elder spirits. With each passing moment, their whispers grew louder, and he felt closer to death's embrace.

Onwé knew he would not live long enough to move down to Namarjo with Tíwé.

He also felt a certain absence within himself; his budding faith was broken, and where it used to be, there was a hole now. A hopeless, empty pit, like the one in the ground on Numi's Ridge. None of his prayers had been answered. No gods of Indians or Christians had heard his cries. No spirits had come to rescue him. He was overwhelmed by the realization that his people were all alone in the universe—all alone with these *things* that feast on humans.

"I love you, Dad," Tíwé said, leaning against his father's arm.

Onwé turned his head, trying to hide the tears that came bursting from his eyes. It had been years since his son had said those words to him.

"I love you too," he replied. "You'll never know how much."

EPILOGUE

Moya spent the final days of her life wandering the woods behind her home. Her blindness had inexplicably lifted, banished by the mysterious energies of the Black Wall. She barely spoke anymore, having nothing left to say after fulfilling her purpose. She'd delved into *Knûth-Sōkáān* and retrieved her son's remains. In the twilight of her life, Moya clung to the belief that Akántha's soul was now free and journeying to the world of his ancestors.

For this, a price had been exacted. The Bishop had willingly given up a valued possession, and had demanded something even more valuable in return—a strong spirit who'd endured a lifetime of unfathomable suffering. Knowing Moya, Onwé was certain she'd agreed to those terms. A person scoured entirely of fear would make a coveted prize for such a monster.

Moya River Stone went missing ten days after Akántha was laid to rest. No search party was dispatched; she had prophesied her end to John Tall Rock, telling him she refused to bear another winter on Pale Peak. John knew better than to challenge her. She was last seen by two men hiking to Mirror Lake for ice fishing. They'd spotted her near the cave where Ashthenôví had died years prior.

The Bureau of Indian Affairs was content not to

investigate the matter. They would not risk the bad press of the disasters on Autumn Ridge, and that spring, an effort was launched to discourage the people from talking about them. The plane crashes and strange disappearances were eventually dismissed as "Indian nonsense," and those who told of them were silenced. This effort, the feds learned, dovetailed conveniently with the culture of the Nauktí and Pozi, whose belief systems discouraged unnecessary discussions of the dead. Through coercion, the Ineho were similarly brought to heel.

In time, as the government had hoped, tall tales of "Indian magic" faded from memory like strange dreams. The people forgot, much as they had forgotten their languages and histories. Over generations of brutal study, the government had learned that forgetful tribes were easier to manage than ones who could fully recall their identities.

When the BIA collapsed the caves of Pale Peak, the supernatural activity on the mountain fell dormant. The bones of the strange old house on Numi's Ridge were eventually cleared, but its foundation was still fit to serve as the cellar of an upscale cabin. Several were built over the coming decades, attracting buyers from Orchid Valley and the more distant cities to the east. By 2017, a dozen houses stood on the mountain, just outside the borders of the rez.

Down through the years, Tíwé Lopez had often hiked the area to survey its development. He'd watched new families come and go, and occasionally assisted the rangers with tracking down missing tourists. He'd explored the trails his father had forbidden him to walk in his youth, and had even discovered a cave the BIA hadn't shuttered. But he remembered his father's warnings and dutifully upheld the hiker's code. Parts of it, at least.

One evening after visiting the abandoned ruins of Autumn Ridge, Tíwé returned to his home in Lake Namarjo to find a note from his son:

Dad,
Pike called again.
         -Nathan

Tíwé sensed the possibility of another lost fisherman. He dialed the ranger station at the western foot of the mountain, whose number he knew by heart.

"Rocky Mountain National Park Service," an old man grumbled, "William Pike speaking."

"Bill, it's Tíwé. You rang?"

"Ah, good thing," Ranger Pike said. "Was about to rotate out. Say, you been up the slopes at all?"

"Just today, in fact," Tíwé replied, glancing out the window at the ominous peak. "Didn't go that far, though. Snow's too thick this week."

"Tell me about it," he said. "Uh, you see any weird shit up there lately?"

"What's going on, Bill?" Tíwé asked. The ranger sounded unusually tense.

Pike hesitated, trying to find the words.

"There's a couple'a city kids who got spooked up there at the Spencer cabin. Said some shit about dreamcatchers and voices out in the woods. They think someone was lookin' in the windows at night."

"Nobody here plays tricks like that," Tíwé said curtly. "Our people don't even make dreamcatchers."

"No, no," Pike said. "I don't mean it like that. You see, the boys and I helped them kids down the mountain this morning, and I'm tellin' you, they were scared shitless."

"Nobody missing, though?"

"Everyone's safe," Pike replied, "but I'm heading back up

there tomorrow to take a better look around. Was wonderin' if you'd like to join me."

"Sounds more like a job for your boys, doesn't it?" Tíwé said. "I don't know anything about crime scenes or whatever it is you're investigating."

"To be honest," Pike said grimly, "them kids got me a bit weirded out with their creepy stories. Was hopin' maybe you and Nathan wouldn't mind keepin' me company. If it ain't too much trouble, that is."

Tíwé looked out the window toward the jagged horizon. It would be dark soon, and the wind had begun to elicit strange noises from the trees.

"You there?" Pike asked.

"Yeah, sorry," Tíwé said, trying to shrug off the sensation of dread taking root inside him. "Suppose I could use the exercise anyway. Alright, Bill. The Spencer cabin at noon tomorrow. We'll be there."

About the Author

Felix Blackwell writes in the horror and thriller genres. His work is heavily influenced by Lovecraftian horror, and its plots and settings are often informed by his academic background in History. He suffers frequent, vivid nightmares, which are the primary inspiration for his stories.

For more creepy things to keep you awake, visit
www.felixblackwell.com

Printed in Great Britain
by Amazon

THE
CHURCH
BENEATH THE
ROOTS

Felix Blackwell

The Church Beneath the Roots